A1

Hope you enjoy
the Book.
        Walt

THUNDER AND LIGHTNING

THUNDER AND LIGHTNING

Amateur Sleuths

a novel by
Walt Bagley

iUniverse, Inc.
New York   Bloomington

Copyright © 2009 by Walt Bagley

All rights reserved. No part of this book may be used or reproduced by any means, graphic, electronic, or mechanical, including photocopying, recording, taping or by any information storage retrieval system without the written permission of the publisher except in the case of brief quotations embodied in critical articles and reviews.

This is a work of fiction. All of the characters, names, incidents, organizations, and dialogue in this novel are either the products of the author's imagination or are used fictitiously.

iUniverse books may be ordered through booksellers or by contacting:

iUniverse
1663 Liberty Drive
Bloomington, IN 47403
www.iuniverse.com
1-800-Authors (1-800-288-4677)

Because of the dynamic nature of the Internet, any Web addresses or links contained in this book may have changed since publication and may no longer be valid. The views expressed in this work are solely those of the author and do not necessarily reflect the views of the publisher, and the publisher hereby disclaims any responsibility for them.

ISBN: 978-1-4401-4913-9 (sc)
ISBN: 978-1-4401-4914-6 (ebook)
ISBN: 978-1-4401-5096-8 (dj)

Printed in the United States of America

iUniverse rev. date: 7/10/2009

To my loving wife Jean,

Thank you for your continuous encouragement and support; also, my abiding gratitude for all the time you spent in editing and proofreading. I love you.

W.B.

Acknowledgement

I would like to thank the following individuals who have given so generously of their time and talents in support of this book. First and foremost to my wife Jean ... she is my first and primary proofreader and copy editor.

Thanks also to Nancy Lucas, Serena Stevens, Tracey Walsh, Lori Beck, and David McCarter for their input, suggestions, questions, editing, and proofreading. This book would not have been possible without their help.

Prologue

The master of ceremonies at the three-day economic conference approached the podium and began, "Ladies and Gentlemen, let's get started. As you know, our theme is *How to Thrive and Grow in Times of Economic Slowdown.* You probably don't know our next speaker, John Lynch. However, his subject is very interesting and timely." After fumbling with some papers, the M.C. read, "His topic today is *A Look at Corruption in Business Accounting.*"

The M.C. continued, "John graduated from high school ranked number two in a class of over four hundred students. I'm told he missed being valedictorian by one percentage point. In five and a half years at Penn State, he has managed to obtain a Bachelor of Science Degree in Civil Engineering as well as a BS Degree in Accounting ... two different fields of study. He has also received a Master of Science Degree in Business Administration and a Master's in Economics. He's currently finalizing his Doctorate in Business Management. His thesis, *A Look at Corruption in Business Accounting,* has been defended and is currently being reviewed by several different sources for validation. I had lunch with this young gentleman and found him extremely interesting and highly intelligent. Ladies and Gentlemen, it is my distinct pleasure to introduce to you one of the youngest presenters at this conference ... Mr. John Lynch."

John stood on a raised dais. With his height of six foot three inches, he had no trouble scanning over the room filled to its two hundred-seat capacity. Although the attendees were mostly male, there were about a dozen females seated throughout the room. During his two-hour long presentation, he had the opportunity to pick out three particular people in the room. Forewarned earlier about a late arrival and early departure, John picked out his father as he entered the room after John began to speak. His father left the room while he was still answering questions. Another person John thought he noticed was an old friend from high school. However, he lost track of him during his Power Point presentation. The third person he picked out was a good-looking young woman. He didn't know her, but planned to rectify that after he concluded his session.

The question and answer period extended beyond the time John had expected. However, the attendees didn't seem to mind since most stayed for the entire session. Based on the applause after the speech, it appeared to John that his presentation had been well received. He was pleased that numerous attendees congratulated him on the research he had conducted on the subject.

After the session, John tried to catch up to the young woman in the audience who had caught his eye. He thought he remembered seeing her at the Paterno Library at Penn State.

A slightly overweight red-haired man rushed down the hall of the hotel where the conference was being held and approached John from behind saying, "I see you're as brainy as ever." John slowed down somewhat after hearing the comment. The redhead followed and in a louder voice continued, "I bet you could have been at the top of your class at Lewistown High School if you wanted to."

Recognizing the voice from his past, he stopped following the woman and said, "Woodpecker." Then he turned around, "How the hell are you?" As he shook hands, John continued, "Harvey, I thought that was you in the conference room. I haven't seen you since high school."

Harvey answered, "Sorry I didn't hear your entire presentation. I was scheduled for another session and decided to skip the beginning of it when I saw your name as a presenter. I was curious to see if it really was you. From what I heard, you sure know your stuff. Do you have time to sit and talk?"

"Sure," replied John, as he motioned to a nearby doorway. "Let's get a table in the coffee shop."

After they were seated and ordered drinks, Harvey commented, "I can tell from listening to the M.C.'s introduction that you've been busy getting all those degrees."

John answered, somewhat embarrassed, "You know me. I always had my head in a book when I had a chance. I just figured I'd adsorb as much as I could while I was in college." Anxious to change the subject, John continued, "What about you? What have you been up to?"

"Well, after leaving Lewistown, my family moved to Charlottesville, Virginia where dad had a job teaching at the University of Virginia. Because dad's benefits included reduced tuition for the family, I attended the university and got my degree in economics. After college, I started working for the federal government and have been there for over two years. I now live in Reston, Virginia, west of Washington, D.C."

John remembered that both of them had been considered nerds in high school and that Harvey had been a junior in high school when he was a freshman. He also recalled that his nickname, 'Woodpecker,' was a natural because his red hair was always disheveled. For the next hour, the two old friends talked and brought each other up to date on each other's lives. The reunion was cut short when 'The Woodpecker' answered his cell phone and said he and his boss had to return to their office downtown. Both men assured each other that they would keep in touch.

PART ONE

Chapter 1

It was an unseasonably warm evening. The trees were a dreary gray winter color, typical of the mountainous terrain in central Pennsylvania. Luke and his two brothers, identical twins Mark and Matthew, were finishing a session on weightlifting at the apartment complex where they lived. Amenities included the exercise room, swimming pool, basketball and tennis courts, and bus service to and from the University. Students living in less lavish facilities often referred to the complex as "The Resort." This particular complex was owned by their roommate's father Harold Lynch. Mr. Lynch was the reason they didn't have to pay rent for their four bedroom apartment.

Their apartment was located just off Penn State's 5,500-acre University Park Campus. The boys knew why most of the 40,000 students attending the main campus in State College, Pennsylvania called it "Happy Valley." They recognized that the university's reputation for high quality programs in education, engineering, research, and excellent athletic programs made for an ideal college environment. The party-like atmosphere didn't hurt either.

Matthew and Mark had seemingly identical bodies. Matt stood six foot, four inches tall and weighed about two hundred thirty plus pounds while Mark was taller by a half inch and weighed a few pounds less than his brother. For the most part, everyone had a difficult time recognizing one from the other. Their seventeen inch biceps and twenty inch necks made their forty-four inch chests appear normal. With thirty-two inch waists and nineteen inch thighs, they could be clones of Charles Atlas. Although their brother Luke's physique was pretty much similar to theirs, he could easily be identified by his dark coloring.

The three brothers had been working out at the complex gym for the past five and a half years. They trained regularly on the weightlifting equipment, treadmill and punching bag. Because of their size, no one else in the gym was willing to spar with them. Their bodies showed the results of weight training which they had been doing since they were in high school. Throughout their college years, the three brothers acted as personal trainers for anyone interested in joining them. Tonight there were seven other participants, including two young women working out with free weights. Normally, during these sessions, John, their roommate, would be on the treadmill running at his customary five-to six-mile per hour speed.

On his way home from the economics conference in Washington D.C., John called Luke who by then was back in their apartment. "I'm just outside of State College. I have to drop some papers off at the construction site."

Luke asked, "Will you be here for your weekly tutoring session?"

"No problem," replied John. I'll be there within an hour."

"Okay, I'll see you then."

That call was over two hours ago. Luke began to worry because he knew that John was too conscientious to be that late without letting them know why he'd been delayed.

Luke called John's cell phone several times during the

past thirty minutes but didn't get an answer. Luke told the others that he was canceling the tutoring session. When the two boys and three girls had left the apartment, Luke asked the twins to go with him to the construction site where John had said he was dropping off some papers he had looked at for his dad.

"He probably met some cute little thing along the way and forgot all about us," said Matthew.

"Yeah, sure," replied Luke, "when was the last time you saw him pick up a girl without us pushing him into it?"

"You could be right about that, but for the last year or so, I've seen him go after a chick or two who caught his fancy," smiled Mark. Saying that, he thought *how many times we've had to coerce John into introducing himself to a girl. And how many times have we had to use John to introduce ourselves to other girls? 'My friend over there would like to meet you but is too shy to talk to you himself.'*

"Something's wrong," answered Luke nervously.

"Okay, you two go and I'll stay here in case he comes back to the apartment," answered Matthew. "Take your cell phones with you," he yelled as Luke and Mark started down the stairs.

"Got mine," they replied in unison.

Leaving the apartment complex, they drove Mark's car, only because it was parked closer than Luke's pickup. They headed toward the site where John's father had recently started construction of a dormitory/parking garage project for Penn State. Ten minutes later, they approached the opened gate surrounding the construction site. They found John's truck parked outside of the lighted office.

"See, he's still in there," stated Mark. "Let's leave so he can finish whatever he's doing. It'll give us something to razz him about later."

"No, something's wrong. I can feel it," answered Luke.

Mark blew the horn as Luke jumped out of the car, looking

around the empty site. He headed for the office and quickly yelled, "Call 911." Luke saw that John was ghostly pale and that he was lying in a pool of blood. He appeared to be seriously hurt.

The ambulance and EMTs arrived within minutes. They examined John relatively quickly and rushed him to the nearby community hospital. Mark told Luke, "You stay here and wait for the police and I'll go to the hospital to be with him." He then hurriedly called Matthew and asked him to call John's parents. While Luke was waiting for the police to arrive, he looked around the office and alertly tried not to touch anything, thinking it may interfere with the crime scene. He considered that someone had apparently searched what little there was in the file cabinet and left a mess of files scattered on the floor. Luke found a short piece of two-by-four with blood on it near where he had discovered John.

After what seemed a long time, a police officer finally showed up at the scene. "Glad this wasn't an emergency," stated Luke sarcastically. The officer looked up at the large muscular frame and replied in a friendly tone, "Actually, I'm a little late. Sorry about that, but, to us, it appeared to be a problem for the campus police, not us. We lost that battle. So here I am. What's up?"

After Luke explained the situation, the officer was very apologetic. "We thought it was a simple break-in. There doesn't appear to be much to steal here. With your friend being attacked it's possible this is more than a robbery going bad."

"The officer continued, "Can you stick around and answer some questions? I have to call in some crime scene techs."

"Yeah, I'll stay," answered Luke. He then called Mark and found out that John was in the emergency room and still being treated by the trauma team. He also found out that Matthew couldn't get in touch with John's parents. Therefore, Matt had called his own parents, Martin and Janet Bowman, who were good friends with John's parents. They would try to track them down to tell them what had happened.

The crime scene techs arrived and did their job in a professional manner. The detective, Lieutenant Andrews, started asking Luke questions, "What's your friend's name?"

"His name's John Lynch. His father owns Lynch Construction, the company that's building this facility."

The detective continued, "Do you know if he had any enemies?"

"No. He's too nice of a guy to have any enemies," Luke replied.

"Are you sure there was no cash in the office?"

With a shrug of his shoulders, Luke answered, "It's a construction site. I don't see any reason for there to be any cash here."

The officer continued his investigation until he couldn't think of anything else that might be relevant to this case. The crime scene techs went about their work quietly.

Lieutenant Andrews said, "That mess in the office could easily have been vandalism. I'll talk to the guy who was attacked later at the hospital."

"That may be a little hard since he was unconscious when he left here." Luke mumbled to himself.

Mark was getting nervous because he hadn't heard anything new about John's condition. Finally, he managed to get the attention of a good-looking, dark-skinned nurse from the E.R. "My friend was brought in with a head injury. Can you tell me how he's doing?"

The nurse said, "He's recovered consciousness and needed stitches to close the wound on his head. However, the doctor's still with him and has ordered some more tests."

After his conversation with the nurse, Mark called Luke to let him know what was going on. Luke indicated he would be with the police for awhile and would see them later.

As Mark left, one of the people in the waiting room

speculated, "He must play on the Nittany Lion football team because of his size. I wonder what position he plays."

Several of the people in the waiting room pondered that he had to be an offensive lineman, but all of them agreed they wouldn't want to face him over the scrimmage line.

Seconds after Mark departed, Matthew entered the waiting room from the opposite door. He got everyone's immediate attention because they thought they had just seen him leave through the other door.

When Matthew didn't see his brother anywhere, he went straight to the emergency room desk and asked the nurse about John's condition. "My friend John Lynch was brought in with a head injury. Can you tell me how he's doing?"

"Boy, do you have a short memory," she replied. "I just talked to you about his condition."

"I'm sorry," said Matthew apologetically, "you were probably talking to my twin brother." Then with a smile, "but I'm better looking than he is."

The nurse walked away, still believing she had already given him the information and that he was giving her a line of bull. Back in the waiting room, Matthew saw Mark standing outside and went out to wait for John's parents to arrive. One of the people in the waiting room spoke up, "I'm seeing double and I haven't had a drink for two days."

"Wow!" said the lady next to him, "are they big, and not an ounce of fat on either of them."

Chapter 2

"Boy," said Matt as they reached the sidewalk, "I sure hope John's going to be okay. I wonder what really happened in the office."

Matt replied, "I don't know, but if I find out who hit him I want five minutes alone with that son of a bitch. I'll tear his head off and hand it to John on a platter."

"I'd be more than happy to help you," stated Mark. "You know, we owe a lot to him and his family."

"Not only do we, but mom and dad as well," answered Mark. "They've been with the construction company almost from the time Mr. Lynch bought it and have worked their way up through the ranks ever since."

"Not only that, but they've ended up being such great friends with the Lynches as well," stated Matthew. Then after some thought he added, "How about if I go get Luke and meet you back here?"

"Sounds good to me," replied Mark.

Mark sat on a bench outside the hospital entrance and reminisced about the first time they had met John. His mind wandered and he thought to himself. *We were at the swimming pool the summer after our first year in high school. While we were doing push-ups, I got into an argument with him and* that little red-headed kid they called 'The Woodpecker.' That's also when I met Luke.

Still thinking back, his mind continued to wander. *I can even remember what we argued about. Harvey and John were talking about something related to science. John had moved to the area after his dad took over the Lewistown Construction Company. I called them stupid little nerds and asked why they'd even talk of something like that outside of school. I remember that John answered with 'I learn things all the time. You don't have to be in school to learn. It's something you should keep in mind.'*

I then sarcastically said, 'What are you, some smart-assed bookworm?' John then commented, 'Yes, I guess a jock like you would consider me a bookworm.'

Even though I heard the word jock, I pretended I hadn't. 'Who the hell are you calling a jerk?' I yelled as I stood up and pulled John to his feet. I remember that he didn't even flinch. He wasn't afraid of me and that pissed me off. I had him by a couple of inches and outweighed him by at least thirty pounds. I hit him two or three times and he didn't fight back. 'Kick the shit out of him,' was all I could think of when a pair of big brown arms grabbed me from behind and pinned my arms to my side. Here was another kid I didn't know. He was much bigger than me at the time. It turned out to be Luke who looked like he was going to crush me until Matt pulled him off.

With his eyes closed Mark continued thinking. *Matt and I were getting the best of him until John jumped on my back and knocked me down. I'd brush him away, but like a mosquito, he kept coming back.*

All four of us were getting pretty well bruised up, but John was getting the worst of it. It took the lifeguard and three park security guys to pull us apart. They called the police and they took all four of us down to the precinct. Our parents were called. Ultimately we all got kicked out of the pool for the rest of the summer.

Mark saw his brother pull back into the parking lot. "Where's Luke?" he asked.

"He's still with the police. I told him to call when they were finished."

"You know, while I was sitting here, I was just thinking about when we met John and Luke," Mark told him. We had that fight and got kicked out of the swimming pool for the rest of that summer."

Just as if Matthew could read his twin's train of thought, he said, "As it turned out, the summer we had that scuffle with them was the best thing that ever happened to us. The park wanted to press charges until John's dad intervened. Mr. Lynch talked mom and dad and Luke's parents into letting us work for him 'just to burn off some of that youthful energy.' He said he was looking for some summer help and we'd do just fine.

"The rest of the summer was a great workout for us," Mark remembered, "better than the workouts with barbells three times a week. Boy! Do you remember how Mr. Lynch sure worked the four of us hard? John didn't get any preference just because he was his son. We all tried to keep up with Luke who was as strong as a bull. We didn't know until later that he used to help his dad, who was a bricklayer. Mixing the mortar and carrying blocks kept him in perfect shape."

Matthew remarked, "That sure was a big year for us. I think we each grew three inches and gained thirty pounds of muscle from all the manual work we did. Luke, who already was big, just got bigger and John filled out, as well. Mr. Lynch knew what he was doing by making us work on the same crew. At first, it was a little uncomfortable, working with two guys we had fought with, but in the end we became the best of friends. That's also the year we picked up a couple of nicknames."

Mark then recalled, "Yeah, like, "The Big Dogs," and "Fat Cats." Someone started calling us, "The Four Apostles," because of our names. Or, maybe it was because we hang out together all the time ... who knows? The one nickname that really stuck was, "Thunder and Lightning."

Matthew laughed. "Remember that newspaper article where the sportswriter wrote, 'John Lynch is as fast as lightning and the Bowman brothers are the thunder that goes with the lightning. With the Bowmans on the line and Lynch in the backfield, the scores added up like pouring rain.' All his articles thereafter referred to us as Thunder and Lightning. We only lost two games that year. Remember how we made up for those two losses by going undefeated and won the league championship the next year?"

Mark cut in. "Boy! Wasn't it something that after football season in our senior year Mr. Lynch offered us the unbelievable deal to pay our college tuition if we'd work for his company during the summers and a minimum of two years after graduation?"

Matthew said somberly, "Do you realize that it was also that spring that Luke lost his parents in that terrible accident on Old Route 522? Because he didn't have any other relatives, mom and dad immediately told Luke he would be living with us until other arrangements could be made. 'No question about it, and don't even think about other options' was what they told him. They adopted him nine months later, and we officially got a little, if that's the right word, brother."

Then Mark laughed and said, "We definitely wouldn't have made it out of high school if John didn't take it upon himself to tutor us. It helped that he has a photographic memory and has a real knack for teaching."

"Yeah," said Matthew with a little skepticism, "I can't believe he got two BS degrees in less than three years and then stuck around to get two Masters and a Doctorate just so he could help us get our degrees, or so he says."

"You and I both know we could have made it without his help," commented Mark. But I admit he helped occasionally. Sure have had lot of fun with him these last eight years,"

"He was always an easy mark for our pranks," answered Matthew. As he checked out a car coming into the parking lot, he said, "Look, here come mom and dad ... wasn't expecting them to come."

Martin Bowman shook hands with his twins. Their mother Janet gave each of them a hug and kiss. "The Lynches were at a banquet down in Chambersburg. They're on their way and will be here shortly," Martin said as he looked at his watch.

"Where are your coats?" their mother asked. "You're just wearing T-shirts. Are you trying to impress someone?" Janet looked around the area for young women who magically appeared when her boys were showing off.

"It's warm out, Mom, and besides we were in a hurry," said Mark while Matt headed for his car to retrieve two jackets.

The twins gave them a quick overview of what had happened and directed them to the emergency room. Mr. Bowman, although shorter than his sons, resembled his sons' build. His chest and arms showed the bulk of someone who had worked hard for many years. His rough hands appeared small when compared to his muscular forearms, just like "Popeye." His many years of experience as a laborer, carpenter and superintendent made him very knowledgeable in the construction industry. As a supervisor and troubleshooter for Lynch Construction, he was a good listener who dealt with problems in a quick and decisive manner. He was very well liked by all the employees, from laborers to foremen. Over the years he had become a confidant to Harold Lynch.

Because he knew his sons would have gotten all the information they could from the nurse, he decided to wait for the Lynches to arrive, instead of inquiring further.

Harold and Margaret Lynch arrived and the hand shaking

and hugging routine was repeated. After being briefed by the others, Harold and the others approached the E.R. and gently knocked on the door. When no one responded to his knock, he rapped on the door a little louder, but politely. When the E.R. nurse opened the door, he told her who they were and asked if he could see John and talk to the doctor. The nurse's eyes got big as she looked over Mr. Lynch's shoulder at the identical twins standing there and said, "Just mom and dad, please. I'll see if the doctor has a few minutes to talk to you."

The nurse closed the door. She thought, *There really are two of them, and identical in every aspect.*

Forty-five minutes later, John's parents rejoined the Bowmans in the waiting room. "John will be okay. It took fifteen stitches to close the wound. He has a concussion and is a little blurry-eyed, but he appears to be coherent. He said when he pulled up to the gate it was open and there was a light on in the office. He didn't give it much thought. When he stepped through the door, he thought he heard a noise behind him, but was hit on the head before he could turn. He doesn't remember anything else until he woke up in the E.R."

"They're going to keep him here overnight," stated Mrs. Lynch, "just to make sure he's okay. The doctor wants the radiologist to look at the X-rays."

"They're going to give him something for his headache," interrupted Mr. Lynch, "and let him sleep. The nurses were trying to keep him awake, but the doctor says it's okay if he sleeps now."

Mark interjected, "He's probably tired. He was at that conference in D.C. for three days. He drove back here after today's, or is it yesterday's session, and stopped by the construction site before going to the apartment."

Margaret Lynch spoke up, "John called on his way home and said he had a meeting with the three of you and wanted to get back to the apartment. Incidentally, he told me he ran into Harvey Harrison, that little red-haired schoolmate who used to live up the street from you."

Mr. Lynch looked around the waiting room and asked, "Where's Luke?"

"He's still at the construction office with the police," replied Matthew. "It appears that the office was ransacked and Luke thought it would be best if the police were called to investigate."

"Why would anyone break into a construction trailer? There's nothing of value in the office," replied Harold Lynch.

"Beats us," shrugged Mark. "We told Luke we'd meet him back at the trailer, so we'd better get over there. If the four of you would like to sleep in our apartment tonight, you can use our apartment if you want. I know that John put fresh sheets on his bed before he left for Washington."

"No, we'll stick around here for awhile and stay in town until John gets discharged," answered Mrs. Lynch. "We made reservations at the Atherton on the way up. Let's meet for dinner when John is discharged."

"Okay, we'll be done with classes by mid-afternoon," replied Matthew.

"We can't stay either," stated Martin Bowman. "We have a meeting with the attorneys on that matter we discussed," as he looked at his boss.

"Okay, I'll be in the office on Friday," replied Mr. Lynch.

After checking with the nurse again to make sure John was going to be asleep for several hours, the twins said goodbye to the Lynches. They headed back to the trailer to meet up with Luke and then to try for a few hours of sleep themselves before they attended classes in the morning. Classes would end in a week. Then, after two weeks of final exams, they would complete their post-graduate work.

The meeting John's mother had referred to was a tutoring session her son conducted each week. Contrary to what most people thought, the sessions were not for the three brothers. None of them were having trouble keeping their GPA above-average; the tutoring sessions were just another reason to get together. Most of the time, other classmates or friends would sit in on their sessions, sometimes to learn, sometimes just to talk. Every session was co-ed, even though some of the women weren't enrolled in the courses being studied. They were there because it was a good place to be noticed.

John had always had a real knack for reading a textbook and being able to explain the meaning in terms everyone could understand. In high school he had been tested to determine if he had a photographic memory, but the results were inconclusive. John denied screwing up the test on purpose. Most friends who knew him well didn't believe him. John's parents were the only ones who knew his actual IQ, but anyone close to him knew it had to be over one hundred fifty.

Chapter 3

John was discharged from the hospital before noon the next day. He still had a slight headache. He was glad he didn't have any classes, although most of his time was spent in a professor's office or in the library, instead of in a classroom. He spent part of the afternoon with his dad and mother going over the documents he had reviewed while in Washington. Mr. Lynch was in the process of buying out Harrisburg Industrial Electronics and wanted John to look over the profit and loss statements. Martin and Janet Bowman were not staying in State College because Martin was meeting with lawyers concerning that buyout.

Harrisburg Industrial Electronics was a relatively small company, with just one location, specializing in motion control and programmable logic controller products for some of the top manufacturers in the industry. They also supplied various electronics needed to operate complex machinery, elevators, and circuit boards for a wide variety of purposes. Their estimated net worth was fifteen million dollars. The owner was selling out for sixty cents on the dollar. The current owner was retiring, but would manage the company long enough for Harold Lynch to train another manager.

Luke and the twins were sitting in the restaurant area of

the Nittany Lion Inn, located on the southwest corner of the Penn State Campus. Owned and operated by the university, it was one of the premier hotel and restaurants in central Pennsylvania. The brothers were waiting for John and his parents when four good-looking young women entered. One of them was the nurse whom Matthew and Mark had talked to at the hospital. The twins nodded and smiled at the foursome. The girls, smiling in return, thought something was funny because they started giggling. The one who was a nurse was overheard to say, "Now that's what I'd call three good looking prospects."

The Lynches arrived shortly after the girls, who were now seated nearby. Mrs. Lynch spied the young women and hurried over to thank the nurse for looking after John and being so nice. Back at her table, she gave hugs and kisses to the boys. Nodding over her shoulder toward the girls, she said, "If you boys were smart, you'd go over there and introduce yourselves. They seem like very nice young ladies."

Thinking she would just sit down, John replied, "Gee, Mom, why don't you do that for us?"

"Just for that smarty pants, I will," she said emphatically and immediately went back to the girls and talked to them for a few minutes. Apparently she said something funny because all the girls started to laugh. The four young women stood and followed Mrs. Lynch back to her table for introductions. The men hurried to their feet as she began, "This is my husband Harold Lynch and my son John."

As John acknowledged the women, he realized that one of them was the woman he was trying to catch up with in Washington when The Woodpecker stopped him. Their eyes met and he could feel his heart begin to beat faster.

Mrs. Lynch, in the meantime, continued with the introductions, "These two little darlings are Mark and Matthew Bowman. You'll have to ask who's who because I can never tell. And this is their brother Luke," which made all four women's eyes go wide in wonderment.

The ladies introduced themselves as Helen Francis, Joan Largent, Kathy Livingston and John's nurse Mary Anne Johnson. Now totally embarrassed by his mother, John did the polite thing and asked the girls if they would like to join them for dinner. After the girls looked at each other and nodded okay, John asked the waiter for a larger table. The ten of them were moved into a nearby private dining area.

Mrs. Lynch took over the seating arrangements by suggesting that the women sit on one side of the table with two ladies on each side of her. She placed her husband opposite her with the twins on his left and right, John on the far left and Luke far right, opposite Mary Anne.

"Now," she began, "just so there's no need to talk about the weather and other little bits of conversation, I suggest that we go around the table and one at a time give some facts about ourselves ... such as where we live, where we work, what our hobbies are. The boys will go first, starting at that end with John," as she pointed to him.

John, shook his head, and thought to himself that he couldn't believe she really was doing this, and said, "I apologize for my mother. Now that the four of us are about to finish college, she believes we should continue our education by meeting some nice young women, of which you surely qualify. I think she'd like for us to be taught some manners and the softer side of life, and then settle down. So, if any of you are ready to do that, please indicate by saying 'Aye'."

"Aye," quietly replied one of the girls, but John didn't notice who it was that said it.

"John!" said his mother sternly, but with a smile on her face.

"Okay. Since my mother has already told you my name, I'll tell you a little about myself. My hometown is Lewistown, Pennsylvania." John was too humble to list all of his degrees.

Instead he said, "I have a BS in Accounting and a Masters in Business Administration. At this time, I'm looking for a job that will be commensurate with my talents." This statement got a raised eyebrow from his father.

John continued, "I have loving parents, at least three good friends," motioning to the right, and I enjoy reading, swimming and traveling, and I like games involving strategy. If any of you are interested in marrying me, please fill out an application and turn it into my mother who will be doing the interviews."

"John!" his mother said sternly, still smiling.

While John was talking, the woman across from him was paying particular attention. She thought to herself... *I think he's about an inch or so over six feet tall and probably weighs about one ninety. His eyes are as dark as coal. I'd like to run my hands through that dark brown hair. He's obviously very intelligent. And, notice that deep tan ... must work outdoors. His hands show that he must be a hard worker. With those good looks he could be mistaken for a movie star.*

Then Matt began with "John doesn't want to brag. He has a couple more degrees that he didn't mention." After pausing briefly, he continued. "I'm Matthew Bowman. My friends call me Matt. I have a twin brother, but I'm better looking than he is and considerably stronger." That got a laugh from the table. "Like John and the others, I'm from Lewistown; have a BS in Engineering and in two weeks I'll have completed the requirements for a Masters in Business Administration. Unlike John, I have a job lined up and expect to start a job two weeks from now for John's dad's company. I enjoy one-on-one sports like boxing and weightlifting. Someday I'd like to settle down and have a family. But, for now, I'm interested only in short-term flings."

"Matthew!" said Mrs. Lynch again, still smiling.

"I'm Harold Lynch and I run a construction company. I've been married for forty years, most of them happy."

Thunder and Lightning

"Harold!" his wife said sternly again, but this time she wasn't smiling.

"Okay, okay. I've enjoyed all of them very much," continued Harold as the waiter returned with the drinks they ordered. "Let's order before we continue. Order what you want, my wife's buying."

After they placed their order, Mrs. Lynch stated, "Mark, it's your turn."

"My name is Mark Bowman and regardless of what my little brother says, I'm the better looking one and also much smarter and stronger." That comment got smiles from the other side of the table. "My mother likes me best. I have a BS degree in Environmental Engineering, and like my brother, will obtain a Master's in Business Administration in a couple of weeks. My degree will help me to do something productive for mankind."

"Luke," said Mrs. Lynch exasperated, shaking her head.

"Don't believe a word these two say," commented Luke, pointing to Mark and Matthew. "Mom really likes me best. After all, she didn't have any choice with them, but she wanted me. My real parents were killed in a car accident and Mr. and Mrs. Bowman adopted me." This seemed to explain a lot to the women.

"He doesn't know he's black," interrupted Mark. "We never bothered to tell him."

"Be quiet, white boy" said Luke smiling. "Sorry, ladies, you must know by now he's not very nice. I'll graduate with a BS in Electrical Engineering, and a Master's in Micro Electronics in a few weeks, but I'm not sure I'll be working in that field because I'll also be working for Lynch Construction."

"I need to talk to you about that," interrupted Mr. Lynch.

"Okay, sir. Unlike these three, I'm laid-back; enjoy reading mystery novels and spending days just hanging out with my friends ... although I do pump iron and hit the punching bag several times a week. I love to fiddle around with electronics."

Matthew butted in "Sure! You're just lazy and never do any work," as he pretended to squeeze Luke's biceps.

"Girls' turn," said Mrs. Lynch. "You start, Mary Anne."

"I'm Mary Anne Johnson," she began. I'm from Harrisburg and currently working at the Nittany Hospital. I plan to move back to Harrisburg in the near future to continue my nursing career at Harrisburg General. If I meet the right fellow, I'd like to settle down and have a family. In the meantime, I want to enjoy the single life ... have fun, go dancing, travel a little, and see where that leads me."

As Mary Anne was speaking, Luke thought to himself. *She's so attractive ... her light brown skin seems to shimmer. Her short hair looks cute with just a little natural curl. I noticed that her eyes just sparkle when she talks. I think she's about five feet seven and what a curvy body! Boy! I'd like to get to know her better.*

Two of the other women told their new-found friends that they also were nurses and worked with Mary Anne. They explained that one of them was happily married and the other was looking forward to be married next June. They stated that they lived in the State College area and said they were happy in their nursing careers.

Margaret Lynch explained that she had worked for her husband's company for many years but was now retired. She said that she stopped in the office periodically, just to keep an eye on what was going on. She told them that she spent a lot of time doing volunteer work in Mifflin County. "One thing you need to understand about these two," she said, pointing to the twins, "is they often reply to questions simultaneously. I don't know how they do it."

The last person to introduce herself was Helen Francis. She said she originally was from Baltimore and held a BS in Business Management, with a minor in Economics. She told them that currently she was a graduate student at Penn State and was completing her Master's in Marketing. She told the group that she would soon be moving to Harrisburg to work in her uncle's consulting business.

While Helen was speaking, John found that he was impressed by her. He knew from experience that Penn State's Smeal College of Business only allowed minor degrees for exceptional students. He thought to himself *Wow! She's some looker! And, she appears to be bright and energetic.* As he listened to her, he decided she had a pleasant voice that was easy to listen to, and, of course, her goods looks made one pay attention to what she said. John estimated she was five foot ten inches, fairly tall for a girl. He looked at her shiny dark brown hair, large brown eyes with the whites gleaming, classic straight nose, and perfect complexion and thought that with those attributes modeling agencies would look at her a second or third time. He noticed that her body was well toned with more than adequate bumps in the right places. *Yes, I'd like to find out more about this woman,* John thought to himself.

As she spoke, she looked directly at John as if he was the only other person in the room. She said, "I was at the Economic Conference earlier this week. I heard your presentation and was very impressed. You're an excellent speaker."

"Thank you," replied John thinking, *No wonder she caught my attention at the conference ... she's beautiful.*

Harold Lynch then asked her, "What does your uncle do?"

"His name is Bateman Masterson and he owns Masterson Business Consultants."

No one noticed that Harold and John raised their eyebrows a little at that answer.

Mr. Lynch explained that he knew Helen's boss, "Old Bat Masterson, I know him very well. He was the one responsible for my buying Lewistown Construction. At the time I had a small remodeling business in Williamsport. He called and asked to meet with me. When I arrived, he got straight to the point. He told me he knew of a construction business that was for sale and asked right out if I was interested in buying the Lewistown Construction Company. He said he had investors interested in financing the purchase. He also said that he would broker the financing and make all the necessary arrangements. He told me upfront what the value of the company was and what I would have to pay for it, as well as certain other stipulations. Within a month, all of the negotiations were completed and I took possession two months later."

Helen was a little confused about that statement. She didn't understand why a business consultant was so involved in such a transaction. However, she let the remark pass without comment.

By the time their meal was served, the conversation was flowing quite well and everyone was enjoying themselves. Mrs. Lynch paid particular attention to the interaction between Luke and Mary Anne and between John and Helen. As they were leaving, everyone expressed their desire to meet again and thanked Mrs. Lynch for the invitation and told her what a superb meal they had. John asked Helen if he could call her later. She agreed by giving him her phone number.

John went with his parents and they talked for nearly an hour in the car outside the men's apartment. Margaret was concerned about the blow to John's head, as any mother would be. She asked a question to determine if his memory was okay, "Tell me the names of the women you just had dinner with."

John saw through her question, "Mom, just because I got a concussion, there's nothing wrong with my head."

She insisted, "Tell me about them."

Because he knew she wouldn't stop until he gave her all the information. He told her each name, gave a description of each, their occupation, plus other details he had heard during dinner. This apparently satisfied her worries. She didn't pursue that line of questions anymore.

Later, when John settled into a comfortable chair in the apartment, the roommates discussed Mrs. Lynch and the evening's entertainment. Mark began with, "You know I love that lady, but she must think we can't get girls on our own. It was a nice evening but I, for one, thought she was pushing a little too hard for us to get married."

"I don't know," stated Luke. "I enjoyed meeting those girls. I think it was a great evening."

"Yeah, you would. You couldn't keep your eyes off Mary Anne, although I admit she's very nice to look at," said John.

"You weren't exactly disappointed with Helen sitting across from you. She and you appeared to be looking deep inside each other's souls," interjected Mark.

"She's easy to talk to and even easier to look at, and boy ... is she put together!" said John. "I got her phone number and I'm going to call her in a few days. Maybe I can help her cram for finals."

"I know what you'd like to cram. You'd teach her Sex Education 101," stated Matthew. "Just like that porn flick you starred in. You know, if your mother knew about that tape, she wouldn't be fixing you up with any women she knows."

"You'd better not have any more of those lying around," shouted John. "That could destroy mom. She'd never understand. You promised me you burned them all."

Mark shrugged his shoulders and raised his hands to indicate maybe.

"When we were in high school, every kid had a copy of that tape," laughed Luke.

"Sure did," said Mark. "We made a lot of money on that one. Don't worry, John. Nobody ever knew it was you on the tape."

"That may be true, but mom and dad might recognize

the lake house. That was one of the worst pranks you ever played on me," said John. "Or was it one of the best? I'm still not sure."

Chapter 4

The lake house John was referring to was a large rustic building, built over a century ago. Harold and Margaret Lynch owned the house and its surrounding twenty acres. At the time of purchase, the property was rundown and in desperate need of repair. Harold had his construction crews remove most of the interior walls to create a wide-open living and dining area. The stone foundation and chimneys were rebuilt and the aging wood siding repaired and covered with vinyl siding that resembled wood. All new windows and a modern metal roof had been installed. A new kitchen, complete with all the conveniences, was recently added. A half-dozen rocking chairs were placed on the front porch, overlooking the lake and grassy area leading down the slope to the pristine water. Over the years, the house had served as the Lynches' getaway site. In more recent years, John used the property more often than his parents. The house sat at the end of a mile-long gated private drive.

"Let's see. How did we arrange that?" laughed Luke. "You once told us that you were a virgin ... that's what gave us the idea. So we suggested that we go swimming at the lake. You went up to the lake house with the twins in their car. I said

I had some errands to run but would meet you there a little later. I did have an errand ... I had to pick up a hooker."

Matthew continued, "We knew John would eventually take his normal forty-five minute swim in the lake. When Luke arrived, the two of us went into the house, set up the video cameras we had rented, and later took the hooker inside. Then we left and took both cars."

"I saw the cars weren't anywhere around and knew right away something was up," interjected John smiling, "but for the life of me I never expected what was to come."

"Yeah, come is the right word," said Mark as he started to laugh.

"Figuring I didn't have any choice but to play along with whatever you three were up to, I decided to take a shower and get dressed," continued John. "I was soaped up when the shower door opened and this voluptuous girl stepped in the shower stall wearing nothing but her birthday suit. When she put her arms around my neck and rubbed her glorious big breasts across my chest, I got as hard as a diamond immediately. Those melons initially felt like soft pillows, but I later found out they were as firm as well-stuffed cushions. She started kissing my neck and worked her way down. By the time she put a lip lock on my love muscle, I was ready to explode and I did. After that, she looked up and sang 'Happy Birthday' to me."

"I wish we could've seen your face on the video, but it wasn't to be. Not that we didn't try. We just didn't have time to check the camera angles," said Mark.

John continued. 'That was a little quick,' she said. 'I owe you more than that' and she grabbed my now limber timber and pulled me into the bedroom where she used my hands to explore every crevice on her body."

"She didn't have to do any coaxing," interrupted Luke. "You may have been a virgin, but what you didn't tell us, and we should have known, was that you had memorized several books about sexual stimulation. By the time you were done, she enjoyed it as much as you."

"I didn't know you were filming it or I wouldn't have been able to perform," said John. "I still don't know if she was faking or not, but she sure did seem to enjoy herself. When she rolled me over and got on top of me and I entered her, I thought I was in heaven. She would bring me to a peak and then she would stop and wait for me to settle down again. She did that two or three times until there was no stopping me. By the time I came, I was totally exhausted and she was breathing pretty hard herself."

"After lying there for awhile, I didn't know what to do, so I asked her if she was hungry. She thought I wanted her to start over again. I couldn't have gotten it up again if Jennifer Aniston asked me to make love to her," laughed John. "When she realized I didn't mean more sex, she said, 'I was beginning to think there was more left in you. I don't think I could have taken any more myself.'

'I was told this was your first time,' she said. 'I don't believe that for one minute, and no, I'm not hungry but a cold drink would be nice. Can I take a shower first?'

"When I got off the bed, I could hardly walk."

Matthew laughed, "When we returned at the agreed-upon time, you two were sitting on the porch like you were old bosom buddies, and we thought we had failed, or that you turned her down. While we talked for a few minutes, Luke retrieved the cameras then drove her back to her car."

"You had even stripped the bed and had the sheets in the washer," laughed Mark. "What a nerd!"

"It was two or three weeks later," said John, "that one of our classmates stopped me in the hallway and asked if I had seen the video that Mark and Matt were selling." "He proceeded to tell me the contents of the film and I soon realized that it was me and the hooker at the lake house. I was so scared that my parents would see it and want an explanation. After you showed me the tape, I was a little relieved, but to this day I'm still concerned."

Luke interjected, "The hooker cost us five hundred dollars, and after the expense of editing and copying the tapes, we still made a profit. A lot of the guys who watched it with their girlfriend said it led to the best sex they ever had."

Chapter 5

Luke and John followed through with their desire to get further acquainted with Mary Anne and Helen by double-dating several times.

Classes came to an end. The four friends finished their final exams and they received their degrees. John's overall GPA for all his degrees was 3.97. The twins contended that John had purposely missed a question or two on his final exams. The other three also finished their college education with a GPA of 3.0 or higher. At the graduation ceremonies, Harold and Margaret and Martin and Janet glowed with pride for their sons' accomplishments.

Because the four friends had worked for Lynch Construction part-time while they were in high school and worked full-time during summer months and extended breaks, they were in mid-management positions with the construction company by the time they were in college. If necessary, they could all act as supervisors on small construction projects. However, Lynch Construction had stopped building small projects many years ago, and their profit margin increased accordingly.

After graduation, Mr. Lynch met with the three brothers individually to advise them that he that wouldn't hold them to their agreement to work for him. All three indicated they still wanted to work for his company.

Harold Lynch was talking to Luke. "Lynch Construction is in the process of buying Harrisburg Industrial Electronics. If you're interested, I'd like for you to work at that company. You can spend a short time working at various positions before moving into management. Eventually, I'd like you to take over the management. Would you be interested in taking on that responsibility?"

Luke was really enthused about the opportunity and replied, "I appreciate the opportunity, and the trust you've put in me. Of course, I'm interested. I have a million questions going through my mind."

"We'll get to them in good time. Thank you for accepting this challenge."

During his meeting with Mr. Lynch, Mark found out that his work with Lynch Construction would consist of designing and inspecting all construction sites, making sure all regulations and specifications were being followed. His job would also entail training employees and establishing safety guidelines at all job sites. Harold explained, "This particular job is not what I ultimately have in mind for you. I'm not in a position to discuss it at this time. Please keep this information between you and me. It may take some time for me to develop what I really want you to do."

Matthew met with John's father to review his job opportunities. Mr. Lynch began by saying, "You know that you and your brothers are like sons to me. I want the best for all of you. Saying that, I think the best place for you in our organization is here in the office. I want you to utilize your engineering background and experience for estimating project costs and preparing construction bids. Ben Dominic, who is currently working in that department, will be retiring in the relatively near future. I need someone to assist him and learn the details of the bidding process. It's gotten too tough for me to handle anymore. Together with Mark, you'll be responsible for hiring and training all new employees. Eventually, when I retire, I think you and your brother would be an asset to John when he takes over the business. You both will work on special projects as the need arises."

"I'll be happy doing whatever you need me to do," exclaimed Matt.

John and his dad had talked many times about John's role in the company. Technically he would be controller for both the construction company and Harrisburg Industrial Electronics. John would initially work as liaison with the project superintendents. Mr. Lynch knew that John would eventually take over management of the construction company.

With the essentials out of the way, Harold Lynch shared his immediate plans with the boys. He offered some well-deserved R & R, and described a beach house he had rented for the next few months in Jensen Beach, Florida. He told them they could spend two weeks at the beach house. Harold said that their parents were planning to use the house occasionally during the summer. He also indicated that the house would be offered to other employees of the construction company.

The four friends, after very little deliberation, decided to invite four companions to join them for two weeks of fun and games in the sun.

As it turned out, Luke invited Mary Anne Johnson and John asked Helen Francis to accompany him. Matthew's and Mark's guests were two sisters whom they had known since high school. The women stayed in two of the bedrooms and the guys in the other two rooms. At least that's how their story went.

When they returned from their vacation, Mary Anne received notice of when she was to begin her job at the Harrisburg Hospital. At her farewell party, Mary Anne's friends kidded her about moving to Harrisburg to make Luke an honest man. If that was the case, Luke seemed to be falling right in line.

Luke moved into an apartment on the outskirts of Harrisburg to be close to his work. John moved into his own apartment east of Lewistown. After asking Mr. Lynch, the twins decided to stay in the apartment they had lived in for the last five years. They would convert one of the bedrooms into an office so that they could work from home, as needed. They insisted that they would pay the same rent for the apartment as the other tenants.

The three brothers spent the first two weeks at the office where they attended many meetings, got caught up on various projects, and learned about other factions of Mr. Lynch's businesses. Because of their past work experience, they had already showed their abilities and work ethics. The other employees exhibited no animosity toward Matthew and Mark for filling positions of authority.

John had worked for his dad since he was twelve. Therefore, he knew most of the employees and their families. The company treated all employees as family and provided them with good wages and benefits. As a result, the company had very little turnover of employees, making the twins' orientation duties almost negligible. It was generally understood that John would eventually take over management of Lynch Construction.

Luke and John spent two weeks at Harrisburg Industrial Electronics to review files and to meet with the owner. Luke then started his own self-imposed training by working on the docks, filling orders, and loading trucks. He planned to work in various positions for the next several months to learn as much as possible about the supply business. The owner said he would stay for a year and then work part time for another three to six months. The employees were not overly concerned about the sale of the company. Even so, John and

Luke met with key personnel to assure them that no layoffs were planned.

John and Mark visited each of the projects under construction. Currently, there were sixteen projects in various phases of completion. John was surprised to learn about several episodes of missing materials from three of the sites. Nothing major was missing from any of the projects, but enough to cause him to wonder if there was a problem. On most construction jobs as big as the projects they normally worked on, materials were misplaced or used by sub contractors without the foreman knowing about it.

While he was at the dorm project in State College, John called the police department to find out if there had been any progress made on the break-in at the construction site office. Detective Andrews advised John there were no fingerprints of anyone other than those who would normally be in the office. He also stated that because there was no other evidence, the case had a low priority and it was not being investigated actively. Although the information didn't sit well with him, John said he understood.

In the next two weeks, two more cases of missing materials were reported, none of which were cause for alarm and surely not enough to report to the insurance company. To file a claim for such a minor amount of missing materials would raise their rates for years to come.

During one of their twice-a-week meetings, John questioned his dad, "Have we ever had this many reports of missing materials before?"

"Not this many," replied his father. "There are always some, but this is strange. Maybe we should double up on our security at each site?"

"I don't know if that's necessary yet," stated John in reply. "We don't want to hire temporary help and then lay them off at the end of the job. If we hire a security company for each site that would be more expensive than what we've lost."

"You're right, but keep checking to make sure it doesn't get any worse," responded Mr. Lynch. "By the way, there's a regional contractors dinner meeting set for tomorrow night. Will you go in my place? Your mother and I are going to the Heart Ball with the Bowmans."

"Sure, I can do that. Hope you and mom have a good time."

The next evening at the dinner, John sat with some of his dad's old friends he'd known since he was young. During the course of the meal, one of the contractors remarked about some suspected petty thefts that had taken place at several of his projects. Two of the other contractors reported similar occurrences, which got John's immediate attention. John didn't feel it was his place to discuss company losses with these gentlemen, so he didn't mention their own missing supplies.

While the group socialized after the meeting, John mentioned what the other contractors had said about missing materials to several others around the bar. Two more contractors acknowledged an unusual amount of materials being mislaid or missing. John now became more and more interested in these events. As far as he knew, he was the only one who connected the thefts to a wide range of contractors.

The next day John reported his findings to his dad. "Sounds like strange things are happening. Better spread the word to our foremen to keep a better eye on our supplies."

"I did that this morning, replied John. "I also ordered fences to be put up around the three sites that don't already have them."

"Good. Let me know if there's anything fishy going on."

The day after that discussion, John was in his office when his secretary said he had a phone call from an old friend. "John," began the caller, "I happen to be in town on business and wondered if we could meet for lunch ... just the two of us. To tell you the truth, I want to pick your brain about something I'm working on."

"Sure," replied John, "I have to finish what I'm doing...How about an hour from now at the 'Ye Old Bar and Restaurant' on Route 322 at the east end of town?"

"That's okay with me. I get the bill since this is work-related," stated John's old friend.

When he got to the restaurant, John shook Harvey's hand and said, "I didn't ask you before how are your mom and dad doing. I haven't seen them since you moved."

"They're doing great," replied Harvey. "Both of them are retired and live in South Carolina. They're having a ball. They have lots of new friends and have been trying their hands at golfing. How about your parents? What are they up to?"

"They're also great. Dad's still working. Mom keeps herself busy with volunteer work ever since she cut back working in the office two years ago."

Harvey questioned John. "What ever happened to those brothers you were friends with? You and they were referred to as the four apostles. Remember I used to call you Apostle John."

John laughed, "Yeah, I remember. We're still the best of friends. They work for my dad."

After getting caught up on each other's lives, Harvey got around to the purpose of the meeting. "John, my boss was at your presentation at the economic conference. He thinks you may be able to help us with a problem we have." He continued with, "I didn't go into detail before, but I work for the Department of Justice." Harvey proceeded to give John some background information on his job. "My department's looking into some affairs of a company that you often work with. I'm doing a background investigation and would like to ask you some questions. I'm asking that you keep this in the strictest confidence."

John asked, "Do you think we should cut all ties to this

company? If so, I feel an obligation to advise some other contractors."

"No. Don't do that. If anything comes from my investigation, there's no way it will affect you or the other contractors. You're doing nothing that would put you in a difficult position. Remember, this is just a preliminary look into the company's financial background. We're just a little suspicious at this time. We have no proof. I only came to you because of our friendship and because of the research you did for your PhD." Harvey then proceeded to ask his questions and explained why his department was interested in the company under investigation.

John told Harvey as much as he knew. He questioned Harvey several times if he should disassociate Lynch Construction from the company that was being investigated. Harvey assured John that was not necessary. They left the meeting after John promised Harvey that the information discussed would remain confidential.

CHAPTER 6

John's schedule was very busy for the next couple of weeks. One day, after he had checked the status of a construction project, he decided to stop in Hagerstown, Maryland to visit an old friend of the family. Mike Roberts owned a small heating, ventilation, and air conditioning (HVAC) company.

When John met with him, he found out that Mr. Roberts was planning to sell the business and retire. His wife had died a few years before and he had no other family to leave or sell the business to. None of the employees were interested in buying it. The company had franchise rights in four states from two separate companies which manufactured high quality air conditioners. At the time Roberts acquired the franchises, both manufacturers were very small and unknown. Both had dealt only in window-type room air conditioners and whole house heating and air conditioning. Now each of the companies was becoming well known. They produced units of all sizes, including large units for business and industrial purposes.

John had always liked Mr. Roberts and spent some time talking with him. They eventually got around to the asking price when he sold the business. When John heard that, he told Roberts, "My dad may be interested in buying your business. Would it be possible if I took the company books home to review them? ... I'll return them within a day or so." Mike agreed because he had known the family for quite a few years and knew that John would keep his word.

When John reviewed the books and tax returns, he found that the company was making a relatively good profit. It could probably do better, but the owner didn't want to expand and hire more employees, all five of whom were nearing retirement age. John returned the books a few days later and told Mr. Roberts, "Your asking price appears to be reasonable. I'd like discuss this with dad when he returns from Florida."

Two weeks later, John received a call from the superintendent of a construction project near Johnstown who reported the theft of fifteen six-inch water valves. These materials were definitely not misplaced. He told John that he had checked them in himself and knew exactly where they were stored. The following day when the plumbing foreman went to get them, they weren't there. The superintendent said he had checked the entire site and knew for sure that they had been stolen.

The next day John learned that three skids of rubber roofing fabric were missing from another contractor's project. Again, nothing major, but a pattern was starting to develop.

John called all the superintendents of Lynch's construction projects and asked them to fax him a list of items missing over the past several months.

Several days later, with the list in hand, John stopped in Mark's office and asked him, "When you get a chance, can you look over this list of materials and give me your best guess if they could be used in the same project. And if that's the case, give me your guess about the type and size of building that would use these items? I'm in no big hurry. When you get a break, I'd like to know what you think."

"How about by the end of the week?" replied Mark. "I have a bid due by Thursday and I need to finish it up."

"Sure. Next week's okay with me."

"Matt and I are taking dates down to Ocean City, Maryland for the weekend," stated Mark. "Do you want to come along?"

"No thanks. Helen and I made plans to spend the weekend with her mother. What are Luke's plans?"

"Mary Anne is reeling him in, just like Helen is doing to you. He's going to her family reunion. Matt and I have a bet on which one of you gets hooked first."

"Whoever has Luke, wins that one. Have a nice weekend."

On Friday morning, Mark opened the door to John's office. "Got a few minutes? I looked over the list you gave me and came up with some ideas, but nothing I can nail down exactly."

"Sit down," John motioned to the chair. "Tell me what you think."

"Well," started Mark, "I want to make it clear that this is all conjecture. I don't want to hang my hat on this."

"Okay, I understand," said John knowing Mark's information would be better than a guess.

"The list of what's missing consists of items that could be used on any number of projects. Almost all of the projects would use ninety percent of these materials. However, two items stick out ... one is the water valves; the other is the rubber roofing. If they were used for the same building, it's my opinion that the project would have to be fairly large ... say at least ten to fifteen million. Also, if those two materials were used on the same building, I think it'd be a medium rise building.

"The water valves, in particular, indicate a building with many water distribution zones. Assuming three zones per floor, this would mean the building is five stories high.

"The rubber roofing is enough to cover about one twelve hundred square feet. This would also be consistent with the three water zones per floor." Mark continued, "Based on previous bids and information in our computer, a five-story office building would cost about twenty million for average fixtures. A dormitory building the same size, on the other hand, would require more partitions and bathrooms and consequently raise the cost by about ten million dollars.

"Of course, I could be way off-base. There's no real way of knowing. Now, tell me what the hell you are really looking for." Mark folded his arm across his chest waiting for a reply.

John then confided to him that he had learned of missing materials from various construction sites throughout central Pennsylvania. "I believe it could be another contractor stealing supplies and using them on his projects. It's not a secret, but we've been keeping the lid on this hoping the thefts would stop. The list you have is everything I know has been stolen recently. As you can tell, the overall amount is adding up."

John continued, "Tomorrow I have to drive down to State College. I'm going to stop in and talk to Pat Lewis, the superintendent, to get his opinion of what he thinks is going on. He's one of our most experienced men and I'd like his input. In the meantime, could you go through our files and old issues of *The Pennsylvania Bulletin* to check if any projects that match your opinion were advertised in the past year? It might give us a clue as to where to start."

"Okay," answered Mark, "let me know what Pat thinks."

The next afternoon John drove onto the State College construction site and parked his truck. He looked up at the building under construction and, once again, felt proud of his dad's accomplishments. Penn State's University Park campus was running out of space and the board decided to try a new concept in building dormitories. The first three floors of the building would be for parking, and the remaining five stories were designed for one-and two-bedroom apartments for students. Seven months ago, there was nothing on this location. Now, a new dormitory for three hundred residents and a parking garage were taking shape. Soon it would take its place as a well-known building on the Penn State campus. To date, there was no name for the building, but he had heard rumors that it was to be named after a former alumnus, one who had made a sizeable donation to the university.

John stopped in the office and greeted the four employees there. When he asked where he could find Pat, he was directed to the northwest corner of the new building. "Hi! Pat," John said as he approached. Pat had just finished talking to two men, "She's starting to look like a real building now," as he pointed toward the dorm.

"Just hope we can get the exterior completely done before winter sets in," replied Pat. "It would really set us up to get the job done ahead of schedule."

"Got a few minutes?" asked John. "I need to pick your brain about something."

"Sure. Let's sit over here and enjoy the nice weather. It will turn cold again soon enough," said Pat, as he went over and sat on a pile of two-by-fours that had just been delivered.

John joined him and told him about the list of stolen items he had compiled. He also told him what Mark thought about the type and size of building for which the materials may be used.

"Let me see the list," Pat said. After looking it over, he continued, "I agree that the only two real indicators are the roofing and the water valves. The other stuff could be used anywhere. Even the water valves are suspect. They may not need all of them or may need many more than the ones listed here. Then, they might buy just a few so it wouldn't look out of line. Of course, that could also be the case with the roofing materials.

Normally, you want all the roofing to be bought at the

same time. There are some variances in the thickness of that fabric. Any reliable contractor wouldn't want to mix them if possible. At least, we don't want to mix them. Let's see," as he turned and did some calculations on the top of the two-by-fours. "I think Mark's a little over his estimate on the building size. There's a lot of cutting to do when putting down a rubber roof. Most contractors order about twenty percent extra when it comes to the roofing. That way you have enough on hand to fix any mistakes, and there usually are mistakes with that stuff. My guess would be a hundred by hundred building. Why don't you check with the contractor it was stolen from?"

"Never thought of it," John said, as he realized how easy that would have been. "But, I'll do that tomorrow when I get back to the office. I have Mark checking which buildings fit the criteria that have been advertised recently. If we find the building size, we can narrow down the list of contractors who may need the stolen supplies."

"Thanks for your input," said John as he got up to leave. "Let me know if you think of anything else. See you later."

"Have a good one," replied Pat. "Tell your mom I said hi."

"Will do," as he shook Pat's hand and walked away.

Two days later, Pat called and told John to add another item to the list that kept getting longer. "Overnight we lost a whole load of two-by-fours. The watchman swears he was here all night and didn't see anyone drive through the gates. He locked the gates after he pulled his car onto the site at ten o'clock and didn't unlock the gate until six. He said he walked around the building once every hour and a half as we asked him to do. He didn't see or hear anything unusual."

"Someone could have taken the materials earlier in the evening," stated John.

"It's possible, but I was here until after six o'clock last evening."

"That leaves four hours that the site was unprotected," continued John.

"Right, but I questioned the janitor in the building next door and he didn't see or hear anything either. He was in and out of his building several times between four o'clock and midnight. I've already ordered more wood. It'll be delivered tomorrow morning."

"Okay, I'll tell Dad. In the meantime, think about who might know the watchman's schedule, as well as yours."

"Okay, I'll get on that," said Pat and hung up.

This news upset John. The rest of the day he thought more and more about this situation. The more he thought about it, the more he was pissed off. Until the matter was resolved, he knew it would be a priority for him.

The next morning right after John arrived at his office he received a call from Pat. "John, I have some important information for you concerning the material stolen from our project. Can you come up to State College? I don't want to talk about it over the phone."

"Sure, give me an hour to wrap things up here and I'll be there by ten."

When John arrived at the construction site, Pat motioned him outside and they walked around the building to where their materials were stored. "Recognize anything here?"

"No," said John, except it looks like you got more two-by-fours."

"Right on," replied Pat, "now look closer at the pieces."

John looked closer and saw some numbers written on top of a few pieces. "I still don't understand."

"Well, remember when you asked me about the size of the suspected building? The numbers on top of this pile of two-by-fours are the ones I wrote while I was doing my calculations. This is the same shipment we had the other day … the same exact wood."

"Well, I'll be damned," said John. "Who sent you this shipment? Was it the same supplier as the first order?"

"Claybourne Enterprises. And, yes, both orders were from them. We've been getting materials from them for years." John's mind flashed back and he remembered some other information he had heard about the company.

"Can you check to see if the other materials stolen were from them too?" John said.

"Can and did, and, yes. Everything stolen came from them. They're one of the biggest suppliers in Pennsylvania."

"Good job, but keep this information under your hat. Let's not jump to conclusions. We need more information before we can determine who did it," said John.

John spent the rest of the day going to several other construction projects that were being developed by his dad's firm. He learned that two thefts from these sites were originally delivered by Claybourne Enterprises. However, only one was reordered from that company. *At last, we may have gotten a lead into the missing materials,* John thought to himself.

During the next week, John contacted some other superintendents at companies which had materials stolen to question them where their stolen supplies were purchased. By the last call, he was not surprised at all to learn that most of the items stolen were originally obtained and then reordered from the same supplier, Claybourne Enterprises.

Another piece of information that John discovered was that in all the burglaries, the items stolen had been either on skids or were bundled with metal straps to hold the items together. At the time John contacted the other contractors; he hadn't given much thought to this because most shipments were handled that way.

With the facts in hand, John approached his dad to let him know of his findings and questioned what the next step should be. "We should turn all of this information over to the police and let them handle it," Mr. Lynch said.

"But which police department?" questioned John. "The thefts took place in at least eight different jurisdictions. The State Police would be a good place to start, but I don't think we have enough facts to get any convictions."

"You're probably right, but let's not get carried away with this. It's still very much suspicion on our part. You don't have any real proof. How about waiting until I check with a few friends before you start to accuse people of wrongdoing?" replied Mr. Lynch.

"Don't wait too long. I get this feeling in my gut that there's more to this than we know about so far."

"Right now, only you and I and Pat Lewis know who may be behind this. I told Pat to keep quiet about it," said John, "but I'd like to bring Luke and the twins in on this. Mark already knows part of it and he may have told Matthew and Luke about my suspicions."

"Okay, but don't jump off the deep end."

"I've got something else I want to bounce off of you," John said to his dad. "I stopped in Hagerstown to see Mike Roberts. He's selling his business. I got interested and looked at his records. Based on the two franchises he owns, I think it might be a good idea if you'd consider buying his business." They spent the next couple of hours going over the pros and cons of buying the business.

Ultimately, Mr. Lynch agreed that the outlook appeared good and made plans to contact Mike Roberts. If he concurred with John's assessment, Mr. Lynch would contact his attorneys to conduct final negotiations and draw up the necessary papers.

Chapter 7

John called his three friends. "Let's go up to the lake house for the weekend." Luke asked if he could invite Mary Anne. When John said, "not this time," Luke knew the weekend would be more than a get-together.

The four arrived late Friday afternoon and spent the evening and well into the night enjoying what felt like old times. Luke and John got a lot of ribbing about seeing Mary Anne and Helen exclusively, quite a difference from the many women they'd dated and bedded in the past eight years. This, in turn, brought up some other conquests. In particular, one episode came to mind where the twins and Luke bet on who could lift the most weight over their heads.

"As I recall," said John, "we were seniors in high school and it was at a basketball game. You three were arguing during the first half about who was the strongest. Finally, not being able to take it anymore, I suggested that we settle the argument by going downstairs at half time to the fitness room and use the barbells to find out, once and for all, who was the strongest. I didn't know the gate to the lower floor was locked."

"When we couldn't get in downstairs," interrupted Mark, "I suggested that we could settle this by using a girl to press over our heads. Whoever could do the most reps would be the winner."

Matt continued, "We called three girls over whom Mark and I had dated and told them what we had in mind. They were skeptical but agreed. After they made their bodies stiff, we lifted them up to shoulder height. We then pushed them upwards over our heads and then brought them back down to shoulder level. This constituted one rep. We were each up to twenty reps before one of the teachers broke through the crowd that had gathered and told us to stop."

"I could've done five more reps," stated Mark.

"Me too," said Matthew.

"I could've done at least ten more," said Luke proudly.

"Bullshit!" shouted the twins together.

John interrupted before they started the never-ending argument about who really was the strongest. "After the game, when we were walking to the cars, Luke said he didn't like the way five guys from the other school were acting. I guess it was his intuition. We stayed out of sight nearby as most of the crowd left the parking lot. A few minutes later, two of the girls, whom we had used as weights, started toward their cars. Five boys approached them and indicated they wanted to put their hands on the girls' chests, 'Just like those three clowns did earlier'."

Mark continued, "The girls ignored them, but one of those stupid assholes grabbed one of the girls. Luke was on him before any of us knew he had moved. I swear that guy flew fifteen feet in the air and landed hard on his right arm after Luke lifted him off the ground and tossed him away. By then, the three of us were on them. John took one out with a kick to the ribs. I got two to the ground with a block which sent them sliding across the gravel lot. Matthew grabbed the last one in a bear hug and kept squeezing until he heard a crack."

"Twenty seconds later, the ruckus was over. The girls were in their cars and out of the parking lot ... and five guys were on the ground. The one Luke had hit was screaming so loud I thought someone was bound to hear him.

"Man! We were out of there within seconds," said Luke. "The next day the police showed up at school to question some students and teachers about a fight that had taken place after the game. None of the teachers knew anything about the fight and apparently neither did the students. Or, if they did, they weren't talking.

"Later, we found out that, of the five idiots who attacked the girls, four were treated at the hospital. One had a broken wrist; another one had two cracked ribs; and two had cuts all over their arms and forehead. How did we miss the other one?"

John interrupted, "Rumor has it those guys said they were attacked by ten or twelve guys for no reason whatsoever."

"Yeah, that episode led to some great dates," stated Mark. "Every girl in school heard about it and wanted to thank us for protecting the sisterhood."

The four friends had more stories to tell and talked and laughed well into the night.

The following morning after exercise and a late breakfast, Luke broke the ice by saying, "Okay, boss, what's up? We know you asked us here for a reason. What's on your mind?"

"You're right," replied John. "You always could read me. I just want to run a few things by you and get some opinions." John told them everything he knew about the missing materials and some of his, as yet, unconfirmed suspicions about Claybourne Enterprises.

"Dad's trying to find out if we have enough information to take to the police, but I don't think there's anything conclusive," said John. "I'm afraid the police can't help yet, and if we get them involved now, they may start asking questions which could put a nix on catching who's responsible."

"Sounds like we need to catch someone in the act and beat

the shit out of them until we find out everything we need to know," said Mark.

Luke butted in, "How come you always want to kick the shit out of someone?"

Mark smiled and shrugged his shoulders.

"Catch them, yes," said John, "but I'm not sure about beating the shit out of them."

"You want to take all the fun out of it," replied Mark.

The group spent the rest of the morning and most of the afternoon brainstorming ways to find out how many people were involved. John, in his typical manner, had charts and diagrams taped all over the walls of the lake house. He left no possibility unturned. Nothing was to be considered sacred and no one was above suspicion. John pointed out that many individuals who worked for Lynch Construction were too well known or had way too much to lose if they were caught doing something so low. He told them that as far as he knew there were no morale problems within the company and the workforce was very stable with very little turnover in personnel.

After they discussed the possibilities, the four friends decided not to involve the police until they had more information. This decision was based on the foursome's belief that once the police were involved, word would get back to the thieves and the illicit activities would be moved elsewhere. Instead, they decided that the four of them would begin working the graveyard shift at four of the construction sites. They would be working undercover, so to speak, because no one, other than Mr. Lynch and the four of them, would know what they were doing.

Their objective was to watch the sites and, in the event of a heist, follow the culprits to their destination, thereby piecing together more of the puzzle. They agreed that no one would take it upon himself to try to capture those responsible.

They decided that during each night of the stakeout, they

would take notes on their laptops to determine if any patterns developed. They would then e-mail the notes to John who would compile them and e-mail the combined notes back to each of them. Also, at designated times throughout each night, they would call each other on cell phones … vibrate only … to check on any activities and keep each other awake.

If they discovered any thefts, they would call the closest person to their site and tell them to come running, although immediate help was not expected because the closest construction site was at least a half hour away. The first person called was to relay the messages to the others. It could take as long as two hours for the others to arrive, depending on which direction the thieves would take.

By evening, the only item remaining to finalize their plan was to get it approved by John's dad. John said, "My time's flexible enough to avoid a replacement, but we may have to get someone to replace the three of you."

Matt laughed at that, saying, "You don't do anything constructive to begin with."

Back in his office, with a plan now in hand, John spent an hour reducing the notes and charts on the walls to a manageable form on his laptop. He rearranged them in a logical order and e-mailed them back to the others.

By design, the plan didn't go any further than following the culprits to their destination. They would regroup and decide what the next step should be after they completed the first step.

When John explained their plan to his dad on Monday morning, Mr. Lynch was not at all enthused about it. He thought everything should be left to the police to investigate. "I think it's too risky for you to get involved with this," he exclaimed.

"But," said John, "you have to agree that the police don't have enough information to proceed with a viable investigation. Until we get enough evidence, they don't have a thing to go on, and if anyone of authority starts asking questions, they'll spoil any efforts to catch the culprits."

"Yes, I can see that," replied Mr. Lynch. "Are you sure you won't get hurt?"

"If anyone tries to hurt any of us, they'd better bring an army with them. Haven't you noticed the size of those three? And you know my training."

"Okay, okay, you've convinced me," said Mr. Lynch, "but if anything happens to you or those boys, your mother will have my ass. I'll get someone to cover for them for a while. It won't hurt to have others trained to do their jobs anyway."

When John realized that his dad was at least partially right about the risks involved, he made a call to his old friend to tell him about their plan and ask for his input. Harvey was skeptical but gave him some suggestions. Then, he asked John, "If you get any information, please let me know before you take any action."

John wondered why, but said, "I don't see any problem with that."

Two weeks later, all their plans were in place to begin the stakeouts. They decided to trade each other's vehicles periodically. In that way, the same vehicle wouldn't be observed each night.

If the first night of the stakeout was any indication, future nights would be almost unbearable. *Man it was cold.* John breathed on his hands and then rubbed them together. He couldn't turn the car on to run the heater, because a running car would be too easily noticed.

John couldn't believe he was sitting out here at three a.m. in a T-shirt and jeans. He was freezing his ass off. It had been warm that afternoon, but a cold front from Canada had dropped in late in the evening after John was already in place for the stakeout. He heard thunder and saw lightning for the past half-hour. To top it off, it had started to rain hard.

John was ready to call it a night when a sedan pulled up

to the site. He noted that a middle-aged woman climbed out of the car. John sat up a little straighter. *This is an interesting development.*

The woman opened an umbrella and ran toward the construction office. Just as she got to the steps, the door popped open. The night watchman stood there with a grin on his face. After she entered, the watchman kissed her and closed the door.

A mysterious woman was visiting the night watchman. John made a quick note of the time and the description of the woman. The woman left an hour later after receiving a good-bye kiss from the watchman.

John thought to himself. *Sure it's cold, but the other three are putting up with the same conditions.* He gave up on leaving early. So, he stayed and continued to get colder. Talking to the other three at the scheduled times didn't help because he realized they were smart enough to watch the weather forecast before they left and had dressed for the expected cold spell. *It's very enlightening to find out how really stupid you are*, John thought to himself, *It's not like I'm new to the area, new to the area. I know it can get cold at night at this time of the year. There's only so much a high IQ can do for you, you dumb ass.*

The next two weeks sped by fairly quickly. The four exchanged vehicles every night. They shifted locations to better positions when necessary. As the weather turned warmer, they found that sitting in the vehicles was more bearable. Each morning John would obtain the notes from the previous night's surveillance, retype and organize them and e-mail them back to the other three by mid-afternoon.

They discovered a few interesting facts. For instance, the mysterious woman … John called the project superintendent, "It's come to my attention that the night watchman on your job has a woman visit him a couple of times a week in the middle of the night."

The superintendent laughed. "Yeah, I know. It's his wife. She fills in at the nearby hospital. She has a strange shift. She gets off work at three a.m. They eat their lunch together and then she leaves. Her husband asked me if was okay. When I didn't see any harm in it, I agreed. Do you have a problem with that?" he asked seriously.

Because he didn't want the superintendent to know about their surveillance, he replied, "Not really. Someone told me about it so I thought I'd follow up on it."

The superintendent continued, "The night watchman does his job and makes his scheduled tours around and through the construction site. I didn't see any problem so I let it happen. Do you want me to put a stop to it?"

"No," John answered. "Let them enjoy their time together. Forget I called."

Luke reported that he observed that another watchman drank a bottle of beer with his meal. He also continued to do what was expected on his job. Therefore, the fact that he drank on the job only ended up as a note in John's file. After all, John sometimes also had a drink at lunch.

The only concern John had was about one of the watchmen on Mark's project. Mark reported that the watchman was elderly and had a difficult time walking up the six stories three times during his late night shift. John made a note to have the old timer transferred to a project that didn't have as many floors.

By the end of the third week, John was totally bored with the stakeouts and called a meeting with the other three to review their plan. "I don't know about you," he stated, "but this plan isn't working out like I expected. I thought we would've finalized this by now. Let's do some brainstorming to see what we can do to speed up the process."

"Brainstorm, my ass," said Mark. "I don't think I have a brain after three weeks of doing absolutely nothing except sitting on my sore ass and typing an occasional note into my computer."

Matthew broke in with, "God bless people who work at night all the time. How the hell do they sleep during the day? I never realized now much noise there is in our complex."

"John," said Luke, "do you know if there've been any other contractors who recently have had materials missing?"

John replied, "To tell you the truth, I haven't given it a thought. I just assumed that our plan would've worked by now, and we would've caught the crooks. I'll have dad check it out with some of his friends."

"Well! Because we have nothing else to do all night long," said Luke, "I've been thinking about ways to get real evidence against the thieves. Is there any way to determine that all, or at least most, of the merchandise stolen is being sold back to other companies? So far, we can only verify one shipment of two-by-fours that was the same as what was stolen and that might be purely by accident."

Matthew butted in, "You know, for a change, you're right, Luke. Maybe there's a better way of getting the necessary proof. I think anything would be better than sitting in a car all night waiting for something to happen."

"It shouldn't be too hard to meet with six or eight contractors to find out if any of their supplies were stolen recently," said Mark. "Maybe it's time that all the contractors are brought up to date on each other's problems. So far, we've been the only ones looking into this."

"I agree," John said woefully, "but the more people who get involved, the more chances are that the crooks will get wind of it and stop stealing supplies before they're caught. Dad will know whom he can trust to keep the information quiet. Maybe we could come up with a code to mark all incoming material and ask all the superintendents to check for the codes on all reorders."

"Another good question would be is how each shipment

is packed." interjected Matthew. "There may be something in common that would make it easier to reload the supplies."

The next morning John met with his dad and brought him up to date on their surveillance. John asked his dad, "Will you call some of your contractor friends and arrange a meeting to discuss the options?"

"Okay," said Mr. Lynch, "I'll call them this afternoon and set up a dinner meeting as soon as possible. In the meantime, you'd better give up with the stakeouts."

"Call me when you have the meeting set up. Can Luke, Matt and Mark also be there? I think it's time they meet some of the other contractors anyway."

"Okay. While you're here, you'd better stop and see your mother. She was complaining the other day that she hasn't seen you for a while. And tell the boys to see their mother too. Those two women are blaming me for working the four of you too hard."

"Speaking of working," said John. "How are you coming along with the negotiations on the buyouts of the two businesses?"

"Harrisburg Industrial Electronics is virtually wrapped up. All that's left is to finalize buyout payments. The Roberts' HVAC buyout is moving along okay. We've agreed to the price and it's in the attorneys' hands for now," replied Mr. Lynch.

"Do you have any particular method of financing in mind?"

"I thought we might want to use banks, instead of Masterson's group. Use them if we have to, but utilize banks as much as possible."

"Good," said John in reply. "I'll talk to you later today or in the morning."

Then, John went to the office to get caught up on the paperwork he had neglected because of the time he was spending on the thefts. He spent several hours calling some of the financial institutions they worked with to verify their credit status and to discuss possible financing of the two businesses that his dad was planning to buy.

He was surprised to discover that his dad apparently hadn't discussed financing Roberts' HVAC Company with the banks. He wondered about that because transfer of ownership was only a few weeks away.

Later that day Mr. Lynch stopped in and told John he had set up a dinner meeting for the day after tomorrow. He invited five other contractors. "We've been friends for many years and have been subs on each others' projects in the past," stated John's dad.

Two days later, Matthew, Mark, Luke, and John, together with Mr. Lynch, and the five contractors met in a private dining room at The Atherton. After dinner, Mr. Lynch addressed the group, "I personally think that was a mighty fine meal, but, as you know, I didn't invite you here just for dinner, as nice as it was to talk with all of you. My son John has been working on a problem that involves all of us to one extent or another. I'll ask him to explain it and what he recommends."

"Thanks, Dad," began John. "The four of us," referring to his three friends, "have been doing some investigative work concerning the numerous thefts that have occurred in the past several months. That's why I asked them to attend tonight."

John then brought them up to date on everything he knew and suspected concerning the missing materials without referring to his notes.

One of the contractors said, "I know Andrew Claybourne. He's been sick for a couple of years. Someone said he was on his deathbed. His two sons have been running the business since he got sick. I never liked either one of them. They're two smart asses … all they want is more of everything and when they get that, they want even more. I hear they're bleeding the business dry. They've been in and out of trouble for years ... a real hardship on their father. I heard one of them was arrested for drugs, but no charges were filed, that I know of."

John realized that the group probably had a number of questions because the room had become quiet. He decided to start a question and answer period.

One of the contractors began, "For myself, and I think I can speak for the others, we thank you for your efforts. However, I don't think there's anything we, as a group, can do about this. It appears to be a police matter, although I understand why you haven't involved them so far. My company doesn't have the expertise or manpower to help you with surveillance, if that's what you want. The losses involved for each of us are not all that much, probably a little more than previous projects, but still below anything we can submit as insurance claims. I know that our insurance costs would skyrocket."

"What do you want us to do?" asked another contractor. "We want to help, but you have to be more specific."

"Well," said John, "primarily, we wanted to pick your brains to see if you have any ideas about where to go from here. So far, we only have one incident that we know of for sure."

"Unfortunately, the information we have can't be proved. We need more documented data to take to the police."

"I have a plan of how you could help us get the proof we need. However, I have to ask for help to initiate the plan. It requires a little time on the part of your superintendents or other trusted employees."

"All right, let's hear what you have in mind," said the first contractor.

"My plan is simple enough, I think," said John. "We could mark each shipment received with a recognizable mark and then check each subsequent shipment for these marks and keep accurate records on these materials. If what I suspect is correct, we only have to worry about large items or materials that are bundled and tied together. Based on my research thus far, it's only high-priced materials or entire truckloads that are being stolen. If any of us find one of these marks, it's essential that it be noted and verified by at least two persons. They may have to testify in court about their findings. I'll call your project managers each Friday for updates for the next few weeks, if it's all right with you."

One of the contractors commented, "I'd be willing to put that much of an effort into this if it helps to catch those crooks." After several other questions, all five contractors agreed to this plan.

The next morning, John had twenty-two indelible stamps made, with a separate mark for each of the construction projects. Three days later they executed their plan.

CHAPTER 8

Most contractors in the northeastern part of the United States try to complete any outdoor work that could delay the completion of their project before the cold weather sets in. Such was the case on seven of the twenty-two projects where materials were being tracked. Three of the seven buildings were very similar in design and required the same type and size of doors and windows.

Five days after "the plan" was initiated, a truckload of doors and windows was delivered to a construction site in Clearfield County. The next day it was discovered that the materials had disappeared. Two days later, doors and windows with the markings of that project were delivered to a construction project in Blair County, sixty miles away. Both orders were received from Claybourne Enterprises. The foremen verified and documented the shipment. They reported that there weren't any other materials missing during the next two weeks.

With cold weather approaching, there was an increase in orders for materials needed for interior work. Because John talked to the various superintendents, he knew the status of each of the twenty-two projects. He devised the second phase of his plan by asking Pat Lewis, foreman of the State College dormitory project, to order a truckload of metal two-by-four studs, a common partition material, from Claybourne Enterprises. The studs were to be delivered the following Wednesday. He then asked the superintendent of an office building project that was being constructed by another contractor to place a similar order to be delivered a few days after the State College delivery.

John met with the three brothers at his apartment on the Saturday before the deliveries were scheduled. After explaining what he had done, John asked for input, "How do you think we can go about getting enough evidence to put these crooks in jail where they belong?"

"Why don't we set up a stakeout again," said Mark. "We'll catch them and then kick the living shit out of them," using his favorite phrase.

"Sounds like a good plan to me," Matthew said excitedly. "We'll pound them to a pulp so they'll never be able to lift a finger to steal again."

"As much as I would like to do that," interrupted John, "because I still want a shot at the clown who hit me on the head, it probably wouldn't work. The guys who are doing the actual work are probably not the ones behind this whole thing. They're just small fish. We want to find the brains behind this."

"Don't you think it's about time we bring the police in on this?" stated Luke, the sensible one.

John answered, "You're right, Luke. To get the evidence is one thing, but it's a different matter to take any further action. Let me bring you up to date and tell you about the next couple of phases of my plan." He then proceeded to tell them what he had in mind.

"Well," said Matthew, "that takes some of the fun out of it, but it leaves enough to make the juices flow a little."

"I still think we should kick the shit out of them," said Mark, trying to act angry.

"Luke, how long will it take you to get the equipment we need and make it work?" asked John.

"I probably have some of it in my apartment. I'll have to order the rest of it to make it work." answered Luke. "It'll take a few days for me to put it together."

"Forget that. That's too long. Can you get what you need here in town?"

"Sure. There's a good electronics store out by the mall."

"Get what you need and put it on this," replied John, as he handed Luke his credit card.

"Holy shit," said Mark quietly. "That's like giving fifty bucks to a kid in a candy store."

"Shut up," said Luke with a smile on his face. "I'll be good," as he winked at Mark.

"Okay," explained John, "let's drive over to State College and look at locations we can use."

"Good," said Mark, "There's a game today and the place will be crawling with women looking for a good time."

"Somehow I don't think Mary Anne would like that idea," interjected Luke.

"What Mary Anne doesn't know, won't hurt her," replied Mark under his breath.

On Wednesday, the appropriate bait was delivered to the construction site. The driver looked around the site and unloaded the truck next to the fence along a side street. As Luke and John filmed the process from the third floor of the dormitory building, John suddenly realized how the materials were being stolen without anyone observing anything suspicious. The superintendent marked the merchandise. As he had been instructed, Luke went down and got a closer picture of the stamped marks on the studs.

The four amateur sleuths met to get the equipment Luke had bought and to finalize plans. "Gee, Luke," asked John, "wouldn't walkie-talkies do the same job as these two-way radios? These are top-of-the-line. The Seals and the Delta Forces probably don't have equipment like this."

"Not really," replied Luke, winking at the twins, "I was afraid we needed more range and if one of us gets into trouble, he surely wants to be able to reach the others. And I, for one, want my hands free in case I have to defend myself."

"What about these video cameras? Do we really need four high quality, low-light cameras?" exclaimed John.

"Well, you did say it would be dark when the thieves strike, and we'll need different angles to cover all points," answered Luke. "Don't worry, I'll return them all when we're done with them."

"Yeah, sure you will," said John quietly. "Did you by any chance buy any tripods?"

"Of course," replied Luke, then under his breath, "four high-quality ones."

An hour after the workers left, the four amateur detectives arrived at their prearranged positions, hopefully to wait for the thieves. Because John thought he knew how the theft would take place, he asked Luke to set up a camera on a tripod half a block away pointed in the direction of the stockpiled material. "Can you rig this to start recording by remote control?" asked John.

"Of course," replied Luke, "I bought all the goodies I thought we might need."

"Why am I not surprised?" John said not so quietly. "Show me what to do."

"Just press this button," replied Luke as he handed him a remote control unit. "Now I have to get back up to the third floor without letting the watchman see me go over the fence. My camera is ready to go."

"Okay, get going and don't do anything stupid. Mark and Matt, can you hear me?" John said into the microphone on his headset.

"That's a 10-4," they replied in unison.

"Okay, keep an eye open and be ready to follow the truck if they make a move tonight. Also, film as much as you can."

"Will do," they answered together.

When it was dark, a pickup truck drove up the side street and slowed down near the construction site fence. John thought he saw some motion but wasn't sure. Before he could press the button to start the camera, the truck moved on up the street and drove away. "Luke, did you see that?" asked John.

"Yes, the truck slowed down and I think someone threw something over the fence," said Luke. "I got it on film. Do you want me to go and check?"

"No," John said, "stay out of sight." Then he continued, "Mark, a green pickup's headed your way. See if you can get the make and license number."

"See it now," replied Mark. "I've got the film running … two guys in the front seat, one in the back of the truck. You want me to follow it? Oh, forget that … it's pulling into the Bigler Road parking garage."

"No. Stay put."

"Hold it," said Mark. "The truck's coming out again. Two men are sitting in the front. Don't see anyone in the back."

"Are you still recording?"

"Right on, boss."

"Stay alert, everyone. Something's going down tonight," stated John.

It was near midnight and nothing had happened until Matthew spoke, "Got a jogger heading toward Park Avenue. He's dressed in jeans and a dark jacket with a hood. Sort of odd, don't you think? Hold on there. He stopped opposite the gate and is tying his shoe. Oops! He just moved behind the bushes in front of the building across the street."

"Can he see you?" asked John.

"Not unless he has X-ray vision," replied Matthew.

A half hour later, the night watchman left the office to

begin his scheduled walk around the construction site. Five minutes later, Matthew reported that the jogger had left his hiding place, looked around and ran across the street and climbed over the fence. "I've got it all on tape," Matthew said, "but I don't see him now."

"I got him," stated Luke from high above. "He's headed toward the stockpiled materials."

"Where's the watchman?" asked John.

"On the other side of the building," answered Luke. "He's already checked the supply area. It takes him twenty minutes to make his rounds."

"Keep filming that load of two-by-fours," stated John.

"Okay. There's a guy attaching something to the load of studs. There ... now I can see. He's attaching straps to the bundles. He must be done. Now he's lying down behind the studs. Here comes the watchman."

The watchman reentered the office trailer and opened his lunch bucket. He pulled out a set of earphones, put them on and started to eat a sandwich. As the watchman sat there eating his lunch he was oblivious to what was going on outside.

Mark said, "Got an empty flatbed headed your way ... no markings. Matt, after it goes by, you'd better move down the block to get a better picture. No doubt in my mind that this is what we've been waiting for."

"Make sure no one sees you," John said.

When the eighteen-wheeler passed Matthew's hiding place, it stopped and a man got out of the front and climbed on the back. After the lights were turned off, the tractor trailer moved around the corner and stopped next to the fence where the metal studs were located. The man in the back swung a hydraulic crane over the fence, and the man inside the fence attached the lifting straps. Within minutes, the truck was loaded with the supplies strapped down and was heading down the road.

Matthew said, "John, you were right about how they steal the material without being seen. They just lift it over the fence."

"Give credit where it's due," said John, "they sure are organized. Okay, Mark and Matt, go follow the truck as planned. Luke, what's happened to the guy inside the fence?" No answer. "Luke!" said John more loudly.

"Be quiet," replied Luke. "There's been a change in plans."

Oh no, John thought to himself. "Are the other two of you following the truck?" he asked the twins.

"I'm a block behind him," answered Matt.

"And I'm a block behind Matt," stated Mark. "We're headed east on Route 322."

"John," interrupted Luke. "I'm on foot following the guy from the site and I believe he's headed for the parking garage off of Park Avenue. Get your gear and head in my direction." Five minutes later, Luke continued, "He's going to the garage. Pick me up out front. I have to find out what he's driving." Several minutes later, Luke said, "He's driving a red Mustang."

John picked Luke up and dropped him off at his pickup. They caught up to the red Mustang and followed it east on Atherton Street through State College and onto Route 322 toward Lewistown.

"John, this is Matt. I'm still on 322 eastbound. I have to pass the truck because it was moving too slowly going over the mountain. Mark, there's no place for him to go, so you'd better stop and let him get a good head start."

"Okay, brother," John heard in his earphone.

John then commented. "We're following a red Mustang headed in your direction. Mark, I want you to watch out for us. When we pass you, you follow the car and we'll drop back and take turns following the trucks. That way we'll have less of a chance of being seen."

"Okay," was the only reply.

Thirty minutes later, after playing hopscotch with the Mustang and the eighteen-wheeler, Matt announced, "They're pulling into the truck stop at the Reedsville Interchange."

"If they go inside, one of you'd better stay with the tractor trailer," said John. "Luke and I will go inside if they do."

"Wait a minute," said Mark. "They're disconnecting the trailer."

"Okay, we see them," replied Luke, I've got the camera on."

A few minutes later, Matt observed the tractor portion of the rig being driven away, leaving two men in the parking lot. One got back into the red Mustang and the other got into a green Chevy pickup. "What do we do now?" questioned Matthew.

"Do we have pictures of all the license plates and the faces of the men?" asked John.

"I've got everything, including close-ups," replied Mark.

"Me too," said Luke happily.

"Let them go," replied John. "I'm more interested in that load of metal studs. We'll take turns watching that trailer. Luke and I will take the first watch. You can get something to eat or take a nap if you want."

Near daybreak, a truck pulled into the parking lot and backed up to the trailer load of stolen materials. "Isn't that nice?" said Luke, as he recorded the event. "They bring a truck with their logo clearly printed on the side." The truck driver finished his work and went into the restaurant.

"I'm fairly certain where that truck will go after the driver finishes his breakfast," stated John.

"Harrisburg's a good bet, but we'd better follow it anyway," continued Mark.

"No," replied John. "No use for all of us to go. You and Matt head for home and we'll follow him. See you back at my apartment about eight tonight. I'll stop and get some sleep at Luke's place before I head back."

"Okay, but you should leave now and let him pass you closer to Harrisburg. We'll wait until he leaves and take pictures of him heading east. We'll follow him past Lewistown to make sure he's heading your way."

"That sounds good to me. Sorry I didn't think of it first," answered John. "Let us know when he gets to the Narrows. After that he has to keep going. We'll wait at the first interchange."

For the next two hours, John and Luke followed the truck to Harrisburg. They periodically filmed the truck and road signs to document the direction the truck was traveling. The tractor trailer arrived at Claybourne Enterprises. The driver parked the truck and went into the office. Luke considered getting closer to see who the driver was talking to, but realized he couldn't do it without being seen and looking out of place.

Fifteen minutes later, the truck driver left the office and got into a blue Buick and drove away.

John asked, "Do you think we should stay here and follow the load, or do you think you feel sure you know where it's going?"

"No use staying here until tomorrow's scheduled delivery time," answered Luke. "Let's go to my place and catch some zees. We can start the film again when the studs are delivered to the other site."

As expected, the next morning the superintendent of the other construction project phoned John's office to let him know he had received the stamped material. He was told that John was out of the office, but the message would be relayed to him. To his surprise, John arrived at the construction site fifteen minutes later. John talked to the superintendent and the other witnesses and filmed the marks on the newly delivered merchandise. He also made note of the names of the two witnesses verifying the delivery and who had delivered the merchandise.

Later that day, John made a phone call to Washington and brought The Woodpecker up to date on their activities. The redhead indicated that all tapes should remain intact, showing the date and time the film was made. He told John he should send them to Washington by special messenger to his attention. "With that documentation, I can get approval to delve a little deeper into the financial aspects of the company," Harvey indicated. "Don't do anything until you hear from me."

"Okay, but don't drag it out," answered John.

"I'll have an answer within a few days. Talk to you later, and thanks."

John and his three cohorts reported back to their jobs to get caught up on the real work at their respective offices. John talked to his dad several times about the investigation. Mr. Lynch was thankful that they hadn't done anything dangerous and told John he must advise the other contractors about their activities. John agreed with the understanding he wouldn't tell the other contractors about the Washington connection.

Although John was getting anxious about what was happening in D.C., he managed to spend the next several days reviewing the financing for the upcoming purchases. He and his dad made many long phone conversations to several banks with whom they had worked with in the past. Although they had an excellent 4A credit rating, two of the bankers John talked to expressed concern over how slim of a margin they would be working on.

"If you go forward with these purchases, you could be jeopardizing the financing of a construction project later on," said one of the bankers.

"What about the payments we get throughout the construction phases?" inquired John. "Wouldn't that take precedence? We'd have money coming in from those periodic payments."

"Of course, it helps and I'm not saying it's impossible," replied the banker. "What I'm telling you is that our board may question your overall cash flow. You know better than I do how much it takes up front to get a major project started. Your mobilization alone can add up to a half a million dollars and payment for materials begins thirty days after notice to proceed."

The banker continued, "First payment from the owner usually doesn't begin until one hundred or a hundred eighty days after you start construction. On top of that, what happens if you start another development of your own?   That's total financing. There wouldn't be any money coming in until you started renting after the construction was completed."

"Okay," said John "I understand what you're saying. Thanks for the information."

Chapter 9

Two more weeks went by and John still hadn't heard from The Woodpecker. He wanted to call him to ask what the situation was but realized it wasn't his place to question a federal agency. Consequently, as John delved deeper into the purchase of the companies his father was interested in, an idea in his head became more appealing. He would have to discuss it soon with his father.

Finally, three weeks after taping the burglary, John got a call from Washington. "John, sorry it took so long to get back to you, but some things can't be done overnight," said Harvey.

"Just tell me you can catch these guys," replied John. "There've been two more thefts that we've documented."

"Well, we're fairly sure a case can be built against the three we know about, but we believe that they're not the ones in charge of the ring. Anyway, these thefts don't come under my agency's jurisdiction. We'll turn it over to your state police when the time comes. However, these thefts could be part of a larger problem that does come under my agency's jurisdiction. Is there any way you can come down to Washington and we can discuss our concerns? To be truthful, we want to pick your brain on the subject of corrupt business accounting."

"What do you mean by these thefts being part of a larger problem?"

"I can't explain it to you now, but if you come down to D.C., I'll be able to give you more details. Can you come?"

"It certainly gets my interest. Are you telling me we won't be able to turn our information about the thefts over to the police?"

"I'll tell you more if you come down, but yes … we may ask you to hold off reporting the theft of the materials. Could you come down and talk to us?"

John replied, "Sounds intriguing. Yes, I can drive down and meet with you. John checked his calendar and asked, "How about Monday afternoon?"

"That would be great. Do you know where our office is?"

"No."

Harvey gave him the address and told him he would leave word at the gate for his parking permit.

After the phone call, John went to his dad's office to bring him up to date and asked, "Is anyone using the lake house the rest of the week?"

"No," was his father's reply, "but I was thinking of sending a crew up to do some work that I haven't had time to do myself."

"How about if I take Luke and the twins up for a few days and we'll do what needs to be done?" stated John.

"Sure. A few days away from the gym won't hurt them."

"Don't worry about that," replied John. "I'm sure there's a lot to do up at the lake house that will give their muscles a good workout."

"If you get a chance, could you cut down that big maple tree on the left side of the road? Mom and I were there last week and made a list of things that should be done. It's pinned to the corkboard in the kitchen."

"No problem," answered John, "a few days of hard labor won't hurt any of us. If we get it done by Friday, we'll probably ask the girls up for the weekend."

"Make sure they sleep in their own rooms," Mr. Lynch said, somewhat seriously.

John then called his friends and told them about the plans, to which they readily agreed. After that, he called Helen and asked her if she could join them on Friday. "Sounds great," she replied. "I'll call Mary Anne and make arrangements for her to drive up with me. Who are the twins bringing?"

"I have no idea," answered John, "but they already had plans with the two women for the weekend. They were happy to change the location. Matt gave them your phone number so they could call you to give them some details on what to expect."

After cleaning up some loose ends at the office, John headed home to change clothes and to buy needed supplies for the weekend. He decided that he had to stop at the beer and liquor store, as well as the supermarket. And since it may be too cold, at least for the girls, to swim, he also decided to stop and pick up a few DVD movies at the local video rental store. He also picked several DVDs for the guys to watch before the girls arrived. Then he headed off to the lake house.

On the drive to the lake house, John thought a lot about his relationship with Helen. They had been dating steadily for some time and John was pleased that both of them seemed to be enjoying each other. They talked about many different subjects, including their desire to get married and start families after they had a chance to get established in their respective careers. Helen indicated that her job was a little different than she expected. She couldn't tell him about it without first clearing it with her uncle. John thought he knew what she was talking about but didn't pursue it. He let his mind drift to the fun they were having and to future possibilities, which for the time being he would keep to himself.

When John got up at his usual time and dressed in sweats, he did his regular 60-minute exercise on the flat section of the front lawn. He didn't know that for the last fifteen minutes of said exercise, he was being watched from a distance. The observer was impressed with what he saw.

Luke arrived as John was starting to prepare breakfast. John threw more eggs and bacon into the skillets, and they ate together. "Do you eat like this all the time?" asked Luke.

"No way," answered John, "only when I know I'll be working it off in the next couple of hours."

"I thought you worked out every day," replied Luke.

"I get a few days a week in at the gym and run a couple of other days," answered John, "but extra work means extra nourishment. I treat myself to breakfasts like this every so often, just to change my intake."

"It tastes good. It's a little different from the protein drink I usually have every morning."

"I didn't bring any protein mix with me, so you'll have to eat what I eat unless you want to go without," said John sarcastically.

"Don't worry. I always have mix with me and I'm sure the twins do too. When you pump iron like we do, it becomes second nature. But you're right, a meal like this occasionally won't hurt, especially if you sweat it out later; speaking of which, when do we start?"

"Just as soon as we clear the dishes," was the reply.

By the time the twins arrived, Luke and John had cut down three smaller dead trees and were working their way toward the big maple Mr. Lynch had mentioned. "Nice that you could join us," stated Luke. "It must be nice to sleep in late."

"Sorry about that," answered Mark. "We dropped my

car off for our dates to use on Friday. We decided to have breakfast with them."

"Well, get your puny little asses in gear. We've got work to do," was the darker brother's reply.

With that, the four started a marathon day of hard labor. The maple tree, as well as three other trees, were dropped, trimmed and cut up into pieces small enough to handle. Because of the number of trees cut, they decided to build three wood storage racks, one closer to the house and one about two hundred feet away to keep the wood relatively dry.

The shed closest to the house would be used for fireplace wood and the one farther away would hold medium-sized pieces to be cut up later or left until the following spring or summer. They built the third rack closer to the first so that the smaller branches could be used as kindling.

They used John's pickup to drag larger logs to a pile deeper in the woods, where they could be stored, or left to rot to provide shelter for wildlife. Mark made a comment to John, "Don't you think it's time for you to trade in this heap and buy yourself something nicer?"

"You're right." "I've been looking. I'll probably buy an SUV so I can still haul things when I need to."

Luke heard John's comment and said, "I'm thinking of buying a van."

It was dark by the time the four workers called it a day. Thinking back, John realized they hadn't even stopped to eat, even though they had consumed a fair amount of liquid. John started dinner while the other three took showers and changed. He planned the menu of salads, steaks on the grill, and baked potatoes for this evening's dinner. He would have served a nice wine, but John knew beer would be their choice because he saw that each of them had taken a bottle to the shower. Matthew was the first to return. John turned the grill work over to him while he went to shower.

After dinner, they spent the remainder of the evening relaxing with some interesting conversations. The CD player stayed on all evening, playing a variety of music including rock, country, jazz and pop. They didn't even consider turning on the TV or the DVD player. In addition, no one mentioned the thefts they were investigating. By midnight, all four had drunk enough beer to guarantee them a good night's sleep, but not enough to cause early morning hangovers.

In the morning John got up, put on clean sweats and headed toward the road that ran next to the lake. A mile into his run, he came across the owner of the vacation lodge that adjoined the lake house property. "Good morning, Mr. Everett, haven't seen you in a long time. What gets you up so early in the morning?"

"Good morning, John, and you're old enough to call me Frank," answered Frank Everett. "I'm just out for a walk like the doctor told me to do. He says I have to build up the heart muscle or have another attack."

"I'm sorry," stated John sincerely. "I didn't know you were having trouble."

"Yeah, I had a heart attack three months ago. Doctor said it was a major one. He wants me to stop working. It's too much strain running this place," pointing over his shoulder toward a lodge.

"Sorry to hear that," continued John. "How's your wife feeling?'

"The wife's not feeling well either. She wants to sell this place and move down to Georgia to live near our daughter Jen. Can't say I blame her. As a matter of fact, I had the appraiser out here last week. He says the building and fifty acres are worth four hundred fifty thousand. If I could sell it for that, I'd leave tomorrow. Business has been off a little. I guess it's because I've let the place get rundown. It's gotten to be a lot of work for my old bones."

"We sure would miss you if you moved," said John earnestly. "Have you considered leasing it to someone?"

"I've been thinking about a lot of things the last three months. I haven't been able to do any manual labor for a long time. Right now there's a lot to be done to close up before we could move. We're considering locking everything up right now and put it up for sale as is."

"When do you expect to leave?" asked John.

"We'll leave just as soon as I can get someone out here to close it up. It's probably going to cost me an arm and a leg since I can't do much myself."

John continued, "What all needs to be done?"

"We've been working on a list so we can get a good estimate from some of the local handymen. Guess I'll have to prioritize it so I don't spend more money than I have. Maybe I'll get lucky and have enough to have the important stuff done."

"Let's go look over your list and I'll give you an idea of what it will cost. That way you'll know what work you can afford to have done."

"You don't have to do that. I know you're busy enough over at your place. I heard the chainsaw working hard."

"Don't worry about it," returned John. "I'm working on a list of things Dad wants done. It's not critical to get it done this week."

"Well, it sure would help me to know what to expect."

John went in to say hello to Frank's wife, Ruth, and then looked over the list.

"Looks like three or four days work for one handyman," mumbled John. "Tell you what. Mrs. Everett, are you still as good of a cook as you once were?"

"Of course she is," answered Frank. "She always gets compliments from the guests who stay here."

"Well, if you'll agree to go over to my place and cook dinner for six, including the two of you, I'll put a dent into that list of yours," spouted John. "I just stocked the freezer and cupboards yesterday."

"I couldn't let you do that," said Mr. Everett. "Besides it's way too much for you to do by yourself in one day."

"Who said anything about doing it by myself? There are three of my muscle-bound friends only a mile away just waiting to flex their muscles."

After a few minutes of arguing back and forth, the Everetts agreed to let John and his friends do some of the work. However, Mr. Everett tried to get in the last word, "I'll stay here to help you. That way we'll be able to get it done sooner." He didn't see Mrs. Everett shake her head 'no' behind him.

"Forget it," said Mrs. Everett. "You won't be doing anything close to manual labor. You'll just sit here on the porch until it's time to go over to John's for me to start dinner."

"No, you're not going to sit here and watch us work," said John. "Both of you will go to my place and sit wherever you want until it's time to start preparing the meal. It would drive you crazy if you just sat here watching us. Now, I'm leaving and I'll return in about an hour. If you're still here when I get back, I'll turn around and go home." John then got up and left without another word.

After running back to the lake house, John explained the situation to his comrades, who were just finishing their morning exercise routines. "Sounds good to me," stated Mark. "Now how about I start breakfast while you three get dressed and one of you can finish up while I change clothes."

"Okay, little brother," replied Matt. "I always have to finish your work for you anyway."

"Get your puny ass out of here," answered Mark.

"You know, I'm getting tired of people calling my ass puny," remarked Matt, faking anger as he walked away.

A short time later, they all jumped into John's truck and drove over to the Everetts, who were just getting into their car as the pickup pulled into the driveway. John beeped the horn and kept driving up to the lodge.

The Everett Lodge was located on the same road, but one mile closer to the main highway than the Lynch lake house. Both buildings were of the same basic design ... wood-shingled siding and logs, river stone foundation, chimneys, and wide porches. The only modern features were the green metal roofs and the rustic-looking metal windows and doors. Frank Everett had contracted John's dad to remodel the Everett Lodge many years ago. At that time, Harold Lynch had bought the adjoining property and rebuilt his mountain retreat at the end of a private road next to a mountain lake.

By late afternoon, the four workers had completed the list of projects on the Everetts' list. Mark looked around the lodge and outbuildings. When he joined the others he said, "There are some projects that still could use some attention. Why don't we stay and put a dent in them?"

The other three looked at each other and nodded their okay.

John called the Everetts to have them delay dinner for two hours. The four spent the extra time working on those projects. When they were finished, they believed that the Everetts could leave as soon as they packed their personal belongings. They had accomplished everything that had to be done to have the lodge ready to be sold.

When they were finished with all the work that had to be done, Mark started an interesting conversation by saying, "With a lot of work and a little money, this place would make an excellent location to use as a training facility."

"Funny you should mention that," continued John, "I was thinking something along the same line. My scenario revolved fixing it up to rent out as a secluded conference center."

Without knowing what John and Mark had just commented about, Luke walked up and stated, "Matt and

Thunder and Lightning

I were just talking about what a nice place this would be to send some of your key personnel for R & R."

"You've got to be kidding," yelled Mark. "You heard us talking, didn't you?"

"Huh?" was the confused reply.

They discussed the subject on the short drive down the road. John stopped the truck for a short time as they discussed the possibility of buying the lodge.

Back at the lake house, the foursome took showers and changed their clothes. They then sat down with the Everetts to enjoy a meal that consisted of many more carbohydrates than any of the four normally ate. The boys never would have eaten that much food at one sitting. That is, except for the fact that they knew that if they didn't take second helpings, Mrs. Everett would be offended. Each of them extended his praises to Mrs. Everett for such a delicious, but too filling, meal.

"Well, Grandpa there helped by going down to the store to buy some of the ingredients I needed," she commented. "It also kept him out of my hair," she said, almost under her breath.

Mark said, "Hey, guys, pointing to his brothers, how about we clear the table and do the dishes? John needs some time to say good-bye to the Everetts."

"Sure," they replied in unison.

"Frank, Ruth," started John after they were seated in the great room, "are you sure you really want to sell the lodge and move closer to Jen?"

"We've made our decision," stated Ruth. "We're planning to call the realtor on Monday and put the whole place up for sale. Then, we'll head South within a few weeks and hope someone's interested in buying the lodge."

John asked carefully, "What will you do with the furniture, boats, and the farm machinery in the sheds if you do sell it?"

"We talked about that also." replied Frank. "Hopefully,

someone will buy the lodge and equipment and continue running it as a lodge. If not, we'll probably ask some farmers in the area if they have any use for it. We could try to sell it separately, but it's probably not worth the effort. There's some money to be made if someone wants to put the time and effort into updating the place. I don't have the strength or desire to do it anymore."

"What about the liquor and beer license?"

"Technically, it's only worth five hundred dollars, but if there's a demand, like down in the city, they're worth as much as five to ten thousand dollars. Not much of a demand out this far, so five hundred's a reasonable figure. Whoever buys the lodge would probably want the license as part of the deal. We really didn't do a bar business, just had it as a convenience to the customers who were staying with us."

"Tell you why I'm asking," continued John. "I know a group that may be interested in buying and continuing to operate the lodge. They'd want their own appraiser to look at the land and buildings, including the equipment and tools. I suppose it would take at least a week to make all the arrangements. Could you stay here long enough for me to check into this? If the group's interested, it could save you about six percent in fees for the realtor and would probably reduce the stress of finding a buyer while you're so far away."

"Yes, we could do that," answered Frank.

"I'll talk to my friends and if they're interested, they'll get the appraiser to come out as soon as possible," continued John. "In the meantime, do you mind if the four of us," referring to the three brothers and himself, "come over Saturday morning for a good look at the property?"

"That would be okay," replied Ruth with a questioning look. After a few minutes more of general conversation and appropriate thanks from both sides, the Everetts left for their home.

Chapter 10

"Man, that was a delicious meal," exclaimed Luke, "If I ate like that all the time, I'd weigh three hundred pounds within a week."

"Isn't that for sure!" added the other three.

They spent the next few hours discussing the Everett property as well as what items from the Lynches' list had to be worked on the next day. "I feel really good about what we did for the Everetts today," stated Matt. "Not necessarily because of the money we saved them, but it just seems that was the right thing to do."

"You're right, little brother," replied Luke. "Someone up there," pointing upward, "just put a checkmark in our books of good deeds done."

"Speaking of good deeds," interrupted Mark, "what do we have planned for the girls when they come up tomorrow night?"

"I can think of some good deeds they could do for us," answered Matt, with a devilish smile on his face.

"I think a little recreation may be in order," said Luke, "and not the kind you have in mind," as he nodded his head toward Matt. "Maybe we could play some volleyball or take a hike in the woods. If the weather holds, we could take the paddle boat out on the lake."

"Why don't we wait until they get here," Mark said. "We didn't tell them to bring hiking boots, or for that matter, a dress to go out to dinner."

"Who'd you invite?" John asked, referring to the twins.

"It's a surprise," laughed Mark. "We met them about six weeks ago and have been out with them a few times. You'll like them."

The next morning John, as usual, got up early and dressed for his exercise. This time he walked down to the lake and proceeded with his three-days-a-week stationary, as opposed to his three-a-week running, routine. For the second time in a week, someone watched his exercises from a distance. The one who was watching was more impressed than he was the first time he had seen John doing this routine.

That day they discovered that the work at the lake house property was not as strenuous as the previous two days. The four of them worked so well together that each knew what to do without any directions or discussion. If one or another needed a helping hand, it just seemed that one of them would show up like magic, assist where needed. Then, he'd go back to check off another item on the list, which was becoming shorter by the hour. By mid-afternoon, they looked at the list and found that they had completed all of the work. The work crew then went back to the house to enjoy a beer on the porch.

"Well, that certainly was interesting these past three days," stated Mark. "I'd think that with all the iron I usually pump my muscles wouldn't feel the strain."

"That's because you're just a little weakling," challenged Matt. "If you were as strong as I am you'd be able to endure much more than a little clean-up work."

John thought to himself *here we go again*.

"Screw you too, piss ant," returned Matt. "I can run circles around you when it comes to hard work, or for that matter, lifting weights."

"You're both full of shit," butted in Luke, "neither one of you is as strong as I am. You're both puny little asses."

"I'm fed up with this puny little ass routine," shouted Matthew. "Get your lazy ass up off that rocker and I'll show you who's the strongest," as he looked around for something to use as a barbell. "We'll use one of those logs outside and see how many bench press reps each of us can do."

"You're on," the other two brothers replied together.

"I'll be the referee," stated John, knowing he couldn't compete in any feat of strength with these three.

They went to the wood pile farthest from the house and Matt picked out a suitable log and said, "I'll go first. What do you think this thing weighs?"

"Somewhere around two hundred pounds," answered Luke as he and Mark lifted the log over Matt.

After telling his brothers to move the log this way and that, Matt said, "Okay, I'm ready, start counting."

"One ... two ... three ... four," John said, as Matt did each press. "Look, there come Helen and Mary Anne. They're a little early." John and Luke headed toward the driveway to welcome the girls.

"Oh, what the hell!" Mark said. He also left to greet the women.

Meanwhile, Matt continued, "Eight ... nine ... ten ..."

Twenty minutes later, the ladies and their luggage were settled into the house after they exchanged hugs and kisses. "Where's Matt?" asked Mary Anne.

"He's taking a nap out in the back yard," answered Mark, while shrugging to the guys.

Several minutes later, Matt entered and said hello and hugged the women as he ignored the men. "Excuse me," he said, "I have to go and shower. I'm a little sweated up after doing two hundred fifty-six bench presses."

"Like a horse's ass, you did," said Mark.

"I think the word is puny ass," laughed Luke. The women just looked at each other, not knowing what was going on.

Helen commented, "Matt, I talked to your dates yesterday. They called to ask what kind of clothes they should bring ... Sounds like they're very nice."

Matt said, with a smile, "I gave them your phone number so they could make arrangements with you. You're right about one thing. They're very nice."

"Pam and Sam, right?" she questioned. "The four of us talked for two hours on a conference call. I'm anxious to meet them. They said they'd be here about five to five thirty."

"In that case, I'd better get a shower and change clothes," Matt said as he bounced lightly up the stairs to his room.

"Do you two want to freshen up before we go upstairs to change?" asked John.

"No, we'll use the bathroom down here," answered Helen. John and Luke each grabbed a suitcase and took them to their rooms.

Later, the two couples were sitting in the great room when Mark and Matthew came down the steps dressed in casual, but identical clothes, which they only did when they were up to mischief.

"Something's up," Luke said as he looked questionably at John, who just shrugged.

"Our dates just called on the cell phone," stated Mark. "They'll be here in a few minutes. Please stay here while we go meet them so you won't ruin the surprise."

"Now you've really got us interested," said Helen. "What do you two have up your sleeve?"

"You'll see," as they heard a car approach and went outside.

A few minutes later Mark entered and said, "Everyone let me introduce you to Pam Fellinger."

Oh my God, she's gorgeous, Helen thought to herself, as they stood to meet her, *and what a body!*

The door opened again and Matthew said, "Folks, this is Sam Fellinger ... that's short for Samantha."

"Oh my," Mary Anne whispered to Helen, "They're identical twins and they're drop dead gorgeous. Life sure isn't fair to us lesser women." The new set of twins was indeed remarkably well built and nearly identical. They stood about five foot seven; were skinny by some standards, which only emphasized their cone-shaped and perky breasts. Their natural blonde hair was cut to a medium length, and they had beautiful faces. Any man would have a hard time looking into their blue eyes without looking down at their cleavage, which was displayed without apparent embarrassment.

"You'd better close your mouth now," expressed Mary Anne to Luke, "before you slobber on your shoes."

They were introduced to each other and soon everyone felt comfortable as if they'd been friends for years. "Where can we freshen up a bit?" asked Sam.

"You can have either room on the right side of the hallway," answered John.

"Which one is Matt's?" she replied, which settled the unasked question ... did the sisters want to sleep together?

After the female twins were finished freshening up in their respective rooms, they returned to the main room to exchange more information with their newly found friends. They fell into a relaxed conversation and immediately felt at ease. Sam said, "We moved to the area from central Ohio about three months ago."

Pam continued the comment with, "We went to college in Columbus. I have a degree in Human Resources and Sam in Labor Relations. We moved to State College when an opportunity to buy a small personnel agency became available."

The group continued to get acquainted until John asked,

"Who wants dinner? "We have to decide whether to eat in or go out."

"We've already discussed that at length and made a few decisions," answered Mary Anne. "I'm the designated speaker. Here are our plans ... this is going to be a casual weekend. We didn't bring any dresses, so no fancy restaurants. Tonight you'll take us to a nice casual place to eat, even a local bar will do, as long as it's not too redneck. We'd like a hearty breakfast in the morning and a light lunch. Tomorrow evening, we'll eat in. We'll cook if you agree to clear and wash the dishes. On Sunday morning we'd like to go to early church services ... it doesn't matter which church. After that, you'll take us to brunch, maybe over at that restaurant on the other side of the lake. In the evening you'll drive us home. You have to promise not to do any work on the house or around the property. And, you won't bring up any business while we're here. If you agree to these rules, you may get lucky. If you don't, tell us now and we'll leave. Do any of you have any questions?"

"No, no questions, we agree," each of the brothers said together.

"I agree also," John said timidly, a little surprised that the women had discussed getting 'lucky,' "but there's one little problem. We had planned to go down the road to our neighbors, the Everetts, to help them with some repairs. We'll be gone less than two hours if it's okay with you."

Mary Anne got a nod from each of the women and said, "That's okay. Now, let's go out to eat." After they returned back to the lake house, each couple retired to their respective room.

The next morning Helen and Mary Anne joined John for a morning run. The run was actually a slower jogging pace. All of them were feeling a bit tired after a night of drinking and dancing at three different bars and later more intimate activities.

Thunder and Lightning

When the three of them returned, they found the three brothers doing upper body training with weights they apparently had stored in Mark's car. The better-looking twins were sitting, if that's what you could call it, in the middle of the floor of the great room doing yoga exercises.

"I'm glad to see they have to do something to keep those wonderful bodies fit," commented Mary Anne to Helen.

"Do you think yoga would make my boobs look like that?" asked Mary Anne hopefully.

"No, forget it," Helen replied quietly.

"Like I said before, life isn't fair," interrupted Mary Anne.

The rest of the weekend went fairly much as dictated by Mary Anne's terms. It was very relaxing and all eight of them thoroughly enjoyed their time together. The women felt they were lucky to be dating these four handsome men who appeared to really like them. The guys, in turn, were lucky too ... several times in fact.

On the way back to her apartment on Sunday evening, Helen asked John, "I need to ask you an important question. But before I do, I have to tell you that I've dated other men since we met. I've only dated two men and both only two times each. We didn't have any sex. I have to know where you and I stand. I'm not asking for a commitment, but I have to know if we have a future," and she lapsed into silence.

"Well, you're not one to mince words," answered John. He pulled his truck into a convenient pull-off and turned off the engine.

"Helen, I like you very much, maybe even love you, even though I'm not sure how to define love. You're my best friend, at least my best female friend, but I'm not ready to get married. I've only been out with one other woman since we met. We've had dinner at least six times. Sex was out of the question. However, when I was a baby I suckled on her breast for eleven months."

He held up his hand to let her know he was not done, "I'd love to continue our relationship as is, but I don't want to hold you back from dating other men. I myself don't need that option. I don't plan on dating other women."

"John, I love you," she sobbed and jumped into his arms for a long soulful kiss. "I also agree to continue our relationship and date no one else."

John said, "Guess it was a good thing I pulled over." It was at least fifteen minutes later before she let go of John and dried her eyes. There were tears of joy in his eyes also, but she didn't notice or they might have been parked there much longer.

In the morning, John talked to his dad to let him know what they had accomplished at the lake house the previous week. "Got a question for you," John began. "The Everetts are going to sell their lodge. What you do think about me and my friends buying it as a business?"

Harold Lynch thought about this for a moment. Then he replied. "Frank and Ruth always seemed to make a decent living from the business." He paused again. John knew from experience that his father was evaluating everything he knew about the Everett Lodge.

Harold continued, "Assuming the price is right and the books show a potential, it's at least worth looking into." Then, after another pause, he questioned, "You know there's no way all four of you can make a living out there?"

John smiled and answered, "We all have good jobs. If we'd get involved with this, we would have to have someone else run it."

"Won't cost that much to look into," replied the boss. "Nothing ventured ... nothing gained. Give it a try."

"Thanks for your input," replied the father's only child. "You and Mom might want to visit the Everetts soon. They're moving to Georgia as soon as they put the lodge up for sale.

I've asked them to hold off for a week before they call a realtor."

John then called a real estate appraiser and told him what he needed. He also contacted his attorney concerning a mortgage financing question that involved a sale by article of agreement. He made one final call and left a message on an answering machine where he expressed thanks for a great weekend and extended his love. He then grabbed his overnight bag and drove to the Nation's Capitol for his scheduled meeting.

Chapter 11

Three and a half hours later, John drove into the Independence Avenue SW parking garage. The garage was mostly underground, below the office building above. Instead of a ticket machine at the entrance, there was an attendant. The parking attendant stepped out of the booth. "How are you today sir?" he asked.

"Just fine," answered John. "I'm John Lynch. I'm here to see Harvey Harrison." The attendant looked at his clipboard and recorded John's license plate number and the time.

Before John asked where to go, the attendant stepped back into the booth. The crossbars rose. The attendant leaned out and said, "Go to the fourth floor. Mr. Harrison will meet you there."

John gunned his engine and pulled into the garage. The sunlight dwindled, replaced by a florescent glow. John wondered why the agency wasn't located in the Justice Department.

After he stepped out of the elevator, John waited for his friend. Harvey met him and showed him into a nearby conference room. "John, this is Dave Becker, who I work with, and Joe Robertson, our immediate supervisor. After they shook hands and talked for a brief period, Harvey continued,

"I've discussed your problems and we've reviewed the tapes you sent us. By the way, those tapes were of excellent quality. The fact that you had more than one camera running will help if these people are ever taken to trial."

"There you go again. What do you mean? If they go to trial," John said with some emotion.

"Well, you never know," replied Joe. "They may plead guilty or do a plea bargain agreement. But in reality we're not too concerned with them. They can be arrested anytime. We want their boss, or bosses. We believe we have an idea who they may be but can't prove it yet."

"The reason we asked you to come here," continued Dave, "is that we believe you can help us dig deeper into this matter. We believe it's much bigger than the petty thefts you're concerned about."

"How can I help you?" returned John with a surprised look. "You're the big boys in this. You have the federal government behind you. I'm not even a rent-a-cop."

Joe Robertson picked up the conversation. "John, our agency is an investigative one, part of the Department of Justice. We don't do enforcement. Under certain circumstances, we could arrest someone, but in general, we leave that to the other agencies. You believe Claybourne Enterprises is responsible for stealing and reselling building supplies. You may be right, but we don't care. Based on results of an investigation we've been involved with for over a year, we believe they're involved with much more. At this time, I'm not authorized to tell you what other agencies are involved but suffice it to say there's more than one."

Joe stopped to take a drink of water then continued. "We've been at a standstill on this case for a good while. The reason Harvey asked you to come is only partially true. Our accountants have reviewed all of the financial statements and tax returns from Claybourne Enterprises, but they can't really determine if they're accurate or not. Let me restate that … all statements and returns are accurate, but some of them don't make sense when you compare one to the other. That's where your expertise comes in. You may be able to detect something we may have missed. Our boss was at the conference you spoke at and he was impressed with you. He tells us you've done extensive research on corrupt business accounting and are, in fact, an expert on the subject. We're hoping that your research will get us a lead."

John had the feeling Joe didn't appreciate that John had been asked to help with this case. Joe's expression was like someone just stuck him with a needle.

Regardless, John asked, "Do you believe that the person or persons stealing materials is the same as the ones you're checking into?"

"We feel it's a definite possibility," answered Harvey's boss. His voice was polite enough, but the tone had an edge to it.

John decided to push a little harder on the needle. "I'll help, with some conditions."

"What conditions?" questioned Joe Robertson, somewhat skeptical, with a real edge to his voice this time.

"I'd like it if I, as well my three friends, would be involved in the rest of the investigation."

"That's not possible," exclaimed Joe in a loud voice. "You don't have any authority to be involved. You don't have training for this work."

"You could hire me," interrupted John, knowing he wouldn't quit his current position anyhow. Pushing the needle deeper, he added. "Besides, what particular type of training do you need if you let someone else make the arrests?"

"I couldn't do that if I wanted to," stated Joe almost shouting. "There's a hiring freeze for our agency until next year's budget is passed. That's almost a full year away."

"You could hire my company as a consultant under the emergency acquisition act," continued John without emotion.

"Or, I could take the other copy of the tapes to the Pennsylvania State Police. Of course, that may put your suspects on guard and put a stop to your investigation."

"You son of a bitch, you're trying to blackmail us," shouted Robertson. "Anyway, you don't have a company," as he calmed down only a little.

Apparently, someone overheard Joe's loud voice. When the door opened, a distinguished looking older man entered the room. "Is there a problem?" asked the stranger.

"No, Pete." Joe answered, "Mr. Lynch and I were just discussing terms under which he could help us with the Claybourne case."

"Hello Doctor Lynch," acknowledging John's Ph. D., "My name is Peter Black. I'm director of this agency," as he came over and shook John's hand. "What is it you want?"

"I'd like to have my friends join me in the remaining part of your investigation. In return, I'll review the documents, which you've probably obtained illegally, and I'll work diligently to resolve your problems. Unlike other federal contractors, I'll only charge for the work we actually do and won't include overhead and profit percentages."

"Joe said you don't even have a company," stated the head of the agency.

"I plan on having one. It'll be a limited legal partnership," John answered smoothly ... "named Thunder and Lightning. I'd like you to have the paperwork prepared and have it notarized."

"And, why do you think we'll do this for you?" Peter said, much more smoothly than necessary.

"Because you're stuck in your investigation, which is bigger than you or Joe are willing to admit," John answered smugly. "If I don't find anything in your, quote unofficial documents, unquote, I won't charge you and won't ask to be involved in the investigation. Now, do you still want me to look at the documents?"

"You know, Joe's right, you are a SOB," stated Peter without emotion. "Get him the files. It may take a while to prepare the partnership papers. What should we state is the purpose of the partnership?"

"Make it general enough to fit any circumstances. I'll provide you with the partners' names, but leave the agreements open to add more partners," was John's reply. "Your lawyers will know how to do that."

"Holy shit, John," exclaimed Harvey when everyone else had left the room. "You've got a lot of nerve. What the hell do you think you're doing? You really are a SOB."

"Relax, Harvey," he smiled. "Joe rubbed me the wrong way, so I thought I'd push a little. I just wanted to see how anxious they were for me to look at the documents. I really didn't expect that I'd actually get my way. I would've done it without a fee if push came to shove."

"How did you know we're in a bind?" Harvey asked.

John smiled and replied, "When I got off the elevator and was waiting in the hall, someone came out of this room and entered the office next to this one," pointing behind him. "I heard him say, the video's ready. Go get Mr. Black."

"I knew who Peter Black was because I looked your agency up on the internet before contacting you the first time. I figured the top boss just doesn't attend meetings on petty theft, so this must be a major case. The video's probably still running so whoever is recording this can tell Mr. Black today's a freebee. But I still would like to have the partnership papers drawn up. I'll also need a notice to proceed with a letter dated tomorrow and reservations at a nearby hotel for tonight."

Four cardboard boxes were delivered to the conference room. John noticed that the boxes were separated according to years, beginning with the current and going back the previous three years. After Harvey left the room, John took the oldest box and separated the contents into state and federal tax returns, monthly bank statements, profit and loss statements and copies of the general ledger books.

John wondered how the hell they had obtained copies of all the documents. *Is big brother really watching or do the Feds have someone on the inside,* John thought to himself.

It took John two hours to go through the first box of records. Thanks to his photographic mind, he took very few notes. The Woodpecker stopped in once to see if John wanted anything or if he needed help. "No thanks," John answered. "The files are well organized. Someone put a lot of effort into arranging them. Can I take them to the hotel with me?"

"No. They won't allow that, but you can stay as long as you like." Harvey pointed to the far wall and said, "The camera's turned off. You're not being watched, but they may search you when you leave. Incidentally, we reserved a room for you at the Willard Hotel. It'll be billed to us."

"That's what I like about you Feds, you don't trust anyone. Thanks for the room. I'll stay for a few hours and come back in the morning."

"Okay," Harvey replied. "I can't stay with you. I have a dentist appointment scheduled."

John continued to review the files for several hours. He finished two of the four boxes when he decided to call it an evening. He made several notes, or more accurately several words or phrases on a lined sheet of paper, which he left lying on the table. He waved good-bye to the camera, which supposedly was turned off. He exited through security and headed for the hotel.

After a light dinner, John went to his room and checked his voice mail. He had four messages, but not the one he was hoping to hear. After that, he spent some time writing notes. If they were compared to the notes he had written earlier, there would be a similarity, except with more details. Before crawling into bed, he called Helen to say goodnight, which was becoming a nightly routine.

The next morning, John moved some of the furniture and did his exercises in his room, followed by a low-carb breakfast. By seven o'clock, John returned to the conference room to review the other two boxes. He made a mental note that the files and his notes had been moved, however slightly. By noon, he had completed his review and had three pages of notes. These notes and phrases were seemingly placed in an arbitrary manner, some on the left, middle or right side of the paper, and some separated by one to four blank lines. There appeared to be no rhyme or reason for how they were placed.

To the casual observer, it would appear that John had propped his feet on an adjoining chair and fell asleep. A trained observer would have noted the small movements of his hand and fingers and the occasional motion of his head, indicating a yes or no.

After he completed his mental review, John checked his notes and re-read various parts of the files he had scattered around the table and on chairs. He made several more notes.

Finally, when he was satisfied that he had done as much as possible, he repacked the files into the boxes in the exact order they had previously been organized. He opened the door and said, "Could you please tell Mr. Harrison and the others that I'm finished. You'd better have them bring a stenographer too," as he sat at the head of the table.

The four individuals whom he had met the previous day had apparently been notified that John was cleaning up the files because they arrived in less than two minutes. They arrived so quickly that John wondered if the camera was still on.

"Well, what did you find out?" asked Joe Robertson, somewhat smugly.

"Good afternoon to you too," answered John sarcastically.

"Sorry about that," apologized Peter. "You'll have to excuse

Joe. He's been on this case for awhile ... he's a little tense because we can't find something to get our teeth into."

"Yeah, and I don't like being blackmailed either," Joe said under his breath.

"Doctor Lynch is trying to help us," stated Peter, "and he's entitled to payment if he does, in fact, help us. So, now that you've reviewed the files, what's your opinion?"

"Thank you," continued John. "Please call me John. My doctorate is just too formal." Then he said, "Whoever collected this information did a nice job of arranging them in a logical order. My opinions are based on several factors. The first is that you must have an inside source. Some of these papers could only be obtained from company files. I need to know that they're, in fact, copies of the actual official documents."

"You may make that assumption," answered Peter.

"The second factor or question is do you have similar documents going back one or two additional years?"

"Yes, we do ... three additional years."

"One more question. Are the other three years comparable to the oldest one I looked at?"

John looked at each of them in turn. When he noticed that Peter gave him a nod, Joe Robertson replied, "Yes, the files from the other three years were completed in the same manner as the oldest box, except for the actual numbers. Our accountants said it would be like filling out a form, just plug in the numbers. That's why we didn't give you the other files. The accountants noticed a difference in the manner of how all the documents were prepared starting three years ago."

"Have you checked to see if they changed accountants between the third and fourth year?" John asked.

"Yes, in a way. They stopped using a firm they had used for years and started doing the work in-house," answered Joe. "One of the sons has some background in accounting and handles the books now, or at least he oversees how the books are prepared."

"So … John said, "the inside person is one of the bookkeepers who knows something is not kosher," as he held up his hand before any of the four could answer. He then turned to the stenographer and asked, "Can you hear me okay? If I talk too fast, tell me to slow down. I won't be offended."

"Thank you" was her reply, "but I can also check the tape."

John realized she was referring to the room next door. That comment verified that the camera and apparently a tape recorder were still on. *Well, live and learn*, he thought to himself. He then began with his opinions, "If you tried to use the different styles in accounting in a trial, it would probably be disregarded because there's nothing illegal about how the books are kept. Each accountant would do it differently, except for the big accounting firms … their procedures are performed exactly the same nationwide.

"Assuming the first year's records are reliable, the first thing that seems strange to me is that they bought this small building supply outlet on the east coast of Florida. Not so much that they bought it, but the fact that they have a truck drive from Pennsylvania to Florida and back on a regular basis. They probably explain it as shipping supplies back and forth, but that doesn't make sense from a business standpoint. Why wouldn't they have the supplies shipped directly to either location? They own a house in Stuart, Florida on the ocean, and charge the expenses for the trip as overhead expenses for managing the smaller company. But, why use a truck when they drive down to the outlet? Why not drive a car or fly? They also have some fairly high boat expenses for the Florida outlet. That may be stretching the limits of business expenses, but it's not that unusual.

"Another point that stands out is the sudden increase in the profit margin. Four years ago, the profit percentage was one and a half percent of gross income. That appears to be a reasonable profit. The next year it goes to two percent and now is up to five percent. There's nothing wrong with a five percent profit margin, but their gross income has increased dramatically and their expenses haven't increased at all. That's why the profit margin has increased to five percent."

John continued, "My sources tell me that the two Claybourne sons are now running the business because Mr. Claybourne is very ill. When they took over the business four years ago, they hired a guy named Paul Adams. I don't know what he does, but he gets paid extremely well. Based on these files, Paul Adams makes six hundred thousand a year, which is way above the norm for central Pennsylvania. The interesting thing is that this Paul Adams works as a private consultant ... no taxes are taken from his paycheck.

The two sons also pay themselves six hundred thousand per year, which is high and somewhat questionable. Even with the additional expense of these three salaries, their bank deposits have been increasing steadily for three years. One item that sticks out is the cash deposits. They own a building supply business. Unless you know something I don't, there's no retail store, other than the Florida business, associated with their operation. So where does all this cash come from? A fair amount of their income comes from companies I've never heard of. I guess they could be shipping to an area where I don't know the names.

The first thing I'd do is to verify that they don't have another source of cash income, such as another building supply outlet warehouse or a damaged goods store. With all the materials they handle, I'm sure there's some damaged merchandise. How do they get rid of those supplies?

If I could," John said pointedly, "I'd spend some resources to find out how these three spend their leisure time. I think it would be a good idea to perform a background check on this Paul Adams guy."

"Tha...tha...that's all folks," mimicking Porky Pig. "Now, if I've helped you in any way, I want in on the rest of the investigation. If not, say so, and I'll be on my way."

"So leave," said Robertson sarcastically.

As John got up to leave, Peter Black spoke up, "Hold on, John. I made an agreement with you and I'll follow through with my part. You did give us some insight and you deserve to be involved. Your partnership papers are almost finished. You do know that it's not necessary to register a partnership agreement, don't you?" John nodded that he knew this. Peter continued, "It's easier and quicker that way. If you don't have any problem with that, you can consider you and your partners as federal contractors with a notice to proceed dated tomorrow. We'll find some other way to pay you for today's work."

"Thank you," said John, "but there's no charge for today. If you could give me a disk including the partnership papers and the NTP, as well as some sort of letter or identification showing us as proper officials of the Federal Government, I'd appreciate it or, better yet, e-mail them to my office."

"We can do both," answered the head of the agency. "Joe, make sure the papers are completed today," stated Peter. "Thunder and Lightning, LLC is now a contractor for the federal government. They're being contracted to work on Harvey's and Dave's team."

"I don't like this idea," replied Joe Robertson sharply.

"We all do things we don't like to do," answered his boss.

Harvey and Dave asked John to accompany them up one flight of stairs to their office to review a few more details of what could or could not be done to further the investigation. Harvey said, "John, I do believe you're becoming a real asshole. Joe's pissed that Pete let you get involved."

John replied, "He's got a real chip on his shoulder. I guess I did lay it on a little thick. Maybe I'll get around to apologizing later."

"He's not as bad as he seems ... or, at least I don't think he can be that bad," Dave said. "He has a lot of pressure on him. This agency is fairly new. Joe came over from the Drug Enforcement Agency, which is another part of the Justice Department. Actually, he was forced to leave DEA. He married one of the big wig's secretaries. DEA has a policy that married couples can't work in the same division. One of them had to leave; so when a position was created here, he applied and got the job. He's not well liked because he lets everyone know he's well-to-do and flaunts his wealth. Apparently, he received a sizeable inheritance when his parents died. He isn't entirely convinced our division is worth the effort. We haven't caught any of the really big boys yet, but we're making progress. Most of the times when we get enough evidence to stop corporate fraud, the big timers have lawyers to get them off the hook."

The three of them worked for three more hours as they tried to decide in which direction their case should go. John explained the plan he had mentioned to his friends. In the end, they agreed the plan had merit. John stated that his new partnership would try to obtain information from the suspected thieves. However, they would not do anything until the federal agency had gathered more information on the three individuals now running Claybourne Enterprises.

Harvey and John had dinner together before John headed back to Pennsylvania. They talked about their personal lives and their respective college and work experiences. One exception was that John told Harvey that he had noticed that his files and notes had been moved during the night. Although John had no problem with anyone looking at his notes, he said it seemed odd since the other four people in the room had assured him that nothing would be disturbed. Harvey was more upset about it than John, but he didn't belabor the subject. He assured John that he would be in touch.

Chapter 12

On the way home, John retrieved his voice mail messages. One of messages was from his attorney. Because John knew this call would take some time and would require his full attention, he pulled off the interstate highway and returned the call. When he told her about the new partnership agreements he had arranged, she was impressed that the papers were prepared in such a short period of time. She agreed with John that she should have a close look at them as soon as possible. She also promised to have a letter of intent as well as a draft of an article of agreement ready by Friday to be delivered to John's office.

Then he called the three brothers to advise them of the good news he had received from the appraiser whom they had hired to check out the Everett property. "Let's meet Friday night at the lake house," he said. "We need to review our options and make some preliminary decisions about buying the Everett Lodge. In the meantime, we'd better think about our own about our own financial picture and how far in debt we want to go. I think it might be a good idea if we leave the women at home this time. Because of the finances we'll be discussing, I know we won't have enough time to spend with them."

The following three days were hectic for John. He spent most of his time working on the financial plans and meeting with bankers about the purchase of the two businesses his dad was planning. He also managed to discuss the Everett Lodge property with two of the bankers whom he believed to be the most receptive to the idea. The work on all the individual purchases was taxing the entire office staff. By Friday afternoon, the secretaries were ready to hang him for all the extra work they had to do, making one change after another.

Before he left on Friday, John met with his dad to go over more details of all the negotiations with which his dad was involved.

"As you know," Harold Lynch began, "the Industrial Electronics purchase is firmed up. The price we agreed upon is to be paid in three installments; the first by the end of the month; the second by March 31st of next year. The final payment will be made by the end of January of the following year. This works out best from a tax standpoint for both the seller and for us."

Mr. Lynch continued, "As far as the Roberts HVAC Company is concerned, Mike Roberts wants a lot less for the business than what your analysis indicates the company is worth. The property which the business sits on is worth as much as the buildings. Some of those buildings will probably need to be replaced. I've given some thought about buying everything outright without any bank financing. But that may not be the way to go at this point."

"Cash payment!" John exclaimed. "You're joking, right?

"I knew you wouldn't like that idea, but I did consider it for a short time. It really doesn't matter. The deal's been approved and will be finalized in a few months."

John said, "I noticed you borrowed some money from Lincoln Bank. I'm not familiar with that bank. Should I contact them about lending us the money?"

Harold paused momentarily, and then replied, "No, don't go to them." He looked into John's eyes to see if he was going to ask more questions about Lincoln Bank. John didn't pursue it.

"You know," stated John, "when this all happens, we're going to have to reorganize our entire corporate structure. We're spreading ourselves too thin and should consider separate corporations ... several corporations would be better. Since you bought the construction company, it's grown way beyond a family-owned business. Dad, you know that without multiple corporate structures, you're leaving yourself and the overall business open to all kinds of liabilities?"

"Yes, I do know," replied Mr. Lynch. "You mentioned this before and so have our attorneys. In fact, they've been doing some preliminary work and will recommend some changes."

"Something else you should give some thought to," John said. "It's time for you to start looking at semi-retirement. Sell the construction company, or at least divide it into separate corporations. Keep one for yourself if you want, but take advantage of the laws and get your money out of the company. Start traveling while your and mom's health is good. Enjoy yourselves. You've earned the right to retire on your own terms."

Mr. Lynch interrupted, "I've worked in construction all my life. It's difficult for me to stop thinking that I have to work twelve hours a day to make ends meet. My employees are important to me. What happens to them if I sell out?"

"That's my point exactly. Sell the company, or, as I suggested companies, to the employees. Let them get a bigger piece of the action. Research shows that working for a company one owns is better than working for someone else. Even if it is a company that treats them as well as you've always treated them. Under ESOP (Employee Stock Option Plans) rules you'd still be helping them finance the buyout, but you'd be able to stop working those long hours immediately. You'd still be here to help them make a solid transition. In five years, you could be completely bought out and free to do whatever you wanted to do."

John continued, "We'd have to be careful on how much the employees could purchase because of what happened at Enron and WorldCom. Those employees lost much of their retirement savings by over-investing in company stock in their 401(k) plans. Studies have also shown that ESOP firms pay about five to fifteen percent higher wages than non-ESOP companies. That would add some extra costs to the companies.

One other thing you should consider. The rental properties and the associated office support should be placed in one or more corporations. There are too many lawyers out there just waiting for the chance to sue you. You have to consider corporate structure, if for no other reason than to protect yourself from a major lawsuit."

John continued, "One last thing you have to consider. This one is a little touchy, but it has a lot of merit. What are you going to do about the Bowmans?"

John's dad was about to say something but changed his mind and said, "You're right. Martin and I have been cutting back a little, and we've talked about retiring, but nothing definite. We'll cross that bridge when we come to it."

"Okay, but it's something you have to do, not me," John said. "I've been talking to several banks about financing the Industrial Electronics Company. It wouldn't be a problem, but it may limit any other development you may want to start. Should we consider going to Masterson?"

Harold answered quickly, "No, that wouldn't be necessary. I've got something else in the back of my mind. I'll tell you about it after I firm up a few things. Don't worry about bank financing. I know a bank that will finance whatever we need."

John wondered what his dad was up to, but didn't say anything.

Harold continued, "Okay, I see you've put a lot of thought into dividing the business into several corporations. You're probably right. As I said, let me think about it and we'll talk about it again. I need to get some input from your mother, as well as my attorneys and accountants. Now, tell me a little more about this proposed venture you and the Bowman boys are considering."

John brought him up to date on the details about the Everett Lodge and the possibilities for its use. Mr. Lynch agreed that the price for the property was right, but was skeptical about the best use of the lodge.

"Make sure you all agree with this project." Then, after a pause, "I'll ask you the same question you asked me. Have you given any thought about going to Masterson?"

"Yes, I thought about it, but to tell you the truth, I think that venture's a little too risky to take to them. We'll use the Small Business Administration guarantees for the banks."

"Sounds okay, but you know I'll back you if you want me to. Think about it."

"Sure," answered John, "and how about giving some thought to the corporations? If you're going to do it, now's the time." John left his dad's office and stopped in his office to call one the best restaurants in town. He charged four gift certificates on his credit card and made arrangements to have them delivered to the four secretaries who had worked extra hard the past few days.

Harold and Margaret Lynch later had several meetings with Martin and Janet Bowman. They discussed the sale of the company to the employees and possible retirement plans.

Chapter 13

A few days later at the lake house, the four friends sat casually around the great room and discussed their thoughts, concerns, and financial status with regards to the Everett property. John let the brothers take the lead in the discussions, knowing full well that the decision to buy or not to buy was up to them. He was outnumbered three to one.

The three brothers had obviously discussed the proposed project at length between themselves. Luke summarized, "Let's start with a few assumptions. First, we only assume we could rent the facility out as a training center. There's nothing like it around to use as a comparison. Second, we can't run the business ourselves. We don't have any experience in this field. Third, the lodge and the other buildings need repairs and improvements. And fourth, and most importantly, we don't have enough ready cash to buy the property outright.

Let's look at them in reverse order," Luke continued. "We need four hundred fifty thousand to buy the property. I'm guessing another one hundred thousand to make the minimum improvements, fifty thousand to run a decent advertising campaign, and on top of that, at least two hundred thousand for operating expenses until the facility gets enough cash flow to pay for itself. That's eight hundred thousand minimum ... an even million would seem more likely. The four of us have a total of one hundred thousand in available cash. We could probably borrow another hundred thousand each without security, which still leaves us a half million short."

John thought *we're not going to use much of our own money if I have anything to do with this project. The rule in business is to use someone else's money ... not your own.*

Mark butted in, "That's fifty percent financing. Any bank should be willing to do that type of a deal, particularly if the property's used as collateral. They'd only be putting five hundred thousand at risk."

"Yes," replied Luke, "but it also means we wouldn't be able to purchase something else we may want, such as a house, for example."

"You're the only one who may want to buy a house in the near future," laughed Matt. "That's assuming, of course, that Mary Anne would say yes if you asked her to marry you."

"Yeah," Luke said, "at least I know the girl I'm with. You don't know if you're dating your girlfriend or her sister. Remember the tricks you used to play. They may be doing the same thing to you."

Matt wasn't amused, and answered somberly, "I should be so lucky."

Luke resumed, "Continuing with my summary... the building needs some work. We can do a lot of the work ourselves. But can we get it done in a timely manner? Also, in order to promote the facility, it should be completely done when we open. Word-of-mouth advertising will be very important to the operation. If we're still under construction, that kind of advertising may not be good enough."

"You sound like you don't want to go through with this deal," said Mark.

"No, it's not that," said Luke quickly. "I'm just making a summary and pointing out that there are problems we haven't completely resolved yet. Now, if I may continue. We need to hire someone to run the facility and to staff it. In my opinion, this is the easiest hurdle to jump. We could hire the manager and let him or her hire the rest of the staff."

"In my opinion," stated Mark, "we hire a firm to oversee the hiring of the manager and to assist the manager in hiring the staff if he or she so desires."

"That may be the right thing to do, but it costs money, which seems to be somewhat of a concern," returned Luke. "The other concern is can we attract companies to rent the lodge?"

Matthew spoke up, "John, you're sitting there being awfully quiet. What do you think?"

"Well," started John, "We've been discussing this for three hours and I still feel the same as I did a week or so ago when we first came up with the idea. I'm excited about the prospects. I believe the project can be profitable, but it won't make us rich. There are some major hurdles to overcome, but I do believe it's possible to work our way through them if we take them one at a time."

John continued, "The first decision we have to make is whether or not to tell the Everetts we're interested in buying the lodge. Unfortunately, they want to put it on the market within the next few days. The other major concern I have is how much it will cost to make improvements to the lodge. Our estimates are far from accurate at this point. We need a better plan so we can get a good estimate of the work to be done."

Mark asked, "You indicated previously that you weren't sure if the Everetts knew that we were the ones interested in buying the lodge. Do you think the Everetts would delay placing the property with a realtor if they knew that it was us who were interested in buying the lodge?"

"Umm," mumbled John slowly, "I guess it's a possibility. We could ask. The worst they could say is no. Another thing that we may want to consider is hiring a business consultant to check out some similar facilities in other locations and advise us on what improvements need to be made for our center."

"And I assume you know of such a firm," stated Mark, knowing John was referring to the company Helen's uncle owned.

"Yeah, I can think of one firm that would do it," John said with a smile on his face.

"Sure you do," laughed Matt. "And I bet you have a possible solution for the improvements also."

"Now you're catching on," returned John still smiling. "I talked to one of the architects dad used recently. He has some experience and has started his own business. He's available to start as soon as we need him. He's also willing to delay billings until after we're open and then we'd make monthly payments."

"Great!" Luke exclaimed. "When can we meet with him?"

"He'll be here at nine tomorrow morning, unless I call him before eight. The question is twofold. Do we want to risk spending thirty to forty thousand to hire some pros to get the information we need, and should we extend an option to buy to the Everetts?"

"I'm willing to put up my share," said Mark quickly.

"Me too," replied the other two brothers simultaneously.

"Then, it's a go," stated John somewhat triumphantly. "I'll call Mr. Everett now and see if we can meet with him tomorrow morning."

The next morning John and the three brothers drove to the Everett's lodge to make their proposal. After Matthew and Mark drove out to the main highway to meet with the architect, John and Luke continued their discussion with Mr. and Mrs. Everett.

John said, "Let's review what we discussed. Our

partnership "Thunder and Lightning" agrees to pay you ten thousand non-refundable dollars for the option to buy the property. That includes all of the equipment and furnishings and licenses. If we decide to buy, we will pay you four hundred fifty thousand dollars. The first installment of forty thousand dollars, plus ten thousand that is non-refundable, would be made upon signing an Article of Agreement to Purchase. The remaining four hundred thousand dollars, plus an interest of five percent per year, would be paid in four equal annual installments."

John and Luke signed a Letter of Intent and Option to Buy on behalf of the partnership. The Everetts agreed to sign the document after they asked their attorney to review it.

The following weeks were hectic for the four friends. They held numerous meetings in the evenings to brainstorm the work that required attention and to assign duties to each of the partners. After all the preliminary tasks were started, all that any one of them could do was sit back and wait for results before they could make the final decision to drop the idea or to proceed full speed ahead.

John was surprised that financing the project fell into place so easily. Two banks agreed to lend up to three-quarters of a million dollars each to finance the proposal. At first, John thought that the two banks had agreed to the financing because they were also his dad's best sources for financing his construction company's projects. After he thought about it some more, John knew that the banks had to have additional reasons to lend the money so readily. He would check his suspicions later if they decided to proceed with the project. In the meantime, what the Bowman brothers didn't know wouldn't hurt them.

Chapter 14

No sooner had things slowed down to normal routines, when Harvey Harrison called and asked John to meet him and Dave Becker for dinner within the next few days.

Two days after the phone call, John met with Harvey and Dave at a nearby restaurant. After they exchanged small talk, Harvey began to speak, "We've done some background investigation on this Paul Adams fellow who works for the Claybourne brothers. It seems his real name is Paul Hanover. He has a record, mostly drug violations with a couple of assaults. He did two years at a federal pen in Texas."

Dave picked up the conversation, saying, "Hanover doesn't spend a lot of time at the Claybourne offices. He has two girlfriends in Florida and splits his time between each. One lives near Naples and the other in Jensen Beach in houses that are owned by Claybourne Enterprises. Those two properties don't appear to have any mortgages. It appears that the women don't know each other. Hanover's cover is that he works as a traveling salesman for Claybourne Enterprises from Harrisburg, Pennsylvania."

Dave butted in, "Our sources state that he hasn't sold anything for the supply business for as long as he's been on the payroll. Two or three days a month he flies in a private jet, leased by Claybourne, to one of the major cities along the east coast. By coincidence, one of our people who was tracking him spotted fairly large boxes being unloaded off the plane. He saw the boxes were loaded in an unmarked van. They left the airport. Our agent tried to follow, but lost the van in traffic."

Harvey continued, "The plane is leased from a reputable firm. They've been cooperating with us. They indicated that on each flight this Adams fellow was accompanied by another individual, named Rocky, who looks like a National Football League lineman."

"It's our opinion that Adams, or Hanover, whatever you want to call him, is using Claybourne Enterprises as a front for something more sinister, maybe drug-related."

"And how does all this affect me?" asked John, somewhat concerned. "Surely, you don't expect me to get involved with a drug operation?"

"Well," stated Harvey, "since you asked. We believe that if the Claybourne brothers had pressure put on them, say for robbery, fraud, and cooking the books, they might make mistakes that could lead to getting something concrete on that Adams guy and his operation."

"This sounds like it could get dangerous," indicated John.

"I don't think so," exclaimed Dave hurriedly.

Harvey glanced at Dave and said to John, "You'd be working on catching some minor thieves, not a drug lord. We just want you to put pressure on the thieves. Let them know that you know about them stealing the building supplies. They either cooperate or you tell them you'll turn the tape over to the police. We hope to use them in turn to get to the Claybourne brothers. You won't ever be near that Adams fellow and his friends."

"I'm a little skeptical about this, but I'm willing to listen to what you have in mind. You'll have to be more specific."

An hour later, John asked, "Why don't you get someone from your own office to do this?"

Harvey answered, "We are a very small agency. We don't have the personnel or the time necessary to run a detailed and prolonged investigation. Our director has managed to get some casual assistance, in the form of research, from another federal agency, but no one full time."

"What about state or local police?" John interrupted.

"We don't want to bring them on board. We don't want any more people knowing about this than necessary. You're already involved ... you and your three friends."

"Your plan could get us in trouble with the local police departments. How do you get around that?"

"The Thunder and Lightning Partnership is already under a federal contract for yet unexplained services as per your own wishes. We'll back you up if any other authority questions your involvement."

John replied with, "We're not professionals. For instance, what happens if we violate someone's civil rights? Will we have to testify in court? What will those criminals do to us? I'm not sure you guys have thought about this and how it would affect us."

"We don't expect you to be in any situation where it'll be a concern. The worst that could happen is that some low level criminal gets off because of a technicality. It'd be convenient for all of us if you don't use your official status unless absolutely necessary."

"And you really believe that what you want us to do isn't dangerous," John stated in a concerned manner.

Harvey shrugged his shoulders and replied, "I don't believe you'll be in any real danger. You'll be doing investigative work. You won't have any direct contact with the culprits. You won't be making any arrests."

"Funny thing is," stated John, "there haven't been any reported thefts since the day I met with you in Washington,"

"That's strange," said Dave. "Sort of makes you wonder, doesn't it."

"Makes me wonder if they don't already know that they're under the microscope," stated John. "Did you ever find out who looked at my notes that I left in the conference room?"

"No. To tell you the truth, I didn't even check it out."

They continued discussion with more questions than the federal agents could answer. Finally, Dave put an end to the meeting by saying, "Call us in the next few days and let us know what you decide." With that, they shook hands and went their respective ways.

Later that night John had a hard time falling asleep because he had so many different problems to ponder. As much as he wanted to catch the thieves, he didn't want to put his friends in harm's way. But he knew that Harvey's plan, with some adjustments he had already thought of, wouldn't work without their involvement.

The next day John met with his dad and explained the entire plan which Harvey Harrison had devised. He omitted the revisions he thought were necessary to make the plan work. When he was finished, John asked his dad, "What do you think?"

Mr. Lynch replied, "I think you're nuts. Why do you want to get involved in this? Let the police do the work." He paused and then said, "But I know you. You got that little grain of sand in your sock. You won't give up until you find the grain or wear it down to a fine powder. It's like when you were eight or nine and you wanted to know why there was a man's face on the moon. The simple answer of 'It's just mountains on the moon' was not enough for you. I had to take you to the library and show you pictures of craters on the moon."

"And from whom did I inherit that trait?" stated John. "Mom and you have always said not to be satisfied with the answers unless you understand them. And, if there's more than one answer, there has to be a logical reason."

"Okay, okay. How long will this take?" Mr. Lynch asked.

"It'll take a day or two to organize everything and check out some suitable locations for our performance. After that, we should be finished in a week or two."

"Get this done and over with as soon as possible. We've got other issues to consider and a lot of decisions to make in the next few months," stated the self-made multi-millionaire. Harold knew he had no choice but to let his son finish this bizarre task.

John returned to his office and called the three brothers to arrange a meeting at his apartment to confirm that they still wanted to be involved, although he knew the answer would be positive.

The morning after meeting with his friends, John called Harvey to let him know they would participate in the scheme. Harvey said, "A package with your ID cards, together with all the backup information we have on the three known thieves, will be sent to you tomorrow. Call me when you're ready for us. Be careful, and remember, we don't want it known that you work for us unless it's absolutely necessary."

A week later, the foursome met to review the results of the background checks that had been conducted on the three suspects by Harvey's and Dave's agency. All the friends had to do was to verify some of the information and follow the three men for several days to establish patterns which would make it easier for them to initiate their plan.

Mark began, "The thief who drove the pickup truck picks up garbage during the day. He's not married, lives by himself and apparently doesn't have many friends. He calls himself Doug Hammer which may or may not be phony. He's had dinner by himself in different restaurants for the last three nights."

"My fellow," stated Luke, "the one, who was driving the flatbed truck, is married, has two children. His name is Tony

Marlow. He does small remodeling jobs when he can find work. He appears to be a good family man but has had a run of bad luck, job wise. I'm told he's a good carpenter and all-around handyman. We might be able to threaten him into revealing what he knows about the gang of thieves."

"I had the guy in the red Mustang," said Matthew. "His name is Paul Adams. He has a record as long as your arm, mostly small-time robbery, a few assaults, and half a dozen minor drug violations. Harvey's information indicates he could be high up in the drug lord organization. There's no record of where he works, so I assume he doesn't have a paying job. He had at least one meeting with the guy who picked up the trailer at the restaurant. What's his name? Is it Brubaker or something like that?"

"It's Barry Brubaker," interjected John. "If everything I hear is true, he's another bad apple like Adams. Let's avoid Brubaker and Adams for the time being. Let's concentrate on the guy without a family. Chances are if we get the information out of him, we can have him put in storage for a while without him being missed. Then we'll talk to the carpenter and this Barry fellow, in that order."

The next evening John and Mark staked out the garbage collector's apartment. They were sitting in their own vehicles and were equipped with the tactical earphones they had previously used.

"Here he comes," said Mark. "At least he cleans up before he goes out for the evening."

"Okay, I see him," replied John. "If he goes left, I'll follow him first. If he turns right, he's yours. We'll leapfrog him until he gets to where he's going. Let's hope he's not meeting someone."

Twenty minutes later, while they were parked near a diner, they watched the prey go inside and sit at a table by himself. "Let's wait until he eats and get him on the way out," stated John. Then into the microphone he said, "Matt and Luke, we're at the diner out near old Route 322. Can you be ready in forty-five minutes or so?"

"No problem," replied Matthew. "We're set up now and checking the recording devices Luke brought."

"Mark, you park your car down the street at the food market. It won't be out of place there. We'll use his car and you can drive it. I'll follow after we make sure no one notices anything strange."

"Will do," was the only reply.

By the time the truck driver came out of the diner, John had moved his truck to line up with their prey's car. Mark appeared to be using the phone in the phone booth at the side of the diner. John and Mark timed their arrival at the man's car as he unlocked his car. John called fairly loud, "Doug … Doug Hammer." When the man turned, John gave him a sharp stab in the neck with his fingers. As the man began to fall, apparently unconscious, Mark caught him and had him in the rear seat of the car within seconds.

How the hell did he do that? Mark thought to himself, wondering if he really saw what John had just done.

"Hurry," said John, "he'll only be out for five minutes or so. Stop at a parking lot and wrap the tape around his hands and feet. Gag him and put the bag over his head like we planned. I'll follow in a few minutes as soon as I make sure no one noticed what just happened."

Later at an empty warehouse in a secluded area of town, they led Doug Hammer to an area of bright lights in the middle of the floor. After they tied his hands and feet to a chair, they removed the hood from his head. He struggled for a few minutes trying to get free, but finally realized that this only made matters worse. It was then that he realized he was alone, or at least it seemed that way. "Hey," he shouted, "what the hell's going on? Why are you doing this to me? Where am I?" He kept this up for several minutes until he realized no one was there to hear him. Luke and Mark had heard him, so they turned up the volume of the tape recorder on which Luke had copied sounds from a gangster movie.

Hammer thought he heard something seemingly far away. It sounded as if someone was being hit, like a slapping sound. As he listened closer, the sound stopped and he could hear a voice. "Tell me ... let you go. I have Hammer next door ... you can save him ... just want to know who hired you." More rhythmic sounds, like garlic being smashed with the palm of your hand. He heard someone moaning. Then, "Let him go ... out for awhile. Let's ask this Hammer guy some questions."

A few minutes later, two muscle-bound men appeared in the bright lights surrounding him. All he could see was the lower part of their bodies and the massive arms and shoulders. One was white and the other light brown. Both wore muscle shirts, drenched in sweat and they each had leather gloves over their hands. And what hands they were ... like ten-pound hams swinging on the ends of four-by-four sculptured forearms.

"First question, what's your real name?"

"It's Doug Hammer ... Douglas Joseph Hammer's my real name."

"We want to know about the building supplies you stole. What did you do with them? Why did you take them? Who else is involved? Answer and we'll let you go. We have your friend Brubaker over there. One of you, or more likely both of you, will tell us what we want to know before we leave here."

With that, the brown one stepped closer and said, "Next question ... how many of you guys involved?"

"I don't know what you're talking about," which caused him to get slapped lightly, first with a ham swinging from the right and then like a pendulum with the ham that swung from the left. He knew the slap was not full force, but it still felt like a brick hit him twice. His first thought was that the gloves were lined with lead weights. His second thought was to tell them anything they wanted to know.

"We have videos showing you stealing supplies. So, we think you do know what we're talking about. Now I'll ask you again. How many of you are involved with stealing building supplies?" Just as he was ready to answer, the frightened Mr. Hammer heard someone moaning from the adjoining room. "I'll talk. I'll answer your questions. Don't hit me again."

"Let's go see what your friend Brubaker has to say for himself. Mr. Hammer, if you'll excuse us we'll be right back." As two of them walked away, Hammer heard "turn on the radio, in case this one can hear us. That way we can see if they give us the same answers."

Hammer heard the radio and what seemed like someone was being punched. He thought things through. *They have videos of us taking the building materials. I'd better tell them what they want to know. They may kill me if I don't tell them what I know. The videos will show I'm telling the truth.*

A few minutes later, the two muscular men returned. "Well now, your buddy Brubaker had some answers for us. Now it's your turn. How many people involved with your scheme? You'll answer either now or after we loosen your tongue a little."

"No need to get violent," Hammer replied. "I only know of four other people, but there may be more."

"Now that's better. What are their names?"

"There's Barry Brubaker, whom you apparently know about. He's from Philadelphia. Craig Arthurs did a few jobs with us, but he moved to New York. He was replaced with a guy named Tony Marlow, who only did one job that I know of. Also, a guy named Paul Adams. They're the only ones I know."

"That's very good Mr. Hammer. Now, who hired you?"

"Barry Brubaker made me do it. I owed him some money on bets I placed. He convinced me that the debt would be wiped out if I helped him with a few jobs. It ended up being eleven jobs. I tried to get out, but Barry told me he'd decide when it was over, not me. I think Craig Arthurs had some gambling debts also. The way it was set up was that there had to be someone else involved. We dropped the load off at the parking lot of a restaurant and it was picked up by guys in another truck. I'm fairly sure none of the others came back to get it."

"How did Brubaker get involved?"

"I don't know for sure, but he's connected to the mob. I think he does drugs too. He's a little unstable and scares the shit out of me."

"What about this guy Marlow?"

Hammer didn't hesitate, "Tony's a good guy. I was forced to find someone to help us when Arthurs moved. Tony's name came to mind. He was only with me for one job. I really didn't want to get him involved, but I was desperate."

"How's this Paul Adams guy involved?" asked Luke.

"I think he's also from Philly," replied Hammer, "he seems to be in charge, although Barry does most of the talking.

They're the only ones I know about. Who are you guys anyway? What's this all about?"

"If we tell you that, we may have to make sure you don't tell anyone else."

"Hold on," stated Hammer. "I don't want to know anything that may get me hurt."

"No problem. Names don't matter. Let's just say that Brubaker and some of his friends stepped over the line. It's our job to make sure they know where the line is and to keep them from crossing it again. Your story checks out, so you're safe for now. However, how can we be sure you won't contact them to tell them about us?"

"I don't know them that well, or how to contact them, so how can I talk to them?"

"Good point! But, how can we be sure?"

Hammer's mind was in overdrive. *How can I get out of this? Maybe I can kill two birds with one stone.* He replied nervously, "How about if I leave town for awhile. I have some vacation time that I have to use or lose it. I've been thinking about visiting my brother in South Carolina. I can be out of here in two days and stay away for a month. Maybe get a job down there. Will that help?"

"It could. Wait here for a minute," as the gruesome twosome walked away.

"Like where could I go," stated Hammer.

A few minutes later, one of them returned and said, "My friend will return you to a suitable location in your car. You'll have to keep the bag over your head, so you don't see his face. That's for your benefit. If you saw him, it might require drastic actions on our part which could prevent you from identifying him or me. Just remember one thing. We have long arms and will find you if you talk to any of the others."

"What about Brubaker?" asked Hammer.

"Don't worry about him. He'll need some medical attention before he does any more work. We'll see that he gets what he deserves. One more question. Tell us what you know about the assault on the son of one of the contractors. He was hit over the head with a two-by-four."

"I don't know anything about that. Please believe me. I didn't do anything like that, and I don't know who may have done it."

After Mark yanked the hood over his head, he drove Hammer to the food market where he got out and disappeared in the traffic. Five minutes later Luke picked him up.

When everyone was back at the office, John spoke, "That went as well as could be expected. We hadn't planned on Hammer leaving town, but maybe it works out for the best."

Luke interrupted, "We may have left a crook get away. It's possible we may never see him again."

"You're right, Luke," replied Matt, "but he's just a small

fish in the scheme of things. We wanted the thefts to stop. And apparently they've stopped."

"We need to get to Brubaker and Marlow ASAP," stated Mark, "before they miss Hammer."

"You're right," continued John. "I get the feeling Brubaker is our best bet for finding out who actually hired the trio. But let's talk to Marlow first. I'm guessing we don't have to pull the same trick on him as we did with Hammer."

"I think you're right," said Mark. "Why don't you invite him to the office tomorrow morning? We'll tell him it's for a job interview. One of us can be here to back you up."

"Good idea," said John, "I'll have my secretary call him tomorrow morning. We also need someone that's not involved with any of us to call Hammer and his employer to make sure he does leave the area."

"I know two people who will do it for me," said Mark. "Pam or Sam could say they're verifying Hammer's employment record. I got a phone number for Hammer's brother in South Carolina. I told Hammer we'd be calling him there in a day or so."

John said, "Mark, meet me here in the morning and we'll talk to Marlow. Matt, you've been tracking Brubaker. You and Luke follow him around tomorrow to see if he sticks to his established pattern, particularly if he tries to contact Hammer or Marlow. All of us can meet about five tomorrow afternoon to discuss what to do next."

The next day, John's secretary announced, "Mr. Marlow is here for his appointment." John replied, "Thanks Lucy. Ask him to wait for about five minutes. Will you call Mark and tell him Mr. Marlow has arrived. Tell Mark to follow my lead."

When Mark entered the office, he winked at John and took a seat where he would be able to see Marlow's face. Also, he positioned himself between Marlow and John just in case if Marlow became aggressive

Thunder and Lightning

"Good morning Tony, I'm John Lynch and this is Mark Bowman. Please have a seat." They exchanged handshakes and John continued, "Would you like some coffee or something else to drink?"

When Marlow saw each of the other two had coffee cups in front of them, he said, "Coffee would be nice," as he seated himself in the only available chair.

Mark poured coffee for Tony and refilled his and John's cups, and returned to his seat. They spent several minutes talking about the outcome of last night's game and the usual weather topics. John's first impression of Tony was that he was a bright young man who was involved with something over his head. John stated, "Tell us a little about yourself and your family, such as your educational and work backgrounds."

"Okay, I'm twenty three years old, married and have two children, ages three and one. I attended Penn College and have an Associate Degree in Carpentry. Before I got a job in home construction and remodeling, my wife and I lived on a farm. I've worked in construction for two years. Unfortunately, I've been out of work for the past year. The company I worked for went bankrupt and there's not a lot of home building going on at this time. I've stayed in the area so my wife can help with her ailing mother. I do some remodeling and handyman work when I can find it. I have a CDL license and drive tractor trailer when I can find the work. It's tough out there right now. That's the basics. Now, can I ask you a question?"

"Sure, go ahead," replied John.

"What made you call me? I filled out an application a couple of years ago, but got a letter stating that there were no openings at that time. I wouldn't think you kept applications that long."

John looked at Mark and turned to Marlow, "I won't lie to you. I didn't pull your application out of our files, although it's probably still there. Actually, our workforce has been very steady for quite some time. When we need someone, we often hire members of families who already work for us.

The reason we asked you to come here was to find out what you know about missing materials that have been removed from numerous construction sites in this and surrounding counties."

As Tony was about to deny involvement, John continued, "Don't deny it. We have videos of you participating in at least one heist. It just happens to be from one of our construction sites. I took some of the pictures myself; Mark took some others."

"I...I don't know what you're...," started Marlow, with tears beginning to form in his eyes. "Oh God, am I in trouble! My wife will kill me," as he put his face in his hands and cried openly.

Mark and John let him compose himself for a couple of minutes. Then, Mark looked at John, who nodded, and said, "We're not here to make trouble for you, although we may not be able to prevent the police getting involved. What we really want to know is who all is involved, who hired you and everything else you know about the thefts."

After a few quiet moments, with Tony sobbing in his hands and mumbling to himself, he poured it all out, seemingly in one breath. "It only happened one time. An acquaintance of mine, Doug Hammer, knew I needed work. He asked if I would fix some porch steps. I said yes, and he gave me a hundred dollars up front. I spent the money on groceries on the way home. My wife and I had a garden in the yard, but we were almost out of food. The next day, when I went to the address he gave me, there were no steps that needed repair. The entrance was at ground level. I called and asked him about that and he said he was mistaken; just to return the money. I couldn't because I'd already spent it on groceries. When I told him this, he got mad, but later said he would forget about the money if I helped him on another job. I said okay, but I didn't know what I was to do until we met two days later, where I met his friend Barry Brubaker."

"Brubaker explained what they wanted me to do and I didn't like the idea. I tried to get out of it, but Brubaker threatened to hurt my wife and children. I didn't have any choice, so I helped them."

After a pause, while Marlow was still crying, John said, "Tell us exactly what you did."

"I'm so ashamed," Tony replied. "They had it all figured out. I met them out on Route 322. I drove a flatbed to State College, following a red Mustang driven by a guy named Paul Adams. Later, I was directed to turn off the lights and drive down a road. I pulled up on the curb next to a construction site. I had to move a hydraulic lift over the fence. Brubaker attached loading straps to the crane and I brought the load over the fence and onto the flatbed. He knew exactly where the supplies were. Then, after the loading straps were tossed over the fence, I helped attach the loaded materials onto the truck. It only took a few minutes, but it seemed like an hour. I thought I'd get caught for sure. Then, I drove the truck to the Reedsville restaurant and dropped the trailer off in the parking lot. Barry told me to keep my mouth shut about what we did or I would suffer the consequences. After dropping the trailer, I went to the next interchange and parked the truck. I got into my pickup and went home just as I was instructed.

"I had to lie to my wife about where I'd been. I've been worried about what I did ever since. Now that I've been caught, it's a relief. I'll accept whatever punishment I have coming. It's going to be hard on my wife, but I'll feel better when it's over. I've been a wreck since that night, knowing that the truth would come out eventually."

After several minutes of solemn quiet, John said softly, "Thank you for telling us about that night. Please excuse

Mark and me for a minute or two," John motioned to Mark to follow him out of the room.

"Well, what do you think?" John asked.

"I believe he's telling the truth," replied Mark. "It matches up to what we witnessed and have on film. It appears to me that he got caught in the middle of something he couldn't control. I feel sorry for him."

"I'm not sure he could've avoided it. I understand the concern for his family," returned John. "I agree that he's telling the truth. It appears that he needs a break. I'm pretty sure I can help in that respect. You go back in and settle him down. Tell him we don't plan to get the police involved. I'll be in as soon as I check out a few things with dad."

It actually took more than a few minutes. John returned to the office and said, "Well Tony! I've got good news and bad; first, the good news. As Mark told you, we won't be prosecuting, or at least we won't initiate it. It's still possible that the police may want to pursue it, but that's not likely due to something we can't discuss with you. Don't worry about it. We'll cross that bridge if and when we get to it.

The bad news is that we don't have any need for a carpenter at this time. However, my dad's willing to hire you as a general handyman to take care of some rental properties he owns. The pay isn't great, but it comes with the benefits he gives to all of our employees. If you're interested, you could start next Monday."

"That's not bad news," stated Tony excitedly, "That's great news. Of course I'm interested. I guarantee you I'll be the best employee you ever had. I'll work for nothing until I've paid for everything that was stolen."

"Thanks for that suggestion, but that won't be necessary," said John, with a smile on his face. "I don't think it'll happen, but if you're contacted by Adams or Brubaker, give me or Mark a call to let us know what they want."

John continued, "I'm tied up the rest of the day, so how

about if Mark takes you to lunch and digs a little further into your background and abilities. We'll consider it your interview. Please don't talk to anyone about this, and whatever you do, don't talk to Brubaker about our meeting." He then turned to Mark, winked and said, "Take your time. Later I want your thoughts about a custodian for the Everett Lodge."

Mark got a confused expression on his face and then caught on. "Okay. I'll work on that." Then he said, "Tony, welcome to the Lynch Construction Company. Let's go have some lunch," as he got up and started for the door.

Tony, still dumbfounded, said, "Thank you Mr. Lynch. I really appreciate what you're doing for me. You won't regret it."

John replied, "I know you'll work out very well, and the name is John. My dad's the only one we call mister around here and that's only in public."

Chapter 15

Later that evening the four friends met to discuss the next phase of their plan. Mark began by telling the other three about his lunch with Tony, "He's really a nice guy. He's had some tough breaks and I'm sure he'll work hard for your dad." Incidentally, he doesn't know anything about who tried to knock some sense into your head with a two-by-four."

"Back to the matter at hand," stated Luke. "Matt and I took turns following Brubaker. He's a shifty fellow, who looks around his surroundings constantly. It's like he expects someone to attack him at any moment. We learned that he has an apartment in Harrisburg, but his official residence is in Philadelphia."

Mark asked, "Do you think he knew he was being followed?"

"No," replied Luke, "I just think he's cautious ... either that or he's paranoid. What's the next step in getting him and his companions out of our proverbial hair? We don't know for sure what Brubaker and his friends at Claybourne are up to. I think we should do a little eavesdropping and find out a little more about these guys. I want to bug their office."

"Isn't that illegal?" asked Matt.

"Probably, but who cares?" answered Luke.

"Can you do it without getting caught? What if they run checks for bugs and taps? It won't hold up in court. Can they be tracked back to us? What would the Feds think?" the other three asked, seemingly all at the same time.

"Okay, okay," replied Luke. "One at a time. First, yes, I can do it. Second, with the high-tech stuff I have access to, together with a few of my own modifications, they won't be detected. The tests I've conducted indicate the bugs are sensitive enough to hear most of a phone conversation, as well as anything said in the room. And finally, we need more information before we can continue. Harvey and his crew are working behind the scenes and are hampered by laws and procedures which we don't have to follow."

"How would you plant the devices or get access to their office?" asked John.

"I don't need access to the office … just need fifteen minutes or so at the outside window. Also, I happen to know that the whole area is currently having trouble with their phone lines. An excavating company dug through the main phone lines. It'll take them at least three days to fix the problem. The phone company will be up and down the surrounding alleys. They'll be attaching new lines to many of the homes and buildings. It won't be hard to get at their office window under the guise of working on the phone lines. If that doesn't work, I'll do it at night. Their office window faces an alley so I won't have to go over their fence to get at the window."

"You've given this a lot of thought," said John.

"Been thinking about it for awhile," replied Luke, "but when the excavator ripped the phone lines apart, I figured we couldn't let the opportunity pass. I have all the necessary components to do the job tonight or tomorrow."

"We've got nothing to lose," stated Mark. "Where will you put the recording equipment and how often will you have to check it?"

"I have to drill a quarter of an inch hole in the window frame and install the bug. Then, I'll glue a thin, almost invisible, wire which will run from the bug to the window pane. The device is voice-activated and has a battery life of plus or minus sixty days depending on how often it's activated. The bug sends a signal to a recorder with a clock that will record the real time for sixty days also. I have to place the recorder within three hundred feet of the bug to be effective. I can retrieve the data as often as necessary in less than five minutes by parking nearby. The batteries in the recorder can be replaced as needed."

After discussing it a little further, Matthew said, "I say we go for it. I'll help you in any way I can." Everyone nodded in agreement and the planning continued.

"Based on what we now know," said John, "we're reasonably sure that Brubaker and Adams will not be as easy to get information out of as Hammer and Marlow were. Also, the Claybourne brothers may be involved up to their teeth. We don't know about the elder Claybourne; he may or may not be involved. Let's give Luke a week or so to see if he comes up with any useful information. If that doesn't work, I think it's about time we use the direct approach and stir up the old hornet's nest."

"Let's hear what you have in mind," stated Luke. The other two shook their heads in agreement.

"Well," John began, somewhat skeptically, "if we go directly to either of the two we think are the ringleaders that won't get us anywhere. If we tell them what we know and what we believe we know, they'll just close down and start up again when things cool down. However, what happens if we, or in this case I, go directly to the old man or one of the sons and put a little pressure on them by showing them the film we have connecting them with the theft at our construction site. If that doesn't work, we could threaten them with an IRS investigation, like they did with Al Capone."

Matt butted in, "I'm still not sure why we're doing this. Why can't Harvey and his buddies take care of these guys?"

"We've talked about this before," said John. "The Feds are afraid that if their involvement's discovered, the entire operation will shut down and a year of hard work will go down the drain. This way they can deny that we're working for them. They never said that, but you and I both know if things go wrong, it's us not them, left holding the bag. The credentials they gave us are more to keep us from being arrested by the local police, not for scaring criminals."

"I want to catch the guys involved with the missing materials as much as the rest of you," stated Matt. "But I never thought that I'd be acting like a detective actually doing investigative work. Not that I don't like it ... in a way, it's fun. I'll be very surprised if this next part of the plan doesn't lead to some sort of violence. Just understand that if I'm threatened in any way, I'm going to defend myself."

"Good," answered John smiling and gesturing to the others, "I'm counting on that. You can deck anyone who even looks like they mean to harm any of us in whatever manner you feel appropriate. Agreed?"

"Agreed," they replied in unison.

"Okay," John said, "I'll clear everything with Harvey before we take any action. What Harvey doesn't know about our bugs won't hurt him."

"Sounds good," Matt said, "what about weapons? Are we licensed to carry guns?"

"The only weapons you need are attached to your shoulders, vertically and horizontally. If you think someone may use a gun on you, use your head and get out of there ASAP. Now, let's decide how we continue from here." They spent the next few hours brainstorming various steps and actions that they could take to resolve the matters at hand. In the end, they concluded that there was only one solution that seemed suitable and agreeable to everyone.

"Okay," said John. "In the meantime, I've got some good news on the Everett Lodge project. The architect finished the feasibility studies. Masterson's also finished checking out other similar companies. I've arranged meetings with our consultants for Wednesday at the lodge. Mr. and Mrs. Everett decided to leave for their daughter's home so the lodge is empty."

"That's great news," exclaimed Luke. "I have a hundred questions and twice as many ideas I want to discuss."

"Me too," butted in Mark.

"Hope you don't think I don't have as many ideas and questions," said Matt excitedly. "I've got a whole notebook full of them."

The next day, John called Harvey to bring him up to date on what they were going to do. Harvey was a little upset that they had let two of the thieves off the hook. "Look," said John, "you told us to proceed as we saw fit. The two guys we talked to are just small fish in this whole mess. That's not who you're looking for, and it doesn't make sense to pin this on them. What are you after ... a conviction or a shutdown of the entire operation?"

"You had no right to let them go. Besides we can still prosecute based on the film you gave us," stated Harvey angrily.

"Don't count on it," John said, just as angry. "I could testify that the film was doctored."

"You'd do that?" shouted Harvey questionably.

"Who's to say," stated John, satisfied that he got his point across.

"Well, we're on hold until you get back to me," John said. After a few minutes of small talk, John placed the phone back on its cradle. *I guess everything I've heard about federal agencies is true. Only top management can make a decision. This could take a long time just to make sure the supervisor's neck isn't hanging out too far. Or probably to make sure someone else can be blamed if something goes wrong,* he thought to himself.

Chapter 16

John made a conference call to his partners and gave the details of his phone conversation with Harvey. "Since we have time, let's meet at the lodge Tuesday, instead of Wednesday to go over all of our questions and ideas. We can use the extra day to put our concerns in a logical order and maybe answer some questions before the meeting." After the call, John wrote down some notes and scanned them into his computer.

By Tuesday afternoon, the four partners had narrowed down their concerns to three basic items: Was there enough financing available to finish all the work needed at the lodge? How long would the remodeling and new construction take to complete? When could they start advertising for employees and clients? At no time did any of the four consider that the project wouldn't be a success.

By late Tuesday night, the partnership agreed on an advertising strategy and had a tentative timeline for the numerous construction activities.

On the following morning, the four friends gathered before meeting with the consultants. Mark made a statement, "I believe we should meet with each consultant individually to determine what their findings are. Then we may have to get them all together to see if we can pick their brains on the right decisions to make."

His twin said. "I have no problem with that. However, I believe that the decision's already been made to proceed to develop the lodge."

Luke followed up with, "I really want to continue with the project, but let's go into these meetings with an open mind. If the results are against us to go with it, we really have to give a lot of thought to our idea. I, for one, don't want to get into this too far over my head ... a little over my head's okay, but keep an open mind, please."

"Luke's right," said John. "We need to keep our options open. How about if we meet with Helen and the Masterson Business Consultants first? Then, we'll meet with the convention expert and, finally, with the architect?"

"Sounds okay to me," Matt replied. "But I feel it in my bones, this is a go."

John left the room and returned with two people. He began, "All of you know Helen and that she works for Masterson Business Consultants. Helen, will you make the introductions?"

Helen introduced Charley Wilson as manager of Masterson's. He began his presentation, "As you requested, we contacted twenty-five companies with a specific list of questions for each. We then followed up with pertinent remarks and other questions. Actually, we contacted thirty-three companies in order to get twenty-five who'd talk to us. By the time we finished with the first five interviews, we pretty much were asking everyone the same follow-up questions. Generally, the contact person was from accounting. However, some were from the human resources department and others were a combination of both."

Charley continued, "As per our instructions, we have results from five companies with ten to twenty employees, ten companies with twenty to fifty employees, and ten companies with over fifty employees. All of the firms are located within a hundred miles of the proposed facility.

"Our report shows the results of our inquiries in various formats. You can read these results at your leisure. For now, I'll start with the items most of the companies desired or ones I thought to be most important. The most important item each company wanted, regardless of size, was a comfortable, relaxed atmosphere to hold their conferences with all the necessary technical equipment on hand for their individual needs. Eighteen of the twenty-five companies listed this as their highest priority. Not surprisingly, this wasn't a concern of the five smaller companies.

"The five smaller firms' highest priority was to be treated the same as major corporations. They wanted the same perks and attention as the larger companies.

"The next biggest concern for all companies, regardless of size, was a reasonable price. Not necessarily inexpensive, but to get a good bang for their buck. Of course, the big companies didn't list this as their second highest priority. The rating was given based on all the companies collectively. The hard copy of the report shows more specific details of the answers we obtained.

"The next item of interest was to have a facility where employees can gather informally to relax, to have a drink, maybe listen to some music or watch a game, without the typical barroom drawbacks. An attractive room with soft cushioned chairs -- something other than bar stools to sit on appeared to be what they had in mind. Part of this answer included a private party atmosphere without the bar being open to the general public."

Charley looked around the room and noticed that John and the other three nodded their understanding. He noted that they all were taking notes. Helen winked at him to assure him that he was giving a good presentation.

"One item that came to the surface was consistent pricing.

This was separate from the low prices. What they wanted was an all inclusive price, regardless of the rooms, conference rooms, meals, other amenities, etc. It'd be difficult to include the bar bill, but one price that would include everything is what they're looking for. In that way, it wouldn't require detailed explanations on their expense accounts.

"The last item that appeared on the consensus list was a facility where spouses had some activities to do while their partner attended the meetings. I was surprised that this didn't mean shopping, swimming, or sightseeing. What they had in mind was some place where the wives, or husbands, could go do their own thing, such as arts and crafts classes, playing cards, a comfortable spot for reading, a relaxed setting for conversations with other spouses, were some of the examples. I think one of the comments we received summed it up. They wanted something similar to a bed and breakfast, only with more conference-type amenities.

"We expected to learn that bedrooms with deluxe features would be a concern. That didn't come out. In fact, it was just the opposite. Nice clean rooms with private baths were all they'd expect ... even a TV was not a major concern, as long as there were common areas to go and watch special programs. Of course, access to the internet was a concern. DSL and wireless connections also are almost a necessity nowadays.

"If you turn to page fifteen in the report, I'll go through the rest of the questions and how the answers were broken down into various categories."

"Charley" stated John, "how about if we hold off on that for the time being. We'll get to it later when everyone sits down together to discuss ideas."

"Sure," he answered somewhat concerned that John didn't like his presentation, but was relieved when John smiled and winked at him.

John asked Charley and Helen, "Based on your research,

how many rooms do we need to make our facility viable for the three categories you mentioned?"

Helen answered, "It's difficult to give a direct answer to that, but in our opinion, meaning Charley's opinion, you'd need at least fifty rooms and amenities to match."

"Thank you. Stay here with us as we listen to the other presentations. I think we'll need your input after the others are finished. I'm sure you'll be able to answer some of the questions the four of us will have."

"Here," said Matt, holding out his arms to Helen, "you can make yourself comfortable on my lap."

"You've got more than you can handle already, big boy," was her reply, as she squeezed his checks and kissed his forehead.

"Hey," shouted Mark indignantly, "I thought this was a business meeting."

"It is," stated Luke laughing, "and I believe Matt just got the business."

"Okay," said John, "let's bring Andy Olsen in to tell us what the major convention centers are doing to get companies to spend their money at their properties. Keep in mind that he's in the dark about what we have in mind."

Andy entered the room after Luke went to ask him to come in. "Thank you for the opportunity to work with you on this upcoming project. I'm sure as your project proceeds our company will be able to be a significant part of your development team. We'll be an invaluable asset to your architects as they put our ideas to paper."

Mark snorted an 'Hmm' and gave John the evil eye.

John, in turn, covered his mouth to hide a smile.

Andy continued, "Our firm is the most respected company around with regard to supplying developers with expert advice on what corporations require of their conference and convention centers. We've worked with convention centers in Orlando, Boston and Pittsburgh. We've done work for Hilton,

Marriott, and Sheraton for their on-site hotel and convention facilities."

He continued, "When we heard about your proposed development, we just knew we wanted to be part of the project. The size of this property is ideal for a conference center. I'm a little concerned about the overall location, being so remote and away from the metropolitan area, but we're willing to listen to what your thoughts are and assist you in any way we can."

John interrupted, "Andy, I don't believe you're on the same track as we are on this project. We have no plans of developing this property by tearing down all the existing buildings and constructing a new hotel and conference center on the site. When you contacted us after you heard about the project, you told me you had some information that could benefit us in determining what to include in it if we decided to pursue developing a conference center around the existing facilities."

"You're right," answered Andy, "we were under the impression that you were building a whole new facility. However, I'm sure our company can help you with what you have in mind and that our involvement will guarantee that major corporations will want to utilize your center. For instance, did you know that the Fortune 500 Companies spend an average of fifty thousand dollars per event just on rooms and meals every time they have regional meetings? Also, they don't meet anywhere that doesn't include at least a four-star and preferably a five-star restaurant."

"Let me ask you a question," interrupted John again. "What are the five top items you believe are necessary for smaller and mid-level conference centers?"

"Well," Andy said, "we haven't had a lot of experience with remodeling existing properties, or for that matter, working on conference centers for medium-sized groups. I'm sure that if you hired us, we would be able to research the subject and work up a plan which would meet your requirements."

"How would you go about researching what's needed?" asked Mark.

Andy, now appearing a little nervous, said, "I ... I'm sure there are standards we can utilize. We'd research these standards and compile a list of items we think are required. We'd provide a summary of our research in report form and make appropriate recommendations."

Matthew, who by now was ready to escort Andy out via the nearest window, stood up and said, "Andy, we really appreciate your coming to talk to us today. At this time, we're not sure this is a project we're going to pursue. Please leave a business card with us. We'll contact you if we think your firm can be of any service to us." He then walked up to Andy, shook his hand and put a firm grip on Andy's shoulder and gently led him out of the room.

"Where in the hell did that guy come from?" exclaimed Luke.

"My fault," stated John. "When he contacted me, he told me he had essential information regarding conference centers. He said he'd provide this information in hopes of getting some work from us as the project unfolds. I read him wrong, sorry."

Matt reentered the room and said, "It will be colder than the proverbial cold day in Hell, before I agree to hire that clown. He had the nerve to say we wouldn't be fully informed without the information his firm could provide. What an ass!" and then, "Oops, sorry Helen. I forgot this is a business meeting."

"Forget it," she said. "I'm sorry word of this got out. It probably came from someone we contacted although we never gave them your name."

"No problem," returned Luke, "word will get out soon

enough once we begin. No harm done. I'll go get the architect. Looks like he needs some help with the plans he's carrying."

John interjected, "I invited another participant also. His name is Bob Goodfellow. He's worked with Charley before and analyzes personnel requirements for various businesses, including hotel and resort facilities. Better bring him in with you if he's here."

"You didn't mention him when we talked two days ago," stated Matthew.

"Just thought of it yesterday," replied John. "Helen says Charley told her this guy really knows what he's talking about. He may have some good input."

After introductions were made, John explained to everyone that the partners would like their input and that they should feel free to participate fully.

The architect, Ben Houseman, started his presentation. "The main lodge, which includes fifteen bedrooms each with private baths, is in remarkably good condition. It was rebuilt thirty years ago and underwent some modifications fifteen years ago. Structurally, the building is sound and meets today's standards and codes. One of my recommendations is to replace all fifteen heating and cooling units in the bedrooms and upgrade the central heat and air conditioning for the common areas. This may require some modifications to the existing electrical wiring, which is not a major issue. Also, the woodwork needs a fresh coat of paint."

Ben continued, "The metal roofs on each of the three largest buildings are in excellent condition. I'm somewhat surprised that the original plans didn't specify slate roofs. With only minor repairs, all the fireplaces in the respective buildings can be used.

In essence, the Everett Lodge could be rented out the way it is. With just a coat of paint and some updated decorating, it's my opinion that the main lodge could be used as soon as the work was completed."

Ben paused to see if he had everyone's attention. "A couple of weeks ago, John asked that I meet with Charley. We went over some of the items Charley thought were needed to make this a desirable place to hold conferences for small to medium-sized businesses. The meeting included two of their employees and two architectural students who are working for me. It was very productive. If you wish, I can go over some additional suggested improvements, which would be best done before the building's occupied. I believe these improvements would be more in line with the ultimate facility you're trying to develop."

Luke looked at his other three partners and answered, "Of course. Let's hear what you're considering."

"Thanks," continued Ben as he set an aerial plan view of the existing building layout on an easel. "Here is an overhead view that shows the original layout when the lodge was built. As you can see, the lodge was built between some of the buildings that were part of the original farm. This building," pointing to the house, "was built about seventy years ago. It's where the owners lived until the farm was sold to the Everetts. The Everetts moved into an apartment they had built on the first floor of the lodge when it was constructed. The house was used as a dormitory by various employees over the years. From the information I've been able to assemble, it's been vacant for the last five years; it's in fairly good condition. The barn, shown here," as he pointed to a building behind the lodge, "was built at the same time as the house. It hasn't been used for farm animals for thirty years. The other seven buildings were constructed at various times before and after the lodge was completed to serve as equipment storage and workshops."

"Now," he said turning over another sheet, "here's what I propose based on the results of inquiries by Charley's team. First, use the Everett apartment square footage to make four additional rooms and baths. Next, remove the kitchen and prep areas."

"Hey," questioned Mark, "where would the guests go for meals?"

"I'll get to that in a minute. With relatively few modifications to the existing kitchen area, you could have two additional rooms with baths. That would give you a total of twenty-one nice sized rooms as a start. Then, again with a few modifications, we would eliminate the bar and expand the lobby area to make cozy sitting areas for casual conversation and reading."

Ben continued, turning another sheet, "Now, put an addition here, attached to the lodge and barn, as shown, to house a modern kitchen and larger banquet rooms. These rooms could be divided into smaller meeting or dining rooms as needed. The design I have in mind could be expanded again if needed at a later time. I propose to use the lumber from the outside of a couple of the storage buildings to make the banquet rooms look rustic.

And then comes the barn," he continued. "Again, with a few modifications, you could turn the first floor into a nightclub or entertainment area. The second floor could be used for meeting or game rooms. Of course, heating and air conditioning would be needed.

The outside area within the 'U' formed by the three buildings could be used as a courtyard, or as an outside dining area. Now, it's time for questions."

A full thirty seconds went by in complete silence. Then John voiced, "Thank you, Ben. That sure gives us a lot to think about. We certainly appreciate your time and effort. What's your estimated cost for completing the project you just explained?"

"The initial cost would include the addition, kitchen appliances, new rooms, the heating and air conditioning, remodeling, painting and redecorating, and landscape work.

My estimated cost is two hundred seventy thousand dollars, which doesn't include any new or refurbished furniture. It includes some work in the barn, enough to make it usable but not to make it a highlight of the property. The estimate includes a wild guess of technical equipment for each meeting room."

John again broke the silence, "Charley, how does this proposal match with your research?"

"For the most part, I think it meets most of the criteria, except that Ben only mentioned twenty-one rooms. I still think fifty would be a more attractive alternative. I'm also a little concerned that the spouses will not have enough to keep them busy. How do you keep them occupied?

"I understand your point about the rooms. Let's ignore that for the time being. I'll also get to the spouses shortly. Bob, you've been listening to all this and taking some notes. What's your take on it? You haven't had much time to consider this but how would you proceed, assuming the project continues forward?"

"Thanks, John. I like the overall idea. Ben indicated that he followed Charley's suggestions. I'd like to know how they arrived at their recommendations, which appear logical, even though I've never given much thought to the needs of small and mid-sized companies."

"We'll send you a copy of their final report," said John.

"Thanks again. I can't say for sure how many employees, or what positions, would be needed. My suggestion would be to hire a reliable general manager and let him be involved with selecting additional personnel. My company could advertise and receive applications and narrow down the field. If you'd like, we could conduct, or at least sit in on, the interviews. Our expertise would be helpful to determine what training and experience is adequate. Give me a day or so, and I'll give you a good guess about how many employees will be needed and some general ideas on wages.

"When you calculate your cash flow projections, I suggest you add up all your known and expected expenses and then add another twenty-five percent to it for unexpected costs. When calculating income, it's best to assume a seventy to eighty percent occupancy rate. Very seldom will you ever reach one hundred percent occupancy. Even at seventy percent, I don't think you'll be that full all the time."

"Thanks, Bob, we appreciate your input. If we proceed, we'll give a lot of thought to a contract with your company. If you have the time, I know these gentlemen have some questions you may be able to answer. I think that a conservative estimate would be fifty percent most of the time."

The next two hours passed very quickly with questions and answers flowing freely. Finally, Bob said he had to leave for another meeting. Charley Wilson also had to leave because of other appointments. After the partners assured Bob that he would be contacted if they decided to proceed, Bob and Charley drove away leaving the four partners, as well as Ben and Helen, to further discuss the pros and cons of continuing with the project.

John returned to the meeting and said, "I wanted to wait until Bob left before having Ben tell you the rest of his plan. Ben, you're up again."

Ben cleared his throat and began, "Now comes the expensive part. At John's request, I did some designs to incorporate the suggestions Charley came up with. In order to increase the number of rooms to near fifty, I drew up a rough sketch of another addition, which would be placed on the other side of what is now the Everett apartment." Ben placed the drawing on the easel and said, "For practical and aesthetic purposes, the building should be just like the other buildings. If you leave the empty house in place, you could get another twenty rooms in the addition. If the empty house were torn down, a building for as many rooms as you want could be added. A rough estimate of adding the extra twenty rooms is about three hundred seventy-five thousand dollars including furnishings, storage, and a new laundry." Silence ensued.

"Boy! Am I confused," said Matthew. "It's my opinion that the lodge concept is a good one, but would we be able to recover our costs in a reasonable amount of time? Do it cheap or do it right. My wallet says cheap but my head says do it right."

"I'm in the same boat, little brother," said his twin. "Flipping a coin doesn't seem like the right way to go either. And what about the fact that we need to double the number of rooms?"

Luke had his say, "Look, I don't know about you guys but I really want this project to be a success. However, my pockets aren't all that deep. I'm thinking about getting married and can't afford too much more than I've already committed."

"Well, congratulations," said Helen, "Mary Anne hasn't said a word about that."

"Oh! sugar," stated Luke, "I forgot you were here. Helen, please keep this under your hat. Mary Anne and I haven't seriously discussed marriage yet."

"You know she can't wait forever," Helen said. "Sometimes a girl has to move on if her fellow isn't willing to settle down." She smiled at Luke and didn't even look toward John.

The twins meanwhile poked John in the ribs behind Helen's back.

"Your intentions will be our little secret; it's safe with me," Helen said with a straight face. *Maybe your best friend will take the hint,* she thought to herself.

"Okay, let's see if we can resolve any of the issues," John said sheepishly.

Mark whispered into John's ear, "You'll do anything to change the subject."

The three brothers smiled because of their friend's discomfort. John, however, didn't see anything amusing,

Thunder and Lightning

but made a point of not looking directly at Helen. Ben, who observed all of the interaction, caught on quickly and smiled as well.

"Ben," asked John, "assuming we decide to go forward, how long will it take you to finalize plans for the improvements and the first addition?"

"The improvements are no problem," he replied. "They can be completed in a couple of weeks. Most of the work is already done. It's just a matter of getting final approval. I'd want to talk to a kitchen designer first. Then, the recent addition will take me at least a month to design; then another month to get it approved by the Department of Labor and Industry. Construction time would depend on how long it takes to advertise and bid the project. A good contractor could finish the addition in a couple of months. You understand that the improvements and addition don't cover everything Charley's research deems necessary, but it would get you open for business. We have to discuss additional enhancements to the property."

"Okay, we understand. Can you and Helen come back after lunch? Maybe we can wrap this up by nightfall."

"Sure," they both replied.

Several hours later, after much thought, many questions, and several cost estimate adjustments, John said, "Let me see if I can summarize everything. The improvements to the main lodge can begin as soon as we make the decision to proceed. I'm sure the Everetts will allow us to begin before the closing. The estimated cost for the lodge improvements is seventy five thousand dollars. If the existing bar and furnishings are used, and the improvements to the barn, the estimate is approximately forty thousand. The addition, including kitchen, meeting rooms, restrooms, etc. would be ninety to one hundred ten thousand dollars. Heating and air conditioning for all three buildings would add another fifty thousand ... add to that another thirty thousand for replacing some of the furniture."

Ben was amazed that John was taking all this from off the top of his head. John's notes looked like chicken scratch and to Ben didn't make any sense at all. The other five participants, including him, had been taking notes frantically and had used numerous sheets of paper. John had three sheets, and those weren't even full and he hadn't misquoted anything yet. The other four apparently didn't consider his memory as anything unusual.

John continued, "An additional seventy to ninety thousand is needed to make cosmetic improvements to surrounding buildings and the grounds, plus another twenty-five thousand for equipment and other miscellaneous items. That's four hundred thousand. I agree with Bob Goodfellow, we need to add another twenty-five percent for unexpected expenses. That brings the total to over five hundred thousand dollars, not including start-up and operating costs or the price of the property." And he thought *that still gives us some room for extra expenses, based on the amount approved by the two banks.* "Did I miss anything?" he asked.

Everyone looked at their notes and shook their heads no. "In that case, Ben and Helen, thank you for your time and all the work you've put into this thus far. If you don't mind, we need to talk among ourselves to discuss remaining expenses and to make decisions about proceeding with the project. Ben, I'll get back to you within the week." And to Helen he said quietly, "Thanks, love, you did a great job. Are you available for dinner this Friday or Saturday?"

"Thank you, sir," she replied into his ear. "How about if you pick me up for dinner Friday and we'll have breakfast at my place Saturday morning?"

"Hmm, that would be nice."

When the two of them left the room, Luke commented, "I'm getting excited about this. Did anyone other than me do their homework? I have some cost and cash flow estimates."

Matthew answered first, "I've done some estimates on profit and losses, but they're based only on financing half a million. The total cost is now nearly one million. It won't take long to make the adjustments."

Mark spoke up, "I did some rough costs based on what I think are reasonable room prices. Construction costs are higher than what I expected, so my figures will have to be adjusted too."

Luke said to John, "Okay, bright guy, why are you being so quiet? What words of wisdom do you have for us today?"

John replied, with a serious look on his face, "Before I tell you what's on my mind, let me ask each of you a question." He looked each one in the eye and knew their answer already. He continued, "Based on what we heard today and the revised figures and the cost estimates each one of you has completed, do you really want to proceed with the project? So far, we've spent twenty two thousand dollars, plus or minus. Are you willing to put all the money in your savings at risk to continue with this project?"

"I'm in," said Matt and Mark simultaneously.

"I'll give you a check now, if you want it," replied the other brother.

"Okay, I'm in also," John said smiling. "Let's make this place look like "The Sagamore" that William A. Durant and Alfred Vanderbilt built up at Raquette Lake, New York." Two of the brothers looked confused at that statement. Only the one who had researched camp-like facilities knew what John was referring to. "And, if we're going to do it right, it's my opinion that we go with the extra twenty rooms now, instead of later. Or, maybe we could open with that addition still under construction."

John continued. "For your information, the financing has been tentatively approved for up to one and a half million.

If we buy the property under an article of agreement, that will allow us to do everything well within the approved financing. The papers need to be finalized, but I'm sure there's no problem. I arranged that when I was working on some other financing for the construction company. When the opportunity came up unexpectedly, I didn't think you'd mind if I did it without consulting with the three of you. Now that we've made the ultimate decision, let's decide where we go from here, and who's going to do what and when."

Mark and Matthew asked a question simultaneously, "How did we get that much approved?"

John gave the only reply he could, "I'm a little puzzled myself, but using an old proverb, 'don't look a gift horse in the mouth'." The twins were confused but didn't reply.

After they made the decision to buy, plans to organize logical steps leading to opening day went smoothly. As the partners talked, they divided the workload evenly. None of them even considered that the work wouldn't be completed in a timely manner. They decided to hire Bob Goodfellow's firm to advertise and to participate in selecting the manager and head chef. Pam and Sam's personnel agency would handle the paperwork to hire the remaining staff. They would hire a public relations firm to develop an advertising campaign to help attract customers.

"One more point that needs our immediate attention," said John. "We're going to need a responsible person to be in charge of the grounds and general maintenance of the buildings. He should be here right from the beginning. Mark and I have someone in mind. Mark, do you want to tell them a little about our guy?"

"You bet. Both of you are a little familiar with our man. His name's Tony Marlow." Mark then brought his two brothers up to speed on what they had learned from Tony and why they thought if he got a break, he would do a good job.

"If you two believe in him, it's okay with me," said Luke.

"Me, too," said Matthew, "but can we afford to hire him now?"

"He's working for dad now," replied John. "I think I can convince dad to keep him on the payroll until we can afford to hire him."

"Speaking of moving him," said Mark. "I have another suggestion. Let's move the old house, which we all believe will be too close to the lodge addition. Let Tony and his family move into it as part of his salary. I think he and his wife would jump at that idea. Also, it would allow us to make the addition big enough to accommodate the fifty rooms."

"Sounds goods to me," said Luke as he looked at the others, nodding their heads. "Why don't you bring it up to him? If he's willing, we could have him move in by the end of the month."

"There's a little problem here," said Matt, "moving that house isn't going to be cheap and we don't have the money to do that now."

John answered, "Good point, Matt. Mark, hold off talking to Tony until you hear from me. I have any idea, but need to bounce it off of someone first. We may be able to get this done rather inexpensively."

After the four had made the major decisions, the partners broke up their meeting and headed home for a good night's sleep; if, in fact, they could sleep with all the concerns that were swirling around in their minds.

The next morning John contacted one of the subcontractors who worked for the construction company. After he talked to him for several minutes, John asked, "Allen, have you ever had a chance to test that lifting device you've been developing?"

"No, not really. We did some rough testing out in the yard, but didn't have anything big enough or heavy enough to prove our design. Why do you ask?"

"I have a house that has to be moved and I thought you might be interested in testing your new toy."

"And you want it moved for nothing, is that it?"

"How about if we split the actual costs? That means you don't get to add in your usual three hundred percent markup or inflate the man hours needed," John said jokingly.

"Okay, I'm interested. Guess you need it moved tomorrow."

"No. We can wait a couple of weeks or so. Let's set a date and a back-up date in case of bad weather."

Allen replied, "Good. When can I see the house?"

"Anytime you want. I'll have one of my men contact you. His name is Tony Marlow."

"Sounds good. How about a drink sometime?"

"If you move that house," replied John, "I'll buy you and your wife dinner and drinks at the restaurant of your choice."

"I'll hold you to that, but we'll still split the costs of the move, right?"

"It's a deal," replied John.

He hung up and went to Mark's office to let him know what had transpired. "Go ahead and ask Tony if he wants the job and the house as part of his wages. If he doesn't want the house, we'll have it torn down. If he does, tell him he has a month to decide where he wants the house situated and that he'll have to build a foundation." John continued to give him more details and explained that everything had to be coordinated with Allen.

Chapter 17

Later that day, John met with his father to bring him up to date on all the projects he'd been working on, both for his dad and his own. John decided it was time to ask a question that had been in the back of his mind since the banks agreed to finance the Everett Lodge. "Did you agree to co-sign the loan for the lodge, or did you put up any of your money?"

Mr. Lynch paused for a moment, and then answered, "No I didn't agree to co-sign your loan and, I didn't use my money to leverage the loan." John wasn't sure that was the full answer to his questions, but knew his dad wouldn't lie to him.

Later, John spent some time writing notes about his activities for the past several days. He reviewed the notes and scanned the papers into his computer for storage.

John spent the weekend with Helen. They enjoyed their time together, just sitting around talking about their futures, both in their careers and in general. They discussed marriage and family size openly. The only actual business they discussed was when Helen told John that working for her uncle was different than what she had expected. "There's more to his business than consulting," was all she said. "I can't discuss it with you without asking Uncle Bateman first, so please don't ask." At the time she didn't know that John already knew about the other side of her uncle's business.

Several days later, Luke called John, "I've been listening to recorded conversations from the Claybourne office and uncovered something interesting. Let's get together to see if you agree with my conclusions."

"Okay, how about if we meet at your apartment tomorrow night to go over the details? I'll call the twins and tell them to meet us there."

"That's good. It'll give me time to get things in order and condense the items that I believe are important."

When John and the twins entered Luke's spare bedroom, they were amazed to see all of the electronic and computer gear neatly arranged on tables and shelves along one wall of the room. "I owe you an apology," said Mark. "All along I thought you were spending all your spare time with Mary Anne, but I can see now that you've put a lot of time into organizing this room."

"Well," replied Luke, "you know I've been interested in electronics all my life, and now that I have access to equipment at wholesale costs, I just went off the deep end. This lab represents many years of knowledge, training, and experimenting. I guess I did go a little overboard, but there isn't anything I know of that I can't do electronically with the equipment in this room."

Mark picked up a couple of items off of the work area and asked, "What are all these things?"

Luke replied, "It's a collection of circuit boards, transistors, and micro circuits. Items I use to build some of my toys."

Matt questioned Luke, "What's with all the forms with the U.S. Patent Office logo?"

Luke answered, "I've applied for patents on three of the devices I built, including the bugs, or more specifically the technology used in the devices. I'm working on a couple more projects that will require patents."

John asked, "Isn't it a little expensive to obtain a patent?"

"Yes it is, but I've worked out a deal with a young patent attorney who's willing to wait until the patents are approved. If I don't get approval, he'll allow me to make monthly installments at a flat fee."

John, ever the business major, said, "Keep track of anything you spend on any materials you buy. That's a business expense."

"Don't worry I have detailed records, including costs to develop and any equipment I have to buy. Now let me show you what I did at the Claybourne office. I drilled the hole for the bugs, four of them in different windows. I filled the holes in with wood putty and placed wires behind spackling compound. It turned out much neater than I expected. The receiver's located on a telephone pole at the end of the alley. It looks like its part of the telephone equipment. Every other day I stop near the telephone pole and download the recordings, which I listen to at night. It takes about two hours to listen to each day's activities."

"For the most part, it's strictly business conversations, although I do know that someone in the office closest to the warehouse is having an affair with another employee. I'm sure a film of several of the private meetings would be rated triple X."

"Here's the conversation I want you to hear. It was recorded in the fancy office at the corner of the building."

As Luke pressed a button, the recording began with the ringing of a phone.

'Hello, Dave speaking.'

'This is Rocky, listen up. We need a truck at the house in Stuart next Friday.'

'I can't get a load ready that fast; give me another week.'

'We can't do that; we need it by Friday.'

'Paul Adams said I'd always have a couple of weeks to get a truckload ready.'

'Listen, I don't care if you send an empty truck. We need our shipment out of here on Friday at the latest, and don't forget the cash.' A buzzing sound followed a slight click.

"The next call was made immediately after the first," said Luke. "I checked the dial tones. The call was made to Lou Claybourne's house."

'Lou, this is Dave. I just got a call from Rocky. He needs a truck in Stuart by Friday.'

'Holy shit! That doesn't give us time to get a load together. Tell him no way.'

'I didn't get a chance to tell him. He told me to just to do it and hung up on me. Do we have enough cash for the shipment?'

'Two million, right. Yes, we have it, but, damn it, this pisses me off. I'll give Paul a piece of my mind when I see him.'

'Don't piss him off. That son of a bitch is crazy enough to kill you if you upset him.'

'You're right. He scares me, too. I guess we'll have to ship good merchandise along with the surplus. Call Brubaker and tell him he has a trip to make.'

'Okay. I guess we have no choice. See you tomorrow.'

Luke interrupted again. "This next call was made fifteen minutes later. It was made to Barry Brubaker in Philadelphia."

'Yes' was the only answer they heard.

'This is Dave. We need someone to make a trip to Florida to drop off a load at the outlet and bring back a load from Stuart and drop it off in Richmond. He has to be in Stuart by Friday.'

'Sorry! I can't do it that soon; got other business to take care of.'

'You have to … We've got no choice.'

'It'll cost you double.'

'You rotten son of a bitch, you're trying to rob me.'

Thunder and Lightning

"Well, it'll cost you double if you want me to have someone go that soon."

'Tell him to be here tomorrow; the load will be ready.'

'Yeah, whatever" ... click.

"Well, what do you think?" asked Luke.

"Sounds suspicious," stated Mark. "Wonder how we could find out what's in the shipment to Virginia."

"Don't think it's up to us to find out," replied Matt. "I suggest we tell Harvey about this and let him find out what's cooking."

John paused, then answered, "You're right." "Let's call him now and let him take over."

"It's eight o'clock," said Luke. " Do you think we can get in touch with him?"

"I have his home number," answered John, as he headed for the phone. "Can you put this on the phone for him?"

"What do you think?" Luke said smiling.

"Harvey, this is John," Harvey listened when he picked up his phone at home. "Do you have the means to record some phone conversations we taped?"

"Not here at home. Can you leave it on my voice mail at the office? I believe you have the number."

"Okay, but listen to it as soon as you get in tomorrow," replied John as he hung up somewhat pissed off at Harvey's lack of interest.

John dialed Harvey's number at the office and asked Luke to record the phone calls on to Harvey's voice mail. "Well, I guess that's all we can do for now," stated John. "I have a real bad taste in my mouth. A couple of beers would taste good right now."

Luke retrieved four beers from the refrigerator and before they had finished even half a bottle, the phone rang. When Luke answered, the caller yelled, "What the hell are you assholes up to and how did you record those messages?"

161

As a big smile spread across Luke's face. He made the statement, "John, I believe this call is for you."

"This is John, who's this?" he inquired.

"You, asshole. I just retrieved my messages from the office. So, what the hell are you doing taping phone calls? You're going to blow our entire operation out of the water. What the hell are you thinking? I'll have your ass in a sling by the end of the week." This tirade went on for a full minute before the caller took a break for air.

John said, "Hi! Harvey, what's your problem?"

"You bastard, you asshole, you son of a bitch, I'll have your ass for this." John pushed the receiver away from his ear while Harvey continued his rampage.

"Calm down, Harvey, calm down and tell me what you're talking about." John again held the phone away from his ear until Harvey ran out of steam.

When finally it was quiet on the phone, John said, "Harvey, now let's talk about this like adults." After a pause and no reply, John continued, "We got this information … it doesn't matter how. We thought we'd better pass it on to you so that you, if you want, can track the truck to Florida and back. It may give you some useable information that may help put these SOBs behind bars." John heard nothing from the other end of the phone and John began to think Harvey had hung up.

"John … John, you could be put behind bars for tampering in a federal investigation." Harvey said, still angry. "Wiretaps are illegal unless appropriate steps are taken to assure no one's rights are infringed upon."

"Harvey, believe me, there were no wiretaps." *That really wasn't a lie,* thought John. "We just happened to be at the right place at the right time."

"You're lying and I know it," stated Harvey, "although the information may be of some use. I'll get in touch with Peter Black to see if he'll authorize trackers on the truck. In the meantime, get the damn tap off the phone before they discover it. Also, this conversation never took place," as Harvey hung up a little too forcibly.

John gave the others a word-by-word account of the conversation and asked Luke, "Are you sure the bug can't be detected?"

"I built it and I can detect it, but without recreating the technology used, I'm sure it's safe."

"How long do we have on battery life?" asked John.

"Several weeks, but I can replace it with a new device in five minutes. The bug itself won't have to be recharged for a year, that's one of the patents," returned Luke.

"Make sure you don't get caught," exclaimed Mark.

"No problem, bro."

"Show us what all this equipment does," said John. A few beers later, with Luke beaming like a little kid, the trio was astonished at the numerous functions that could be done with the room full of electronics.

Chapter 18

The following Wednesday, John received an e-mail from Woodpecker …'Call 302-345-4532 at four o'clock from a public phone. The number is untraceable.' So, at four o'clock John called the number. "This is Woodpecker," was the answer.

"This is Apostle John, why all the secret agent stuff?"

"Are you alone?"

"I'm in a phone booth, what do you think?" John said smirking about the intrigue. "And what's with using a public phone?"

"Listen, I'll do the talking … no questions. It's possible our office phone calls are being monitored. Peter is really pissed about the phone tap. He'll get over it, but stay out of his way for awhile." John thought that was an easy request since he had no contact with Peter Black since the meetings in D.C. Harvey continued, "He told me not to contact you, but I wanted you to know that you were right. We tracked the trucks to Stuart and back to Richmond. Part of the shipment was unloaded there, but about a third of the shipment was taken back to Harrisburg.

"We managed to get someone inside one of the warehouses to verify that the merchandise was, in fact, various forms of illegal drugs. DEA's now involved and are waiting to track the drugs when they leave the warehouses. They believe this is a very major drug ring and they want to catch everyone involved. The information you gave us was passed on to them, without telling them where it came from. This is a big feather in our caps. Peter will eventually get around to thanking you, but don't expect anything soon. He's concerned that he'll get called in to testify about where the information came from."

"Should we continue with our side of the investigation?" asked John.

"Stay out of it. I'll be in touch," and Harvey hung up.

John hung up the phone and returned to his car a block away. After he sat there thinking for a while, he drove back to the office where he called his three friends to arrange a weekend party at the lake house. The four would invite the girls. Helen and John had been seeing each other quite often in the previous weeks. Helen was excited about the party when he called to ask her if she was available.

Later that evening, John received a phone call from Peter Black, who wasn't as aggravated as he apparently had been earlier. He told John that he and his team were off the case. Peter didn't bother to explain the reasons, and John didn't ask.

The next day John met with his father. "I got a call from Harvey Harrison's boss last night. He told me we're officially off the case. I think it's now bigger than we, or his small agency, can handle. The case has been turned over to the Drug Enforcement Agency." John thought it best not to tell his dad that Harvey had also called him with more details.

"I'm certainly glad that you're getting out of it. I just had a bad feeling about what was going on, but I knew my anxiety wouldn't keep you from investigating the thefts. Tell me what happened." John then told him only some of the details.

"Good to know it's finished. Your mother will also be

happy. Now, let's talk about more pressing business. My attorneys have been very busy."

Mr. Lynch continued, "Sometime in the next four months, the Lynch Construction Company will be broken down into separate companies. In essence, there'll be five companies … general construction, site preparation, concrete products and paving, steel erection and heavy equipment, and lastly, office services."

"Mother and I will own twenty-seven percent of each business, and you'll have ten percent of each. My partner will continue to own fifteen percent. The other forty-eight percent will be offered to the employees currently working in each company. The employees will be able to buy out forty-eight percent immediately. And the remaining twenty-seven percent can be bought after five years. The final buyout will be no later than ten years."

"The attorneys are working on details on how much each employee can buy. None of the employees will own more than five percent of the business, at least not for the next five years."

"That's nice, but…" started John, but was interrupted by his dad.

"It's a done deal," continued Mr. Lynch. "The rental properties will be separated into commercial and residential companies. You'll own forty- eight percent of each. Mother and I will own the other fifty-two percent."

"Each company will be incorporated and headed by a board of directors. You and I will serve on each board and will assume executive positions for the next five years. You'll be the economic advisor for each company. My partner will also be on each board for at least the first five years. His involvement as a silent partner will have to cease at that time the sale is announced."

"At the end of the fifth year, I won't accept any position with any of the companies. You can continue any position that the board votes on. Of course, you'll still own the third highest percentages in each of the businesses," stated Mr. Lynch, smiling.

"Your friends will be given the opportunity to work for any of the companies and participate in ownership in the same manner as the other employees. At least, that's the current plan. I'm currently looking at other scenarios." John questioned this comment, but didn't say anything.

"The attorneys recommend that an accounting firm should be hired for each company. I've taken the liberty to have an ad placed in several newspapers requesting resumes to be sent to a blind post office box. I'd like you to interview the applicants and hire one accountant, preferably a CPA, for each company. I asked the attorneys if you could own the accounting company, but they thought that could lead to a conflict of interest."

"You know I'm going to be involved with developing the Everett property," John began. "How is that going to affect your plans? Also, what is the current status of the Harrisburg Industrial Electronics and the Roberts HVAC companies?"

"I know that developing the Everett property will take a lot of your time, as well as that of the Bowman boys. My partner and I recognize and accept that. As for the other companies, you'll own twenty-five percent of the Industrial Electronics business. Luke will continue to manage that company. In the next ten years, he'll be able to buy as much of my share as he wants.

Roberts HVAC company is a different matter. You'll own twenty-five percent of that also. You'd better hire someone to manage it. Mike Roberts will stay until July of next year. His employees, all of whom will be retiring, have agreed to stay until the following January to help train new employees. I have an idea about Roberts HVAC, but I'm not prepared to talk about it yet either." John's curiosity was awakened again, but he still didn't comment.

Harold continued, "You know that fifteen percent of all the Lynch companies are owned by my partner. That probably won't change. However, his involvement as a silent partner will have to cease."

"Gee, I'm speechless," stated John. "When I said you had to break up the company, I just assumed you would stay in control of each. I appreciate all that you're giving me and your confidence in me, but are you sure that's the way to go?"

"You either get it now, or inherit it when we're gone. It's better to do it now to keep the legal eagles and IRS out of it later. I'm taking your advice. I've already started to back out of full-time hours and I'm going to continue to do so as conditions permit. One or more of those CPAs you hire better be well versed in tax laws. We're going to need a lot more guidance in respect to the tax implications of all of these changes.

"I've been advised that because of your ownership in each of the companies you'll have to be very careful how you handle the treasurers' positions and the accounting work."

"Boy," started John, "when news of this breaks, the employees will be asking a lot of questions. They'll be wondering how this affects their jobs. We'd better find a way to tell them as soon as possible."

"I've given some thought to that," replied Mr. Lynch. "The employees are receiving a notice of a company dinner in tomorrow's paychecks. The invitation just says that their spouses or significant other are invited and that it's important that they attend this event. By now the office grapevine has already started working. All employees will be wondering what the fuss is all about.

"I'm putting you in charge of making the official announcement. The dinner is in two weeks. This is in addition to our regular holiday dinner. You have two weeks to decide how to explain the details of the split-up. I'll have the details of the plan delivered to your office by noon Tuesday. Good

Thunder and Lightning

luck and thanks for giving me the idea about splitting up the company," said Mr. Lynch as he walked out of the office, without glancing at John.

John returned to his office and was intercepted by his secretary Lucy. "Tony Marlow's here in the lobby," she said. "He's been waiting to see you."

"Send him in," replied John, his head still spinning from the conversation with his dad.

As Tony walked into the office, he began by speaking very quickly, "Mr. Lynch, I just wanted to thank you for the job offer and for allowing me to move into the house on the lodge property."

"Hi! Tony," John said, motioning him to a chair. "It's John, not Mister, remember? We didn't do it for you. We decided it was a good idea because we couldn't afford to pay you what you're worth at this time. The house is to offset some of the difference. Besides, it will be more convenient for you and for us if you're there full time."

"My wife and I love the idea," returned Tony.

"How's your mother-in-law?" asked John.

"Thanks for asking. She's feeling better. Emily's very happy about my job and moving into the old house. She likes the idea of bringing the kids up in that location. She's already checked out the schools and plans to introduce herself to some of the locals as soon as we move in."

Tony, obviously nervous, took a deep breath and continued quickly. "Listen, Mr. Lynch, I mean John, I don't want to take up too much of your time, but there are some items we need to discuss before we move the house." John nodded his head okay and Tony continued. "There's an area about one hundred yards from the lodge that Emily and I believe would be an ideal location for the house. If it's okay with you, we'd also like to add a room to the house and have Emily's mother move in with us. We'd also like to use the field behind the house to plant a garden."

"I think I know where that is," replied John, "but show me," as he pulled out a contour plan of the area. Tony pointed out the location he had proposed for the house and the garden.

"Good spot. Go ahead and move the house there, and add the room too."

"Well, there's a little problem. We'll have to move the house down the embankment, up this road, and then back up the hill. That could be tricky."

"Why not take the direct route across here?" asked John, pointing at the plan.

"We'd have to cut down the trees along here to get the house through," answered Tony. "I don't think I can do all that work, plus building the foundation in a month."

John laughed and said, "I'm sorry, you apparently were left under the impression that you had to do that by yourself; that's my fault. I've already arranged with dad for the equipment and manpower to do the necessary work. You'll just be overseeing and assisting the crews when needed. Here, call this number when you're ready. They can be there within a day or two."

"I can build the foundation," stammered Tony. "I just can't cut down and move all those trees without some heavy equipment."

"Don't worry, you'll have lots of help," laughed John. "Do you have any other questions?"

"A couple, but only one for now ... Can I use some of the rough-cut wood in the big shed back in the woods?"

John look confused and asked, "What shed and what wood?"

"Here," as Tony pointed at the layout of the property. "The shed doesn't appear, but it's clearly on the property. It's full of rough-cut wood, mostly oak, but some cherry and maple. The wood was cut from timber located along this area," again pointing at the map. "There's a real nice sawmill set up at this end of the building. Looks like it was all hand-built, runs off of the power attachment on the farm tractor."

"Have a seat," John replied as he picked up the phone and said, "Lucy, would you please get Frank Everett on the phone for me. His number's in the Everett file."

"Frank, this is John Lynch," as he started the conversation over the speaker phone, "Got a question for you. I understand that there's a shed full of rough-cut wood in the northwest section on the property. Tell me about it."

"Sure," answered Mr. Everett, "I built the shed about ten years ago as a storage bin for the wood I used in the lodge. Every winter after the lodge was closed for the season, I'd spend time out there cutting trees and running the wood through the mill. Since I've been sick, I haven't cut any wood for about three years. I reckon the shed is pretty full. Everything should be good and dry by now. Why do you ask?"

"When we walked through the property, you didn't mention it. The surveyors aren't finished yet, and I just wanted to be sure it's on the property and that we can use it."

"Never occurred to me to tell you about it," answered the former owner. "Use all you want. It belongs to you. There are layers of oak, pine and maple and a little cherry. When it's full, the shed holds about fifty layers of one-by-fours and one-by-sixes in lengths from four to twelve feet. I believe there are a few layers of two-by-fours and four-by-fours in there also. I built all of the sheds and storage buildings from wood I cut and dried myself. If you plan on using the saw and planer, make sure you clean and sharpen them before you connect the tractor."

John hung up after he asked about the family and gave Mr. Everett an update on what they were going to do.

"There's your answer … use what you need," said John. "If there's any left over, maybe it could be used for the lodge and barn remodeling."

"There'll be plenty left over," replied Tony. "Tell me what you need and I'll cut the wood and run it through the planer."

"Thanks," answered John. "Do me a favor and call Ben Houseman, our architect, and tell him about the wood. Ask him if he can make use of it in the remodeling. Lucy will get you the phone number."

"No problem, I'll call him today."

Tony left John's office after he discussed moving the house and setting a timetable for the men and equipment that would be needed. John began to wonder if he was capable of doing everything he and his dad had talked about. *'Well,'* he said to himself, *'when swamped with work, delegate it.'*

John spent the next four hours and part of the next day making notes on the computer. In the end, he sat back, placed his feet up on the desk and grinned, satisfied that he had a plan for coordinating all the aspects of the different projects he was now juggling. *It's time for me to mix a little business with pleasure.*

First, he called Helen to see if she was able to join him for the weekend. He told her it was business related. They would leave directly from work for the lake house on Thursday evening. Helen was excited and said she could get away. "Wait until you hear my news. I'll tell you on Thursday," and hung up before John could ask any questions.

Next, he called his three friends and partners. He told them to be prepared to discuss business matters at the lake house Friday evening and Saturday. He also told them that they should also invite their girlfriends.

He made two more calls to order the food and beverages needed for the weekend get-together. He made arrangements to pick up the orders on the way to the lake.

Late Thursday afternoon, John arrived at Helen's office to pick her up. Helen wasn't in her office. Behind her desk sat an older gentleman whom John knew immediately must be Bateman Masterson.

They introduced themselves as Masterson said, "Nice to meet you, John. "I've heard a lot of good things about you. You're going to go far in the business world."

"That's very kind of you," replied John. "My dad has nothing but praise for you and your business. It's nice to finally meet you. I look forward to working with you in the future."

"It's my pleasure, but you won't be dealing with me in the future," replied the elderly gentleman. Your dad probably told you that I'm not one to beat around the bush, so I'll get straight to the point. My niece Helen is very dear to me. I have plans for her to take over my business when I'm no longer able to work. I've always thought of her as my daughter, even more so since her dad died. I look after her and don't want anyone to take advantage of her or hurt her in any way. Therefore, I'm asking you, man to man, does she have a future with you?"

John was taken aback by this question and almost told the old man that it wasn't any of his business. Instead, he said, "I understand your concern for your niece. I also don't want to see Helen hurt in any manner either." He continued. "At this time, she's my best female friend ... no, correct that. She's my only female friend with whom I have a romantic interest. I'm still learning the definition of love, so I don't know if I love her. I can tell you I enjoy being with her. I foresee us getting married and spending our future together. However, I believe we both want to climb that proverbial ladder in the business world before we make that commitment. I believe Helen feels the same way about me."

"Thank you for telling me that. I'm only intruding into your privacy because of my concern for my niece. I apologize if I offended you. Helen would kill me if she knew I was interfering in her love life."

"No apologies are necessary. I'm happy that you're so concerned about Helen's future. And, I'll let this conversation be our little secret."

"I'm sorry I can't be with you for the next few hours. I'll bet the conversation will be interesting," Masterson said with a twinkle in his eyes. "But I find that I can no longer keep up with you young folks." He looked at John, who was obviously confused, and said, "Helen will tell you everything soon and she has my blessings to do so. Have a great weekend," as he walked away.

Helen entered the room and smiled at John. "Uncle Bateman said he wanted to meet with you before we left. What was that all about?"

"He just wanted to inquire about some business matters."

She turned to John with a tear in her eye, and said, "I have some important news. I'll tell you on the drive up to the lake."

Later, in John's new SUV, Helen began her story about her boss. "Uncle Bateman is my mother's older brother. She and I are his only living relatives. He has always looked after me and helped mom and dad through some tough times. He paid for all of my education from private elementary and high school through college. He never married. Mom told me he had one true love in his younger days, but she died when they were in their early thirties. He was devastated and never pursued another woman. He' devoted his entire life to his work.

Uncle Bateman's been discussing his business with me. He told me you probably know that he's an investment banker. Most people think the consulting end of the business is the only thing he does. Actually, the business consulting is the smaller of his two operations. The general public doesn't know about the investment bankers.

When I graduated from college, Uncle Bateman had me

work for Charley for a short time. He did this so I would have a general idea what the consulting end of the business did. Lately, he's had me traveling with him more and more, meeting people and sitting in on business meetings. These meetings are always very private and confidential. Before any business is conducted, Uncle Masterson pulls this gadget out of his briefcase. It looks like a big black book and is fairly heavy. It's full of electronics which check to see if there are any listening or recording devices in the room. This gadget is cumbersome but necessary." John made a mental note of this device ... *maybe Luke could refine it.*

Helen continued, "I don't go into the meeting until Uncle Bateman meets with the individual first. After he explains my role, he asks for permission if I can attend the meeting. So far, no one has refused to let me attend. At first, I just sat and listened. Now, Uncle Bateman's been getting me more involved. After I review the files, he asks me to make suggestions about what to do. If he doesn't like my suggestion, he tells me why and asks that I come up with another idea. He doesn't tell me what he thinks until I explain my reasons for the suggestion. I now attend some meetings without him.

When he begins a meeting, he's very direct and gets right to the point. He'll start off by saying, 'I know of a company, business, or an individual, that needs help. Here's what they need, are you interested? Or, this business is for sale, do you know anyone who may be interested in buying? Or, business XYZ wants to expand, can you help, or do you know anyone who can help?' If he can help a company, the terms are simple ... pay a flat percentage fee and pay it back within five years. A ten year payback can be used if the amount borrowed is high enough. Then, keep investing for another ten-year period to become one of the investment bankers. Of course, the business is actually owned by the investors, under the name of one of many different holding companies, until the loan is paid off. Do you understand?"

"Yes," said John, "I understand and, in fact, I know some of his investors. They're also known as venture capitalists."

"I'm sorry," she replied. "Of course, you'd know about them. Your dad and some of his friends are investors."

"Correct, again. There's a rumor that Masterson has a file on every entrepreneur in Pennsylvania and surrounding states."

Helen said, "This stays between you and me, but, yes, it's true. You wouldn't believe what kind of information he has. I'll tell you more about that later. Supposedly, he got his nickname 'Bat' after a difficult transaction in which he put his entire company, and all his money, in hock to make the deal go through. One of the businessmen involved said that when Bateman Masterson went to bat for you, you could bet that you had a hit. Bateman was shortened to 'Bat' and the name stuck. 'Old' was added later as age began to creep up on him. Contrary to popular belief, he loves the nickname."

With tears in her eyes, Helen continued. "Yesterday he called Charley Wilson and me into his office. Without preamble, Uncle Bateman stated that since he's getting older and won't be around much longer, he wants the company to continue when he dies, so he has decided to make us partners and co-owners of the company. A gift for our hard work, he said. The legal papers will actually show the company was sold to us with financing provided by the owner.

There are two separate businesses involved, although for practical purposes, the company's name is Masterson Business Consultants. Charley will own and manage the business consulting portion, and I'll own and manage the venture capitalist portion. He wants the businesses to remain in our respective families."

After a deep breath, Helen continued. "There are several stipulations to the sale of the businesses to us. One is that upon his death, which God forbid doesn't come soon, I'll be bequeathed the building, known as 'The Masterson Mansion,' from which all the business is handled."

John knew that The Masterson Mansion was located on Front Street in Harrisburg, near the Susquehanna River. The four-story building was built on a knoll, which had kept it dry during the times when the river flooded over its banks. The white brick building made many people think it was the governor's mansion, which in reality was located several blocks to the west. The mansion was well kept with beautiful gardens surrounding the building.

Helen continued. "Another stipulation in the sale is that I agree to hire the family, who for three generations since the company was founded, has worked for the Masterson businesses. There are currently four members of that family who gather information and keep files on individuals and businesses throughout the East Coast. These files contain information pertaining to ownership, financing, management, and investment opportunities for a wide variety of businesses, banks, and investment groups. That family is to work independently with little guidance from me ... although I can ask them to gather information on individuals and businesses as I see fit. Officially, their business is an independent contractor which works exclusively for Masterson Business Consultants."

She continued, "Unlike J. Edgar Hoover's files, these files were developed with the intention of providing help for flourishing businesses and opportunities for the overall business community. Uncle Bateman showed me the files on you and your friends. He's had them since you were in high school. The four of you are expected to go far in the business world."

John questioned why Masterson had this information, but would have to believe that Helen knew what she was talking about.

"Both businesses are small, she stated. Charley has a

staff of eight but I have only one assistant on my staff. Uncle Bateman explained that Masterson Business Consultants started as a front for the investment bankers. In itself, it's a very viable and profitable concern, thanks to Charley, who has worked there for thirty years. The office will continue to be located in The Masterson Mansion, where Uncle Bateman now lives on the third and fourth floors." Helen's eyes filled up with tears as she thought of Bateman's death even though it could be years away.

"I'll be the only one with access to the files and the family members who collect the data. I haven't met the family yet, and I don't know where the files are. Everything's done by a high-tech computer in Uncle Bateman's apartment on the third floor. He wants me to be responsible for initial contacts with clients and prospective clients when he can no longer make the rounds. He defines his, and now, my role as acting as a matchmaker for businessmen and investors."

"Is your uncle sick or is he dying?" asked John.

"No! No!" she exclaimed. "He's healthy as a horse. I'm worried I won't be able to keep up with him. He's always going somewhere. He has a company plane and his own pilot. He hires a driver when he has to make short trips and does a lot of work while riding in the car."

"So what's your problem?" John asked seriously.

"I'm afraid I won't do as good a job as he does. I want a life outside of work. I'm afraid I won't have time to spend with you and our friends. I want to be successful in my career, but don't want to work twenty-four-seven."

"Have you talked to your uncle about your concerns?"

"Yes, and he told me that I should have a life outside of work. We talked about you and our relationship. He can see that I'm happy. He told me about his one true love and how he regretted how he had lived his life. 'All work and no play is no way to live,' he said. 'Enjoy yourself, get married and have a family,' is what he told me. I'm sure he likes the idea that we're getting serious."

"So," stated John, "work hard while at the workplace and play hard whenever possible. As far as you and I are concerned, let's make the best of the time we have when we're together. Busy or not, I want to be your best friend, confidant, and only lover. The fact that you're busy won't in itself make me go out looking for another woman, unless you close me out all together. I love the fact that you're concerned about our relationship. Both of us will be very busy in the upcoming year, but I really love the idea that we're spending most of our free time with each other. We're good for each other, and I'm discovering what love means and how much I love you."

With that comment, Helen wrapped her arms around John's neck, which nearly caused him to run off the edge of the road. John managed to pull off the road, near the same spot he had pulled off many months before. Some minutes later, John broke away from Helen, filled with joy, "Let's finish this at the lake house. After that I'll tell you my exciting news."

"Don't waste our time getting there. We've got a lot of hard playing to do tonight," she replied.

They spent most of Thursday night and all of Friday morning playing hard, over and over again. Each of them realized that their relationship was blossoming into something that was destined to grow as they spent more time together. Both had expressed what they wanted from life. They had discussed the idea of marriage but didn't make any serious plans about their future together.

Chapter 19

John waited until Friday afternoon to tell Helen his news about the sale of his dad's construction company. They spent a considerable amount of time going over John's plans to announce the changes at Lynch Construction. Before their friends arrived, John and Helen still had time to drive over to the Everett Lodge to check out the work in progress.

Helen told John, "I'm surprised to see how much construction has been accomplished in such a short amount of time. The addition between the Everett apartment and the barn is already under roof. What's the problem with the wing of the building?" The second addition was only partially completed.

John replied, "They're doing as much work there as they can before the house is moved. Once the house is moved they will extend the building to accommodate the additional rooms."

When they returned, the Bowman brothers and their dates had already settled themselves into their rooms and were seated in the great room. The brothers questioned John about the rumors concerning changes at work, but John politely asked that they hold off questions until the next morning when he would explain everything.

Thunder and Lightning

They spent the evening with light-hearted conversation about each other and told stories about comical things that had happened in their workplaces. The eight of them began to relax and to enjoy the break from the stress of their jobs. Of course, they consumed a generous portion of beer and wine which helped to reduce the stress. The gathering broke up and the couples retreated to their rooms.

Early the next morning, John was out on the small pier at the lake doing his stationary exercise program. Once again, John didn't realize that someone observed him doing this exercise. Forty minutes later, Helen then joined John for a slow run along the lake road. When they returned, they observed the other six individuals doing their yoga and weightlifting routines. At breakfast, John stated that he needed the others to help him brainstorm and ask questions about a project he was working on. They all agreed without exception.

After they had cleared the breakfast dishes, John started, "Okay, here's the deal. I need Pam and Sam to assume they work for Lynch Construction, the same as these three," pointing to the brothers. "Helen and Mary Anne will act as spouses of Lynch Construction employees." Both women think to themselves, *I'll make that happen some day.* John continued, "All of you will have the opportunity to ask any questions you may have. As a matter of fact, that's exactly what I need from you."

As he saw all seven nods, he continued, "My dad has decided to sell Lynch Construction." All of them, except Helen, expressed surprise that showed John he had their undivided attention. "The attorneys are currently finalizing documents to divide the existing company into five separate companies. Portions of those companies will be sold to the employees. Each employee will be given the opportunity to buy into the company they currently work for. They will participate in company profits, based on the percentage of the company they own."

Then John continued by giving the details of how an ESOP worked. He stated that since no actual stock shares existed, the percentage owned by employees would be broken down into individual units, based on the value of the new company.

John then explained how the company would be split into five separate companies. "Please keep this information confidential. The official announcement will be made at the dinner that's planned in less than two weeks. I'd appreciate it if you could also help me with some of the details at the dinner.

Now, each of you has a legal pad in front of you. Please take the next ten minutes to write down any questions you have. Don't worry about covering everything. I'll ask for more questions later. Don't throw away your papers, I'll need them."

"Somehow I don't believe that statement," said Matt.

"Holy shit," Mark said quietly. "I have a hundred questions already in my mind. Where do I start?"

At the end of the ten minutes, John started to speak again. "Let's begin with Matt and go around the table."

"My initial question is personal," began Matthew, "I work for all of these companies. Where do I fit in?"

"That hasn't been worked out yet, but each employee will be given the opportunity to work for any of the five companies," answered John. "Pam, it's your turn."

"I work in accounting," she began. "Is that considered office services, and if so, where does the income for that company come from?"

"That's a very good question. Accounting will be part of office services. Each company will pay a fee for your services," replied John …at least, that's the initial plan. We have to put some more thought into creating that company."

Mark asked, "How much of the company can I buy?"

"There's a formula based on your years of employment,

your pay rate, and your position. I won't know the full details until early next week. I do know that forty-eight percent of the business will be offered immediately, with another twenty-seven percent offered over a five to ten year time period."

Sam broke in, "I don't have any extra money to buy into the company. Does that mean I can't be an owner?"

"By no means, that's another option in the formula. Some people will be able to invest now and others will do it through payroll deduction or by taking out a separate loan. Details on that are still to be worked out. Luke, what's your first question?"

"This is also a personal question. I don't work for Lynch Construction. Can I buy into any of the companies without being employed by them?"

"I don't know the exact answer to that question. The attorneys will have to have input on that one. However, as you know, my dad's buying Harrisburg Industrial Electronics, so I believe you'll have an opportunity to buy into that company as an alternative. Dad hasn't decided if and when he'll sell his portion of that company. You'll continue to manage the company until he's made his decision. Now let's get some questions from the girls playing the role of spouses."

Mary Anne went first. "My husband has been a foreman for the company for many years. He's planning on retiring in the relatively near future. How does the buyout affect him?"

"Good question," answered John, "I don't have a concrete answer to that, but I believe you can only be an owner as long as you work for the company. Also, the break-up won't affect your existing 401k program or your final retirement package. The investment company that handles the existing 401k is now investigating options for anyone who elects to retire now or in the near future. I'll have to get back to you with a final answer. Helen, it's your turn."

"My husband was recently appointed an executive with the company. Will his promotion be affected, and who'll be in charge of the new companies?"

"The break-up will require some changes in management. There will be more managers, rather than fewer managers, so there should be no demotions involved. For the next five years, dad and I will have controlling interest in all five companies. Dad may or may not act as CEO for each. It's up to him, but I wouldn't be too surprised if he starts backing out of the day-to-day decisions." John gave no indication that there was a partner involved.

"A point of interest for everyone is that each company will be incorporated individually, and a board of directors will be selected for each company to oversee operations. The CEO for each company will be decided by the top five owners by percentage. In all probability, it will be the person who currently manages that particular company."

"What about you?" Mark asked.

"I'll serve on each board and will probably be comptroller for each company. Dad is giving me ten percent of each company. I will also buy whatever portion the formula indicates I'm entitled to buy."

During the next four hours, and occasionally throughout the rest of the weekend, the others questioned John. He answered as much as he could while he continuously kept track of all the questions in his head or by jotting notes on paper.

After the initial shock of hearing about the proposed changes, the four couples eventually settled into relaxation modes for the rest of the day. At one time or another, each couple visited the Everett Lodge to see the ongoing work. With heavy equipment supplied by Lynch Construction, the operators had cut a neat path to allow for moving the old house. Within the next week, the stumps would be removed. The equipment was also used to dig out a basement at the new location for the house. Somehow, Tony had found time to plow the field behind the proposed new location. No one but John realized that the plowing was a prelude to develop the site into a planting area of over two acres the next spring.

By Sunday evening, the eight were totally relaxed and none of them looked forward to their respective jobs the next day. However, they all looked forward to a long holiday weekend in a few weeks.

On Monday morning back in his office, John began to make detailed plans on how to make the announcement about splitting up the company. Several times throughout the day, one or more of the office staff tried to pry information from John about the upcoming "mandatory dinner," as it was now referred to. John refused to answer any of their questions or to be drawn into their traps.

On Tuesday and Wednesday, John met with the attorneys away from his office to avoid further questions or more rumors. John's dad had conveniently been called out of town on business. On Friday, Mr. Lynch called into the office to advise them that he and his wife would be out of town until the day of the dinner.

Over the weekend, John reviewed and refined the agenda for the dinner and the announcements. By Monday before the dinner, John finalized his and three other individuals' presentations. He planned to use films, Power Point slides, and displays to help explain the concept. To avoid further discussion at the office water cooler, John had everything typed and prepared by temporary personnel at Pam and Sam's office. He had the list of questions and answers from the weekend at the lake house summarized and assembled in brochure format and reproduced. Likewise, he had handouts of all the presentations that would be distributed after the announcements had been completed. The four presentations would be given by John, one of the principal attorneys, a representative from the banks handling the buyout financing, and an expert on employee-owned businesses from the Small Business Administration.

By the day of the dinner, work at the office had virtually come to a standstill. Even the construction sites showed a considerable slowdown of production. There were many rumors ranging the gambit from pending bankruptcy and lawsuits against the company, to Mr. Lynch being very ill, to larger-than-usual Christmas bonuses. All employees were given the afternoon off to prepare for the dinner.

John had planned the dinner to be a banquet ... from hors'd'oeuvres and complimentary drinks to a surf and turf meal and assorted desserts. After the meal, John stood before a microphone and began, "Ladies and gentlemen." The crowd immediately became quiet. "Welcome, and thank you for attending. I know you're all anxious for this to get started, but first I need a little time to set up and get organized. Take a restroom break, and for those of you in coat and tie, you can remove them and make yourselves comfortable. We may be here for a while, so call the babysitters and let them know you may be late. The staff will clear the tables and move them into classroom format. Please allow room for couples to sit together. There will be water, coffee and sodas available along the two side walls. Help yourselves and be back here in twenty minutes."

The restaurant staff and many of the Lynch employees rearranged the tables while the Bowman brothers and their dates placed notebooks and pencils at each place. Two big-screen TVs and related computer equipment were set up on each side of the podium.

Satisfied that everything was ready and all the chairs were occupied, John again called for attention, "Ladies and gentlemen, thanks again for being here. I'm sure you already have many questions and probably will have many more as I go along. Please write down your questions as I proceed. We'll have a question and answer session later. If we can't answer them now, we'll get answers and pass them on to you at a later date.

Also, everything I'm about to talk about is explained in hand-outs, so you don't have to take detailed notes at this time. Now, if I have everyone's attention ... Here's the news ... my Father and Mother," pointing to the table to his right, "have decided to sell the construction company." The room broke into a loud rumble of various comments and exclamations until John once again asked for order. "They plan," pause, "They plan," waiting for quiet, "to sell the business, or should I say businesses, to the current and future employees. This sale will take place within the next four months."

The other three presenters spent the next hour and a half explaining how the sale, or buyout, would take place and as many details as possible. The question and answer session lasted another hour. John again explained that most of the answers were found in the brochure and handouts. The employees only had several questions that needed additional research. John assured the audience they would provide answers to these questions in the next pay envelopes.

Based on the comments overheard at several tables, John and his father assumed that the sale was generally accepted and most, if not all, employees were enthused about the possibility of buying into the business.

John ended the meeting with, "I have a question. Do we want to take time at the annual party to discuss more details of the sale, or do we want to have a dance band as usual? Let's see a show of hands on having a band." Just a few hands were raised. "Okay, how about if we allow time to further discuss the sale of the companies?" Most of the hands went up. "Okay, we'll discuss the buyout after the annual dinner. If you think of any more questions, please jot them down and give them to me or Lucy in the next two weeks. The next several months will be very busy for all of us. Please remember that we have a business to run, so don't forget that our customers expect a good product and good service throughout the upcoming changes. Good night, safe travels, and sleep well."

John accepted congratulations and thanks from his family and friends for the manner in which he had handled the announcement. Not surprisingly, the older Bowmans left with John's parents for a late night coffee on the way home. John and Helen and Luke and Mary Anne begged off drinks with the two sets of twins and headed for John's apartment where they all prepared for bed and quickly fell asleep.

Chapter 20

The next few days were filled with excitement around the office and project sites. The work pace had slowed down since most employees' thoughts were on the upcoming sale. Then, almost like a switch was thrown, the employees stopped talking about the buyout and resumed work like it had been prior to the announcement. During those few days, John didn't have a chance to spend much time in his office. He spent most of the time at the offices of attorneys, bankers and other professionals and attended to details about his, his father's and their employees' businesses. By the end of the following week, John had completed preliminary plans concerning various aspects of all of the businesses. Because he knew he couldn't do all the work himself, he started delegating work to the people who would ultimately be, and in most cases currently were, the managers of divisions of one of the new companies. John insisted that the managers and their assistants meet with all of the employees within the next two weeks. He advised them to take any questions or comments from the employees and present them to John as soon as they were compiled.

Two weeks after the official announcement, John received

a phone call from Luke. "I know we're not on the Claybourne case anymore, but I've been checking the bugs I put in their offices. It's more or less as a trial run for my equipment. There are two things I believe you should know. First, old Mr. Claybourne is apparently on his deathbed. All the family has been called in to say their good-byes, although from what I understand he's been in a coma and hasn't actually talked to anyone for nearly a year."

"That's too bad," replied John. "I'm sure he's more respectable than his two sons appear to be."

"The second thing I learned is that apparently the Claybournes are planning a major shipment in the next couple of weeks. Listen to this recording. From all indications, it may be the biggest shipment to date. I think we should tell Harvey about this shipment."

After John listened to the tape, he said, "You're right about that. I'll give him a call right now. He'll be pissed that we still have the bugs in the office. Are you sure there aren't any other bugs or phone taps? Or, that anyone knows about your devices."

"I'm sure," stated Luke. "I have a tape from two weeks ago at four o'clock in the morning with someone moving around, apparently not wanting to be noticed. They were placing listening devices in the office. Of course, I picked up the bugs' output immediately. The very next day I recorded a call that ordered a sweep of the office on a regular basis. That night someone entered the office and removed the listening devices that were installed the day before. A guy comes in every few days and checks for bugs, and they haven't found my stuff yet."

"Okay, I'll make the call, but let's stay out of this. It's a federal matter now." Then after a pause, John said, "Speaking about electronics reminded me of something." John then told Luke about the instrument Mr. Masterson used to check for listening devices. He asked him if he could develop a miniature version. Luke told John yes, and said he could probably do it in a few days.

Five minutes later, John called Washington and told Harvey. "Woodpecker needs to go to a public phone ASAP and call Apostle John." John hung up without waiting for a reply.

It took twenty-five minutes before John received the return call. "Please don't tell me you're still working on the case," Harvey said as soon as John answered the phone.

"I'm not, but I have some information you may be interested in learning," replied John. When he didn't hear any objection, John continued, "It appears that the Claybournes and their associates are going to make a major shipment in the very near future. It may be their biggest yet."

"How the hell did you get this information?" yelled Harvey. "We were keeping half an eye on them until we were told to keep out of the case. Drug agents have been watching closer than we have, but they don't appear to know anything either."

"Forget how I know ... just understand that it's reliable information. I'm calling as a courtesy, and because I like you Harvey," said John in a calm voice.

"The bosses are going to be pissed off about this," said Harvey, "but I have to tell Joe Robertson and Peter Black. I'm sure Peter will pass it on. It could be a feather in his cap with DEA. He's pissed at them for not keeping us in the loop on this case. Thanks for the call."

Harvey hung up without further comments or questions. John went back to work, too busy to worry about what the Feds did with the information.

A few days later, John read about the death of Andrew Claybourne, owner of Claybourne Enterprises, Inc. in the local newspaper.

Later in the week, John got a phone call from Emily Marlow, Tony's wife. "Mr. Lynch, I'm sorry to bother you. I know you're busy and Tony would be mad at me if he knew I was calling you."

"What's wrong?" asked John, hearing the concern in her voice.

"I don't know for sure, but Tony's been beat up. He said it had something to do with a job he did before you hired him. I called you because you apparently helped him with this problem before. I think he's afraid that he may get you into trouble."

"How bad is he? Where is he? Is he in the hospital?" John asked concerned.

"It's not real bad and he won't go to the hospital or doctor. I know he's hurting and has some deep cuts. He went out to the house to do some work. He's been out there day and night for several weeks. I'm afraid he might be involved with something he can't control. I don't want him to get hurt or lose his job with you."

"Mrs. Marlow, listen to me," as he told her a little lie, he said. "I'm on my way out to the lodge. I'll stop by and talk to him without telling him you called me. Trust me, whoever did this won't get away with it."

After he hung up, John thought about it for several minutes and called Matt, "Matt, this is John. Can you get away from the office now? Someone beat up Tony Marlow, and I need you to go with me out to the lodge to talk to him."

"Sure," replied Matt. "I'll meet you out at your SUV in ten minutes."

On the way to the Everett Lodge, John told Matt about the phone call he received from Tony's wife. "Let's play this cool and pretend that we just stopped by to check on the progress. Don't let Tony know I talked to his wife."

When they reached the lodge, they saw Tony working on the foundation of his soon-to-be home, but didn't go directly over to him. After they checked on the main lodge, they walked over toward Tony, who may, or may not, have noticed them before.

They approached. "Hey Tony," Matt shouted. "How are things going?"

Tony kept his back to them while he continued to work and replied, "Great, we plan on moving the house within the next two weeks. I'm just finishing up here."

"Looks like you've got everything under control. Looks good," stated John. "Where are the men who were helping out?"

Still keeping his back to them, Tony replied, "I never called them. I'm the one who's going to live here, and I didn't want to take them from more important work."

"You mean you did this all by yourself?" exclaimed Matt.

"Yeah, it took some long days but I thought it was best."

Matt and John looked at each other and circled around to face Tony. "My God, what happened to you?" asked Matthew as he saw Tony's cut and swollen face.

"Nothing, nothing really, I fell over some blocks yesterday and got cut up a little."

"Don't give me that shit," exclaimed Matt. "You've been in a fight and apparently lost. Tell us what happened."

"It's nothing, just a misunderstanding ... nothing to worry about. I'll be okay."

John said, "Tony, you're not the type to start a fight. Tell us the truth. What happened?"

"You don't have to get involved. I told them I wouldn't do something and got beat up for it. I'll do what they want and they won't bother me again."

"Who are they?" asked John.

"There were three of them. I didn't hear the names of any of them. They told me that Doug Hammer and Barry Brubaker said I would do a job for them. They want me to drive a truck up North later in the week. I told them I had a job and couldn't leave, but they insisted. The way they acted, I knew they were up to no good and I didn't want to be involved.

"They slapped me around a little when I said no. Then they started punching. They told me the beating was a sample of what I would get if I didn't do what they wanted. When I still said no, they indicated they'd do the same thing to Emily, my wife, if I didn't drive the truck."

Almost crying, Tony said, "I had to say yes. I can't let them hurt Emily. I'm sorry, but I have to do this. You've been so good to me and Emily, and I don't want to do it, but I can't let them hurt her."

"Did they come out here to talk to you?" asked John.

"No, they were waiting for me at my apartment. It was dark and the first thing they did was grab me and put a rag in my mouth. Then they pulled me around the side of the building and explained the facts to me."

"Why do they need you? Why don't they drive it themselves?" asked Matthew.

"They told me it's because I have a CDL license and they know that the police in the Northeast have been cracking down on unlicensed truck drivers. All state police departments in New England states have major campaigns checking for illegal drivers, unsafe equipment and overweight loads. They're checking all roads, from interstates to back roads."

"Relax, Tony," John said. "There may still be a way out of this. Matt and I have a good idea what this is all about," although he didn't tell Tony what they knew. "Let's go down to the lodge and go over this again. Did they say where you would be driving to? How will you know when it's time? Where will you meet them? Try to remember everything they said."

At the lodge, Tony recalled the episode again and answered questions that John and Matt asked. Tony said, "I remembered that one of the three mentioned weigh stations on I-78 and I-95. They told me that they would call me the night before and that someone would pick me up and take me to where the truck was parked. They also told me that I'd be making several stops and would be gone for at least two nights. Emily was to call into work and say I was sick." Tony said he pretty sure they didn't know where he worked and was positive they didn't know that he'd be working at the Everett Lodge.

John pulled Matt aside and said, "You go with Tony in his truck. Take him to the emergency room. Tell them it was a construction accident. When he's done, take him back to his wife and stay with them for awhile. Tell Emily as little as possible, but that everything's going to be okay. Tell her that Tony will be out of town for a few days working for us. Suggest she stay with her mother until Tony gets back. I'm going back to town and make some phone calls. I'll call you at Tony's."

Seeing a fire in John's eyes that he hadn't seen before, Matt nodded but didn't say anything. Although John appeared to be calm on the outside, he knew that John was boiling on the inside.

John called his office on the way home to let them know he would be at his apartment. From there, he called Harvey, "Contact Peter Black and get him on the phone. This whole thing with Claybourne may be heading in a new direction."

Harvey replied, "Peter isn't here. Besides, you were told to stay out of the Claybourne case."

"Get him and tell him I have new and important information about that shipment of drugs."

"John, you're interfering with a federal investigation, one involving more than one agency. Our agency is not even in on the Claybourne case anymore. We've been told to stay out of the way."

"I don't care who's involved. Get Peter on the phone and

I'll explain what happened and what I want in return for the information."

"John, I'm serious; Peter isn't here. And besides, you're in no position to demand anything. I don't care what information you have."

"Get Peter and tell him I have information that will get another feather in his cap as well as yours. If he wants someone else involved, that's up to him. But I'll only talk to you and Peter, not to anyone in another agency."

"Give me details so I can convince Peter, but I can't make any promises."

John proceeded to tell Harvey about the attack on Tony and what he thought the Claybournes and a certain Mr. Adams were up to.

"How sure of this are you?"

"I'm fairly certain, but hope to have more concrete information in the next few days," replied John.

"Where can I reach you? I'll try and contact Peter to give him your message."

"I'm at my apartment for now," replied John. "But you only have a few hours." John hung up and started thinking how to handle the situation. An hour later, he managed to calm down enough to acknowledge the realities of the problems involved. During this time, Harvey called twice to let John know he hadn't found Peter, or at least that's what he told him.

While he thought about how to proceed, John called Luke at his office and explained the situation. "Do you still have the listening device in the Claybourne office?"

"It's still there, and it's still working, but I haven't checked the recording for a day or so."

He told Luke what happened to Tony. "Can you listen to the recordings and determine if getting Tony involved came from the Claybourne office or if it came from an outside source?"

"Sure," answered Luke, but it will take a couple of hours. "I need to wrap things up here and then go home to listen to the recordings."

"How hard would it be for you to keep track of what's going on in the Claybourne office in real time, like relaying their phone calls and conversations to a remote location?"

"I can do that easily," stated Luke. "To do it quickly means I can't prevent someone else from hearing it on the airwaves if they get lucky enough to find the frequency I'd be transmitting on."

"When can you have it up and running?"

"Let's see," stated Luke, thinking out loud. "An hour to get the equipment; an hour to refine it a little; say two hours driving and installation time; plus some 'just in case' time. I can have it ready by seven tonight."

"Where can you put the receiver so we can listen in to the conversations?"

"The best and easiest place would be in my apartment," answered Luke.

"Go ahead and do it before you start listening to the conversations. Would it help if Matt and Mark came down to help? Can you record the conversations as we listen?"

"Yes and yes," replied Luke. "I can split the recording into segments and all three of us can listen. That will cut down the time considerably."

"Okay, I'll ask the twins to head your way as soon as possible."

After he hung up, John called Matt. "Get your tactical headgear and cameras and drive to Luke's. Better take your federal ID with you. We may need it to help us in a pinch. I'll call Mark and have him meet you there. Tell Tony to stay at his house and wait for our friends to call him. Let him know we'll be somewhere close to that truck for as long as he's driving it."

With the preliminaries out of the way, John calmed

down even further and started to think of ways to bring the Claybourne matter to a close. He was deep in thought and almost didn't hear the phone ring. "John, this is Harvey. I have Peter on the line. Tell him what you know about the possible shipment of drugs."

John proceeded to recite to Harvey and Peter the word-for-word conversation recorded from Claybourne Enterprises' office. When he finished, silence ensued. After several seconds, Peter responded, "John, listen, give us a chance to put a tap on their phone so we can get concrete evidence on them."

Taking a chance, John said, "You put listening devices in their office and had to remove it a day later. I have everything I just told you on tape. In my mind, that's all the evidence you need. Why are you dragging your feet?"

"John, this is bigger than you know. I insist that you leave this alone. We want the entire organization, not just the Claybourne part of it."

John didn't reply, knowing they were right. Just as the silence was getting uncomfortable, an unidentified voice asked, in a somewhat nasty tone, "How did you know we had listening devices in place for a day?"

"Because I have better equipment than you do," replied John, just as nastily.

"I know for a fact that their office is checked every other day for listening devices or taps," stated the unidentified person. "Nothing has been found or they wouldn't be talking so openly."

"Newest technology, patent pending," replied John sarcastically.

Again, the phone was quiet. Finally, Peter said, "John, let's talk about this. We'll get back to you within an hour." A slight pause, and then, "Concerning your listening device. How long have you had it in place? Do you have all the conversations on tape?"

"They've been in place for about six weeks. Every sound made in the office, and in most of the building, has been recorded on a hard drive, not a tape recorder. And, in addition, every pertinent conversation has been tagged for ease of retrieval."

Harvey thought to himself, *I wonder if we can use any of the data after the phone tap was approved, or will the court throw everything out because we started it beforehand?* "How often do you listen to the data?"

"Every two or three days," answered John, "until today. In about three hours I could have someone listening to the conversations, twenty four-seven, until this thing is finished. Something else you need to know. The guy who will be driving the truck works for me. In return for the information we've provided you, I want you to assure me that you'll do everything possible to protect him from being harmed or prosecuted."

John heard some hushed conversations in the background before Peter again stated that they would call back within an hour. "You didn't give me your assurance," stated John.

The unidentified person replied. "We can't guarantee keeping him out of harm's way, but I'll make sure he won't be prosecuted."

"Thank you." John then returned to his inner thoughts. After minutes of deep concentration, John pulled out a notepad and began to write words and phrases on the paper. Satisfied with what he wrote, John called Tony.

After he received answers to a dozen or so questions, he gave Tony some instructions. John jotted several more notations on his paper. Subsequently, he called Luke's apartment and left a message telling Luke about additional electronic equipment he would need.

John then called the twins to bring them up to date and to brainstorm several items in the plan he was developing. When he remembered that Tony wouldn't be available for a few days, John called one of his construction foremen to have a crew finish the work Tony had started on his house. John loaded his SUV with items he may need and returned to his living room to await the return call from Peter and Harvey.

When John received the call, Peter turned the conversation over to the still-unidentified person, presumably from the DEA. "John, here's what we're going to do. Two of my men will be on their way to Harrisburg within the next few hours. They'll follow the truck to its destination and take whatever action they deem necessary, probably nothing but taking note of where and who gets the shipment. We hope to have other men in place to track any of the merchandise to its individual destinations."

"Why don't you put a GPS on the truck to keep track of them?" asked John.

"We plan on putting a tracking device on the truck as soon as feasible. However, if they have a GPS already on the truck, which a lot of companies now have, we won't be able to use ours. The two will interfere with each other."

"How do we know that the driver who's working for us ... by the way, his name is Tony Marlow ... won't come to any harm?"

"We can't guarantee that he'll be entirely safe. We won't be close enough to help should they decide his services are no longer needed. Like I said, there are no guarantees," stated the federal agent. John knew then that the Feds were only interested in the drugs and that wasn't good enough. He would provide his own protection for Tony. The conversation continued for several minutes, but John wasn't paying that much attention ... his mind was working on his own plan.

Later that evening, John and his three friends were at Luke's apartment where they discussed possibilities and what they could do. Mark said, "If I were a drug dealer with a big shipment, I'd make sure I wasn't being followed before I made any deliveries. I'd also have a GPS on that truck to let me know where it was at all times."

When he heard this comment, Luke stated, "Claybourne has GPS systems on all of their trucks. You can tell by the white domes on the back of the cabs. There are companies nationwide that track the trucks and report back to the company as often as the company wants. Some companies run their own systems so they can tell customers exactly when their shipments will be delivered."

"Peter's friend told me they can't put their own tracking system on any truck that has a GPS on it," stated John. "He said that the two would interfere with each other."

"That's true for the most part, or for the time being. I can put a GPS transmitter on the truck that won't interfere with their unit," stated Luke. "Its part of the same technology used in the listening devices I installed at the Claybourne offices. Incidentally, my patent request's almost finalized. I should have a patent in a few months."

"Congratulations!" They all said simultaneously.

"Can you get rich over this?" asked Matthew, somewhat jokingly.

"There's a good possibility of it," stated Luke. "There are a lot of possibilities for this new technology. I think that radio and television stations will be particularly interested. Also, the armed forces and law enforcement agencies will find it useful."

"Oh," replied Matthew, still joking, "I assume your favorite brother will somehow get rich on this also."

"You'll be well taken care of," stated Luke, in such a manner that Matt knew he wasn't kidding. "I'll let you know if there are any situations where you can get involved. Maybe I'll need some of that moldy money you keep in your wallet to start a new business."

"Just let me know," replied Matthew, seriously. "I'll do what I can."

"Me too," stated Mark.

"Hey! Me, too," answered John. Then, after a brief pause, John said, "Getting back to the subject of the GPS. Can you put something together quickly that we can attach to the truck?"

"Yes and not only the truck. I can put a small tracker on Tony also, small enough that it can be concealed rather easily."

"How do we follow them?" asked Mark.

"Microsoft made it easy," replied Luke. "They developed a program called 'Streets and Trips' for computers. All I need is a computer for each tracking device."

"I have my laptop in the SUV," stated John. "We can use that, can't we?"

"Yes," replied Luke, "and mine too. But it will take me some time to put them together. You three will have to listen to the recording without me, so that I can work on them."

"No problem," replied John. "Just show us how and we'll be on our way."

It took three hours for the three of them to go through the disks to get them organized into pertinent files. They separated the calls that could, in their opinion, pertain to the shipment and distribution of drugs.

In the meantime Luke was hard at work making two transmitters to track the truck and Tony. He left the apartment twice to buy several items at an electronics store and to retrieve items from the building where he worked. When he was satisfied that his work was completed, he got the two laptops together and installed the Microsoft program.

When he called the other three together, he said, "Mark, how about if you go to the all-night market to buy some snacks? Matt, how about you pick up soft drinks at another store?" Each of you take a transmitter and take an indirect route to each location. John will track Matt, and I'll follow Mark on my laptop."

When the twins returned, John and Luke showed them the route each had tracked and how fast they had traveled at various points along the routes.

After they discussed their plan for another hour, Mark said, "Looks like we're ready to go."

"Okay," continued John. "I'll call Tony to see if he's heard anything yet."

When Tony answered the phone, John said, "Tony, it's John. Have you heard from them yet?"

"Nothing yet," was his only reply.

"We're set on our end. If you get a call, contact me right away to let us know what they tell you."

"Okay, but I think we're okay for tonight," replied Tony. "I'm going to get some sleep. It may be a long day tomorrow, or maybe not until the day after, or whenever," he continued nervously.

"Hang in there, Tony," sensing his anxiety. "You can't get in trouble with the police and one of us will always be nearby. I'll call you in the morning if we don't hear from you."

John said, "Tony's starting to feel the pressure, but he's hanging in there like a real trooper."

"I don't blame him a bit," stated Matt. "I'd be just as nervous if I were in his shoes."

"You can say that again," replied his twin.

"Let's get some sleep. Tony will call when he hears from them."

All four friends were up early the next morning. John, as usual, completed his five-mile run before meeting the other three for breakfast at a nearby restaurant. "Let's call Tony to see if he got any sleep last night." After the phone rang for a full minute, John hung up. "No answer. He's probably in the shower."

"I don't think so, boss," said Matthew as he sat straight up in his chair. "Tony told me he gets up at sunrise. I don't get a good feeling about this."

"Okay," replied John. "Let's move it. Get your cars and go to the Claybourne warehouse. Don't be too conspicuous. Luke, you make the first pass through the area and tell us what you see. You two follow and I'll bring up the rear. Keep your tactical radios on and report in on what you see. Turn on your cameras before you drive through the area."

As John drove toward the warehouse, he asked himself the question. *How could I be so stupid? Those guys are smart enough not to give Tony a chance to call anyone. They probably just went to his apartment, surprised him, and then forced him to go with them.*

Ten minutes later, John heard Luke's voice in his ear. "There's an unmarked red Kenworth tractor trailer sitting in the loading dock. Don't see any unusual activity. Hold that," a pause, "there's a blue Ford sedan sitting down the block with the driver crouched down. If that's not a government car, I'll buy lunch."

Two minutes later, Mark reported in. "Thanks for the heads up, Luke. There's also a dark green Ford parked on a side street with a driver in it. Since they're so obvious, it makes me wonder if these guys are really pros."

A few minutes passed with no report from Matthew. John asked on the radio, "Matt, where are you?"

No answer. "Matt, can you hear me?"

No answer; then, "Sorry about that. I was stopped at a traffic light and guess what? A pickup pulled up right next to me and our friend Tony was driving. He saw me, but didn't react. There was some guy in the passenger seat, and I didn't want him to notice Tony looking at me, so I just acted like I was daydreaming. A guy in a white Cadillac SUV with fancy chrome wheels is following Tony."

"We got lucky on that one," replied John. "Luke, get the GPS tracker for the truck ready. I've got an idea how to get it on the truck." A minute or two later, John spoke into the radio, "Tony was walking around that red truck as I drove by.

Apparently, there was someone watching the truck. I saw three guys, one of whom is our old buddy, Paul Adams."

After checking the hookups and lights on the tractor trailer, Tony got behind the wheel and started the powerful diesel engine. When the passenger door was opened, one of the men from the SUV got in alongside of him. He was as big as a barn and very muscular. "Didn't know I was going to have company," Tony said.

"I'm not here for conversation. Just drive," was the answer. Then, as an afterthought, the passenger asked, "Do you have a cell phone?"

"Yes," answered Tony.

"Give it to me." The man reached over and patted Tony's shirt and pants. "Empty your pockets."

"That's fine with me." *What an asshole!* Tony thought to himself.

Tony was just sitting behind the wheel, checking over the instruments when his passenger said, "Okay, let's get this show on the road."

"Listen," replied Tony, "if you want to drive, let me know and I'll get out. But if you want me to drive, I have to wait for the air pressure to build up or we won't be able to stop this rig. I'll leave when that gauge is above the green line," pointing to the air pressure gauge. His passenger gave him a dirty look but didn't say a word.

While he waited for the air pressure to build up, Tony checked the manifest to see what he was hauling. This got him a dirty look and a sarcastic comment, "We're fully loaded with coffee beans. What did you think you'd be carrying?" Tony just ignored the question, thinking, *Yeah, coffee beans being delivered from a construction supply company.*

A block after he began the trip, Tony needed every bit of the truck's air pressure to stop the truck when an obviously drunk man staggered from the curb, right in front of the truck. Tony slammed on the brakes but didn't stop in time.

He hit the drunken man. The truck seemed to be still moving when Tony jumped from behind the wheel and went to the aid of the man he hit. As he got to the front of the truck, the man was crawling out from under the truck. "Sumabitch" the man said, slurring his words. "You broke my bottle," holding up a brown bag with a dark liquid running out of the bottom.

"What the hell's going on?" yelled Tony's passenger, as he watched the drunk stagger across the street.

"Thought I killed that bastard," replied Tony. "I guess the Lord does take care of drunks and babies." He headed back to his driver's seat, wondering what the hell John was doing under the truck.

Because they had been forewarned that the truck would be traveling on I-78 and I-95, the four friends headed in that direction ... three in front of the big red truck and one behind. John, who was the last in line, commented into his radio, "Gentlemen, I do believe this convoy has more vehicles than we expected. From here, I'm fairly sure we have a red tractor trailer, one white SUV, two Fords ... one green, one blue, and I think a red Mustang that we've seen before. They're traveling in that order, and before they spot me, I'm pulling off the road."

"Okay, replied Mark. "I'll turn at the next intersection and then fall in at the end of the line. I should be able to film the convoy as they go by. You may be able to get in front of them if use the old road. It runs pretty much parallel in this area, and I'll bet there's not much traffic on it."

Tony, who was much more relaxed than he was an hour ago, looked in his mirrors and stated, "Looks like your friends don't trust us. They're following us."

"Not your concern," replied the asshole. "Just keep driving and let us take care of the trash." This comment made Tony a little nervous as he thought *they know my friends are out there somewhere.*

Later, Luke came on the radio again, somewhat frantically,

"They fooled us. The truck's taking I-81 South, not north as we expected."

Matthew, who was now the last vehicle in line, interrupted, "Relax, I'm still back here, and have them in sight, or at least off and on. Everyone, just turn around and get behind me. I'll make a pass as soon as you get here."

"No problem," stated John, "I've made the turn and will catch up to you shortly."

"Hold on," yelled Matt, "the truck's stopping on the bridge. I have to pass it and keep going."

"Okay, no problem," said John. "I'm behind you and I'll check it out."

"I'm not on I-81 yet," replied Luke. "I'm pulling off."

Mark spoke up, "I'm still north of Route 22. I'll turn and pull off the road and wait for what you want me to do."

After several minutes went by, John spoke again, "The truck's sitting on the bridge out of the traffic lane. It's a wide bridge here." A few seconds later, he said, "The blue Ford also pulled over in front of the truck. The white SUV and the red Mustang are nowhere in sight, so they had to have seen that the blue car stopped. Good move for the suspects. I don't think they're on to us, though."

"I got off I-81 at the interchange just over the bridge," said Matt. The dark green Ford kept going straight, with the white SUV not far behind him. I didn't see the red Mustang. Do you want me to follow them?"

"No, stay put," answered John. "Our only concern is Tony. Matt, which direction are you going?"

"John, this is Mark. I'm parked on old Route 22, facing I-81. I'll wait here. I can be on I-81 in less than a minute."

"This is Matt. I'm parked in a scenic overlook next to the Susquehanna River. I can see the truck on the bridge, as well as the blue Ford."

"Okay, team, we're still intact and in good shape. Don't let them see you if possible. Stay loose and keep cool."

When fifteen minutes had passed, the truck was still on the bridge. "Guys, this is Mark. A white SUV just got off I-81 northbound and got right back on I-81 southbound. I think it might be our suspects."

As he was talking, Matt observed that the truck had begun to move and said, "The truck's moving. They must've got some signal by the guy in the SUV as it drove by."

"Stay put," said John. "We'll know if they get off here. If they don't get off, we can catch them before the next interchange. There's no place for them to hide on I-81."

"The truck's now in the traffic lane and passing the blue Ford. The white SUV is right behind the truck. No sign of the Mustang. Wait a minute. I see that vehicles behind the SUV are stopping. It looks like they all have flat tires. The blue Ford's now moving. Hold it. It's also stopping with at least two flat tires. Traffic on the bridge is coming to a standstill. You two north of the bridge had better consider another way around."

"Wait," said John, "I think this is working out just the way they wanted. Luke, how far away will you be able to track the truck?"

"It's a new device, so I can't say for sure. As an educated guess, I'd say eight to ten miles."

"Stay there for a few minutes. I think I know where they're going. Mark, you stay put. Keep your radio on."

A few minutes later, Luke made a report. "I'm tracking the truck southbound on I-81. They didn't get off at Route 11."

John asked, "Matt, can you follow them southbound? Stay with traffic flow and don't try to catch up with them."

"On my way, but there's not much traffic," was the only answer.

Five minutes later, Matt exclaimed, "Just passed the green Ford. It's parked along the shoulder. The driver's changing a flat tire." Then, "My, oh my, guess who just pulled onto I-81 southbound? ... Our old friend in the red Mustang. I think he was checking to see if anyone was following. He didn't wait long enough. Boy, are we lucky!"

"Okay, guys," stated Luke. "The truck turned east on Route 581, the Harrisburg Beltway."

"Here's the plan," shouted John, triumphantly. "Luke, go down along the river through Harrisburg. Matt, continue to follow the truck and turn onto Route 581. Stay back. Mark, I want you to go north on I-81 to the roadside rest near Grantville, about twenty miles north. I'm going to go east into Camp Hill on a route parallel to Route 581. I'm betting the truck goes around Harrisburg via I-83 and gets back on I-81 northbound. Luke, keep us posted on the truck's location. If you lose it, that'll mean they took another route and we'll have to backtrack as fast as possible."

Every few minutes Luke made the same statement. "Truck's continuing on Route 581; so far, so good." Finally, "John, I do believe you were right. The truck's now proceeding north on I-83. I'm going to cross the Susquehanna River and cut through the city. I'll keep tracking to make sure he stays on I-83 northbound and doesn't head toward the Pennsylvania Turnpike via I-283."

Fifteen minutes went by when Luke reported that he was continuing to track the truck on I-83 northbound. "The truck's turning off I-83 onto Route 22 northbound at Colonial Park. I'm less than half a mile away."

"I'm a mile behind them," shouted Matt.

"The truck's turning onto a side road on the right side of the highway across from a mall," said Luke. "The sign says it's Clinton Avenue. The map doesn't show a name for the road, but it's only a half mile from I-83. The truck's stopped at a warehouse a block away from a school. I'll turn at the next road and see if I can find a spot to watch them."

"Luke, better stay away," said Matt. "I have an eyeball on them. All three vehicles are parked next to a big building with several loading docks. I just pulled into the parking lot of Bob and Jack's Restaurant across the street. The truck's backing up to the loading dock … looks like they're going to load or unload something. I have my camera running."

"This is John. I'll park in the mall lot across the street from the restaurant. Will I be able to see them?"

"If you get the right angle, you shouldn't have a problem," replied Matthew.

John spoke again, "I see a forklift removing a wooden crate from the truck. Tony's walking toward another truck. Matt, can you walk to an area where Tony can see you just to let him know we're still with him."

"I'm sure I can."

John continued, "I've got my camera running. They've moved seven wooden crates to another truck Tony and his babysitter just went to. This truck is a black Freightliner and is pulling a white trailer. Tony's driving that truck now. They're on the move again with the SUV and Mustang behind. I still think they're heading up I-81 to I-78. I'll follow."

Luke cut in, "I can't track the movement. The GPS is still on the red truck."

Matt spoke up, "Luke you'd better go with the others. I'm sure Tony saw me. Right now, there's no one around the loading dock. I'll wait a few minutes and see if I can retrieve the GPS without anybody seeing me."

"Good idea," said John. "The truck's turning right back onto I-83. Mark, we're heading your way."

"Okay," Mark replied. "

Tony felt pretty secure because he had seen Matt when he was getting into the new truck. He thought he had lost everyone when the traffic stopped on the I-81 bridge. "Hey," he said to his passenger. "Do you think I'd be allowed to stop and take a piss? There's a rest area up ahead, and, besides, if you want me to stay within the law, I should stop and fill out my log books in case we get stopped by the PUC or ICC."

"Yeah, go ahead," the asshole said as he pulled out his cell phone and typed in a text message.

"Tony's pulling into the rest area," John said. Mark, since I don't think they'll let Tony out of their sight, I need a distraction while I pass a tracking device to him."

"Okay. Let's do it on the way into the men's room. You'll have to get close to Tony."

Chapter 21

As Tony and his passenger approached the door to the men's room, Mark was leaving. He avoided looking at Tony and bumped into the passenger. While Mark apologized, John slipped by them and passed the device to Tony and whispered, "Coat pocket." Tony didn't slow down and headed directly to the stall, where he inspected the one-inch black plastic square John had just given to him and put the item in the pocket of his jacket.

As the convoy got back on the road, John commented, "I'm tracking Tony."

Luke responded, "My tracker's also working. Matt, how did you get the tracker on the black truck?"

"I couldn't, so I put it on the SUV," he replied. "I figured they wouldn't be separated too far until they reached their destination."

"Good work," stated John. "Tony's turning east onto I-78 toward Allentown."

Mark interjected, "I heard some truckers say that there's a State Police and PUC check on I-78 eastbound. It's up there about ten miles."

"Mark," said John, "you and Luke go ahead and get on I-78 and get in front of them. Get off at the interchange after the

PUC checkpoint and wait for them to proceed again. Stay in front of them. Matt and I will follow you and get off at the interchange before the checkpoint. We'll stay behind them after the PUC finishes with them."

After the State Police weigh team and Public Utility Commission personnel completed their check on the truck and Tony's logbook, the convoy continued east to Allentown. On the east side of town, Tony was directed to an old rundown warehouse where he parked the truck at a loading dock. He did as he was told and got into the SUV and was driven to a restaurant.

The man in the red Mustang stayed with the truck and supervised the unloading of a wooden crate that was moved to a small box van. John and Mark dutifully recorded this activity on film. Matt and Luke sat in their cars. They kept watch on the doors of the restaurant where Tony apparently was having his lunch.

Tony and his entourage returned to the black truck and headed east on I-78 toward Newark, New Jersey. Along the way, they made a pit stop at another rest area, as well as another stop at a weigh station in New Jersey. Tony was directed to a loading dock near the port of Newark. He parked the truck and was driven from the area in the SUV.

About an hour later, Tony was brought back to the truck. As he was pulling away from the dock, he now noticed that the truck was not pulling as heavy a load as it had been when he first started that morning. All of his movements continued to be tracked by two computers. Several cameras took photos of the transfer of the cargo for future reference. Tony hadn't spotted any of his friends since Allentown, but had no reason to think they weren't nearby as he traveled north on I-95.

As Tony approached I-95 at the George Washington Bridge, he commented to his passenger, "If we're going to keep my logbook in order and stay within ICC regs, I'm going to have to stop and rest fairly soon. I'm also getting low on gas."

The passenger typed a text message into the cell phone and transmitted it. A few minutes later, the phone vibrated loudly and the asshole read a message and commented, "You have about another hour to go before we stop." End of message. End of the conversation, such as it was.

North of Bridgeport, Connecticut, Tony was directed to get off of I-95 and head toward a large truck stop and a couple of motels near the interchange. Tony and his passenger went into the restaurant where they ate in silence. When they were finished, his companion took Tony to the motel next door. The asshole handed him a key and said, "Don't even think about trying to leave the room tonight. You can't open the window. And, this will create a very loud alarm to go off if you try to open the door," as he put some kind of contraption on the outside door knob.

Tony entered the room and opened the drapes just in time to see the asshole getting ready to enter the room next door to him. The asshole stopped and said, with a motion of his hand, "Keep the drapes shut too."

As Tony closed the drapes, he noticed the red Mustang was parked in front of the room on the other side of his. He also had time to see a black man walking through the parking lot. *'That will let me sleep a lot easier tonight,'* he thought to himself. As he looked around the room, he realized his traveling companions were not taking any chances. The phone and internet connections had been removed and the window, indeed, could not be opened. He was tempted to open the door just to see what would happen, but decided it wasn't worth the possible consequences.

The evening and night passed uneventfully. John and Luke, then Mark and Matt, rotated their watch every two hours. They had rooms in a motel next to the one where Tony was sleeping. They had a good view of the adjoining motel through a row of short pine trees between the properties. When on duty, they sat in the backseat of Luke's van with darkened windows.

After breakfast the next morning, Tony continued his drive northward on I-95 through Providence, Rhode Island and toward Boston, Massachusetts. The asshole told him to pull over before they reached the Port of Boston. When Tony spotted a convenient place to pull over, the asshole opened the door and jumped out saying, "Wait here."

Tony sat in the truck alone for nearly a half hour as ordered. Finally, the man in the white SUV pulled up behind him. He shouted to Tony to get out and get in the SUV. "Here are your orders," stated the guy Tony knew was Barry Brubaker. "Go straight ahead and enter the gate with the 'RESTRICTED AREA' sign. The guard there will ask you for identification and the manifest included with your papers. They may or may not want to check what's in the truck. Let them do whatever they want. They'll tell you to drive to a dock where part of your cargo will be unloaded. Complete any necessary paperwork and drive back out this way. Stop across the road and pick up your passenger. Someone will be watching you the whole time. Don't speak to anyone and don't leave the truck unless you're told to do so. Do I make myself clear?"

"Sure," answered Tony. As he reentered the truck, he now understood why they wanted him to drive. He thought *I'm the one on record who's driving the truck and if anything goes wrong. It's me, not the asshole, who'll take the blame.*

As Tony approached the gate, everything went pretty much the way Brubaker had explained it to him. He noticed that something was unloaded and then something else was loaded back on the truck.

Two hours after he had left the asshole, Tony stopped and picked up his passenger again. He was then told to get back on I-95 and proceed to Wakefield, a small town north of Boston. There, he parked his truck at the loading dock of what appeared to be an empty store. Tony was then told to go to the SUV where the two men took him for a ride and a meal. Because of the isolated location of the truck, John and his friends couldn't see what had transpired with the black truck. When Tony returned, he found that the black truck wasn't there. In its place was an all-white Peterbilt truck attached to a matching trailer. Both were decked out in more lights than Tony had ever seen on a rig.

As he got out of the SUV, Brubaker handed him an envelope. "This will cover your expenses. We need this rig back in Harrisburg between noon and five o'clock tomorrow, but not before. Back the truck up to the door on the far right of the loading dock. Leave the keys in the truck and get in your pickup and go home. You're on your own from here. Keep your mouth shut and you won't get hurt. Don't stop to talk to anyone. If you do, your wife will pay the consequences. Don't try to call anyone, even your wife. Your phone is tapped so we'll know if you don't follow our orders. Stop someplace and stay overnight. Someone will be watching you, so don't do anything stupid. Here's your cell phone ... the batteries are dead." With that, the SUV pulled away. Tony's former passenger was now riding shotgun in the SUV. There was no sign of anyone else in the area.

Tony had no choice but to drive south to Pennsylvania. While doing his safety checks, he noticed the trailer doors had a lock and a lead seal so they could tell if the door had been opened. He climbed into the cab and started the diesel engine. As he waited for the air to build up, he read the manifest showing him, and/or the ICC, what was in the trailer. Apparently he was carrying a load of nails. *Is there a steel mill around Boston?* He thought. As he pulled out, he felt the pressure on the big engine. He knew that he definitely was hauling a full load.

Tony got the big rig rolling and headed for I-95 southbound.

Thunder and Lightning

The engine in the Peterbilt was well tuned and the 18-wheeler reached a cruising speed of 65 mph with little effort. He kept checking his mirrors, but didn't see anyone following him.

Although he couldn't see them, Tony was being followed, or tracked, by six vehicles. Three of the vehicles were in the front. One was a red Ford Mustang; one was Luke's van, which was tracking Tony. They were approximately one and two miles ahead, respectively. Mark was driving the third vehicle that was four miles in front of the van.

The first vehicle behind the white tractor trailer was a white Cadillac SUV, which kept alternating its distance behind the truck from one-quarter to one mile. The first time the SUV did this maneuver, the other two trailing vehicles almost got exposed. But the tracking device alerted them. They now were two miles behind their friend and employee.

"Wish we had a fourth tactical radio," John said. "We could talk to him at least."

"On the other hand," Mark answered, "if they saw him with it, he may be in deep shit. Why do you think they let him drive by himself, but keep checking on him?"

"Maybe it's a play on the old 'give him enough rope and he'll hang himself' routine or maybe they have something in the truck they don't want to be near."

"How do we let him know we're still with him?"

John's comeback was, "Better yet, how do we get him to pull over so we can talk to him?"

"It's too risky having him stop as long as the other two are around."

"Guys," stated Mark, "I just passed a sign for a rest stop. It said the next stop is forty miles ahead. Let's get him to stop there. If the suspects don't want him to know they're around, they may not want to risk stopping."

"Good idea," stated John. "Matt, do you have anything in your car to make a sign to tell him to stop at the next rest area."

"Hmm ... yes, but I'll have to stop to get it."

"Okay, do it and then pass everyone and head to the rest area."

"Okay boss," as he started looking for a place to pull off the road.

It took Matthew two minutes to retrieve some paper from his trunk and to write a note large enough for Tony to see. He taped it to the inside of his passenger window and sped down the interchange ramp to catch up to Tony. As he passed John, he asked, "Can you read the note?"

"I can read it and so will the driver of the SUV when you pass him," answered John.

"I figured that, so I'll have the window down when I pass him. I already tried it, so there shouldn't be any problem."

"Go get 'em, Mr. Earnhart."

It took Matt twenty-five miles to catch up to Tony's truck. He could have done it quicker, but there was no big hurry. As he drove up alongside Tony, he beeped his horn twice. Tony looked down from his driver's seat and gave Matthew the thumbs-up sign.

"Okay," Matt said into his radio, "he saw me and gave me the thumbs-up sign. Now what?"

"You and Mark better do the contact," answered John. "Luke and I will keep tracking Tony and the SUV. Luke, you pull into the rest area also. If the SUV gets off I-95, so will I."

"What do you want us to tell him?" asked Mark.

"Tell him he's being followed. See if he knows what he's hauling. And, most importantly, tell him to do everything he would do if this were his real job. This may just be a test to see if they can trust him, or if he's going to create any trouble."

Later, Mark commented, "The red Mustang pulled in and the driver, more or less, hid his car. He went into the men's room. He's now in an area where he can see the phones and the men's room door. It's like they expect him to stop here."

"Well," said Luke, "it's been three hours since he had breakfast. I need to go also."

"Good point."

As it turned out, all the drivers had an opportunity to make a pit stop. Matt managed to let Tony see him without being observed by the Mustang driver. Mark positioned himself to keep an eye on everyone as they entered the rest area. He made sure no one would try to follow Tony into the men's room. Once Tony and Matt were finished with their conversation, Tony went back to his truck and brought his logbook up to date.

When Tony got back on I-95, the Mustang driver met with the two guys from the SUV and had a short conversation. The Mustang driver then got in his car and also headed southward. It wasn't seen again. The two occupants in the white SUV got back into their vehicle. They continued to follow Tony.

The SUV was tracked until it turned west on I-284. Luke lost contact with it a short time later. Tony stopped at a truck stop in the Poconos in Pennsylvania. As he had been instructed, he planned to stay there overnight after he ate dinner and had the gas tanks filled.

Tony's friends conducted a thorough search of the area. John then entered the restaurant and sat where Tony could see him. After he made sure that no one was watching Tony, John walked past Tony's table and slipped him a note. Five minutes later, the two met in the restroom for a quick conversation and update.

The next morning Tony continued his trip south and west toward Harrisburg. He was stopped twice in Pennsylvania for PUC and ICC checks. The rest of the trip was uneventful. Several hours later he pulled his rig into the parking lot of Claybourne Enterprises. He parked the truck and headed for his pickup. Of course, he had been tracked and followed the whole way.

Tony drove for two miles and stopped at a traffic light.

He heard a short beep from the car next to him. When he looked over, Mark made a motion for Tony to follow him. After fifteen minutes, and several unnecessary turns, Mark and Tony pulled up at Luke's apartment. Matthew arrived shortly afterwards and made the statement, "You weren't followed."

Inside Luke's apartment, Tony met with his four employers, who were just as happy as he was to have this trip behind them. After they made some phone calls to loved ones, the group conducted a debriefing session and recorded as many details as each could remember.

"Several questions come to mind," said John. "The first concerns the two Feds; at least we think they were Feds. Did the guys in the SUV and Mustang know the Feds would be there? If so, how did they know? Second, why did they go ahead with their plans if they knew they were under suspicion? Next, why did they assume there were only two of them? I'm fairly certain they didn't catch on to the fact that we were also following them. Something doesn't smell right here. Any chance you know the names of any of the guys traveling with you?"

Tony replied, "I know the guy who was driving the SUV is Barry Brubaker. He was with me when we stole the material from the State College site. The only name I heard was when the guy in the Mustang called my passenger Rocky."

They spent some time discussing many other questions. In the end, they didn't know any more than they did at the beginning.

After a brief explanation to Tony, John ended the discussion by stating, "I believe it's time we turn all our information and questions over to our government friends and let them run with it. We've done all we could. I'll call Harvey and let him know what we did. Can we e-mail him the information we have?" he asked Luke.

"Not if you're in a hurry," Luke replied, "too much

information with all the pictures and videos we have. It'll have to be mailed to him on computer disks."

Because he figured there was no use in postponing it, John called Harvey. "Harvey, it's John," was all he said.

"Oh shit," was the immediate reply, "as if we don't have enough problems today. Now you call looking for an update."

"You sound like you had a bad day," stated John, with a smile on his face, "What's the problem?"

"We lost track of the truck the day before yesterday. The two cars that DEA had following the truck lost it on I-81 somewhere near Harrisburg. The truck was heading south, so they've been searching for the rig in Maryland and Virginia with no luck at all."

"You're looking in the wrong direction," replied John. "They headed northeast into New Jersey, then north to the Boston area. They also changed rigs a couple of times."

"How the hell do you know that? Harvey shouted. "No, don't tell me. Your driver called and told you where they went. Tell me what he told you and maybe DEA can track down the truck now."

"Forget it," answered John, "the truck was unloaded and the shipment probably has been moved several times by now. Listen to me, Harvey. We think you and the DEA have more problems than losing track of what could have been a major drug shipment. There's something strange about the way the drug agents lost the trucks."

It took John half an hour to explain to Harvey what had happened and about some of their concerns. John then made arrangements for all the computer disks to be picked up at Luke's office the following afternoon by someone from Harvey's staff. He also arranged to have other recordings from the Claybournes' office picked up by Harvey's staff member once a week.

"Harvey," stated John, "we've gone as far as we can with

this investigation. Peter and you have to take over from this point on. We don't have the manpower or expertise to finish this thing. If you have questions, we'll be happy to help, but as far as we're concerned, the ball's in your court."

"If you remember correctly," Harvey answered, "you were supposed to be out of our way a long time ago. You're the one who keeps sticking your nose into this thing."

"You're right," replied John, "but this time, we're serious."

Before the friends called it a day, they decided that Tony had to stay away from his apartment to avoid further contact with his undesirable acquaintances. Since the suspects didn't know anything about his job at the lodge, they decided to move him and his family there immediately. Tony would pick up his family at their apartment and they would stay in the lodge until their house was moved and was ready to be lived in.

Chapter 22

Back at the construction company the next day, John found his dad in the office and brought him up to date on the investigation. Mr. Lynch was pleased that John and his friends had finally turned the investigation over to the Feds.

By the beginning of the following week, John had put the investigation to the back of his mind and continued his planning for the eventual separation of the construction company. He placed the other projects in a lower order on his list of priorities.

John and Mr. Lynch first conducted numerous, but timely, meetings with the lawyers, accountants and bankers who represented the current construction company to iron out details of the sale, breakup and future management of the various companies that would be created.

Harold and John held a second round of meetings with the prospective new owners and managers of each proposed company. Because the new owners were already managing many of the departments within the existing company, there were very few concerns that would not be settled immediately. The problems that were not settled only required minor negotiations or explanations to resolve. At the suggestion of the Lynches, each new company would hire their own attorneys, accountants and other advisors to review the settlement papers. In that way, there would be no misunderstanding at a later time. They agreed to strict limits for review time in order to allow the split-up to take place as soon as possible. John directed that each new manager meet with the employees to keep them up to date on all matters pertaining to the new companies. He also provided them with specific questions to ask each employee concerning future employment and retirement opportunities.

John deliberately held off the next meeting until last, at least the last meeting of the current round. For practical purposes, he scheduled the meeting with his parents in a private dining room of the Nittany Lion Inn in State College, away from the construction headquarters. The Nittany Lion Inn was a 225-room hotel run by Penn State's hospitality services. The Inn had several restaurants with many private dining areas. Some claimed the Inn, which had always been painted white, was as old as the university itself, but in actuality, was less than a hundred years old. The hotel was known as a place where the "average Joe" could be comfortable with more affluent Penn State alumni.

John entered the dining room an hour earlier than the scheduled meeting time. He wasn't surprised when he saw that his dad and mother were already there. "Well," started Mr. Lynch smiling, "it took you long enough to call this meeting. We felt left out."

"Now, Harold," stated Mrs. Lynch, also smiling. "You did say it made logical sense that the other meetings had to be held first. John, come give your mother a kiss."

"Sorry about the delay, mom and dad, but as you said, everything has to be in order." John was obviously nervous about this meeting, but knew it had to be held.

John's dad replied, still smiling, "You and I both know this meeting had to take place, so let's get it done."

John realized his dad was trying to make the situation

easier for him, so he relaxed a little and stated, "So where do we start?"

"Why not start with the most pressing issue? When will I start to turn over the actual management of the construction company?" said Harold. "The answer's simple ... as soon as the new companies are formed."

The answer surprised John. "Why so early?" he asked.

"Sit down and we'll explain."

John suddenly realized he'd been had. His dad knew all along that John had to ask him to turn over control of the company as soon as feasible. This made the other matters a little easier to discuss.

Mr. Lynch continued, "When Mother and I talked about leaving the business, we assumed it would be turned over to you. We also knew that in order to let you run the company in your own manner, I had to step aside immediately. As long as I remained in charge, it would always be perceived that you were just a puppet for me. Mother and I have complete confidence in your ability to make the company prosper and grow. You've proven that in the way you want to break our holdings into separate companies. I thought of this possibility, but didn't act on it. It makes complete sense."

John interrupted, "But, I don't want to force you to leave. What will you do?"

"Don't worry about that," replied Mrs. Lynch. "We've been looking forward to this for several years. Dad and I plan to enjoy our remaining years, whether it's sitting on the porch by the lake or traveling all around the world."

"She's right about that," stated John's dad. "As you know, I haven't spent much time in the office since you started working full time after you graduated. My managers have actually been handling most of the day-to-day business for a couple of years. The time has come for me to relinquish control of the company to you and the others."

"I'll still be on the board for the next few years. If I have any concerns, you and the CEOs will be the first to know. In addition, I'll only be a phone call away and will still be around if you need a listening ear. Believe me, this is what we've been planning since you were in high school. The issue is not a concern for you or for us ... it's done and over with. Now let's get to more important matters."

"Maybe not as important, but along those same lines," stated John. "What are we going to do about Martin and Janet?"

Harold Lynch answered, "I don't see where that's a problem. They're part of the equation. My leaving won't affect them. Martin is part of management and will continue in that role as long as he likes. Janet, I know for certain, is going to retire. She'll take whatever retirement incentive she's entitled to."

"Do you think I should talk to them?" questioned John.

"I don't see any harm in that, but what they do will be their decision."

John was somewhat relieved but still questioned these comments. "I've been aware of their situation for a few years since I started paying more attention to the financial end of the business. Do they know that I know about them?"

"The subject has never come up, and that's the way they want it. You'll have to approach that matter with them, not me or your Mother."

"I appreciate what you're doing for me and the company, but I still feel like you're being forced into retirement. That's not what I had in mind."

"Listen, son. Believe it or not, the changes you're making in the new format are a blessing. I bought the construction company many years ago and worked my tail off. Years ago, we prayed that you would be interested in taking over the business. Five years ago, I realized that I couldn't continue to work twelve to fourteen hours a day much longer. I started turning more of the day-to-day operations over to my managers. It took almost three years for me to get to this point. I feel comfortable leaving them in charge. When your mother and I are gone, you'll inherit my remaining shares and may end up being CEO. I believe that my decision to let them handle the day-to-day management may have been the best thing for my health … not that I've had any problems before, or now, for that matter. But age does have an effect on how much pressure or work the human body can endure. Look at it this way … as soon as the company is split, I'll take an early retirement. Money isn't an issue. I'm already semi-retired. You've proven you can take over if necessary. So, what's the problem?"

"When you put it that way," explained John, "it sounds okay, but it wasn't my intention to force you out. I thought you'd cut back to three or four days a week. Then, after a certain amount of time you'd go to working one or two days a week before you actually retired."

"I've already cut back, so now it's time for retirement."

They continued their conversation for another hour. At the end, John realized that his parents were way ahead of him. They had already made the decisions without his having to encourage his dad to take early retirement.

"Okay," said John, "You've convinced me. I was so afraid to bring up the matter of early retirement, but you're way ahead of me, as usual. Now, let's talk about the retirement options that the retirement advisors have worked out. Did you get a chance to look over the options I gave you last week?"

"Yes, I looked them over very carefully. You know these options affect me also?"

John answered, smiling, "Yes, I know they affect you. None of these options should be a real concern for you. I don't know exactly how much money you managed to stash away, but I'm quite certain you and Mom aren't concerned about retirement income. Am I right?"

Harold and Margaret both grinned at him as their answer.

Margaret interrupted, "If I don't have to be here, I'm going to the gift shop." She knew she would hear the details of the conversation later.

Harold continued, "I firmly believe that the options available are fair to everyone. More so for those who want to retire in the near future. Do you have a breakdown of how many individuals may opt to take each package?"

"Based on our personnel files, here are the facts," as he handed the list to his dad.

Harold spent some time looking over the various lists. He asked, "How many of those who are over sixty can we expect to retire now?"

"The 401K specialists tell us we can expect half to leave now, and of course, the other half in one to five years. Big surprise ... right?"

After he had read the list, Mr. Lynch asked, "How much did you take into account for each company?"

"I assumed everyone would leave at the same time. I calculated one hundred twenty-five percent of the above figures plus one hundred fifty percent of healthcare insurance for the next ten years as part of each company's costs. If just half of the employees retire now, and half later, it will only mean we'll have more operating capital to work with until they retire."

"How close are the appraisers to finalizing the worth of each company?" asked Mr. Lynch.

"Based on my conversations with them last week, they should be ready to present the figures to you within two weeks. You know that the total value for the entire company is over one hundred million."

Harold continued, "Tell me again how we determine what percentage of each business an individual employee will be allowed to purchase."

"The appraisers first will have to determine the number and price of units for each company," John said. The appraised value will be what you'll be paid for the business. My shares will be subtracted from your units. The number of units in each company varies depending on the appraised value of the company. The appraisers will establish the price of each unit the same for each company so that employees of each company are treated equally. Once they determine the number of units for each company, only eighty percent of the units can be bought by employees. The other twenty percent will be reserved for future employees.

"The formula is a little complicated. However, each employee will be permitted to buy a certain number of units based on the number of years of service in the old company and their position within the new company. It will take a minimum of five and a maximum of ten years for the total buyout. The value of each unit will be adjusted yearly, based on the overall value of that particular company. As employees retire, they'll have to sell their units back to the company."

"What about the property and buildings?"

John replied, "You'll continue to own the property and buildings for the next five years. The management of all five companies has agreed to stay at their current locations for that time period and pay a reasonable rent. After five years, the management of each company will have the opportunity to purchase the portion of the property they occupy.

"I don't want the companies to be burdened with unnecessarily high expenses," replied Mr. Lynch. "I have enough money to retire."

"At this time, I can't picture any of the companies being moved unless they expand to the point where they need more space. I don't know if you're aware of it, but the management of all of the companies has already agreed to operate under the title of 'LYNCH' ... Lynch Construction, Lynch Steel Erection, Lynch Concrete, etc."

"No, I didn't know that," stated Mr. Lynch with a surprised look on his face.

"Well, it makes sense. Why not take advantage of the good name. Outside the industry, no one will know about the sale anyway," stated John.

"That's probably true, but it's still a nice gesture. I'm pleased with how things are working out. I don't have any doubt that the new companies will continue to prosper and provide you with an income for years to come. With that said, you handle the rest of the details and I'll be on my way. I have a tee time in an hour. See you soon." Mr. Lynch stood and hugged his son and walked out the door. John wasn't sure if he detected tears in his dad's eyes or was it just the glare.

Chapter 23

John wondered how he was going to handle the meeting with Martin and Janet. But just as his dad had predicted, it didn't make a difference. One thing that came out of the meeting with his father was that he'd have to check with the attorneys about ownership in an employee-owned business if one of the owners was not an employee.

John sat in silence for a long time, wondering if it wasn't time for a little break. He pulled out his cell phone and called Helen to see if she could get away early and maybe arrive at work a little late tomorrow. She accepted the invitation, provided they'd spend a quiet evening at home and order carry-out. He realized that his relationship with Helen was blossoming into what romantics would call a state of joy.

The next afternoon Tony called John and told him that the house was to be moved the next day. John really wanted to watch this process and called the Bowman brothers and invited them to watch the big event with him.

The four friends arrived at the lodge at daybreak and everyone was ready to put in a long day.

When John saw what had been done to prepare for the move, he was surprised that the house was not up on blocks, ready for the move. Instead, several trenches had been dug on each side of the house and cross beams had been placed under the house. Upon closer inspection, John noticed that each beam was being held up by jacks at the end of each beam. He noticed that hydraulic hoses had been attached to the jacks that were joined with the other ends to what appeared like an ordinary compressor. It was obvious that all the preliminary work had been done. After what seemed like a delay, John asked if there was a problem. The foreman answered no, they were just waiting for the boss and some of his friends to arrive.

When a carload of men arrived, the foreman directed them to a location out of the work area but close enough so they could observe the process. When the foreman sounded a horn, the compressor was started. The owner approached the workers and pressed a button which raised the house two inches off its foundation. Several minutes went by as men measured and re-measured various points around the house. After the foreman saw that his workers were ready, he sounded the horn again. The owner then pressed another button and the house was raised slowly a foot off the foundation. The men made several more measurements and they repeated the process. An hour later, the house was about four feet above ground and a truck backed a set of I-beams on wheels under the other beams. The beams were attached and fastened to each other by clamps. In that way, the house began its short trip down the clearing to its new location.

During the move, John approached the owner of the moving company and asked, "I noticed that you used a new type of jacks with higher lifts and, as much as I am impressed with this, I thought you were trying a new process to move the house."

The owner smiled and said, "Wait, I just did that to show these guys the old way first. The new process begins at the other end. Eventually, we'll be able to use the new process at each end of the move." John nodded and walked along with his friends, down through the clearing, which had been dozed and smoothed for ease of moving the house.

The house was moved without any problems. In a relatively short time, it reached its new location. The foundation of cinder block had been readied, including the foundation and floor for the addition to the house. It wasn't until he got closer that John noticed that there weren't any of the usual U-shaped notches along two sides of the house and two deeper notches in them at the ends of the house. Normally, all the beams would have been lowered into their individual slots, which would allow the house to be supported on the foundation. The beams would then be removed and the missing cinder blocks installed.

Mark commented, "What are those balls on top of the foundation?" After he inspected it a little closer, he said, "They're ball-type rollers. They're the same type of rollers airlines use to move freight in and out of planes. I can see how using them will help move the house off the trailer, but how are they going to remove the rollers? "

"Beats me," was Matt's reply.

The house was backed into position and two jacks were used to make the bottom of the house to line up with the top of the rollers. The workers made several close inspections and adjustments. They attached a cable to a hook already installed at the end of the house. The other end of the cable was attached to a four-wheel drive pickup at the opposite end of the new foundation. It wasn't until the tension was increased and the house began to move with ease that everyone noticed the small rollers installed on the long I-beams. As each cross beam was moved to the end of the I-beam and the house was on the rollers on the foundation, they stopped the movement of the house and the cross beam was slid sideways onto a waiting truck. John was astonished that the house had been moved onto its new foundation in less than two hours.

When the truck which had held the beams was moved,

another truck was backed up to the house. Then several men carried a number of bundles that turned out to be heavy-duty balloons into what was now the basement of the house. A short time later, several hoses were brought out through the basement door and attached to nozzles on the side of the truck. Once again, the owner, now smiling openly, turned a key which started a compressor in the truck. Several minutes later and after some adjustments to the control panel, four workers, located at different points around the house, reported the status in feet, then in inches, and finally "ready to lift." Slowly the house started to rise off the foundation. Once it was high enough, the foreman shouted, "Stop." Four men then reached in and removed the rollers that were on top of the foundation. The house was then slowly lowered back onto the foundation. The balloons in the basement were removed and placed back on the truck.

The foursome approached Allen, the owner, and John introduced everyone. They congratulated him on the move. They asked Allen numerous questions which he answered willingly and with obvious pride. John managed to get close enough to him and said, "Great job. Give me a couple of days. Then, give me a call so I can make arrangements about that dinner I owe you and your wife."

"Sure, and don't forget you owe me for half the cost of the move," he said with a smile.

"Just send the bill," returned John.

When the moving crew and the other onlookers left the site, Matthew turned to the other three and said, "Not much use for us to go back to the office today. Why don't we stick around here and help Tony with the addition to the house? It looks like he's already built the walls and trusses."

Tony, indeed, had the walls and trusses pre-built. He also had cut the wall out of the house where the addition would attach to the house. All they had to do was to remove the temporary plywood Tony had installed over the opening.

Tony put up a fuss about his employers helping him, but finally he realized that their offer was genuine. By dusk they had the walls and trusses up. They also had the roof sheeting in place and the shingles were installed.

Mark said to Tony, "That'll get you out of the weather." And as Tony walked away, Mark turned to John and said, "You know he's done most of this work himself. After you told him to use the construction crew, he changed your order and had them work on the lodge improvements."

"I didn't know that," replied John, "but give him credit ... he's not afraid of hard work. We made a good decision to hire him. I'll take care of the construction crew with direct orders. I don't want him to get physically run-down. We're too close to opening the lodge to have him getting sick or hurt because he's too proud or stubborn to accept help. Let's go check on the status of the lodge improvements."

While the four owners had been helping Tony, workers from Lynch Construction graded the area where the house had been. They dug out the footer for the remaining portion of the addition to the lodge. The footer would be poured the next day.

Back at the lodge, Emily Marlow had prepared a meal for the five tired men. They washed up and then sat down for what turned out to be a very satisfying meal. Before they left, they toured the lodge to check on progress of the remodeling. Much to their surprise, it appeared that most of the work had been completed, except for the end of the addition where the old house had been. It didn't take John long to realize that the progress was due at least in part because of the extra manpower used on the lodge instead of on Tony's house. Upon further investigation, he discovered that with a full crew the lodge would be finished soon.

John confirmed this information the next day when he discussed the status of the lodge with the foreman. He told him to go ahead and finish the needed work. As they completed their assigned work, the workers were to go over to Tony's house and work on the house and not pay any attention when Tony objected.

John also managed to place a call to Bob Goodfellow to check on the process of hiring a manager for the lodge. Bob told him that the list had been narrowed down to four candidates and he would be conducting interviews within a week. When he asked John if he wanted to be involved with the interviews, John politely said that was Bob's job not his, but to let him review the resumes before the final decision was made.

Chapter 24

"Listen to me," said Lou Claybourne. "My brother and I are starting to get really worried about those drug enforcement guys. They know about that last shipment. The fact that we're under investigation means they suspect something. We need to back off and wait until things settle down a little. Better yet, we have to stop making these shipments."

"I told you," stated Paul Adams, "we knew that DEA would be following the truck. I told you about it before it happened. We have a contact in the DEA office who will keep us advised about any actions that they plan to take. Besides, it's not for you to say when you will or will not ship. We control the shipments ... not you. You'll move the goods when we tell you to. It's either that or you lose everything and we eliminate any unnecessary loose ends."

"That sounds like a threat to me," answered Lou. "You can't move the merchandise without us, so don't get high and mighty with me. Not only that, look how easy it is for us to clean the money for you. That paycheck you get is very lucrative and as clean as a newly washed car."

"Don't kid yourself. We can get any stupid fool to drive a truck. Admittedly, the laundering process works well, but you're a small fish in our operation and don't think otherwise.

You've been paid very well for your services. We'll decide when your services are or aren't needed. Don't forget we still have a copy of your arrest record for dealing drugs. If that were to be made public, your company would go down the tubes."

Lou replied, "We're not implying we're going to cause trouble. It's just that a federal investigation scares the shit out of us."

"You and your brother do as you're told. Leave the Feds to us. Our source is impeccable."

After Adams left the office, Lou turned to his brother, "I think it's time we start to think about how to get out from under control of that bunch of slobs. With dad gone and the business doing well, we have enough money to live high off the hog." Lou pulled out a drawer in his desk and took out several pills that he quickly swallowed. He said, "How the hell did we get into this mess anyway?"

"You know as well as I do that our gambling losses got us started," Dave answered. "We lost so much we had to steal back and resell some of the building supplies we sold. We were in so deep that Brubaker told us he had another way for us to pay back what we owed him. All we had to do was to make a few trips down South and deliver goods to various locations up North. The shipments started small and got bigger and bigger. I still shiver every time I think about the time you and I got stopped by that local cop in North Carolina for speeding and you had crack in your pocket. Why he decided to search you is beyond me. We spent the night in jail before we were released. If dad would've found out, it would've killed him on the spot. Brubaker got us out of jail. He told us he had paid off the cops to let us go. I know now it was a setup ... they've used the information to keep us in line. They have us right where they want us, under their proverbial thumb. And speaking of drugs, where did you get those pills you just took? You know you're taking more and more. You'd better cut back."

"That's true," Lou answered, ignoring the comment about the pills, "but the other thing that bothers me is the money laundering process. We have accounts receivable from all those phony companies. We have two problems ... first is the high salary we pay Adams. I covered that by sending 1099 forms to the IRS. Adams doesn't know about that. Top that off with the fact that we have to give Brubaker half of our salaries, tax-free. The second problem is we're not shipping any supplies to those same companies. It makes the company profits appear high, but if we're ever audited the discrepancies could be discovered."

"Like I said, it's time to start thinking about a way for us to get out from under that big thumb without getting killed in the process. It's going to take a lot more than a little luck to get us out of this. For now, we just have to go along with what we're told to do and keep our eyes and ears open for any possibilities that we should consider." When his brother left, Lou went to the bathroom where he locked the door and prepared his next fix, something to counteract the pills.

Had the two brothers known that their conversation was being recorded, they may have considered a plan to go to the police and work with the Feds to sever the "thumb" they were under.

Chapter 25

John realized that events were taking place almost faster than he could keep track of them. The purchase of Mike Roberts' air conditioning business was ready to be finalized. John decided that the company would run as is for the next year or so until the old owner retired. Only then, would he begin to develop the real potential of the company.

    John discovered that the real estate portion of his dad's company was easier to split away from the construction business than he had expected. The fact that his dad had recorded all rental properties in both parents' names was a real plus. All John had to do was separate the personal holdings, such as their primary home, their summer home, and the lake house near the Everett Lodge, from the other properties. The rental properties were then transferred to the newly created corporations. The attorneys could handle all that work about changing the deeds of ownership. John hired a separate office staff to manage the day-to-day activities of the real estate companies, instead of combining them with the construction office staff.

    John began to analyze the data pouring in from all the managers concerning the questionnaires completed by all the employees of Lynch Construction. At first glance, there didn't appear to be many employees who wanted to work for a different company than management had assumed they would. John or one of the Bowmans would meet with each of them on an individual basis to discuss their concerns.

The number of employees who wished to retire, either now or within the next five years, was well within the figures John had presented to his dad.

Surprisingly, there were a considerable number of employees who wanted to contribute money up front to buy into their new company. This had the potential of increasing cash flow and possibly it would decrease the amount each company would have to borrow. It also represented a trust by the employees that the companies were a worthwhile investment. John knew that it had been proven that employees who had ownership in a company tended to be dependable and devoted.

At the same time that John was in his office, Harvey and his partner Dave Becker were seated in Peter Black's office, listening once more to the conversations recorded from the Claybournes' office. Peter said, "It appears that someone high up in DEA is working for or with the drug dealers. How do we go about finding that person without alerting him or her? For all we know, it could be the director himself."

"We could devise some sort of a trap or sting operation to bring them out in the open," answered Harvey. "In my opinion, we can't do it by ourselves. We have to inform someone from DEA about the mole in their office. Let them handle the matter. It's not our job to investigate one of our sister agencies."

"I don't like the idea of spying on another agency," interrupted Peter Black. "I'm sure the director isn't involved. I've met him on several occasions and I think he's an honorable man. He has an excellent reputation with everyone in the Justice Department."

"I find it hard to believe that he'd be involved either,"

stated Becker. "I think we should advise him of our concerns and let him find the person or persons."

"You're both right, of course," replied the boss. "Is there anyone we trust over there, and let them go to the director? ... Harvey, you look like you have something to add."

"How about if we take our information to our Deputy Attorney General and let him take it to the Deputy in charge of DEA? That way we're covered without making a direct accusation."

"Great idea. After all, both agencies share a common boss. I'll make a call and set up a meeting with the Deputy and tell him our concerns."

"Before you do that," said Dave Becker, "I have a very general question. Have we shared everything we have with DEA? If not, they could use it against us somehow ... say we're interfering with one of their ongoing investigations."

"Another good point, but to the best of my knowledge, we've given them at least a summary of everything we know, except, of course, who our sources are. Even though they talked to one of them on the phone, I never told DEA the name of our source. And trust me, I've documented all the information that we sent to them."

"After this," said Harvey, "we may be forced to give them actual copies of all the disks we have. We may even be forced to tell them about our sources."

"If we have to, we will."

Chapter 26

The four young men met with Bob Goodfellow to review the short list of possible managers for the Everett Lodge. Bob had narrowed the number down to four as John had previously instructed him. After John and the other three spent an hour reading the resumes and background checks, he asked the question, "Why don't the four of us write down whom we think we'd want to hire in order of preference?" They all agreed.

When everyone had written down their choices, Luke began, "I like Steve Appleman, Scott White, Harry Portsmith, and Brad Boyson, in that order."

Mark followed with, "White is first; Appleman second; Boyson third, and Portsmith last, although they all look very promising."

Matthew presented his list, "I have Appleman, White, Boyson and Portsmith. Okay John, what's your preference?"

"I like them all also, but my top two are Appleman and White. I also like the fact that each of them has a degree in Restaurant and Hotel Management, in addition to being a trained chef. Bob, have you interviewed these four?"

"I talked to each of them with some follow-up questions, but didn't go into any detail," stated Goodfellow.

"Okay, Bob," said John, "set up appointments with both Appleman and White. We'll make our decision after the interview. Allow two hours for each of them. Use the lodge as an interview site. We'll give them a tour of the facility and see if they have any comments or suggestions."

"Do you think we should have Helen perform any further background checks?"

"No, she's already done a thorough check. The investigators wrote some comments that you should be aware of. Appleman and White have admitted they're a gay couple and live together. They do not, however, make a public display of their relationship. As far as the investigators are concerned, they're well liked by both male and female co-workers."

"Maybe we should hire both of them," joked Mark.

"I don't think we can afford that option," stated Matt.

"Just kidding," was the reply.

Not surprisingly with this group, none of the four even raised an eyebrow about the gay comment; neither did they consider this a problem.

"Based on what we've seen the last few weeks," interrupted Luke, "the construction and remodeling is close to being finished. Should we start thinking about a grand opening?"

"Good point," said John. "Tony and the foreman indicated that the major work will be finished in a week. It'll take another week to clean everything up and another to finalize the minor details."

"Why don't you have a quiet opening," began Bob. "Shoot for a grand opening a month later. That would give you time to work out some bugs and train the staff. It would also give your PR people time to plan the publicity for the event."

"I like that idea," stated Mark.

"Me, too," joined in the others.

"Where do we stand with hiring an overall manager," asked John.

"Well," began Bob, "there we have a little bit of a concern.

We have plenty of young people with somewhat limited experience who may be interested. Several people have what appears to be the right experience, but most of them expect starting wages beyond what you can afford. I was really looking for someone older with a lot of experience, but that too may be expensive. There's one gentleman whom I'd love to hire. He has an excellent background and his experience is top-notch. But, he's retired and is looking for work only to fill in some of his time. I'm guessing he wouldn't want to put in the hours that opening a new property may require."

Goodfellow paused for a few seconds and then continued. "What I consider a viable solution is a little over the budget anticipated, but it has some very good possibilities. I'd hire the older gentleman on a temporary and part-time basis and let him train two other assistant managers who would come from the less experienced group."

Luke asked, "Do you think you can get two of the younger applicants to work as assistant managers. Didn't they apply as managers?"

"You're right about the manager position. The want ads did say 'manager,' but I believe that we can find a few qualified individuals who would want the job as assistants, particularly if there's a possibility for advancement."

"How much over budget are we talking about?" asked John.

"I believe we could make it work for forty to fifty thousand, plus benefits for at least a year, two at the most. Depends on how much the three individuals would be willing to start with and how much the more experienced person would expect. Don't forget that you would have three people, instead of a manager and an assistant."

Matthew hesitated and asked, "Maybe he'd be willing to serve as a consultant and be paid as an individual contractor? He probably doesn't need the benefits. Then, Appleman and White could be named co-managers."

"That's a good idea," replied John, "what do you think of that?" he asked the others with a sweep of his hand.

After the group discussed this idea further, they agreed to that concept. They suggested that Bob Goodfellow should approach the older gentleman with the proposal. If he accepted, Bob should ask him to sit in on the interviews of the others.

Chapter 27

"Peter, your office is supposed to be investigating tax fraud. How the hell did you get involved with a drug investigation?" the Deputy Attorney General of the Justice Department questioned.

Peter replied, "Trust me sir, it's not by choice. When I sent you a summary of how we got to this point, I tried to be brief on purpose." He gave his boss a file folder and continued. "Here's a more detailed version of what made us come to you. We're looking for guidance, so that we don't step on DEA's toes. Our little agency is out of its league here. We'd prefer to let someone else handle it from now on. We're just the proverbial messengers in this situation."

"Okay," said the Deputy, "let's go over the background in a little more detail."

After they had answered all of his questions, the Deputy made a phone call to the Deputy in charge of DEA and requested a meeting and the reason for it.

Three days later and after several phone calls and hand-carried documents were exchanged, Peter Black, Harvey, Dave Becker and Tom Owens, the director of DEA, met in the Office of the Attorney General. Joe Robertson would have attended also, but he was out of town on other business.

The Attorney General who noticed the surprised look on the faces of some, began with, "I asked Tom Owens to attend this meeting because I have absolute trust in him and know, without exception, that he's not involved with any criminal activity. Tom, please tell these folks what you know."

Tom Owens, on cue, said, "I just want everyone here to know," as he pointed to the people from his sister agency, "that I take no offense to what you did. It's commendable; I would've done the same thing in your position. To put your mind at ease, you should know that we've suspected that there was a mole in our organization for a long time."

"I'll state for the record that I've reviewed all your documentation and find it very interesting. I'll also state for the record that we found out who your source was shortly after our phone conversation. They've been under the microscope since then. I apologize that I didn't advise you that I was investigating them ... particularly since you came forward with the information you have. We're convinced that they're not involved with this case in any way other than what you've stated in your documentation. They most definitely are not drug dealers."

The Attorney General picked up the conversation, "Okay, with all of that out of the way, let's discuss what we're going to do with this information and how we're going to put some people behind bars." With that, they continued the meeting in a cooperative manner. The discussion flowed from one topic to another until they arrived at an acceptable solution.

CHAPTER 28

John hadn't spent any time with Helen for the past two weeks and figured it was time to sit back and relax for a weekend. So, after he called his parents to find out if they planned to use the lake house, he called Helen to ask if she could get away for a long weekend. She, in turn, suggested Wednesday evening and Thursday by themselves and then the weekend with their friends. John was somewhat surprised when she told him what to wear on Wednesday and what other clothes to pack. Helen surprised him again by saying she would call the others and make all the arrangements.

For the next couple of days, John put in some long hours, finishing up odds and ends. He thought Helen must be busy also, because both Matt and Mark stopped by his office to say they were looking forward to the weekend. By Tuesday afternoon, Helen had sent several e-mails informing John that Matt would pick up the groceries on his way to the lake house. Helen didn't give any indication of what she had in mind.

John left the office at noon and headed for his apartment to pack. Because Helen had suggested for him to wear a suit, John decided to shave and take a hot shower before he left. Later, he was glad he did. When he met Helen at her apartment, he thought she looked like she had just left a spa. She was wearing her black coat and had her bags at the door when he arrived at her apartment.

He continued to be surprised as Helen directed him to drive in a different direction than the mountain road toward the lake house. Unable to keep his curiosity at bay any longer, he asked, "Okay, now tell me what's going on and why the special treatment?"

"Be quiet," she said with a smile, "you'll find out soon enough. Just sit back and do whatever I tell you." Reluctantly, he did just that and kept the conversation on insignificant subjects. Even with his memory, he wouldn't have been able to remember later. His mind was too busy trying to figure out what she had up her sleeve.

Two hours later Helen said, "Turn right at the next intersection and go about two miles." John knew they were somewhere in the Pocono Mountains and realized they weren't going to be at the lake house tonight. Shortly he saw a sign, which read The Martin Lodge and Restaurant and turned into it as Helen directed him to do so. "Pull up at the restaurant and leave the SUV with valet parking."

"Guess we're having dinner here tonight," said John, mostly to himself.

Helen didn't wait for John to open her door. By the time he got to her side of the car, she was already finished talking to the parking attendant.

When John and Helen entered the building, they saw a luxuriously appointed dining room that obviously had just been redecorated in a rustic design. "Good evening, Miss Francis, Mr. Lynch" said a middle-aged gentleman. "Welcome to the Poconos." John was puzzled.

Helen smiled and said, "Hello, Al." And to John she said, "John, this is Al Fieldman, the manager of this fine resort." John exchanged some pleasantries and complimented Mr. Fieldman about his lovely facility.

Thunder and Lightning

"Your table is ready," explained Mr. Fieldman. "May I take your coat, Miss Francis?"

When Mr. Fieldman took Helen's coat, John almost stuttered as he looked at Helen and said, "My god ... you're beautiful in that dress. It's a good thing your coat covered it up or we'd never have made it here in time for the reservation." He continued to admire her as they were escorted to their table. He thought she looked stunning in the almost backless and low-cut dress.

"I guess this is what is called your basic little black dress," he commented.

"I suppose you could say that," she said, totally pleased with the looks he was giving her. Helen appeared to be embarrassed that everyone else in the room was giving her the same looks.

John continued to be surprised as wine and appetizers were served without the benefit of a menu. The two had a relaxed conversation that covered a variety of topics, nothing of any consequence. John realized that their dinner choices apparently had been pre-arranged because they were served without placing an order. "I'm very impressed," stated John, "about how you arranged everything. How did you find out about this place?"

"All in good time," she replied, "we're not done yet."

As dinner reached its conclusion, they finally were given a choice of desserts. They both refused, but each ordered a cappuccino. "I guess it's time to pay the piper," said John as he reached for his wallet. Helen lightly took hold of his hand and shook her head no. John just raised his eyebrows with a questioning look.

"It's been taken care of."

As they left the room, John was thrilled that Helen was getting admiring glances. Helen, on the other hand, felt like she was being undressed with wishful eyes ... at least John's eyes appeared to want her the most. He would have to wait.

Helen took John's hand and led him down a wide corridor to a room where a four-piece combo was playing that could best be described as mood music. A small dance floor was located in front of tables for two or four people. Al Fieldman met them and escorted them to a cozy table near the dance floor. Shortly after they were seated, their drinks arrived without an order.

"I can't believe this," exclaimed John, "you planned all of this to perfection. It's such a wonderful night. Thank you. I don't know what I can do in return, but whatever it is, it's yours."

A marriage proposal would be nice, Helen thought, but instead said, "I'll tell you later what I expect, but for now I'd like to dance with you." So they danced and danced. There was no rock and roll with this band, just slow moving "hold each other close" type of music. They danced, talked and laughed and enjoyed each other's company. They didn't even notice that most of the other patrons had left the dance floor.

Eventually, Helen closed her hand over John's and whispered, "I think it's time for you to pay the piper." She led him from the room and down another corridor to what were obviously private rooms. She slipped a passkey from her purse into the lock and entered. John wondered when she had gotten the key, but didn't question her.

As soon as she was inside the room, she turned and gave John a very passionate kiss. "I wanted to do that every time we danced tonight." She then reached to untie his tie. "And I know what you were thinking when we danced. I could feel you getting excited."

"Just your imagination, that's all," as he reached to unfasten the top of her dress.

She slapped his hand playfully and replied, "Don't touch until I tell you," as she removed his suit coat. Then as she slowly unbuttoned and removed his shirt and pants, she rubbed her hands all over his body slowly, all the while licking her lips. Several times he reached for her, but each time she moved away. She stooped over and gently removed his shoes and socks, leaving him in nothing but his briefs. Once again, she slapped him lightly as he reached for her.

He was forced to watch as she deliberately folded his clothes and placed them on a nearby chair. Only then did she stand before him and unfasten her dress and let it drop to the floor. She slapped him again as she removed her bra and dropped it to the floor. All the while she pretended to do what John assumed was a strip tease. She made a quick move and gave him a "don't you dare look" that stopped him from grabbing her. She then bent down and picked up her clothes and ever so slowly folded them and put them on top of his clothes.

Once again, she gently slapped his hands and leaned over and began to lower his briefs, which were hampered by a protrusion. She kissed his chest, and then his stomach, and lower to his right thigh and his left thigh. She held her hand against his stomach as she made him raise each leg in turn and picked up the briefs that had fallen to the floor. She looked him square in the eye and folded the briefs and placed them on the chair.

She motioned for him to stay where he was. She seductively walked over to the bed and pulled down the covers, lay down and adjusted the pillows. "It's now time to pay the piper," she said as she patted the bed. "If you finish before me, we'll have to start over again." As it turned out, they started over three times before they both fell asleep and once again in the morning when they showered together.

It was only after the shower that John realized that their luggage was in the room. "You really know how to make a trip memorable," he said. He took Helen in his arms. "What do you have in mind for an encore?"

Her reply was, "Easy, Tiger, you couldn't do it again now, and besides, I'm starting to feel sore."

"How about if I kiss it and make it better."

"Not now ... we have things to do," she replied with a smile on her face and a glint in her eye. "After breakfast, we have a meeting. You'll have to wear a coat, but you don't need a tie."

Helen dressed in a much more conservative business outfit than she had the previous night. John had always thought she was attractive and now he knew she was truly beautiful. As they walked to breakfast, he wondered about this as yet unnamed meeting.

Even though they hadn't placed an order, a continental breakfast arrived. "Thank you for making all these excellent arrangements. It took a lot of planning on your part and I really appreciate everything you've done."

Blushing, she replied, "There's more to come ... the meeting, that is."

"What's this all about?" he questioned her.

"Okay," she began, "no more surprises. I helped to arrange the financing for the owner. When I told him about your project, he suggested a meeting between the two of you to discuss ideas ... maybe you could learn from each other."

"Aw ... great," he said quietly.

As she glanced at her watch, she stood up and said, "Come on, it's time to go."

When they arrived at an office that was out of the way, she knocked on the door and entered. "Excuse me Bill. John, this is Bill Martin who owns this wonderful establishment. Bill, this is John Lynch. Why don't I leave you two to talk business? I'll be around somewhere."

John noticed a raised eyebrow on the face across the desk and asked, "Bill, if you don't mind, I really would like for Helen to stay. I believe she's just trying to be polite."

"Of course, she should stay. Helen knows more about

Thunder and Lightning

me and my business than I do. I'm confident that anything we discuss will remain between the three of us." As Helen and John sat down, Bill continued, "John, let me give you some background information. You know about Masterson Business Consultants, don't you?" When he saw John nod his head, he plunged forward, "I've known Bat Masterson for years. We've done business many times in the past. When I called him the last time, he indicated that he'd be retiring soon and that he wanted me to work with his new right hand, Helen. I agreed to meet with her to see if we'd be able to work with each other. I'm extremely happy that I had that meeting."

With a wave of his hand, he said, "This property was in the process of being completely remodeled when the former owner unexpectedly left town with a large portion of money from three local banks. He has yet to be found."

"The banks got together and foreclosed on all of the loans. In essence, they took over control of the property. Masterson met with me and asked if I'd be interested in the property. I was, but the three banks weren't willing to put up the necessary funds to complete the remodeling. That's where Masterson's investors came in. I could finance the entire project through him and his investors as I've done in the past."

"Helen, God bless her, was a tremendous help in finalizing the necessary financing and the paperwork involved. The remodeling was just recently completed. Even though we've been open for three weeks now and are doing a fairly nice business, we have the grand opening scheduled in two weeks."

Mr. Martin continued, "During one of our many conversations, Helen mentioned your project with the Everett Lodge. I thought maybe I could be of some help to you. She thought I might think that she brought up your project just to interest me in talking to you. I didn't think any such thing. She's too nice of a woman to do that. Consequently, the invitation for both of you to join me here ... Do you have any questions?"

"First of all, thank you very much for having us. From what I've seen, you have a fine-looking property, considerably larger and more luxurious than ours will ever be. I appreciate your willingness to help, but you're just getting started with your project. I really can't expect you to take the time to help me and my partners."

"You're being too polite," said Mr. Martin. "Your real question is ... He hasn't even had a grand opening yet. What makes him an expert?" John began to protest but was interrupted. "I should've told you before. This is the twelfth property I own and operate. In addition, I own or have controlling interest in several other businesses."

John started to speak again, but Mr. Martin raised his hand to stop him. "I plan on doing more business with Helen in the future and I want her to be happy. I could tell by the twinkle in her eye when we talked that she's in love with you and wants to make you happy too. If you're happy, she's happy. And when she's happy it makes it easier for me to work with her. Therefore, you see, if I help you it's in my own interest."

John was impressed that Martin had seen right through his doubts. He also was beginning to feel a genuine fondness for the man. "Thank you once again," said John. "We're in love and she does make me happy. I'd appreciate any help you can provide."

Helen, with a big smile on her face, thought, *You just guaranteed yourself that I'll really make you happy tonight, even more so than last night.*

The three of them proceeded into a long and enjoyable conversation concerning business in general and operating a lodge and resort in particular. John first asked if Mr. Martin would mind if he took notes and then scribbled on sheets of paper in his unique way. After they had a light lunch and when Helen and John were ready to leave, John asked Mr. Martin, "How can I repay you for your hospitality and for all the guidance you've provided?"

Bill commented, "You can invite me to your grand opening," and with a wink of his eye to Helen, "and to your wedding." Helen only grinned at that comment.

John shook hands with Bill and said, "You can be sure you'll be invited to both."

Helen almost fainted, but covered it well. "Thank you for everything," and kissed Martin's cheek to cover her astonishment. Her mind wondered. *Did I hear that right? ... a wedding?*

After they stepped into John's SUV, he said, "That meeting was probably more informative than any ten-week course I had in college. I could really get to like that gentleman. Thank you again for arranging this entire trip."

She said, "Thank you, but I've also learned a lot. Would you mind decoding those notes of yours? I'd like to have a copy of the transcription. Or, better yet, maybe you could teach me your system."

"I'll type them out for you, but you know as well as I do that it's not the system ... it's what I can retrieve from memory. It may take me a few days before I finish transcribing the notes. Is that okay?"

"It's okay, but could you explain the basics to me. Maybe I can use them."

When he realized she was serious, John told her, "I divide the paper into five parts. I write the most important items on the top left, then the top right, bottom left and bottom right. I reserve the center of the page for items that tie the others together, or sometimes use arrows to move items from one spot to another. The words that I write are just reminders of what was discussed in case I forget. That's it."

"But you don't forget, do you?"

"Sometimes I need the words to give me a hint."

"When did you realize you had a photographic mind?"

"It's not truly photographic. There are some things I can't remember. Not only that, but my mind doesn't necessarily store information in a logical sequence. There are times when I can't retrieve information I know should be there. That's why I use notes."

"Who taught you about the note system?"

"I developed it myself and I've refined my system over the years."

"Hmm," was her only response.

On the two-hour trip to the lake house, John and Helen discussed their conversation with Mr. Martin and how John could use the information. Helen was once again astonished that John could repeat a detailed conversation verbatim as if he had a tape recorder in his head.

John didn't mention anything about a wedding, but there were some things that Helen could remember exactly. It didn't lower Helen's enthusiasm. By the time they fell asleep that night in the lodge, John and Helen were, indeed, very happy and completely exhausted.

Chapter 29

At the Claybourne Enterprise office, Lou was talking on the phone, "Of course I know the names. His father's a customer of ours. I understand that the old man is setting it up so that the employees can buy the business. The other three are brothers. One of them is black. The story is he was adopted, but that could just be a cover for the old lady screwing around. Why do you ask?"

The caller then proceeded to tell Lou a long detailed story about how the four friends investigated the theft of building material and how that investigation led them to the drug dealers. "I think they knew they were out of their league and apparently turned the investigation over to the DEA."

"What are you going to do about them?" asked Lou.

"I'm not concerned about them. The real question is what are we going to do about the next shipment?"

"You mean, 'the last shipment,' don't you?"

"Well...yes. It was to be the last one, wasn't it?"

Because Lou was pissed he yelled, "What the hell is this? You told me one more shipment and we'd be even."

"Don't jump to conclusions, Lou. It will be the last trip up north, but I believe we need to talk. There's a lot of money in it for you."

Lou shouted into the receiver, "The Feds are getting too close. They're after me, not you ... and they're getting too close. I want out. No more shipments. No more involvement. I want out ... and I mean out all together. Do I make myself clear?"

"Yes ... clear ... quite clear. We'll talk later. In the meantime, I think you should hire some men to teach the busybodies to mind their own business. Rough them up a little ... but, for God's sake, don't kill them. We have enough problems. Just teach them a lesson."

"I'll take care of it," as he popped several pills into his mouth.

Chapter 30

John woke up at his usual time and got dressed for his morning run without waking Helen. "Where do you think you're going?" she asked. "Oh, I didn't realize it was light outside. Wait for me and I'll go with you. I need a shower first, though."

John went downstairs and looked at his watch and assumed he could probably be back by the time she was ready. However, ten minutes later Helen came downstairs dressed in running clothes and ready to go. John let her set the pace as they ran past the Everett Lodge to the highway and back to the lodge. "Is that the best you can do?" she said.

John gave her a playful nudge and said, "This time I set the pace," and started running. Helen kept up until they reached the highway again. Then she was left behind as John picked up the pace. He was sitting on the steps of the lake house when she arrived out of breath. "Smart ass. Come on, I need another shower, don't you?" A half-hour later she knew that kissing did make it better.

The two sets of twins arrived in the late afternoon in their own cars. Luke and Mary Anne arrived shortly thereafter. They quickly agreed that there would be no talk of business for the entire weekend, just friends who enjoyed each other's company.

Saturday afternoon, Luke and Mary Anne decided to take a stroll while the other six played board games in the house. When they returned, Mary Anne had this tremendously big smile on her face.

When Pam saw the pair, she said, "You look like you just had great sex."

To which Mary Anne replied, "Not yet, but we will," as she held out her hand to show off a large diamond on her hand. "We're going to be married!"

The women were the first to react. John swore he got an elbow in the ribs when Helen jumped up to congratulate them. They all hugged as the women screamed "How?" "When?" "Tell us how he asked." "Did he get down on his knee?" "When's the wedding?"

As the women and the guys drifted into different areas, Mark commented to no one in particular, "Shit, the pressure's really going to be on us now." He turned to John and said, "You're next, man." John shrugged his shoulders saying, "Why me?" But he knew deep down that Mark was right. He and Helen had skirted around the issue several times. Soon they'd have to have a very serious discussion to discuss their future together.

Everyone was in a festive mood the rest of the night and into Sunday. Luke and Mary Anne decided to leave Sunday afternoon to drive home to tell their parents the good news. When the two had left, it appeared to John that the women became unusually quiet and wanted to cuddle. John thought of Mark's comment, *the pressure is really going to be on us now.*

As she cuddled closer, Helen thought *When's it going to be my turn?*

CHAPTER 31

Monday evening, when Luke was getting out of his car, a man jumped from behind the car next to his. Another one moved from the front of the same car. Both men were wearing ski masks that covered their faces and hoods that were drawn tight over their heads. Because it was dark outside, Luke had only a quick glance before he was punched in the kidney and was grabbed from behind and his arms were pinned back. The man in front used a baseball bat like a battering ram and plunged it into Luke's stomach twice saying, "This'll teach you to mind your own business. Don't get involved with things that don't concern you. Stay away from the Claybournes."

The masked man drew the bat in the proper method to hit again, but the attackers now had Luke's full attention. With the first attacker hanging on, Luke made a quick turn to the left which moved the man behind him at least partially in line with the home-run swing that was now underway. The batter managed to slow the swing down enough that neither Luke nor the ragdoll holding him from behind was incapacitated. However, it was enough for Luke to flex his arm and back muscles to allow him to free his arms. As Luke turned quickly to the right, he grabbed the one that was holding him in a bear hug, lifted him off the ground and used him as a shield to move in the direction of the man with the bat.

"Drop him, you asshole," the batter said as he got set for another try at the long ball.

Meanwhile, the ragdoll, who was having a difficult time breathing, cried out, "Ho … ly sh … it, Gene, just hit him."

The swing, when it came, was more like a golf swing than a baseball swing. It was intended as a ball buster, but it hit Luke on the bottom of his foot which he had stuck out by reflex to stop the blow. The pain hurt enough that he released his grip on his shield. When he realized that Luke was hurt, the shield turned toward Luke and threw a right hook. Luke blocked the punch and grabbed the attacker's arm, giving it a quick twist. The attacker's arm or shoulder snapped like a dry twig and the attacker screamed very loud as he fell toward the batter. Luke took a step after them, but his injured foot couldn't take the pressure and he half stumbled.

The batter, who thought this muscular giant may be able to catch one or both of them, threw the bat. Luke managed to get his arms up in time to protect his face, which was the target. The batter realized his mistake as Luke picked up the bat to defend himself. Because they didn't have any other weapons, the assailants knew they were over-matched and fled the area.

Luke looked around the parking lot to see if there was anyone nearby who could help him. When he saw no one, he called 911 on his cell phone to report the incident and then called Mary Anne to ask for her help. Unbelievably, she arrived at the same time as a police officer. After a quick examination, Mary Anne asked the police officer to tell the ambulance to hurry. Luke couldn't walk and may have had internal injuries.

The police officer took Luke's statement while they waited for the ambulance. It was just another attempted robbery as far as he was concerned, but Luke knew better.

At Luke's insistence, Mary Anne called his three friends instead of his parents. They arrived separately while Luke was still being processed, examined, tested and X-rayed and, was generally stripped of his dignity. Mary Anne explained as much as she knew which was only what Luke had told her.

Eventually, a doctor entered the waiting room and asked if there was any family with Mr. Bowman. Mary Anne was the first to stand, almost showing her ring as proof and said, "He's my fiancé. These are his brothers and a friend."

The doctor recognized her, smiled and said, "Hi Mary Anne. Your fiancé's okay." He turned to include the others and continued, "He's bruised and hurting a little, but overall he's okay.

"His foot isn't broken, but, he won't be able to walk without crutches for a week or two. Then, he'll need to use a cane for a while.

"There's no sign of internal injuries, probably due to the high density of his stomach muscles. I highly doubt he'll be doing any weightlifting until his stomach muscles heal a little."

The doctor continued, "Too bad Luke was hurt the way he was, but I guess it could have been a lot worse. Apparently he did a little damage of his own. The police tell me we should be on the lookout for anyone with wrist, arm or shoulder injuries. They're going to notify all hospitals in the surrounding counties to be on the lookout also."

To Mary Anne, he said, "He'll have to watch for blood in his urine for a few days. The blow to his side doesn't appear serious, but as you know, the kidneys are very sensitive." The doctor answered a few of Mary Anne's questions and told them Luke would be wheeled out in a few minutes. As he left, he leaned next to Mary Anne's ear and whispered, "I expect to be invited to the wedding." She smiled but didn't answer.

Luke was wheeled outside and Mary Anne went to the

parking garage to get her car. When she was out of earshot, Luke told the other three that they would have to be careful about being attacked themselves. "Those two guys told me to stop being involved with the Claybournes. I didn't tell the police what the batter had said about minding my own business."

John asked, with a question in his eye, "Will you be safe in your apartment?"

Luke replied, "I have the best security system in the world … even better than yours."

When Luke was settled in the car, his three friends discussed if they should go to Luke's apartment. Mary Anne overheard the conversation and said, "Thank you for coming. But he needs a nurse more than he needs his friends tonight."

The remaining three went to a local diner to decide what action, if any, they should take. Matt made a statement. "I'm not concerned about our apartments and cars. Security is not a major problem, primarily due to Luke's testing one or more of his electronic toys." However, they were not without concern.

Mark and Matthew were more concerned about John than they were about each other. They knew that they had the same advantage Luke had when he was attacked. Size did matter. John shrugged them off.

In the morning, John planned to call Harvey and ask him how their involvement in the drug investigation was discovered. Before they left, they agreed to be more vigilant in their day-to-day activities and to keep alert if someone was following them.

When John called Harvey he told him about the attack on Luke, he tried to remain calm but underneath he was steaming. "Harvey, I just told you what happened. You've got to know that our involvement was leaked from your office, not from this end. What are you going to do about it?"

"John, it wasn't part of the plan. DEA has suspected for a while that they have a mole in their office. We've discussed ways of finding that person. We did think about using the four of you as bait, but we dropped the idea because you're civilians. We decided to pass along some information that would let us know who the mole was but nothing's been done as of this morning."

John finally lost his cool, "I don't believe you, Harvey. You or someone in Washington released our names and set us up. You got someone almost killed and for what? Nothing. And, who do you think is going to be next? Surely not someone in Washington? This stinks. You hang us out on the line ... No, not on a line ... on a line we could move. You tie us hand and foot to a tree and let them take their best shot at us. Then when they're done, you can cut the ropes and put us in a casket. Is that what you Feds call a plan? Please forgive me if I fail to see how such plans work." John ranted and raved on for some time until he got his anger off his chest.

Harvey let him vent and eventually replied, "Too many people have had access to the information. The information was already forwarded before we could get a plan in place. DEA has it narrowed down to twelve people, but that doesn't make it a grand slam. Those twelve are now undergoing intensive background checks, quietly, of course. Personally, I don't understand why they'd go after you anyway. You weren't that involved. Whoever sent them after you wasn't thinking ... period."

John settled down and apologized for his outburst. After he hung up, he thought *wasn't thinking?* Or, maybe he was thinking way ahead ... maybe he was setting up the Claybourne brothers.

Chapter 32

Several evenings later, Mark was walking to his car in a remote area of the shopping mall. Four masked men jumped out of a van and tried to force him inside. "Not a real good idea," he said as he threw the closest one into the side of a parked car. The second man was less fortunate as he got kicked in the back of his legs. He immediately screamed.

Matt popped out from behind some parked cars. "Save some for me," he yelled. He rushed two of Mark's attackers. Matt took both of them down with a well placed clothesline, as it's called in the NFL.

The first attacker pulled a knife from his pocket and did some fancy hand and wrist work to get it open. "Hmm," said Mark. "I'm impressed, but like I told you … not a good idea." He took a step toward his first victim, grabbed the hand holding the knife and just stood there with the hand held high in the air. "Let go of the knife before I take it from you and cut your balls off with it." As he lifted the man into the air by his arm, the knife dropped to the ground and Mark released the arm. The attacker, thinking he had an advantage, swung at Mark's face. Before the punch landed, Mark hit the attacker's head with two quick jabs, followed by a right hook to his side. That blow apparently did some obvious damage.

The man's ribs cracked and he fell to the ground, holding his side. He took short breaths because deeper breaths caused too much pain.

Mark turned to his brother and said, "Do you need any help?"

"Na, these two won't give me any trouble." He gave one a sharp blow of his elbow to the back of the head. Matthew slowly picked up one of the men by the seat of his pants and the neck of his shirt and plunged him headfirst into the side of the van. The remaining attacker tried to run, but Matthew grabbed him and said, "Not done with you yet," and forced an arm behind his back until it reached his head. Because Matthew's left arm was around his chest, the man was held up on the tip of his toes that prevented him from leaning over to lessen the pain.

"Just answer a question or two and I'll let you go unharmed. First, who hired you?" Getting no reply, Matt pushed the arm up higher until he sensed that the arm went a little beyond the tearing point.

"Hurts, doesn't it? I've had torn muscles before and I know it hurts. The question again was who hired you?"

The answer was not a surprise, "Claybourne, Lou Claybourne."

"Next question, who else are you to go after?"

"That Lynch kid. John Lynch."

"Last question, how do you know the Claybournes?"

"We've done some other jobs for them."

"Explain."

"We buy drugs from them, not for ourselves, but to sell. We also do some attitude adjustments and bill collecting when necessary."

Matt looked over at Mark with a questioning look. Mark, who was leaning up against the van, shrugged his shoulders. Matthew then released his captive. "Sit down over there," pointing to the other three lying on the ground. Turning to his brother, he asked, "What do we do with them?"

"We could drop them off at the Claybournes' doorstep, or we could have them take a message back."

The brothers carried on a brief discussion for the benefit of the attackers. Mark went back to the four on the ground and said, "Just thought of a few more questions for you, ah ... gentlemen. How many of you in your gang, and, lastly, are you the ones who attacked our brother?" Matthew leaned over like he was going to pick up the only one in a sitting position.

The answers were quick in coming. "We're not really a gang, just the six of us trying to get by." Misunderstanding the term 'brother,' "The other two were to give the black guy a message."

With a nod from his twin, Mark spoke up, "I suggest that you gather your other two friends and leave for parts unknown in the very near future. The Claybournes' drug business and everyone associated with it is about to become history. You may tell them that if you like. But for your own protection, I suggest you just leave town. If you stick around, my brother and I won't be as kind to you the next time we meet."

After they made sure the four thugs weren't going to cause any more trouble, the twins went to Mark's car and drove away. They stopped around the corner at Matt's car. Afterwards, they followed the van to Route 322 eastbound.

"Do you think we'll be seeing them again?"

"I'd be surprised if we did. None of them will be doing much for a week or two. If they don't leave, they definitely will remain out of sight of the Claybournes. As a matter of fact, I don't think they'll even deliver our message. I'll call John to let him know what we found out."

Later that night, John received a call from Mark who told him what happened. "I knew you two were up to something when you didn't call or talk to me at work for the last two days. What made you think they'd go after you before me?"

"They probably know you're a puss and decided to take us big guys out first. Besides, I spotted them following me just after they went after Luke. We did a little playacting to get them in the dark parking lot. No harm, no foul."

"I do believe you're right about them not getting in our way again. They're just small fries in this game. As a matter of fact, I'm beginning to believe that the Claybournes are just middlemen also. There's someone higher up pulling the strings. Tomorrow, I'll relay the information to Harvey and let them follow up if they want. Let's stay out of it, if we can."

"You've been saying 'stay out of it' for a long time ... hasn't worked yet."

Later, alone in his apartment, John searched his mind to review the pertinent details of what he now referred to as the Claybourne case. Using the notes on his computer to help recall the facts, he soon realized that someone either in Harvey's office or the DEA's office had to be giving information to the drug lords. He believed he had a fair idea on who it could be. He decided that a detailed financial check on the person(s) would be necessary and that would require a special meeting.

The next day he called Helen's office. "Miss Francis's office. How may I help you?"

"This is John Lynch," was all he got out before Helen's assistant replied.

"I'm sorry Mr. Lynch. Miss Francis isn't in the office today. May I take a message?

John continued his interrupted request. "Yes, I know she won't be back until tomorrow. I'd like to talk to Mr. Masterson."

"I'm sorry; I just assumed you wanted to speak to Helen," she replied, obviously embarrassed.

"It's a perfectly normal mistake," John replied, putting her at ease.

"One moment, I'll connect you."

Bat Masterson answered the phone. "John Lynch, I'm surprised you want to talk to me."

After some polite conversation, John asked, "I need something investigated and would like to meet with you to explain the details."

"Why didn't you just ask Helen? She told me she had a conversation with you about her job. She can have an investigation started at her whim"

"I think this request is way over her authority level at this point."

Intrigued, Masterson replied, "I'm eating in this evening. Can you travel to Harrisburg to have dinner with me?"

"Of course," was John's response. Masterson told John to call him on his direct line when he arrived. Masterson would disengage the security system to allow John's entrance.

John met with Mr. Masterson that evening. After a lengthy discussion and numerous questions, Masterson agreed to have the financial records of several federal employees reviewed.

CHAPTER 33

Luke was upset about the attack. He wasn't able to walk without a limp. Mary Anne made him promise to stay at home for a few days and not to do anything too strenuous. He entered his workshop and began working on another miniature device. "When I'm done, I'll know everyone who enters the Claybournes' office or makes a call in to or out of any phone in the building," he said out loud. After he had lost some sleep and missed several meals, Luke finished a design. *Now, build it and then install it without getting caught,* he thought to himself. Had he known about the information his brothers had obtained, he probably would not have proceeded with the construction. Instead, he might have been rigging a bomb instead of a camera and telephone tracking audio/video receiver and transmitter.

Luke knew he couldn't go near the Claybournes' office for fear of being recognized, so he called an acquaintance who happened to be a reformed second-story thief. They had known each other since high school and met occasionally to compare notes on security systems and other similar electronic devices. Luke was sure his friend would do the job for him when he told him why.

The twins and John checked in with Luke several times

to make sure he was feeling better. They told him about the attack on both of them. It cheered Luke up knowing that five of the six muggers would probably need some medical attention. Mark asked Luke, "What have you been doing with your time off?"

"Just working on a project, nothing specific," Luke answered.

The fact that Mary Anne had been staying at his apartment every night had slowed down Luke's progress somewhat, but two days later he had a working model finished and tested. All of the electronics were hidden in a two-inch thick, three-ring binder. He drilled a quarter-inch hole in the edge of the binder to allow a low light camera to view everything within a range of three to thirty feet. Because he remembered the room layout from when he installed the listening devices, he knew exactly where the binder would be located. Luke knew that with time he could make it smaller, but for now size wasn't important. A smaller device would be placed between the wall outlet and the phone line. All of the equipment would be the same stealth format as his pending patent. The only problem he could foresee was the length of the power cord which was needed to plug the binder into an electrical outlet. The device could run on batteries for a week or so, if needed, but a hidden power supply would provide for long-term collection of data. Satisfied with his latest creation, Luke called his friend to ask him over to view the handiwork.

By morning, thanks to Luke's friend, the binder was receiving data from all devices connected to the phone lines, including computers and e-mails. The motion-activated camera was working. Luke could see and hear real-time conversations from his workshop or save it to a hard drive for later review.

Only after everything was up and working did Luke tell his brothers and John what he had done. The twins thought it was a good idea. John's only comments were, "Would the information they collect be admissible in court? And, will you be able to get the phone number of incoming calls?"

"Of course," Luke replied.

John continued with, "It's going to take a lot of time and manpower to keep track of all the incoming and outgoing calls."

"Not to worry. I set up a voice recognition program to record only the voices we are concerned about. Routine business calls can be eliminated fairly easily."

"Okay, sounds good. Get well and see you soon."

"I've already started lifting light weights. This isn't the first time I've been hurt. Say hello to Helen for me."

John briefly considered calling Harvey to let him know what Luke had done, but quickly dismissed the idea. *Why take the hassle from the Feds when what they don't know won't hurt them.*

Chapter 34

When the four friends met with Bob Goodfellow to review the selections for manager and chef of the lodge, they were very pleased with the outcome.

"I have some good news," said Goodfellow, "and maybe some better news, depending on your outlook."

"You have the floor," stated Mark.

"First, the good news. The older gentleman I told you about … his name is Robert Hilton … is very interested in acting as a consultant to train your staff. No, he's not a relative of the Hotel Hiltons. He wants a two-year contract. He'll spend thirty to fifty hours a week at the site for at least the first four months. After that, he'll cut back to no less than twenty hours a week. He wants a flat fee of seventy-five thousand.

In addition, he'd appreciate if you'd consider paying for his supplemental Medicare insurance. He says he can start as soon as he finds and moves into an apartment in the city. He said he's not a country boy."

"What happens about an assistant manager?" asked John.

"That's the better news," replied Bob. "Appleman and White would like the job … to share … they'd like to be co-managers and co-chefs ... whatever you want to call them. They want to share the duties."

"Initially, I thought this was a bad idea. You know, two people sharing a job. In this case, two jobs. But after talking to them, I feel they could make it work. I talked to each one individually and each has their own attributes. Later, I talked to them together. They make quite a team. Eventually, I got around to the gay issue. They thought that was the end for them. They really were concerned that the gay issue would prevent either one of them from getting the positions. I told them it would get out one way or another. After all, they were going to be moving to a much smaller community and someone would find out sooner or later. They didn't care about being found out. They only cared that it might affect the lodge's business. I believe you should interview them and come to your own conclusions."

"What's it going to do from a financial standpoint?" asked Matthew.

"You have to hire two people anyway, so there shouldn't be any difference. I think you can increase their current wages and still be under what you had budgeted for a manager and chef. "

John stated, "I know the gay issue doesn't make a bit of difference to anyone here. But, how does it affect the business? This is, after all, a small city. Will customers come even if the fact gets out?"

"Let's face it," said Mark, "the gay issue won't make a bit of difference. If the meals are good, people will come, no matter if the chefs are gay or not. If the food isn't, we won't make it anyway."

"Is the kitchen finished?" asked Luke.

"Yes. It's ready to go," replied Mark

"Then, let's have a little get-together to see what kind of meals they can prepare. I'm willing to put up some of the cost to see what they can do. If, that is, they're willing to cook for us."

"Well," replied Matthew, "if we're going to do that, why don't we go the whole way? Ask our Mr. Hilton to come and show us what he would do in the dining room. Have the two chefs prepare whatever meals they want to serve. We and our guests will do the set up and clean up."

"We don't have all the supplies yet," commented John.

"Rent what we need and let the chefs order what they plan to serve."

"Bob, what do you think?" asked John. "Will they be willing to put on their dog-and-pony show?"

"Let me call and ask them. What's your schedule?"

John looked around the table and said, "ASAP."

Several minutes later, Bob returned after he had made a couple of phone calls and told them, "Its set up for next Saturday. I told them you'd put them up for the night. All they need to know is how many and how many different types of meals. Mr. Hilton suggested that he'd provide the wait staff and maid service."

After a somewhat lengthy discussion, they decided on four tables of eight and that a choice of six different meals would suffice. Each table would sample all six meals. The guests would include the four owners and their dates, John's parents, the Bowmans' parents, Tony and his wife, Bob Goodfellow and his wife. Bob also suggested that each couple invite another couple.

Chapter 35

He answered the phone. "This is Lou Claybourne, can I help you?"

"You know who this is. We want you to transport a shipment personally from Florida to Boston next week."

"Listen, Paul, I told you before, the Feds are too close. We can't take the chance for another run. Not at this time. Maybe after things cool off a little."

The man known as Paul Adams, aka Paul Hanover, said, "Don't give me any of your shit. Have a truck at the warehouse in Stuart on Friday. Do this and you'll be off the hook with us ... no more trips, no more hassle, no more calls from me. Listen, we know the Feds are looking into this. That's why we have to get the two of you to make the trip yourselves so no one else knows about this run. He added, "Tell you what ... since this will be your last run, we'll give you a bigger share of the goods to use as you please.

"Sounds good, but I still think it's too risky. Get someone else to make this run," and he hung up the phone, swallowing a handful of pills.

Paul Adams slowly hung up the phone and turned, "That guy's pissing me off. We should send someone up there to change his attitude."

"Yeah, I know what you mean. He has to be convinced to make this trip with him and his brother doing the driving themselves. Get a couple of the boys from Philly to get their attention enough so that they make the trip. Make it happen."

"It only takes a phone call," as he turned back to the desk and dialed a Philadelphia number.

Later in the day, Dave Claybourne entered his brother's office in a panic. "Lou, my wife just called. She says two men are holding her. They told her to call me to let me know she'll be okay after we get back from our trip." As he was talking, Lou's phone rang. His wife was screaming, "Two men took me from our house. I'm being held at a house near the river. They said to tell you I'd be released as soon as you got back from your trip. They made me pack clothes for five days. Sharon's with me and she was told the same thing. What's going on?" The phone was disconnected before he had a chance to reply.

"Aw shit! What did we get ourselves into? Even if we make the trip, our wives will kill us when we get back. How will we explain this to them?"

"Right now, I'm not worried about what will happen later. We have to make the trip. I'd sooner face my wife later than have her dead because I didn't do what they wanted."

As if on cue, Lou's private line rang. The caller said, "Hello Lou. Guess you got our message? Now get your ass on the road. You have two days to get to Florida. Miss the deadline and your missus will have reached her deadline too."

"Let me talk to my wife."

"When you get back, you can talk to her all you want," and the phone line was disconnected.

Lou hung up and said, "We'd better do as he says ... one last time. I have to go to the bathroom." He left to get a fix to calm his nerves.

Dave got a good look at his brother as he left. Lou's eyes

were not as clear as they once were. His nose had a raw look, which made him look like he had a cold. He noticed that Lou stumbled when he walked, and his speech was sometimes slurred. Dave had the feeling his older brother was heavier into drugs than he originally believed.

The morning after the phone calls, Luke checked his listening devices. When he heard the calls, he immediately called John to let him know what had transpired. John told him to get everything ready to transmit to Harvey.

Harvey, as expected, went into a tantrum. John ignored him and let him rattle on. Finally, Harvey calmed down enough to give John a private number so Luke could transmit the data from the phone calls to him. "Listen, Harvey, I think these guys finally made a major mistake. The call came from Paul Adams, but he called from a new phone number. We have the number from where the call originated. It could be a lead to the next higher level in the gang. Someone needs to check out who owns that phone."

"How do you know it's a new phone number?" asked Harvey.

"You don't want to know. Just follow the information."

"What the hell have you done now?"

"Don't ask questions. Just follow where the information leads you." With that reply, they both were quiet and finally hung up.

John called Luke with the number Harvey had given him so Luke could transmit the voice data from the call. John then returned to the work piled on his desk, without any thought of what Harvey and the Feds were going to do with the information.

By the time Sunday rolled around, John and his partners were considerably more nervous than they let on. Mark and Matthew had spent a considerable amount of their spare time helping Tony finish his new home and making the lodge and grounds presentable. Luke was uptight because the Patent

Office was asking more questions about one of his electronic devices than he thought necessary. In addition, Luke's mind was racing about projected budget figures for the lodge. John, ever the laid-back person, was trying to tie up loose ends.

The parents of the four young men watched with amusement as the excitement in their offspring's eyes continued to glow. Unknown to the boys, the Lynches and the Bowmans had traveled to Philadelphia and had dined at both the restaurants where the proposed chefs were currently employed. They decided that all of their meals were of excellent taste and quality. As far as they were concerned, the boys had nothing to worry about. Also unknown to the new lodge owners, they had hired a well-known landscaping firm to enhance the inside and outside of the lodge with plantings that would provide color on a year-round basis. Their surprise required a great deal of timing so that the boys wouldn't find out until all the landscaping work was completed.

Chapter 36

"Harvey, I need you and Becker in my office now." Peter Black placed the phone receiver down.

A few minutes later, Harvey and Dave rushed into their boss's office to find Peter and Tom Owens from DEA discussing recent football trades.

"Tom told me something I think you should hear straight from his mouth," as he gave Tom a nod.

"We got an anonymous call about two hours ago, telling us that an eighteen wheeler loaded with drugs was about to leave Stuart, Florida, heading north. They gave a detailed description including the license numbers. The logo on the truck is Claybourne Enterprises and is being driven by two men who I believe are Dave and Lou Claybourne."

"We found the rig by helicopter surveillance and have it under observation now. Two cars are following them. When the information was passed up to me, I immediately recognized the name and decided to bring the three of you in on our plans."

"Do we know for sure it's the Claybournes?" asked Harvey.

"There's no reason to think otherwise." Then after a short pause, Tom continued, "Based on the data you sent us yesterday, we assume that this is a setup. We get a shipment of drugs, and the Claybournes take the fall."

Dave Becker piped in, "Do you think the Claybournes will spill the beans and tell us about the others involved?"

"You can bet on it," said the DEA boss smiling. "You can also bet that when that truck started its trip north, all strings between the Claybournes and any higher ups were severed. Any information the Claybournes give us will lead to a dead end. In essence, we believe that the Claybournes unknowingly are the sacrificial lambs. This type of setup has been done before."

"What about the truckload of drugs?" asked Peter. "Would they be willing to give up that much money to frame someone else?"

"My guess is that the drugs are either tainted somehow, or their value is not as much as one would suspect. Either way, it's included in the cost of doing business. And it takes the pressure off the ringleaders."

"Remember one thing … the Claybournes are not being framed. They're guilty of at least aiding and abetting, and probably a lot more than that. We'll follow them to find out where they may lead us, but when the time's right, we'll take them into custody. After we're finished questioning them, I'm sure we'll add numerous other charges. Right now, we're giving them some rope and hopefully they'll lead us to the next step up the ladder."

"I'm glad we forwarded the information from the phone call to you," stated Peter. "The ball's in your court now but, remember, we still have a case pending against the Claybournes. Any information you get from questioning them should also be passed down the line to us."

"Supply us with a list of questions so we can work in with our questions," said Owens. "We'll work together, but my guess is that our charges will be much more than you can come up with. We'll work together to put them away for a long time. It's the least we can do considering how you've helped us to get to this point." As he looked around the table, he asked, "Harvey, why the puzzled look?"

"Just thinking," said Harvey, "but I'm still concerned that the ringleaders will go after the guys in Lewistown. How's the investigation progressing to find the mole in DEA?"

"I can't tell you the specifics, but we're making progress. Little by little, we're narrowing down the list, but the plan we have in place takes time. We're eliminating one at a time. Only five to go, and, to be honest, if it's not one of them, we're at a loss ... even the remaining ones scare the hell out of me. It could go real high up the ladder."

Harvey said, "I'll tell Joe Robertson when he gets back from L.A."

Owens immediately broke in, "I wouldn't do that. Let's keep this between the four of us." Then, as an afterthought, "I've said too much already. This conversation never took place and isn't to be repeated. Do I make myself clear?"

"Clear enough for me," replied Harvey. The other two shook their heads yes.

CHAPTER 37

While he was talking on a cell phone, Dave Claybourne said, "Listen, we'll explain when we get home. Believe me, it's not something we wanted to do. We were forced into making this trip. Just calm down and I'll make it up to you."

After he hung up the phone, he said to his older brother, "They let our wives go home. Boy, are they ever pissed! Our marriage has been shaky to begin with, and this may push her over the edge. In a way, I don't really want that to happen, but I may not be able to prevent it. She told me to tell you that your wife's packing to go to her mother's. She doesn't even want to find out why they were abducted."

Lou answered, "Let her go, screw her. She doesn't know how well off she is. A week or so with that half-assed family of hers and she'll be begging to come back home. If she doesn't return, fuck her!"

Dave realized his brother was high. *Guess I know what was in the box Paul Adams gave him before we started north. There's nothing I can do about it.* As a reply to Lou, he said, "Well, we'd better come up with a good story. I wonder why they let the women go before we got back."

Lou was mumbling to himself, slurring his words: "First things first … we don't have … whole way up to Boston …

drop it off at the warehouse ... one of our drivers take it north later ... wonder why we had to pick this load up ... what happened to those guys we hired to teach them a lesson ... do it ourselves ... teach those assholes from Lynch a lesson ... butt their noses in where they shouldn't."

Dave was glad that he was driving. "I don't think that if we go after them is a good idea. It can only get us into more trouble. And, besides, why was this information passed on to us? Why didn't those assholes do the job themselves?"

" ... Grease balls don't give a shit ... those guys ... gave us an opportunity to get even ... their interference."

"What interference? We don't know if they're really involved. Besides, we can't go up against those guys with just two of us."

"... Worry ... screw 'em ... big guys with us ... office ... teach them a lesson."

Dave, sensing his brother was going over the edge, said a little cautiously, "Lou, I'm not sure that's a good idea. We can't just walk into their office and attack them. We'll have to get them somewhere alone."

"We'll find a way ... to come to us ... they will come ... grab their old man ... girlfriend ... snatch them into our web ... don't care how ... do it as soon as possible."

"Okay, okay, I'll make some calls to get a few boys from Philadelphia who've done some work for us before. I wish now that when you hit him with that two-by-four, you would have put him out of his misery."

Chapter 38

John realized that the waiting was over, at last. Today the trial dinner would be served at the newly remodeled Everett Lodge. The new owners made arrangements for all the diners to stay overnight, have breakfast Sunday morning, and to participate in a critique from their observations. For the last two days, the three Bowmans and John talked for hours about the possibility that they had made a big mistake buying the Everett property and thinking they could make it a profitable business again.

Mark and Matthew, in particular, seemed the most nervous. The possible loss of their savings, combined with the thought that they could lose their positions at the construction company made them uneasy. "What do you mean?" asked John, "that you're afraid of losing your jobs? There's no way that'll happen. Where did you come up with that silly idea?"

"Well," stated Mark, "nobody really told us how we fit into the new scheme of things at the office. It appears to us that we've been excluded from all the details about ownership of the business."

When John recalled the conversation with his parents about company ownership, he replied in the only way he could, "Don't worry, you'll be well taken care of," and turned to Luke, he said, "and you, too."

Not sure what John meant, Luke wasn't concerned about any losses since he was almost guaranteed to make a profit on his miniaturizations of specialized electronics. He was concerned that it would take too much of his time away from planning his wedding and starting a new electronics business.

John wasn't concerned about money at all. From what his dad had told him, he was guaranteed an income for the rest of his life. John's concern was that if the lodge failed how it would affect his friends' financial pictures.

"It seems we've been discussing these concerns over and over again since the day we decided to buy the lodge," stated John. "Let's face it ... we're committed to opening and at least giving it our best efforts. Go home and get ready for a nice evening. It's party time."

"You're right," answered Luke. "It's too late to change things now. Think positive and positive things will happen."

"Yeah, act enthusiastic and you'll be enthusiastic," quipped Matt, in an unenthusiastic manner.

Later that evening, the four partners took turns as bartenders and circulated around the room, chatting with the invited guests. Mr. Hilton approached John and Matthew when they were refilling drinks, "I have a little surprise for you, as well as for our chefs. I invited six additional people, friends of mine. I want to see how the chefs handle this situation. Hope you don't mind. Too late if you do, here they come now."

"Well," said Matt, looking at John, "why not see if this throws a wrench into the works. Introduce us and we'll introduce them to the others."

Mr. Hilton did just that. Within minutes, the six newcomers, with drinks in hand, were mixing with the other guests. And, like magic, another table appeared and was set with plates and silverware.

After a reasonable amount of time, Hilton approached John and told him it was time for dinner. "How did the chefs take the news about the additional guests?" asked John.

"I haven't told them yet," Hilton said with a smile, "can't spoil the surprise. And, by the way, let the guests order anything they want off the menu. Don't try to spread the six choices around evenly."

John smiled as he said, "You're a devil, aren't you?" as Hilton walked away to give some orders to the wait staff.

Everyone ordered dinner, with limited wine and entrée selections. Hilton divided his time between observing and, in some cases, helping the waiters and the chefs in the kitchen. The diners were offered a delectable selection of desserts but many declined because they were too full.

During the after-dinner drinks, John took the opportunity to introduce Mr. Hilton as the acting manager and chief operating officer. He spoke of Hilton's background and his competence in training a new staff.

Hilton, in turn, introduced the waiters and, then with great applause from the guests, the new chefs for the lodge. Hilton answered a question he knew was on the minds of the owners, "I pulled a couple of tricks on the chefs tonight. First, there were six more people than they expected. Second, everyone ordered what they wanted." The chefs adapted beautifully and, unless I'm sadly mistaken, everyone had plenty to eat." This comment produced more applause from everyone.

Chapter 39

Near I-95, south of Richmond, Virginia, the Claybourne brothers were parked in a lot near a repair garage. "Son of a bitch," yelled Lou. "This is all we need now ... the god-damned truck breaks down with a mess of drugs in the back."

"Calm down and keep your voice low," replied Dave. "We don't need the whole world knowing what's in the truck. Nothing we can do about it now. The mechanic said he'll have it fixed in a couple of hours after he gets a new supercharger in the morning."

"What the hell is a supercharger anyway?" Lou continued to yell.

"How do I know, but it's something to do with all the black smoke coming out of the stacks." Listen, we'll only draw suspicion if we stick around here. Let's check into the motel across the road and get some sleep while we wait for the truck."

"We should keep an eye on the truck," said Lou in a calmer voice. "What if some idiots get the idea there's something in there that they could steal."

"If it'll make you happy, we'll get a room where we can see the trailer and take turns watching it from across the road. If we stay here, someone's sure to get curious. Let's go!"

Little did they know that someone was already curious. Two federal drug agents were already talking on the phone to their office. Tom Owens said, "Stay out of sight and watch the truck. Plan to take turns with the other agents throughout the night."

The job turned out to be more complicated than expected. The mechanic didn't finish the repairs to the truck until late Monday evening. During that time, no one appeared to be interested in the contents of the trailer or any of the other trucks in the lot waiting for repairs.

On Monday, the Thunder and Lightning Partnership met with all of the involved parties to hire personnel, and to make plans for a quiet opening. They would schedule a full-scale grand opening within six weeks. They decided to hire a person to handle publicity, to schedule entertainment, and to take reservations for groups and individuals.

Mark made a motion that was quickly accepted. "Let's reserve next New Year's Eve for us and our invited friends." The motion was quickly accepted by the others.

Matt had the floor. "Pam and Sam will interview prospective employees and give a short list to Robert Hilton. As general manager, he'll be responsible for interviewing and hiring most of the staff. The two managers in training will help him where needed. But their initial responsibilities will be to contact the numerous vendors needed to operate various aspects of the business."

The four owners confirmed their decision to leave the day-to-day operation to those people more qualified, namely Robert Hilton and his staff. At Hilton's suggestion, they decided to hold board meetings every other Tuesday for at least the first six months of operation. In that way, the owners would be kept up to date on the progress on their new business.

CHAPTER 40

Lou Claybourne's blood pressure continued to rise. He popped pills and shot up left and right, but nothing seemed to be working. In addition to thinking about the idiots at Lynch Construction, and the stupid truck breaking down, he couldn't get in touch with the drug lords to let them know they were running late. Top that off with his brother Dave telling him to calm down and stop taking drugs, and ... Boom ... his head was starting to explode. "I don't understand why the fuck we can't get in touch with Adams. Every number I call doesn't answer."

Dave's reply didn't calm Lou down at all, "I'm getting a bad feeling about this whole thing. I keep thinking we're being set up. I don't know why, but the thought keeps popping up in my head."

"Then don't think anymore." To change the subject, he said, "What did you find out about those four bumbling nincompoops from Lynch Construction? And, what happened to those guys we hired to kick the shit out of them before?"

Answering truthfully, Dave said, "I don't know. I haven't been able to get in touch with any of them."

Dave was grateful Lou was talking almost normally. But he knew deep down that Lou was becoming more dependent on the drugs. "Old man Lynch and his buddy Bowman have breakfast together every Wednesday. We can have them snatched and taken to the warehouse on Clinton Avenue. Then, we'll call their kids and tell them if they want to see their fathers again, they have to go to the warehouse. After they get there, we can have a couple of the boys from Philly pound them good and let them know they have to keep their noses out of our business."

"Sounds okay to me," replied Lou, "make sure you use enough men. I don't care what it costs, and I want to be there when they get their beating. "

"Do you think that's a good idea?" asked Dave. "We can deny everything."

"I don't have to deny anything," replied Lou. His head was pounding and his heart was beating fast. He was taking so many different drugs he couldn't remember when he took what.

The drug agents were relieved when they observed the truckload of drugs finally continue its trip north late Monday evening. They almost lost track of the truck eight hours later when it entered Harrisburg, Pennsylvania. The truck went to a warehouse in Colonial Park. The agents didn't know it was the same warehouse Tony stopped at on his trip to Boston. It was backed into a loading dock where Dave got a high lift and unloaded two boxes, leaving them just inside the door. The agents assumed the truck would be there for a while and started driving around the area looking for places where they could continuously view the truck. However, the brothers got back into the truck and left the area. The Feds left two men to watch the loading dock. Then they began to search the surrounding area.

The agents in one of the chase cars got lucky and noticed lights in a warehouse on Clinton Avenue. He saw that Dave Claybourne was closing the door and the truck was clearly visible inside. Another thirty seconds later, the truck and its cargo would probably have been lost for good. Five minutes after the door closed, the lights were turned off and both men left through a smaller door. The two brothers drove away in a late model pickup, which had been parked just outside the garage bay.

The agents stayed at the warehouse instead of following the pickup. This was necessary because the driver in the other car was still at the first warehouse. Within minutes, they called to their superiors to let them know their location and details of the area. They soon learned that both warehouses were owned by Claybourne Enterprises. Upon further investigation, they determined that there was no other exit that the truck could use. The agents could easily watch all the doors. They were told that another team would relieve them in four hours. They would take turns watching both warehouses.

The Feds didn't detect any activity at the Clinton Avenue warehouse for the next thirty hours. At mid-morning Wednesday, they observed six men entering a side door. Two of the men obviously entered against their will. The agents made a call to headquarters shortly thereafter requesting instructions.

Two hours after the men entered the warehouse, the federal agents noticed two of the thugs came back out and were now standing under the hangover near the entrance. It had started raining and the thugs were trying to stay dry.

The agents had established an open line with Washington to keep them aware of what was going on. DEA supervisors began making plans for a multi-task force raid on the warehouse.

Chapter 41

Shortly after the agents saw the men enter the warehouse, the telephone rang and John answered. "Good morning, John Lynch speaking."

"Listen closely. If you want to see your old man and his friend again, you must come to 2435 Clinton Avenue in Harrisburg. Come only with those other three idiots you run around with. Don't even think of calling the cops. Be here in two hours."

John could hardly believe what he had heard. His initial thought was that it was a joke, but deep down he had a feeling it wasn't. He made several phone calls, including one to his dad's cell and verified his feeling. Two hours, that was barely enough time to drive to Harrisburg.

He called Matt and explained the situation, saying, "Meet me at the Route 322 and Route 22 interchange as soon as you can and bring Mark."

He then called the company's pilot to file a flight plan to Harrisburg and to be prepared to leave immediately. He then called Tony. After a brief explanation, he told Tony to bring help and that the plane would be waiting for him.

John called Luke before he met with Mark. He told Luke where to meet them in Harrisburg and asked him to bring some specialized equipment. The company plane took off with Tony while John was halfway to his destination.

They had fifteen minutes to spare when they arrived at the designated address. They used the time to get familiar with the building entrances. It didn't take Sherlock Holmes to realize that there were two thugs standing near the main entrance, apparently waiting for them to arrive.

When the four friends arrived at the warehouse, their descriptions were relayed to D.C. In a very short time, the agents knew who the newcomers were and that they were on their side.

As Matthew entered the doorway to the warehouse, he stumbled, held his knee and said, "Shit! I twisted my knee again. I don't think I can walk on it. Give me a hand," as he reached out to one of the thugs.

The guard quickly stepped aside and said, "Do you think we're crazy? You can't expect us to believe that. Get your ass up and keep moving."

Matthew tried his best to get up, but immediately fell to the floor again. "Let me help him up," said his twin. "It's an old football injury and he just had an operation last week."

Not quite sure if he should believe them or not, the guard backed up and pulled a pistol out of his pocket. "Do it, but don't make any quick moves."

Mark slowly took the few steps necessary to reach his brother and knelt down and pulled up Matt's pant leg, revealing a bandage and brace on his knee. He gently and slowly rubbed Matt's knee, saying. "I told you not to walk on it so soon after the operation."

"I'll be okay. Just let me sit here a moment," was the reply.

Luke and John, not paying any attention to the twins, started to move apart a little, but the guard noticed the movement. "Stay put." Then he yelled, "Anthony, Jose, get out here and lend us a hand." A few seconds later, two more thugs arrived at the doorway. Luke and John shrugged their shoulders as Mark continued to tend to his brother.

"Enough of this shit. Get up and get inside."

As Mark pulled Matthew to his feet, he made a show of placing his brother's arm around his neck to support Matthew's weight. Together they slowly proceeded into the warehouse with Matt in noticeable pain.

As the foursome entered, they looked around and soon determined that they were on an empty loading dock. They noticed that a tractor trailer was parked in one of the three loading bay areas. They observed that there were two windowed offices on their left, separated by a hallway that obviously led to more rooms.

One of the thugs pointed to four chairs in the middle of the room and said, "Sit down." John noticed that only the guard with the gun was paying close attention. He did all the talking, so John assumed he was in charge.

After the lead thug made sure John, Luke, Mark and Matt were seated, he told Anthony, "Go get Lou and Dave."

Lou was in the restroom shooting up. Several minutes passed before the Claybourne brothers appeared. "Well, well," said Lou, "the busybodies have arrived, and just in time," as he looked at his watch.

John put a questioning look on his face and said, "What're you talking about?"

Lou's blood pressure had not dropped in four days. He yelled, "You know damn well what I'm talking about. You butted in matters that didn't concern you and now you're going to pay for it."

"Where's my dad?" John asked. "And their dad," pointing a finger at the other three, "

"They're in the back room."

"I don't believe you." said Mark. "Let me see them."

Lou pointed to two of the thugs standing nearby, and said,

"Take him down the hall and let him see them. Then bring him back. One of you stay there to guard the old men."

Mark was marched down the hall with a man on either side of him. The guards didn't notice that he paid particular attention to the offices and possible exit locations as they proceeded down the hallway.

Back at the dock, Lou looked over at the guard holding the gun. "I told you, no guns. I want them hurt, not killed. Now put that thing away." Luke and John gave each other a raised eyebrow.

The guard mumbled, "Fuck you," but put the pistol back in his pocket.

Mark was escorted to an office near the side of the building. The two fathers were sitting calmly in chairs, their hands and legs tied to the chair. "The cavalry has arrived," Mark said as he entered the room. "Are you both okay?"

"Not bad," replied Mr. Bowman.

"Been better," said Mr. Lynch. "Are you by yourself?"

"Just the four of us," as he smiled and winked.

One of Mark's escorts grabbed his arms and said, "Okay, let's go." Mark could have easily taken him, but decided it was not necessary yet. The other thug stayed with the older men.

When he got back to the dock area, he said in a loud voice, "They're in the northwest corner by the school. One guard is with them."

During the time Mark was being taken to their fathers, John asked, "Just who are you and how did we interfere with you?"

"I'm surprised you don't know us. I'm Lou Claybourne and this is my brother Dave. I don't mind telling you this because I want you to know who kicked the shit out of you. We're going to teach you a lesson for interfering in our business."

"Do you mean we should have let you get away with

stealing materials from us only to sell them back to us at a later date?" asked John sarcastically.

Lou hesitated slightly and replied, "You know damn well that's not what I'm talking about. That's not why we're here."

"Who broke into the construction office in State College?" asked John. No one answered. Lou was starting to sweat profusely. *What the hell's happening to me?* He began to feel really nervous.

John continued, "Are you telling me you didn't steal from us? I have video evidence that it was you, or at least someone from your company, who took supplies from at least five different construction sites and sold them back to us or to another construction firm. Why was the construction office broken into?"

Lou wasn't thinking when he answered, "To find out what materials you would need from us." Lou's eyes began to get blurry. *Why are my legs feeling like Jell-O?* he asked himself.

John then said, "The only reason we haven't turned the information over to the police is my dad's respect for your dad. He was afraid that calling his boys thieves would kill him, but I guess you did that yourselves."

Lou's blood pressure took another leap higher. His eyes were not quite in focus. He shouted, "We didn't kill dad. He never knew what we were doing. Besides, we only did it until we found another way to get the money we needed."

"What did you need the money for?" pushed John. "And why don't you need it now?"

"To cover our gambling losses ... pay for drugs."

"Lou, shut up," yelled Dave, believing that the Lynch boys didn't really know anything about the drugs.

"You shut up, yourself. If you wouldn't have got me started on drugs, we wouldn't be in this position. It's your fault."

Dave went on the defense. "I only gave you a little something to take the edge off. It's your fault that you moved up to the harder stuff and had to find a way to pay for it." Dave realized that Lou was starting to crack up. He saw tremors racking Lou's body.

"It's still your fault. After I was hooked, I had to steal to have money to buy more drugs. You could've stopped me, but no, you wanted more money to live the high life ... you and that useless wife of yours. You know she runs around on you."

"Lou, you don't know what you're talking about," yelled Dave. "Be quiet."

"Wake up, little brother. She's a whore. Just ask Paul Adams. I'm sure he's managed to get a piece of her. He probably had some of my wife too, although she probably went after him."

"Lou, you're high. You don't know what the hell you're talking about," screamed Dave. "Shut up!"

"Who's Paul Adams?" asked John like he was part of the conversation.

"He's the one who told us how to make more money and make it easier," answered Lou.

"Lou, shut the fuck up."

"Fuck you," Lou replied, now showing signs of being heavily drugged. "Adams told us to steal material and resell them to help pay our debt to him. Then he told us how moving shipments of drugs from Florida up the East Coast could pay for what we owed him and still have lots of money left over. We also transported tax-free cigarettes."

John heard thunder in the distance.

John interrupted, knowing Lou would soon be in a state of mind where he wouldn't be able to talk coherently, "Who else was involved?"

"Adams had a couple of friends. I have files ... my office ... with the names ... each time we met ... blackmailed to keep making shipments ... I kept files ... incriminate him ... his friends too."

"What about the money laundering?"

"Their idea ... had ... do it ... file ... office."

Shortly after the friends had entered the warehouse, there was a knock on the side window of one of the drug agent's cars. "I'm Tony Marlow and I'm with those four in there. You'll need one of these if you want to know what's going on." He handed the agent a small receiver with two headphones that he had removed from Luke's van. He commented, "Please stay here for five minutes until I open the back door. Incidentally, don't get gun happy when you go in. Four more of us will be there also." The agents were still stunned when Tony and three others with him walked away toward the warehouse. They put on the earphones in time to hear, "They're in the northwest corner by the school. One guard's with them."

As Tony approached the warehouse, he heard some of the conversation that was going on inside in his earphones. He and one of the others turned right, while the other two went left around the side of the building. They met at the back door opposite a school. It was starting to rain harder. The pilot had told him a heavy thunderstorm was predicted. The rain made it easy for Tony to quietly force the lock on the door with a crowbar. He let the others enter. He noticed that John was the only person sitting in a position where he could see the foursome enter.

Sneaking the short distance down the hall, Tony peeked into the room where the two older men were being held. As he entered, the guard in the room tipped over a chair as he stood up. Before he could do anything, the three men subdued him.

"What was that noise?" said Dave as he heard the chair fall. "You okay back there?" he yelled.

"Yeah, I'm okay, just leaned the chair back too far," Tony answered in a hoarse voice, as Harold and Martin were being untied.

John also heard the chair fall and talked a little louder

to cover the noise, "Tell me, who's Paul Adams? And what's Barry's last name?"

Lou's eyes got wide. His mind was working overtime to decide if he had mentioned those two names. When he suddenly realized that he hadn't mentioned Barry. After feeling a sudden burst in his head, he called out, "You ... son ... of ... bitch ... how do you know those names ... you ... know about ... drugs." With a hand motion to the four seated men, he yelled, "Get 'em ... kick ... shit out ... them ... now!"

In the two seconds it took the thugs to react, the four friends rose and made their move. Matthew was no longer in pain and hit the closest thug in the chest with his fist. The man dropped immediately to the floor stunned and had a hard time getting his breath. Matt turned and backhanded another man. The man who he hit slowed down just enough for Matt to face him. The man put up his fists in a boxer's stance. Matthew shook his head and kicked the man in the balls. "That's one down," he said, as the man dropped to the floor vomiting all over himself. As he turned back to the first thug, he continued, "Your turn again." The man, still stunned somewhat, made a move to hit Matthew but was not fast enough. Matt hit him with a roundhouse right fist that put the man on the deck out like a light. "That's two," said Matt, as he turned to help the others.

Meanwhile, Mark lunged toward the man with the gun and hit him with a chest-high tackle that put the two of them on the floor. As the gunman pulled the gun from his pocket, Mark hit the gunman's arm with his elbow and knocked the gun to the floor. He quickly kicked it across the room. Meanwhile, one of the thugs managed to get behind Mark and locked him in a bear hug. The gunman got up from the floor and hit Mark with a glancing blow to the head. Mark let himself relax and fall to the floor. The man behind him was unable to hold him up and let him go. Mark grabbed the man's legs and pulled. The man fell to the floor with a hard thud. Mark stood up quickly and hit the other thug with a couple of jabs to his face to slow him down. The first man got to his feet and gave Mark a jolting blow to the back, which gave the other a chance to recover and start pounding Mark with blows to his body, which had little affect on Mark.

Matt grabbed one of the assailants in front of Mark and put him in a headlock and told Mark, "You're getting slow."

Mark replied, "Let him go. I don't need your help." So Matt let the assailant go, but not before pushing his head down and raising a knee sharply into the assailant's face.

Luke managed to grab the arm of a nearby thug and twisted it behind the thug's back and shoved him into another thug who was coming at him. Figuring that the odds were against him anyway, he didn't have to be courteous, so he punched the thug in the kidney and created extreme pain that caused him to blackout immediately. The second man decided he couldn't compete with Luke and turned and ran down the hallway toward the back door. Unfortunately for the man, there were six men coming in the opposite direction. Tony raised the crowbar into the air and the man held up his arms in surrender. All the men headed for the loading area. Four federal agents joined them shortly thereafter.

As Matthew released the head of his opponent, Mark turned to the man behind and hit him with four or five combination blows before the man had a chance to react. "You have two choices," said Mark. "You can run now and save yourself some pain or you can take your beating like a man."

"Fuck you," was the reply, as he charged toward Mark.

Mark sidestepped him and with his right arm grabbed the man's shoulder which made him turn and stand erect. Mark showed no mercy as he rained a series of blows to the man's face and body, making his eyelids and lips bleed profusely, before the thug succumbed to a hard blow to his chest.

Mark's other thug was slow to react from the knee to his

face and raised his hands in surrender as Mark turned to take care of him. The man slowly sank into a sitting position on the floor, further indicating that he was no threat.

John was faced with a decision. There were four men in front of him. When he noticed the two Claybournes take a step back as Lou yelled, that reduced his choices. The first thug assumed a boxing stance while the other swung wildly at John's head. John sidestepped the blow and gave a karate chop to the back of the man's head as momentum carried him forward. John turned back to the boxer and blocked the first jab with his right arm and then followed up with his left. The man threw what was intended to be a roundhouse left to the head. John grabbed the fist with his right hand and, with a twist of his hand and body, made the man do a somersault onto the floor.

With both men slightly off balance, John slipped out of his shoes and went into a karate defensive stance. As the first attacker rushed John, he was met with a right kick to the body, followed immediately with a second kick to the head.

John's boxing opponent changed his tactic and rushed toward John intending to wrestle him to the ground. Like a Russian dancer, John dropped to a one-leg knee bend and used the other leg as a broom to sweep the boxer off his feet. John was quickly up on two feet again and used his right foot to deliver a punishing blow to the man's head. The man fell to the floor in pain, but not out of commission.

Matthew was on his way to help John when a powerful grip on his arm stopped him. Luke waved his hand in a gesture of saying no and said, "You may want to stand and watch this instead of helping."

Matt wasn't sure, but stopped to look at John. Mark and the others soon joined the group as both Luke and Mr. Lynch held up their hands to keep the others from interfering. That included the federal agents who had rushed in via both front and back doors.

John heard the word "knife" from the onlookers as the man whom John had hit with a karate chop turned. He lunged at John with a knife intended to pierce John's heart. John grabbed the man's wrist with his right hand as the man lunged forward. With his left hand, he hit the man with a sharp blow to the back of the elbow, which caused a loud crack with the elbow twisted in the opposite direction. The man screamed. Because the man's arm was useless, he began to move his left hand to hold it straight. John felt no remorse as he kicked the man's chin and put him out of commission.

John's boxer apparently had been hit in the head too often to know when he should quit. He again rushed at John, intending to put John in a bear hug. John did a cartwheel and after he had pinned the man's head between his two feet turned and made the man tumble to the floor. John continued his movement and moved over the man's back with a karate blow to the back of his head that made the man go limp.

As he got to his feet, John turned his attention to the Claybournes. When he approached, Dave raised his hands in surrender. Because Lou was under the influence of so many drugs or maybe was just plain stupid, he shouted, "You bastard. You've ruined everything. You rotten son of a bitch."

"You know," replied John, "you're starting to piss me off."

To which Mark replied, "You mean he's just starting to get pissed?"

John grabbed Lou by the front of his shirt, but when he saw the faraway look in Lou's eyes, he let him go and turned his back on him. Thunder rumbled nearby.

Lou reached down and picked up the gun that Mark had earlier kicked across the floor. He yelled, "I should've killed you the night I hit you with the two-by-four," and began to aim the gun at John's back.

John heard the word "gun," as he started his move. He jumped into the air with a move that would make Chuck Norris proud. With the speed of lightning he turned one hundred eighty degrees and landed a kick to Lou's jaw. As John's foot hit Lou, there was a flash of lightning outside. Thunder followed immediately. No one heard the bones crunch in Lou's jaw.

As Lou fell to the floor, Matt was heard to say, "Now, that's what I call thunder and lightning."

When he saw the other men for the first time, John turned to the federal agents and said, "I assume you have enough information to arrest them?"

"I didn't know he knew those types of moves," commented Mark. "How long have you known about that?" he asked Luke.

"A couple of months now," he replied. "I've seen him doing some exercises at the lake a few times when we've been up there. I knew by watching him that he'd been at it for some time. Pretty impressive, if you ask me."

"I'll say it's impressive," answered the twins in unison.

Mr. Lynch interjected, "He started taking karate during high school and maintained the practice to keep in shape. This is the first time I've seen him use the fighting part of it. I always thought he did it just to keep mentally sharp."

"I'll certainly keep that exhibition in mind the next time I start to joke around with him," stated Mark.

"Knowing when to use it is part of the training," stated Mr. Lynch.

By now, the drug enforcement agents were busy handcuffing all of the assailants. The agent in charge approached John and asked, "Are you going to make a fuss over who gets the credit for the arrests?"

"Arrest? What arrest? We don't want anything to do with that bunch. They're all yours, and don't forget to charge them with kidnapping too."

The agent replied, "If that trailer over there contains the drugs we think it does, they'll be in jail for years. Finding drugs next to a school will add years to their sentence." He shook John's hand and said, "Thank you for not wanting any credit. It'll make things a lot easier to explain. After all, we've been following that truck since it left Florida and were waiting for more men to arrive before we took any action. With that school next door, we didn't want anyone to get away."

The agent continued, "If you don't want to be involved with the media, you'd better leave shortly. I'm fairly certain after we check the trailer, there'll be an unidentified call made to the local news media that a drug raid's in progress. We'll make a big deal out of it. You know, put the school next door in lockdown. Call in some local and state police to make it look like a combined effort."

John motioned for Tony to come over. "I don't know if this will help, but everything that was said in this building was recorded. Here's the tape," as he took it from Tony and handed it over to the agent.

"We probably won't need it, but thanks again."

The four friends and their fathers and the others left shortly thereafter. They made sure no one saw them leave the warehouse. Outside, and under an awning on a nearby building, John asked Tony, "How did you manage to get here so quickly? And how did you get the others to come with you?"

"Well," he answered, "I was already on my way to town when you called, and the airport was on the way. I knew that if I waited for help to arrive from the office, we may be too late to help. I remembered there was a construction project near the airport in Harrisburg. So, once we were in the air, I called Lucy at the office and asked for the phone number at the construction site. I called the site and told them your dad and Mr. Bowman were in danger and needed help. These three were in the office at the time and met me at the airport. I think they're a little pissed off for not getting into the ruckus, but I'm sure they'll be telling about the job the four of you did on those thugs for a long time."

"Thanks for coming to our rescue," said Mr. Lynch, "but I don't really think they would've hurt us."

"Hard to say," said Mark. "But as nuts as that one Claybourne is who knows what could have happened."

"Thanks for coming anyway," said Mr. Bowman. As he looked at his watch, he continued. "I could go for a drink." He motioned to all of them, "How about you? I'm buying."

"Both of you'd better make a few phone calls first," said Luke. "By now, the whole company and probably your wives know you were missing."

"Good thinking," replied Mr. Lynch and turned to his long-time friend. He said, "You call the local construction site and I'll call the office. Then we can call our wives."

"Suit yourself, but I'm calling Janet first. She'll kill me if someone else knows we're okay before she does."

"You're right." And they went off to make the calls. "You four had better make some calls too."

"I'm not that henpecked," said Mark.

"I am," said Luke as he pulled out his cell phone.

John didn't know if he was henpecked or not, but decided to call Helen anyway.

Matthew turned to the other construction workers and said, "Lead us to the closest bar," but on the way he made a phone call. Mark hesitated, but decided he'd better make a call also.

PART TWO

Chapter 42

The excitement at Lynch Construction continued to grow as the day got closer to when employee ownership would take effect. However, during the next few days, the office grapevine went into high gear. Talk around the office and the construction sites was centered on how their principal owners kicked the shit out of a bunch of bad-assed drug guys. As the story was retold, each person added a little more to the event. By the time the last person heard the account that day, the foursome supposedly beat the crap out of twenty highly trained assassins. Many wondered what it would be like to be hit by one of the three muscle-bound teddy bears. Others talked about John's talent as a 'Ninja' and how he managed to keep that facet of his life hidden for so long. Everyone in the company thought that the four were very nice young men and that it had been, and would continue to be, good to work with them.

The drug bust had been highly publicized and continued to get front page coverage. Two days later, John received a call from his buddy Harvey. "Well! You didn't solve the case we had in mind, but you certainly put the Claybournes out of business for a long time, probably forever. Peter Black and Tom Owens send their thanks."

"Too bad they weren't able to find out who the real boss of that operation was," replied John.

"The Claybournes are cooperating, especially Dave. Lou isn't doing much in the way of talking since his jaw was broken and his mouth is wired shut. He's having a tough time coming down from the drug-induced high. The doctors aren't sure if he'll make a full recovery, mentally that is. His jaw will heal just fine."

"As far as finding out who the bosses are, there's some headway also. The phone number you gave us didn't help much. It led DEA to a furnished apartment in Trenton, New Jersey. The man and wife who lived there haven't been seen since the day we started following the truck from Florida. We have a description of their cars, but no license numbers. However, the voice recording matched some others that the DEA had on file. There's a fair to good chance that it'll help down the line. The tapes and disks you gave us will also lead to someone who will eventually lead us to the higher ups. So, all is not lost ... something good may come out of this later.

"Another comment on the drug gang ... DEA found the person responsible for leaking information about the investigation. It was Joe Robertson's wife, who was a secretary to one of Tom Owens' assistants. She's refused to talk to anyone except her husband and her lawyer. DEA's considering a plea bargain with her if she agrees to help them track down who she was working for in the organization. Joe is also under suspicion and has been placed on administrative leave. He also hired a lawyer and refuses to talk. Their financial accounts are currently being reviewed to determine if his money really came from an inheritance. We assume it was Joe who looked at your notes. Apparently, he left the office at quitting time, but checked back in after you left the building."

As Harvey was talking about Joe, John was debating whether or not to tell Harvey what he thought. Deciding *what the hell,* John said, "I never had a good feeling about Joe Robertson. I've had investigators digging into his background with a fine tooth comb."

Harvey was quiet for a short time, then replied, "If you find anything interesting, will you let us know?"

"Of course I will. By the way, what was hauled in that truck?" asked John.

"There was a combination of different drugs, from marijuana to heroin and crack. They were shipped in coffee beans, which accounted for a lot of weight. Half the load was cigarettes and cigars, which added another dimension ... tax evasion ... to their problem. So in a way you did get them for taxes. What was unloaded at the Claybournes' warehouse was intended to go to the Philadelphia and the New Jersey areas. The rest was to be taken to New York and points further north. The drugs themselves were of very poor quality and some were tainted with chemicals that may have been more harmful than the drugs themselves. Lou Claybourne apparently took some of the tainted drugs. That could be the reason for his quick mental decline. The general consensus is that the bosses knew about this and used it to get rid of the drugs and the Claybournes. We're still working on how cigarettes were involved."

John said, "Too bad about Claybourne Enterprises. They actually do a good business; the employees don't deserve the bad publicity they're getting. It's bound to cause them some trouble. Who's going to manage the company while the Claybournes are in jail?"

"That's the other reason for this call. Because of the large quantity of drugs and the fact that they were discovered near a school, DEA is in the process of confiscating all of the assets of the Claybournes ... business, homes, cars, boats, and the works. The attorneys are having a field day with this one. The business will be shut down and everything sold at bargain basement prices. With your background and contacts, do you know of anyone who may be interested in the entire operation, lock, stock and barrel?"

John's mind was spinning. Who did he know? Would they be interested? How much would they have to pay? Who was going to manage the business now? Would this increase the prices his company would have to pay for construction materials?

After what seemed like minutes, which could only have been a few seconds, John asked, "Harvey, is there any way of determining how much DEA will ask for everything?"

"Normally, they'd advertise it and put it up for bid. That would probably take as long as a year or so to accomplish."

"Harvey, do you think they'd be interested in selling the business and possessions in a different manner? Shutting down that business will cause a hardship to the employees who work there, as well as companies like ours that depend on them for supplies. What if I can find someone to run it until they make a decision?"

"I see your concern. With all the lawyers involved, I'm sure it will take a long time to actually get control of the properties. How long will it take you to find someone to manage the business?"

"I'm sure I can do it quickly, particularly if you give me the name of the person who initially got you involved in their books."

"John, I don't know if I can do that. We promised we would never reveal his name."

"Tell him that the company may be closed and that he could prevent that by talking to me. I'd never reveal his involvement in the case against the Claybournes. I'm just interested in keeping the business open so our access to supplies isn't limited to someone we don't want to work with. If he agrees, ask DEA to stall on closing the business until I come up with a better plan."

Harvey and John continued discussing the possibilities.

After they finished going over all the questions and answers, Harvey agreed to present the idea to his boss and then to the DEA. He could use John's involvement as a wedge to open the door to further communications.

As soon as John hung up, he made a call to his favorite girl. "How would you like to have dinner tonight with the man of your dreams?"

"I didn't know Brad Pitt was in town," Helen replied teasingly.

"Ouch!" said John, "I guess I know where I stand. And to think I was going to ask you something very important."

Helen thought initially, *Will you marry me?*, but quickly realized that was only wishful thinking, and replied, "Well, if it's really important, I guess I could have dinner with someone in my top ten."

"Thank you, my love. I'll pick you up at seven." John spent the next couple of hours to consider names of a possible manager for Claybourne Enterprises. His biggest problem was that he didn't know anyone currently working at the company. That's the reason he needed to talk to Helen.

John was about to call his dad to ask if he knew who was in charge at Claybourne when he realized that his dad was attending a board meeting for a statewide contractors association. *I'll see him tomorrow,* he thought to himself.

John arrived at Helen's apartment ten minutes early. After a long kiss, he almost said *the hell with dinner.* Helen noticed John's hesitation, smiled to herself and said, "You're actually in my top five," and picked up her coat.

Helen was somewhat surprised at John's choice of restaurant. It was nice and quiet and the food, while not tasteless, was not the best, either. She was further surprised when the waiter seated them in a corner saying, "Is this the table you requested, sir?"

John sat with his back to the other patrons. It didn't take her long to realize this was not to be a romantic dinner.

Throughout dinner, they had a pleasant conversation, but she knew she didn't have John's full attention. When the coffee arrived, she reached for his hand and said, "Okay, we've had dinner. Now, what's really on your mind?"

"You, of course," he lied.

"Baloney! Let's get on with it. Are you breaking up with me?"

"What? What are you talking about?" answered John. "I have no intention of leaving you. I love you too much for that."

Helen was pleased with that reply, since she had made the statement to get his attention, not to ask the question. "I know that, but you got me here under false pretenses. What do you want me to do?"

"I'm sorry. You're right. I have to ask you to use your resources to find out everything there is to know about Claybourne Enterprises, and I need it ASAP."

"Why?"

He then proceeded to explain all the details to her and his thoughts about the matter. One question led to another and then another. Unlike John, Helen needed to make notes as they talked. Several pages of notes later, Helen made the statement, "I can understand why you want to have this taken care of immediately. If that company were closed, it could have a significant effect on many companies and the bottom line on profit and loss statements. This case may require me to change some priorities."

"I know this may cause some problems, but it's the time element. We need this now, not later, that's the problem. Charge it to Lynch Construction."

"Charging isn't the problem, and you should be ashamed to even think that. Now, take me home so I can make a call to get things moving tonight, instead of tomorrow morning."

Chapter 43

The next morning John called his dad to tell him about the Claybournes' closing and to pick his brain about who might be available to run Claybourne Enterprises. Mr. Lynch agreed with his son about the necessity to keep Claybourne open. The only people he could recommend were employed by Lynch Construction, and with the new ownership taking over soon, it didn't seem likely that one of them would take the job. "You or someone like you could manage the business once you got involved."

"You're probably right," answered John. "I already have Helen doing some background checks on the existing staff. Hopefully, someone will rise to the surface. I didn't think you'd mind, so I also have her doing thorough checks on the Claybournes' reputation with banks across the state."

"That's a good starting point, but unless DEA says it's okay, we may be spinning our wheels unnecessarily, although someone has to give it a try. The money we spend will be worth the effort if we can keep the business open. If they close the business, quite a few people will be out of jobs and we'll have to work with another supplier. God only knows how much more that will cost us. Do what you have to do, Son."

For the next few days John contacted several people without giving away information that may jeopardize the Claybournes' complicated situation. Helen checked in a few times to give him updates or to ask him for more information. So far, every rock she'd overturned had been positive about the business. The Claybourne brothers were another story. They left a dirty trail of greed and hunger for power wherever they went, both in and out of state.

Everyone whom Helen's investigators talked to indicated they were unsavory characters. Apparently, as long as their father ran the business, they were kept in line. When he became ill, the sons' real colors began to show. They were known to be heavy gamblers, frequently losing large amounts of money at casinos and with local bookies. Both men were known to have mistresses.

John decided he had waited long enough for an answer from the DEA, but instead of calling Tom Owens directly, he called Harvey at work. "Have you heard anything from your DEA friends?" he asked.

"You have a way of knowing the best or the worst time to call me. How do you do that? Tom and Peter are in the office talking now. But I'll tell you now, it doesn't look good."

"What does that mean?"

"I've been talking to one of my contacts over at DEA and he says the agency has already started the process of confiscating all of the Claybournes' property. They intend to act as quickly as possible to prevent any interference. They say it's standard procedure and sets examples so others with property to lose don't get involved in the drug business."

"Is there anything I can do to help our cause?"

"At this point there's nothing you can do. Peter is your best bet for any compromises. He understands why you want to keep the business open. It's very nice of you to want to help the employees."

"That's part of it," said John, "but I don't want you to think it's the only reason. If the business is kept open, it would mean getting supplies we already ordered at the prices we based our bids on, as well as the unopened estimates we have waiting for bid openings. If we have to change suppliers, they'll have us by the short hair. Believe me, the fact that we didn't use them initially will increase their prices drastically. It will cost Lynch Construction, as well as many other companies, a lot of money. So don't think this is entirely a good-will gesture."

"I understand, and it doesn't change anything. DEA will make the decision and they'll make it soon."

"Okay, thanks Harvey. Give me a call when you know something. I'll owe you."

"John, one other thing ... we had two contacts inside Claybournes. Tim Daniels is the CFO and Martin Peterman is the warehouse manager. They started this whole investigation when they contacted the Pennsylvania State Police who passed it on to us. Both men agreed to talk to you in private. It probably doesn't mean much now. I'm just passing on the information. I'll call you later."

When John hung up, he couldn't believe his efforts were in vain. He spent the next several hours reviewing all his notes and searched his mind to discover if he had missed anything that could have changed the outcome. He didn't overlook anything. On his way to his apartment, he received a call from Harvey. "I can't talk because I'm on my way into a meeting. Peter just called to let me know that Tom Owens agrees with your reasoning. He promised to meet with their attorneys tomorrow morning to see if they can help without setting a precedent. I'll call when I know something."

John's spirits were lifted a little, but deep down he had the feeling that the DEA wouldn't budge enough to make a difference. Later, during a call to Helen, he pretty much gave into the obvious. He told her that after he heard from Harvey he'd start contacting other suppliers to see if he could establish a good rapport. Maybe he could get some prices on major items needed for projects already under construction. He would concentrate on future projects after the bids were opened.

John arrived at the office early in the morning and started to review the data he had the staff gather. He hoped to get a jump on the other contractors who would also be looking for construction materials. He realized that million of dollars were at stake if he didn't get most of the supplies ordered in a timely manner. He knew that construction schedules could be delayed and late penalties would be subtracted from their profit margin. By mid-morning, he had compiled a list of materials for which he'd have to obtain prices and order them. He was literally reaching for the phone when it rang.

"John, this is Tom Owens from the DEA. I have some news for you that I wanted to relay myself instead of going through Peter and Harvey. Our attorneys have checked the law governing this matter and say that we'll be allowed to alter our normal procedures. Hold on a second."

John could hear papers rustling. Shortly, Tom began again, "In order to keep the Claybourne business from being closed for a long period of time, thereby creating major economic problems, our normal procedures will be circumvented. Do you have a pencil and paper handy? Oh! I forgot, Harvey told me you about your ability. You don't need to write anything down. What we're going to propose are procedures that have never been used by our office, but other agencies have used them under emergency situations. Their use has been upheld in the federal court system."

Owens paused and continued. "First, we'll advertise that bids will be accepted on all the Claybourne assets while we're in the process of obtaining the assets. Next, we'll advertise for bids for only two weeks prior to the bid opening. After bid opening, we'll allow thirty days to arrange for initial payment, or down payments, on the assets. Our standard percentage for this down payment is ten percent of the highest bid. At the time of down payment, the winning bidder will be required to sign an agreement to manage the business on behalf of DEA until such time all legal paperwork can be completed. All monies derived from operating the business will be placed in restricted accounts. These funds can be used as operating capital for the business. None of the profits made from the business during this time period can be distributed to owners or stockholders. After all the paperwork has been completed, we will expect full payment of the amount of the bid minus the down payment. Any funds still in the restricted account will be released to the new owners.

The total time period could be as few as nine months, but could go as long as three to three and a half years. All of this will be included in the advertisement. Do you have any questions?"

"Probably a thousand," answered John. "When will you place the first ad?"

"Within a week," was the answer.

"Will the ad indicate exactly which assets are included?"

"Yes, but only those major assets that would be enough to make a difference in the bid amount. Keep in mind that under normal circumstances we only get fifty to sixty percent of the actual value of the assets."

"How will you keep every Tom, Dick and Harry from bidding?"

"Each bid will have to have a letter from a financial institution indicating the bidder's ability to pay the bid amount. The bidder will also have to include an insurance bond with his bid so that if the bidder defaults, the bond will pay the bid amount. I'm sure it's almost the same, or at least similar, to any construction bid you submit."

"Can the Claybournes submit a bid?"

"The Claybournes, and any relative as far as third cousins, are on our shit list. No, they can't bid."

"What if the management team doesn't produce a profit, or runs the business to the ground?"

"That's the bidder's problem, not ours. We get our money one way or the other."

John and Tom talked for another thirty minutes before Tom begged off by saying he had another appointment. John's mind was in full-spin cycle. He could think of several different ways to proceed with this information. Which was the best one?

Finally, he decided the best way to proceed was to approach the two employees at Claybourne and tell them the situation. Maybe they'd be able to give him some input as to which way to proceed. Before he called them, he called his dad to find out if he had any suggestions. Mr. Lynch's secretary told John his dad was at lunch with his wife and Mr. and Mrs. Bowman. He would return later in the day. He decided to take matters into his own hands and ask Helen about her research on Claybourne Enterprises.

Helen's assistant told her it was John calling. Helen answered the phone with her ever-pleasant voice, "Good morning and how may I do you?"

John smiled to himself and said, "Good morning to you too, my love. I can think of several different ways you could do me, but right now I only have time for work." After a few playful minutes of talk, John brought her up to date on the Claybourne situation and then asked, "Did your investigation of Claybournes include employees?"

"Only a few of the higher-ups. Why?" she asked.

"Were Tim Daniels and Martin Peterman on the list, and if so, what can you tell me about them?"

"Hold on until I bring the data on them up on the computer. Yes, they're two of the four we have information on. Let's see ... Tim Daniels is fifty-five years old. His wife's name is Linda and they've been married for thirty years, and they have two children, Tim Junior and Lydia. Both of the kids are in college at Bucknell University. That's the parents' alma mater. Tim Senior has a degree in accounting and Linda's degree is in education. Tim has worked for Claybourne for twenty-five years, first as a bookkeeper and later as CFO. They appear to live slightly above their means, which would not be unusual with two kids in college. They have an average amount of debt and usually pay their bills on time … fair to good credit rating."

Helen continued, "Martin Peterman is also fifty-five. He's worked for Claybourne for twenty-two years. Before that, he worked for several different construction firms. His wife Nancy is the manager of a small retail store at the local mall. They have four children, all under the age of eighteen. They've been married for twenty years. Their financial rating's a little lower than what you would expect for someone that age. That's about as far as we went. Should we investigate further?"

"Not now. Do you think your investors would back them if they wanted to buy the company?"

Helen thought for a minute and said, "Let me bounce that off of Uncle Bat. He's in the office today. Can I call you right back?"

"Sure, I'll wait right here."

Chapter 44

'Right back' must have been a relative term because it was three hours later before John's phone rang. "John, this is Bat Masterson. Helen's on the other phone."

John was surprised that Mr. Masterson was calling. As he normally did, Masterson got right to the point. "There's no way I can risk my investors' money on the two unknowns we're talking about. Based on our initial research, Claybourne Enterprises is worth at least seventy-five million. That's way too much for unknowns. Why did you select Peterman and Daniels?"

"Actually, I was thinking of all the employees buying the company and having them manage it until they were reorganized."

"It won't happen," replied Mr. Masterson, "but I have a better idea, which is why Helen asked me to make the call. Why don't you buy the company? I can arrange the financing for you."

John was dumbstruck. *Did he hear right?* Helen's uncle continued, "John, you have the background, the ability, the financial backing, and, most of all, a desire to keep that business running. Again, I ask, why don't you buy it?"

"What do you mean by financial backing? I'm as unknown as the two employees at Claybourne."

"John, that's not exactly a true statement. You'll have to bounce that one off of your dad and his partner. Besides, when I said you, I meant you and your three friends. I have to go, so think about it. Incidentally, I have some information we discussed at our meeting in my apartment. I'll send it to you tomorrow. Here's Helen." With that comment, he put his phone down and winked at his niece, who was heir to his investment banking firm and all the peripherals that went with it.

Helen, who hadn't spoken during the entire conversation, said, "I told him you wouldn't believe me so I asked him to make the call." The silence at the other end of the line prompted her to say, "John ... John are you still on the line?"

John, who was still dumbfounded, finally answered, "Yeah, I'm here," but he was still trying to grasp what had just been proposed. "Do you really think we should do this? Holy shit! What will dad say? What about Lynch Construction? Would we have to leave them? How do I submit a bid to DEA? How much should I bid? Holy shit!"

Helen, who had never seen John so unsure of what to do, laughed out loud. "John Lynch, you poor fellow. You have a golden opportunity thrown right in front of you and you don't know how to handle the pressure. Wait until your friends hear about this."

"Helen please don't mention this to them. I have to talk to dad and get his permission before I propose this to my friends."

"You know that I won't. This is a business transaction and you know, as well as I do, that my business dealings are confidential. And, I don't think getting your dad's okay will be a problem."

"Thank you, my love. Yes, I know you wouldn't blab this

to anyone. I've got a lot to think about. Tell me, how high can we go with our bid?"

"Well, like my uncle said, the company's worth at least seventy-five million. That's not including any 'blue sky' value. That would probably add another twenty-five percent to it. We can cover the seventy-five million easily. To us, it looks like you can get this company for a very good price."

"Thanks, I'll certainly keep that in mind. I have to start things moving. I'll call you soon. Love you."

"I love you too." And, then she asked a question that had been puzzling her, "What meeting did you and my uncle have?"

"I asked him to do some investigation for me. I'll tell you about it later."

Helen thought to herself, *Someday I'll marry that man, but I just know it won't be in the near future. He won't have time for a wedding. Maybe I was stupid to suggest that John and his friends get involved with Claybourne Enterprises.*

The whirlwind in John's mind continued as he thought of new questions. He went to his dad's office to see if he had returned. When he saw that his dad was sitting behind the desk, he entered saying, "I called Helen today to get the lowdown on two of Claybournes' top personnel to see if they had the background to buy the business. She had to talk to her uncle about that one. Mr. Masterson himself called and told me it couldn't be done. Financially they weren't capable enough for the investment bankers to take a chance on them."

Harold had a smile on his face, but John didn't notice. John continued, "Then he dropped the bombshell. He said the Bowmans and I should put a bid in on buying the company. Masterson said he could get full financing for us, but I don't know how we can borrow that much money. Everything we have is invested in the Everett Lodge."

John paused for a moment and then said, "Wait a minute

... you had to have had a hand in this. I asked you before if you used your money to get us financing for the lodge. You told me no. Is that right?"

"Yes, that's right." Harold grinned at his son. "But, I didn't give you all the information that maybe I should have. I'm still not in a position to tell you everything. Please forgive me, but you'll have to wait a little longer. Trust me ... everything will be okay."

John was still dumbfounded. He didn't know what to do or say. After he thought about it for a moment or so, he asked, "Is there anything you can tell me, or do you have any input?"

"As a matter of fact, I do have some input," replied the man John respected more than any other person. "When you first came to me about DEA's plans, which I felt was more than satisfactory, I assumed you were thinking about me buying it. You asked me for suggestions on who could run the company. I had no idea you meant whom I'd suggest to buy the business. Now you're telling me that the thought of us buying Claybourne Enterprises didn't even enter your mind. Martin and I were on the phone with Bat Masterson for over an hour about this. That discussion led to the suggestion that you and the Bowman brothers buy the company."

With a broad smile on his face, Harold said, "John Lynch, my son, you're slipping. That thought should have occurred to you as soon as you heard about the situation."

"Thinking about it now, you're right," answered John. "Honestly, the idea never crossed my mind until Mr. Masterson mentioned it."

Harold spoke again, "During our phone conversation with Masterson and his prodigy, we discussed many possibilities. Martin and I considered buying it, but decided we were too close to retirement to start a new venture. Helen's the one who recommended that you and the Bowmans run Claybourne Enterprises. That eventually led to the possibility that the four of you should buy the company. She's an extremely perceptive young lady. She'll make some savvy man a good wife. Do you know of anyone like that?"

"You're starting to sound like mom."

"Yes, and your mother's also very perceptive about people."

Harold was about to dismiss John. Instead he said, "After our phone conversation, Martin and I discussed several other possibilities that will affect you and your friends."

John said, "What possibilities?"

His dad's reply was, "We'll talk about that later. I'd like you to be at a meeting here in my office at five o'clock. By then, the staff will be gone. At that time, I believe you'll learn how the financing became available. Mother and all the Bowmans will also be here. I'll see you then," Harold said, dismissing John.

Chapter 45

John left the office thinking that maybe he was losing it. *Why didn't I think of us making a bid on Claybourne Enterprises? I know why ... because neither my friends nor I have that kind of money.*

John wondered about the little lady who had made the suggestion. *Helen brought up the idea. Even so, how did the approval come about so quickly? Dad had to be involved with this somehow, and what's the meeting about?*

John had a couple of hours to kill before the five o'clock meeting. He shut his office door and did a lot of thinking. *The Everett Lodge. What will happen to the construction company? What are the pros and cons of buying Claybourne Enterprises? What about me and Helen?* There was no doubt in John's mind that he wanted to be with her for the rest of his life, to get married and eventually to start a family. *So, what's holding me back?*

John called a florist and ordered two dozen red roses to be delivered to Helen. With a lot of forethought, he asked that a note be added ... 'Marry me?'

John returned to his dad's office at five o'clock where John's mother and Martin and Janet Bowman were sitting around the desk with Mr. Lynch. John was about to sit down when his dad said, "Tell the other three to give us fifteen minutes before you all return." John would've used the intercom system, but apparently the four parents weren't finished with their discussion. The three brothers and John waited anxiously as they had been instructed. When they entered the room, Mr. Bowman invited them to take a seat.

Martin started the conversation, "The grapevine tells us that you three are somewhat concerned about where you fit into the new companies that are being formed." As a group, they began to speak, but Mr. Bowman held up his hand, "I'm not done," which kept all three of them quiet. "I have a story to tell. Let me finish before you question anything."

"To begin with, the three of you would be able to make a nice living from Lynch Construction, even if you don't actually work for the company." That comment caused the three of them to have questioning looks on their faces, but Martin raised his hand again to prevent any discussion. "Wait until I'm done."

He continued, "Years ago, I had a small, but successful concrete business. I had eight people working for me, including your mother who ran the office. Luke's dad, Zack Lincoln, was a bricklayer and also had a nice business. We did a lot of projects together, and we became friends. At that time, Lewistown Construction was owned by Jeff Chamberlain and had been in business for many years. Mostly, because of poor management and a lack of interest, his business never thrived the way it should have. Jeff used to contract most of the work out to subcontractors. Zack Lincoln and I did a lot of work for him."

Continuing, Martin said, "One day Jeff approached Zack and me to say he was going to sell the business. He asked if we were interested in buying Lewistown Construction. Without much thought, we turned down the offer. A month later, he told us that he had sold the business to some guy from up north. It really came as a surprise that he'd sold it so quickly."

Martin paused to catch his breath. "A few weeks later, the new owner, Harold, moved to town. With his good business sense, he began to expand the business by bidding on larger and larger jobs. Because Jeff Chamberlain had told him that Zack and I had done a lot of work for him, Harold kept providing work for both of our little businesses.

"One day Harold approached me and asked if I'd be interested in merging my business with his. Instead of buying the businesses outright, Harold wanted to give your mother and me a percentage of his business in exchange for our companies. When I told Zack about Harold's offer, he told me he had the same offer."

The foursome listened with great interest. Martin continued his explanation. "My share of Lynch Construction was to be fifteen percent and Zack's share, because his company was smaller, was to be five percent. Harold said he'd hire all of our employees and ensure their positions for at least the next two years. After that they would be subject to performance evaluations to keep their jobs. Zack and I discussed the offer a couple of times. Zack told me he was going to do it and I was also leaning that way."

Pausing to take a drink of water, Martin went on. "Before we could accept the offers, Zack and his wife Carol were killed in a head-on accident caused by a drunk driver. The driver, as well as two other people died, in that accident. Luke didn't have any other relatives. Harold and Margaret and your mother and I discussed Luke's predicament. The four of us couldn't decide who Luke would live with … the Lynches or the Bowmans. Both families wanted him to live with them. Ultimately, we flipped a coin to decide with whom Luke would live … and we won.

Harold then wanted to cover all of Luke's expenses. We didn't agree with his offer. A few years later … after many profitable projects, Harold started a trust to pay for all educational expenses for Luke. I didn't know it until later that he had included the two of you in the trust. As you know, we later adopted Luke and had his name changed to Bowman.

The day after the funeral for the Lincolns, Harold came to me and said he was going to propose to Zack's men that they start working for him immediately. I sold my concrete paving business to Harold in exchange for fifteen percent ownership in the construction company. Harold hired all of my men, three of whom are still are working for the company. Harold wanted to call the new company Bowman and Lynch but I wouldn't have it. The name was changed from Lewistown Construction to Lynch Construction. At that time, and ever since, I've only wanted to be a silent partner in the company. Just a peon doing the jobs assigned to me ... I was paid a salary comparable with the work I did. Margaret's duties at the office were increasing along with the business so your mother started working in the office to help out.

Our first several projects were financial successes. We actually started a second business. You'll learn more about that later."

He took another sip of water before he spoke again. "Initially, some of my share of the profit was used to supplement my income. As time went on, I used it to buy rental properties throughout the state. The income from the rentals, in addition to the remaining part of my annual fifteen percent, has made me fairly wealthy."

Martin Bowman looked at his three sons, who were now speechless, and continued, "Now, here's the reason for this meeting. When the paperwork is completed for the new Lynch Construction companies, Harold and Margaret, as well as your mother and I, plan to accept the retirement options offered to all employees."

Holding up his hand again, he said, "At the time of my retirement, each one of you," referring to his sons, "will own a

Thunder and Lightning

five percent share of the Lynch Construction companies and all of its subsidiaries." He went on again, "It's already been decided. Your mother and I will have plenty of assets to enjoy the life we choose. I'm done with my part of this meeting ... the easy part. Harold, now it's your turn."

Before the three brothers had a chance to object or question their dad, Mr. Lynch held up his hand to stop them, and said, "During our earlier meeting, we flipped a coin to see who did which part. I lost, so I get the difficult part.

Seeing that he had their attention, Harold began, "Well, here goes ... the hard part, first." As he waved his hand to include the four younger people in the room, he continued, "You're all fired!" Silence, absolute silence, from all four of them, and confused dumb looks, permeated the room.

Martin and Janet, as well as Margaret and Harold, almost laughed out loud at the expressions on their sons' faces.

"Let me explain. First of all, you're not really fired, but we, Martin and I, with your mothers' backing, suggest that you give up your positions at the construction companies. As Martin said, as soon as the papers are signed, we're retiring. John and I will still be the majority owners until the new owners buy out the shares I'm going to relinquish."

Then he pointed to the three brothers and said, "Your five percent share will not make you major owners, but close enough that you will have a voice in how the companies operate.

Our original plan was for the four of you to work at the construction company and eventually take over the management. However, because of some recent developments that I'll soon explain, it's our opinion that the new companies will flourish better without any of us looking over their shoulders everyday. If you're here, the new management will always question if they made the right decision, or if you are going to override them, or worst scenario, report back to me.

No one, except John, knows that Martin's a silent partner.

John has only known that fact since he got involved with the accounting portions of the company. To his credit, he discovered that within a few months of working on the finances ...something our in-house accountants never picked up. But, they of course, never had access to our personal accounts either. Martin's partnership will have to be revealed before the final papers are signed.

The last part involves some of our other companies. We're only selling that portion of the company which was Lynch Construction. The Harrisburg Industrial Electronics was bought by Lynch Construction, which means Martin and Janet own fifteen percent of that company also.

The same is true for Roberts HVAC. What none of you, including John, know is that Lynch Construction recently purchased Mid-Atlantic Environmental Engineering. It's a company that specializes in consulting services for the construction industry. The company has thirty employees who work in three offices located in Pennsylvania, Maryland and Virginia. We acquired the business after the owner decided to skip the country with most of the company's funds. We were asked to look into buying the company when no one from the firm wanted to buy the company. This company has a lot of potential. The management of two of the three offices is intact."

Apparently the four parents were apprehensive about the meeting with the four sons because everyone appeared to be thirsty. Harold stopped to take a long drink of water. As he set the glass down, he continued. "Masterson Business Consultants researched Mid-Atlantic Environmental and indicated that the company is viable. It has a very good reputation and good employees. We've bought the company for next to nothing.

"The company lacks a true leader who's capable of leading the company. Martin and I are hoping that Mark will take on that challenge."

Mark was about to talk when Harold raised his hand to stop him.

"Roberts HVAC has some good people working for them. They know residential heating and air conditioning well. However, in order for that business to expand, we need someone to take over the management. He'll have to hire more personnel. Move the company into the industrial and commercial arena as well. We're hoping that Matthew will accept that job."

Matt begins to speak, but Harold continued, "We'd like it if Luke continues to manage Industrial Electronics.

It's Martin's and my intent to sell these three companies to the four of you, as separate corporations, of course. Martin and I'll accept the profits from the three businesses for the next ten years as payment. In ten years, you'll own the businesses outright."

Harold continued, "As Martin indicated, early in our business relationship we started a second business. That business is a private bank. Initially, one percent of the profits from Lynch Construction were deposited into this bank. We've increased that percentage after a few very profitable construction projects."

With a motion of his hand that indicated the three other parents, "Up to now this bank has had only four customers. The money in this bank was used to purchase or finance some of our individual building projects. Lynch Construction has also borrowed funds from the bank. All loans are repaid along with appropriate interest. There are still several insignificant accounts receivable due to the bank."

Another pause for a sip of water, Harold kept on speaking, "That accounts for the three of you," referring to the brothers. Then he pointed to John, he said, "What are we going to do with you? John, perhaps you can tell the others about our earlier conversation."

At first, John, who had been thinking about the banking

business, wasn't sure where he was supposed to take the conversation. When he realized what his dad's intentions were he replied, "I plan on taking over the management of Claybourne Enterprises. That is, if we can make a successful bid to buy the company. I propose that the Thunder and Lightning Partnership buy Claybourne Enterprises." That took the air out of the three brothers.

"Let me explain," said John. He then brought them up to date on the Claybourne situation and how they could conceivably own Claybourne Enterprises in the very near future. He didn't tell them how the four of them could come up with the money for their proposed business. He didn't tell them because he really didn't fully understand how they could borrow the money. However, Martin's and his Dad's comments had offered some insight.

Everyone was excited about the facts they had just heard. The foursome expressed their gratitude and had a lot of questions. Matt was the first to summarize the situation. "This means we leave Lynch Construction to manage one of our own companies. In ten years we could own four businesses outright, plus part ownership in the five new Lynch companies."

The reaction of the four young men who would be leaving the Lynch Construction Company, and the details needed to put a bid in on Claybourne Enterprises, took up most of the evening.

Martin Bowman spoke up saying, "Let's take some time for this to settle in. How about we meet tomorrow to pick up this discussion? I suggest we meet at the Holiday Inn conference room for the sake of privacy."

When everyone left the building, John returned to his office and made a few phone calls. He called one of the corporate lawyers. After being connected to his voice mail, he asked that the staff check into the procedure needed to bid on the DEA confiscated property.

He then called his dad at home to question him about the financing of the lodge and Claybourne Enterprises. John began by saying, "I remember when I asked you about borrowing money from Lincoln Bank when I was checking into financing the buyout. You didn't tell me the full details."

John could hear the smile in his dad's voice. "You didn't need to know at that point. Now you do need to know."

John asked, "Am I to assume that the banks agreed to lend us money for the Everett Lodge because you and Martin put up the money in Lincoln Bank as collateral?"

"It's not that easy, but you can make that assumption," was Harold's reply. "Lincoln Bank agreed to be a silent backer of each loan approved by the other two banks. The other banks would be responsible for the paperwork.

John asked, "Can I also assume that a similar circumstance exists with Masterson?"

"You can also make that assumption. But it involves more than that. What we never got around to telling you is that you and the Bowman brothers are the owners of the Lincoln Bank. I decided to wait and see if you would discover that fact yourself. Martin's probably telling his sons about that at this time."

"What!" exclaimed John. "How did you get that one past me?"

"It's been there since the beginning," replied Mr. Lynch. "It wasn't enough by itself to make Masterson bite at the opportunity but it's a significant amount."

"Meaning you and Martin put your share of Masterson's at risk also."

Harold had no choice but to reply, "That's correct."

"Thank you on behalf of all four of us. Is it possible that this generous proposal could affect yours and Martin's style of living in your retirement?"

"I see where you're heading with this and the answer is no. The answer is that both Martin and I have enough to do whatever we want to do. A large portion of our investments at Masterson's would end up in government hands as estate taxes when we die. So, we decided to use it to benefit our children first. If we didn't think the four of you were intelligent enough to manage these businesses, we wouldn't have made those decisions."

John and his Dad talked for another fifteen minutes about the various businesses.

Chapter 46

John then called Helen and said, "Hi," expecting her to thank him for the flowers and the note. He just got a 'Hi' in return. John was puzzled but continued, "Would it be possible for us to get together tonight for dinner and discuss some more details concerning your company's involvement in our future business ventures?"

After a moment of hesitation, she replied, "I guess I could," and hesitated again, "as long as it's a business meeting. To be truthful with you, since we've been good friends for a while, I'm questioning if I should go out with you."

"Why shouldn't you go out with me?" John asked in a very serious manner.

"Well, today I received some beautiful roses with a note that read, 'Marry me?' I don't know who sent it, and until I find out who it was, I don't believe I should be going out with someone I've been intimate with."

John now realized his leg was being pulled and said, "You're probably right. People will talk, and I for one, don't want to drag your name through the mud. So, let's forget dinner. By the way, was there a ring involved with the request?"

"No, as a matter of fact, there wasn't a ring included with the flowers."

"Are you sure? Did you check the stem of each rose? Maybe your new fiancé put the ring there?"

"Holy crap!" she exclaimed as she dropped the phone and ran to look at the flowers.

"You scoundrel," she shouted, not unpleasantly, when she returned.

"Why am I a scoundrel? I just brought up the possibility. I didn't say there was a ring on the roses."

"You're still a scoundrel."

"Well, if there's no ring, I don't think the marriage proposal is official. In which case, it's my opinion that you can go to dinner with me."

"I don't know if I want to go to dinner with you now."

"It's up to you, but I wouldn't miss the opportunity if I were you. Maybe we'll be able to determine who sent the roses with the unsigned note?"

"Okay, you've talked me into it. Besides, a marriage proposal isn't official until it's done in person and there's a ring. Pick me up in an hour." She didn't wait for a reply.

John arrived right on time and knocked on Helen's door. She opened the door and she already was wearing her coat. He leaned down and kissed her, which she quickly turned into a passionate, tongue-exploring event. John enjoyed it instantly and said, "One more like that and dinner will have to wait." They enjoyed the second kiss as much as the first.

"Then it will have to wait." Helen opened her coat to reveal her very beautiful birthday suit. As the coat fell to the floor, she said, "Let's have dessert first." She then jumped into his arms with a kiss that made John diamond hard.

Their first round of lovemaking was quick and completed on the living room floor with John's clothes strewn all over the room. It wasn't until they came up for air later that they realized that some of their entanglement and thrashing had caused the furniture to be moved around. They noticed that some of the chairs had been moved and an end table was overturned, spewing pictures and knickknacks onto the floor.

"Dessert was delicious," exclaimed John. When he pulled Helen to her feet, he said, "but I'm still hungry." Picking Helen up in his arms, he carried her into the bedroom saying, "And the floor isn't a good place to satisfy my hunger." John placed Helen on the edge of the bed and covered her nude body with a robe he found nearby. He knelt before her and placed her hand in his and said, "Helen Francis, you're the love of my life and I'll love you forever. Helen, will you do me the honor of marrying me and spending the rest of our lives together?"

"Yes, yes, yes," was the only audible reply as tears ran down her face.

They never did go out to dinner. Several hours, and a couple of hot showers later, each of them had satisfied their hunger. Lying in John's arms enjoying the aftermath, Helen said in a loving manner, "It still won't be official until I have a ring."

"You're right, my love. Let's not announce it until you do have a ring." Helen slid up in the bed and looked into John's eyes, as she thought *this may be a delay tactic*. When John saw her look, he continued, "And we'll start looking for a suitable ring this weekend." This caused them to enjoy dessert once again and there was nothing quick about it this time.

John stayed the night, without ever having discussed business. When he left for his apartment early in the morning, he had a hard time walking to his SUV.

Mark, who was the first one to see John in the morning, said, "You got laid last night, didn't you?" John only smirked and walked into the hotel conference room where their meeting was to take place.

Luke was the only one in the room and said to John immediately, "You got laid last night, didn't you?"

John wondered *I guess the look on my face shows how much I'm in love with Helen.*

Mark looked at John and began speaking, "Before our parents arrive, someone needs to explain to me how it's possible that a group of investment bankers are willing to let us bid on any company let alone one worth at least seventy-five million dollars."

"Yeah, I don't completely understand what Masterson does," exclaimed Matt.

John paused a moment, then started, "This is not for public information, so it stays in this room." John explained the two separate operations of Masterson Business Consultants, without giving them details of Helen's future ownership. He provided the basic concept of how the business worked and a brief overview of the files Masterson kept on personnel and businesses throughout the eastern United States. "Our fathers, or should I say we, own Lincoln Bank. The bank is backing the financing of the Everett Lodge.

Our parents are also investors with Masterson. I don't know how much money's involved, but it must be substantial. They used their shares with Masterson to leverage the money Masterson is willing to loan us."

When the others arrived, they resumed the previous day's conversation. John told them that the one piece of information he'd managed to obtain from Helen was her research on the financial status and overall value of Claybourne Enterprises … lock, stock, and barrel. He told the group that he found out that the seventy-five million dollar figure, that had previously been mentioned, included the property and equipment only. The value of the company's future potential wasn't considered.

John proceeded, "With average bids of between fifty and sixty percent of the value, it'd be difficult to arrive at a bid that would ensure we'd win the bid. Bidding the estimated value would probably win the bid for us, but we wouldn't want to leave too big of a gap between our bid and the next highest bid." After all of the details were reviewed, the eight of them decided a minimum bid of at least forty-five million would be necessary. They would submit an actual figure after they conducted additional reviews.

The discussion concerning the four friends leaving Lynch Construction proceeded relatively quickly. The longest discussion concerned the fact that each of them was entitled to their share in the ownership of the new companies, in addition to what was given to them by their fathers. The primary question was … did the men have to work for one of the companies to be part of an employee-owned company? By definition, it seemed that they would have to work there.

John answered this question for them. "I talked to the attorneys yesterday. They said that as long as the sales agreement indicates that part of the company was owned by designated individuals, there won't be a problem. I can tell them to make those changes as soon as dad and Martin explain what's happening to a few of the managers. The employees have to agree, because dad doesn't have to sell his shares of the business to them." Other than that minor issue, they all agreed that the changes would be beneficial.

After the meeting, John realized he had some unfinished business that needed his attention and made another call. When the phone call was passed through to the inner office, he said, "We never did finish our business last night. Could we meet for lunch?"

The answer somehow didn't surprise him, "I'm in no shape to go out in public. Come to my office and I'll order in."

"Is your Uncle Bat in the office today?"

"Yes, he's here or at least up in his apartment."

"Ask him if he could join us for about fifteen minutes before we have lunch."

John was already in Helen's office when Bat Masterson

entered. He looked at both of them, then with knowing eyes smiled. "Good afternoon to both of you."

After the initial embarrassing moment, John asked Bateman if he could talk to him privately to which he received a positive reply. The two men left the room and John returned five minutes later.

Helen immediately exclaimed, "I think he knows we were together all night."

"Oh, he knows alright, and I do believe he approves."

"What did you want to talk to Uncle Bateman about?"

"Three things ... first, I asked him for permission to marry you to which he gave his blessings. The second reason was to thank him the information your investigator uncovered about four federal employees. I also asked if he would tell me how much money my dad had invested with you. He wouldn't give me that information."

Helen answered, "I know who some of the investors are, but not everyone. I knew your dad was involved, but I didn't know that you and the Bowman brothers had funds invested until Uncle Bateman told me yesterday. Are you going to tell me who the federal employees are that the investigator discovered?"

"Sure, why not," he replied. "I asked Mr. Masterson for information on Harvey Harrison, Dave Becker, Joe Robertson, and Peter Black."

Helen wanted to ask who John thought was working with the drug cartel, but decided she didn't really care.

John continued, "Listen, I know I told you we'd go shopping for a ring on Saturday, but I need a little more time." When he saw the disappointment on Helen's face, he went on, "No, nothing like that. What I mean is can we set a time after the bids are submitted when we can both take a day off, or at least a half day, to shop for a ring that we both like?"

Helen recovered very quickly after she heard John's reasoning. She looked at her appointment calendar and said,

"You're right ... how about Thursday the 19th, that's two weeks from now?"

"Sounds good to me ... We'll make it a fun day. Since you represent your investment bankers, I believe you should be an active participant in the bid preparation procedure. "Now, a question, can we use your conference room for the next two weeks or so, so that we can discuss details of the bid in private?"

As she checked another calendar on her computer, she said, "Okay" and marked the conference room for her use for the next two weeks.

Chapter 47

The ad stating that bids would be accepted on the Claybourne properties was printed in various newspapers. The news media picked up the ad and re-ran the story of the drug raid and subsequent arrests again.

For nine business days, John, his three friends, and two temps whom they'd hired to do secretarial and accounting tasks worked day and night to gather information relevant to the value of the Claybourne business. They held meetings with bankers, lawyers and, in particular, some employees of Claybourne Enterprises.

In the end, they arrived at a bid, considerably higher than their original estimate of forty-three million dollars. They submitted a bid of sixty-three million, two hundred sixty thousand dollars three days prior to the deadline. The four young men also had a plan for immediate takeover of the company and change of management, with minimal disruption as possible. The bid would be submitted under the name of one of Masterson's holding companies. Later, the company would be bought by an, as yet unnamed, corporation. That was assuming their bid was, in fact, the highest bid.

With Helen's approval, the four continued to use her office as a meeting place to discuss the other businesses they were going to manage. Because Mr. Hilton was willing and very capable of handling any of the problems that arose, matters at the lodge were well taken care of. John and the three brothers had met with him and the co-managers on several occasions to discuss what John had learned from Bill Martin on his visit to the Poconos with Helen.

Because they would all own a piece of each business, the four friends and their fathers spent time working on suitable business plans for each company.

They agreed that Harrisburg Industrial Electronics was in good hands. Luke had already been doing the actual management of the company for some time. He led the group through some of his proposed changes. The four offered comments and suggestions to his plans.

The six of them discussed Roberts HVAC which presented some difficult problems. Matt would have to create an entirely new segment of business for the industrial HVAC equipment. The group spent considerable time on various strategies for advertising the newer products, as well as how to interest architects, engineers and contractors to use the equipment. Of course, they contacted the manufacturers to review their advertising and promotion plans. Matthew wanted the six of them to meet frequently to review the progress and to suggest additional measures for building the company.

Mark reported to the others that he'd meet with the thirty employees of Mid-Atlantic Environmental Engineers ... first all of the employees together, then individually. At the first meeting, he'd explain the new ownership, and question the employees on their current contracts, pending agreements, and other subjects relating to how the company operated. He said that the second series of meetings would deal with each individual's place in the company ...what they wanted out of the business, details on their individual backgrounds and areas of expertise. Mark decided to establish the York Pennsylvania office as the new company headquarters. He told them that several key employees had already agreed to move to that location.

The following Thursday John and Helen wandered through several jewelry stores, shopping for an engagement ring. By John's insistence, they had to visit at least five stores before they narrowed down their choices. They visited two additional stores and revisited two others before they agreed on a style for both engagement and wedding rings. The jeweler whom they selected would design the rings based on their ideas. John's distinctive memory of what they liked in the various styles was a big help in the design. John and Helen nearly had an argument when it came to the actual size of the precious stones. John wanted larger ones than Helen was willing to accept.

"I appreciate your offer. But listen, I'm a small-boned woman and big diamonds would not look right on my hand. In addition, because of my business dealings, it wouldn't be appropriate to wear a ring with a big stone … it might appear too flashy."

Eventually, it was the jeweler, much to John's surprise, who agreed with Helen. He said, "It really is too big a stone for her hand."

John said, "Okay, you talked me into it. However, I only agree if you let me buy earrings that would complement the ring."

Helen didn't object to this purchase and really appreciated his thoughtfulness. "How can I refuse something like that," she said.

The jeweler said it would be at least two weeks before the ring was ready. John asked Helen, "Can we wait until the ring comes to announce our engagement."

Helen replied, "As far as I'm concerned, an engagement isn't official until there's a ring on the finger."

After their shopping expedition, John and Helen were on their way to dinner when his cell phone rang. As he listened, he heard, "John, this is Harvey. I thought I'd pass along some information. There were four bids submitted for the Claybourne properties. The bids will be opened on Monday morning. The bidders can attend if they want. One interesting fact is now coming to the forefront ... most of the property owned by the Claybourne brothers was purchased in the last three years, which corresponds to when their father became ill and they started running the business. The fools bought most of the possessions under the company name and never changed them into their own names. Consequently, there's no way they can file suit to get them back, with the exception of their homes, cars and personal items. They could presumably ask the courts to allow them to retain that part of their properties. DEA's still acquiring properties owned by the Claybournes. The brother, who's still coherent, at the advice of his attorney, is being very helpful, hoping for leniency."

The conversation continued for a few minutes and John thanked him for the information. After he hung up, John realized that he had never told Harvey he and his friends had submitted a bid.

Chapter 48

The next three days were relatively uneventful, considering what was at stake. The four friends met for a couple of short meetings. The only decision to come out of those meetings was that they decided not to attend the bid opening in Washington because they didn't want it known yet that they were involved.

Helen resolved their dilemma by suggesting that she should go. After all, she was a representative of the investment bankers. Her suggestion made sense, so on Sunday evening she drove to D.C., with a promise to call John at her office as soon as she knew the results.

On Monday morning, the four friends and both sets of parents met in the conference room at Helen's office. Bat Masterson opened the door and asked, "May I join you?"

Mr. Lynch was the first to answer, "Of course." He then introduced the others. The brothers didn't know Masterson, but because of the discussions they'd had with their parents and John, they knew what he represented to them.

The time for the bid opening came and went. Helen hadn't called. Everyone was a little on edge because of the time it was taking to learn the results. They knew from experience that with bid openings it only took a few minutes for the bids to be reviewed and then the amount of the bids stated. John was tempted to check to make sure the phone was working. He actually did check to make sure his cell phone was on.

Finally, forty-five minutes later the phone rang. No one jumped to answer it, so Mr. Masterson, who was closest, picked up the receiver. He said, "Hello," and after a few seconds, "yes, it's me. I'm here with the Bowmans and the Lynches, all of them. Please hold on."

Masterson handed the phone over to John who reached for the phone and nervously said, "John speaking," that made everyone laugh because who else would Helen have asked for. "Hold on, let me put this on the speaker."

Helen started by saying, "Sorry for the delay. The Claybourne attorneys had numerous questions and objections as to how the company was confiscated. They also objected to the business being sold without any approval by the Claybourne family. Apparently, these same questions had been asked time and time again since the drug raid. The attorneys were asked to leave when they interrupted every time they tried to open the bids. Finally, they were forced to leave, accompanied by security guards."

Helen continued, "The sections of the legal code which authorized the seizure and sale were read in accordance with federal procedures. In essence, the Claybourne brothers pleaded guilty to the charges, following their attorney's advice. That speeded up the process. The person in charge of the bid opening opened each package. He proceeded through a checklist to ascertain that all necessary documents were included. Then the bids were read aloud. Do you want me to read them off to you?"

By this time, no one was seated. They all had gathered around the table listening to Helen. John replied to the question, "Yes, we all want to know," with what all present recognized was a shaky voice.

"Okay. The first bid opened was also the lowest bid. It

was a bid of twenty-five million. Next, was a bid of thirty-nine million five hundred thousand. Yours was the third bid to be opened. The fourth and last bid was ..." She paused for enough time for all of them to anticipate that the worst was coming ..."fifty-five million four hundred thousand dollars. Congratulations, gentlemen, you now own a building supply company."

The excitement around the table was not immediately apparent. It took several seconds before any of them moved. Helen, who was expecting a loud reaction said, "Hello... hello, are you still there?"

"Yes, my love, we're still here. That's great news. We're just a little overwhelmed. Thanks for all your help. Can you get the names of the other bidders?"

She said, "I have all the information."

"Come home as quickly as you can get here," said John. "Tonight we party." Their conversation ended with John saying, "I love you," which went unnoticed by everyone except John's mother.

The excitement continued through lunch at a nearby restaurant. The other diners knew something special had just happened but didn't know what the reason was for the celebration.

Harvey called John while they were still in the restaurant. "I got the bid results if you're interested."

Because he was within earshot of other patrons, John answered in a businesslike manner, "Of course, please give me the results."

"Well, the highest bid was sixty-three million two hundred sixty dollars. It was submitted by a company in Delaware. They did leave some money lying on the table. The next highest bid was nearly eight million lower."

"Do you know the name of the company?" asked John.

"Yes, but we understand it's a holding company for a group of investment bankers from Harrisburg." Harvey paused for a few seconds and added, "Oh!" Another pause ensued and was followed by, "I assume you know them."

"Yes, I know them very well."

Harvey now realized John didn't want to, or couldn't, discuss the details at the present time. "Well, I've got to go. Congratulations on your new venture. Talk to you later."

On the way home in their car, Margaret Lynch said, "I'm so thrilled the boys got the bid. You know, Harold, I do believe that there's going to be a lot of excitement in our family, not only the new businesses our son's getting into, but I think there'll be a wedding in the near future."

"Yes, I know. Luke and Mary Anne are getting married next summer."

"Oh, I know about Luke and Mary Anne, but I'm talking about our son and Helen. I'll bet you a dime to a dollar that they'll get engaged before he officially leaves the construction company.

What makes you think that?" he questioned.

"Just a mother's intuition … just a mother's intuition."

Chapter 49

The next several weeks John and his dad spent numerous hours concerning the business, mostly finalizing the split-up of the construction company. Their attorneys and bankers completed the necessary paperwork for the transfer of ownership. The new owners/managers were advised that no one from the Lynch family would be actively involved with the management. They were told that Harold and John and the Bowmans would serve on the board of directors for each company.

Martin Bowman's decision to retire and the announcement that his sons were leaving concerned the new management. They initially thought the family had problems with how the company was being split up or that the Bowmans didn't receive an appropriate portion of the business. Harold Lynch met with them and explained about the new companies and the reason the Bowmans were leaving. He asked them that the information be held in strict confidence, at least for the time being. He told them that Martin would receive his normal retirement. His sons would each own five percent of each business, plus their share for past employment in the company.

By the time of the annual holiday party, most of the

excitement had died down and the employees were doing their jobs in their normal efficient manner. Harold and Martin were seldom seen in the office, although they periodically visited each job site where they answered questions from the employees. They also extended farewell wishes to long-time friends. Some of them would also be retiring shortly.

John continued to meet with the accountants, attorneys and the new company managers to review details that had previously been handled by his dad.

At the company party, John gave the employees the opportunity to ask more questions. When the questions revolved around why the Lynches and the Bowmans were leaving the company, Mr. Lynch made the explanation. He explained his and Martin's ownership, which came as a surprise to the employees. He also explained the fact that Martin's sons would be taking over Martin's shares.

John continued his explanation by saying, "Matthew has bought an interest in the Roberts HVAC Company and is going to manage that company. Mark's obtained part interest in Mid-Atlantic Environmental Engineering and will be moving to York, Pennsylvania to manage that firm."

Harold interjected and told them, "My son was approached by a group of investment bankers who were in the process of buying Claybourne Enterprises. They made John an offer he couldn't refuse. He'll be moving to Harrisburg to manage that company."

Several of the employees immediately assumed that Mr. Lynch was part of that group. Little did they know that it was the younger Mr. Lynch.

John took over the meeting again. "The Bowman brothers and I have another piece of information. We recently bought and restored the Everett Lodge. All of you are invited to a grand opening party in two weeks. After the applause died down, John announced, "Luke would like to say something."

Luke came forward and said, "You know that I'm not

a public speaker, so I'll make this short and sweet. Mary Anne, will you join me?" After she reached the podium, he continued, "Most of you know that Mary Anne and I are engaged to be married. We're here tonight to ask you to keep the date of June 15th open so you can attend our wedding." The entire audience applauded and cheered. As Luke passed John, he whispered, "You're next."

John wondered how he knew about his plans and assumed that Mary Anne and Helen had talked earlier. "How do you follow up with that wonderful news?" John said.

Someone in the audience shouted, "How about you?" The entire audience, as if on cue, quieted down. John looked out at them and said, "Why not?" He walked back to his table and knelt down on one knee in front of Helen.

"Helen Francis, I love you with all my heart. I'd consider it a great honor if you would be my wife and spend the rest of your life with me." He then reached into his coat pocket and brought out the ring they had ordered and began to place it on her finger. "Well, what's your answer?"

Helen knew the ring had been ordered but didn't know John had picked it up. She was, therefore, momentarily shocked and said, "Yes, yes, yes." He placed the ring on her finger as everyone stood and applauded as the two of them embraced lovingly.

John's mother, with tears of happiness in her eyes, whispered to his dad, "I told you there was going to be a wedding in the family." Mr. Lynch just shook his head in wonderment.

Epilogue

A few days after the party, John met with several key employees of Claybourne Enterprises to bring them up to date on their plans for the company. As far as the employees were concerned, John was just the new manager, because the news media had reported that a company from Delaware had actually bought the business. The biggest concern of the existing employees was that the company would be split up and sold so the investment bankers could make a quick profit. John eased their concern immediately by explaining that he had left a good position to take over the management of the company.

John made the statement, "In addition, new and improved healthcare and 401K plans will be implemented." That made the employees pleased, thereby making the transition easier. John continued, "I want to institute a policy of employee involvement. Each employee will be given the opportunity to suggest better ways of doing their own jobs, as well as overall company improvements. Any suggestion can be made. If your suggestion is not accepted, you will be told why and given the opportunity to present additional data in favor of the change.

John added one more comment. "Due to the bad publicity

Claybourne Enterprises received since the drug raid, the name has been changed to Mid-Atlantic Contractors Supply." He didn't bother to explain that the new corporation was another holding company established by the investment bankers.

* * *

Within a week of the official takeover, John called his friends together again. This time they signed corporate papers for Industrial Electronics, Roberts HVAC, Mid-Atlantic Environmental Engineering and finally the Everett Lodge. The only difference in the positions in these corporations was the order of the officers. The Board of Directors, including the four friends and their parents, would be the same.

* * *

A week after the corporate signing, the DEA released the documents which authorized John to run the Claybourne Enterprises on their behalf, until final papers were approved. In addition to the supply business, the major items included in the property confiscated included four warehouses, two in Pennsylvania and two in Florida; a discount supply business in Florida; a split-level house owned by the deceased Mr. Claybourne and his wife; two luxurious homes currently occupied by the families of the two Claybourne brothers; a beach house in Maryland; three houses in different cities in Florida; two cabin cruisers; plus all the vehicles and equipment used by the supply business.

The new owners met to discuss what to do with the additional properties. By a unanimous vote, they decided to sell the three properties and personal automobiles that had been owned by the Claybournes back to their spouses. Since there weren't any mortgages on the properties, the sale price was established at one dollar each. The three families were given the opportunity to buy any of the other properties and/or luxury items at a cost equal to one-half the appraised value. As it turned out, only the family homes and automobiles were transferred back to the Claybournes. The attorney who handled the transfer was quick to note that only one person said 'thank you' to the new owner and that was the widowed Mrs. Claybourne. The other two spouses accepted the offer without comment.

Dave Claybourne pleaded guilty to transporting and dealing drugs, kidnapping and tax evasion. As part of his plea bargaining, he received fifteen years in a federal prison. He was never charged with the theft of the building materials.

Lou Claybourne was hospitalized for two months before he could eat without the use of a straw. He underwent three separate mental evaluations before being declared incompetent to stand trial on the drug charges. He was committed to a mental hospital.

* * *

After months of investigation, a team of DEA agents used the information supplied by John and Masterson to prove that Joe Robertson had not inherited sufficient funds from his father's estate to support his and his wife's style of living. Faced with this information, Joe Robertson and his wife both plea bargained for lesser sentences. Their deal included informing the DEA agents of all the details they knew about the drug lords.

Because of the facts provided by Joe Robertson and his wife, the DEA was able to keep track of Paul Hanover, aka Paul Adams, and his accomplice, Rocky. The two were later found guilty of transporting and delivering drugs in a case unrelated to the Claybournes. Rocky and Paul were sent to prison for a fifteen year sentence.

In a separate trial, Paul Hanover was found guilty of tax

evasion. That was a direct result of the 1099s submitted to the IRS by Lou Claybourne. He was tried and convicted. The judge sentenced him to an additional ten years after he completed his drug sentence.

* * *

Luke eventually received fifteen patents on his electronic devices. The federal government bought the rights to seven of the devices for an undisclosed sum. With a portion of the profits from the sale of his inventions, Luke established trust funds for the education of any children he and Mary Anne might have, as well as any children of his three best friends. His friends would not learn about these trust funds for quite a few years.

Because of the government's purchase, Luke was also able to establish a manufacturing firm which would produce innovative devices as a result of the other eight patents.

* * *

Harold and Margaret Lynch and Martin and Janet Bowman retired on the day that the final papers were signed for the buyout of Lynch Construction. They would continue to collect the profits from all the companies now owned by their sons for the next ten years.

* * *

By previous agreement, the four received reasonable salaries for the jobs they preformed. For the first ten years of operation, they wouldn't receive any profits from the businesses they owned.

* * *

Luke and Mary Anne were married and wasted no time to start a family. Ten months later, they became proud parents of a baby girl. Mary Anne was thrilled that Luke was such an attentive father.

* * *

Within a year from the time the four friends had taken over the management of their respective companies, the companies exhibited signs of growth and profit potential. The four of them met every other week to bring each other up to date and to discuss possible solutions to the various concerns of each company.

By the end of their third year, the four young men started to train managers to handle the day-to-day operations of each of the companies to allow them time to oversee their entire business ventures.

* * *

John and Helen were married the year after Luke and Mary Anne. They agreed to wait several years before starting a family. Because Helen's Uncle Bateman experienced a stroke which caused some paralysis, John and Helen moved into the Masterson Mansion to care for him and to take advantage of his still sharp mind.

* * *

Two years after their wedding, John received three calls within days of each other which could have a direct influence on his life. Helen called John during one of the bi-weekly meetings with the three brothers. Without preamble she said, "I have a client who's interested in expanding his vinyl manufacturing company. They manufacture vinyl siding, fencing and railings. The owner would like to stay involved but is willing to part with a portion of the company. My initial analysis indicates that nearly five million dollars would be needed to take control of the company and take it nationwide. I believe it's an excellent opportunity for Thunder and Lightning to expand. Are you interested?"

John's answer was, "It would have to be fifty-one percent for us to become interested. Maybe he'd be willing to manage the company for us."

Helen replied, "I'll pass that information to him, but my initial reaction is that it might be a possibility."

After he talked with Helen for several minutes to obtain more information, John said, "Let me talk it over with the other three and I'll tell you our decision tonight." He then relayed the information to his friends which he had just heard. They all were interested and agreed to meet in Helen's office later. That would allow her to have more time to delve deeper into the business's value.

The second call was from The Woodpecker. After a minute of catching up with each other's news, Harvey said, "John, we believe we have a problem with the manner in which a company's keeping their accounting records. Any chance you could review their books for us?"

John replied that he was willing to drive to D.C. the following week to review the records and would give his opinion on the findings.

The third call held interesting possibilities. "Doctor Lynch, this is Bill Nelson calling from Penn State. I'm chairman of a committee from the University. We're in the process of reevaluating some of our business management courses. Your name was suggested as someone who may be able to provide some insight on criteria for our business courses."

Those phone calls left John with much to ponder.

About the Author:

Walt Bagley is a retired professional civil engineer. As an avid reader of mystery novels in his leisure time, he decided to try his hand in writing a mystery. This book is the result of over four years of challenging his imagination.

Walt and his wife Jean live in Altoona, Pennsylvania. They have been married for nearly fifty years and are the parents of four grown children who have provided them with nine grandchildren.

Printed in the United States
221021BV00001B/4/P